# SINFUL PROMISE

## A DARK MAFIA ROMANCE

VOLKOV BRATVA
BOOK THREE

ZOE BETH GELLER

KINKY INK PUBLISHING, LLC

Sinful Promise

By Zoe Beth Geller

# INTRODUCTION

Roman is the youngest brother in the family, and he's angry that a shipment his brother trusted him to handle has been stolen. He wants revenge but has to be careful to avoid an all-out war.

He finds out who stole his weapons and travels to obtain more information with his right-hand man, Alex. They have intel on where their nemesis will be, but they didn't plan on assisting a runaway bride.

Join Roman and his captive on his quest for revenge. He believes Dasha is his nemesis's bride-to-be. But who is she?

Find out aboard his yacht as secrets flow like the currents in this dark mafia romance.

If you like mafia lite and mafia tropes, then this is for you. Sink into the underworld of morally grey men and the women who bring light into their world with book 3!

This contains the tropes of a Cinderella-esque woman who becomes a willing captive looking for an escape, an anti-hero who is oblivious to love, touch her and you are unlived, with plenty of spice. This is a mafia romance suspense.

# PREFACE

I loved writing this series and hate to see it end. Maybe Alex will get a book! I love writing mafia suspense. I plan to intertwine the series by building a huge mafia world in New York City. Some of these characters will appear in other books.

Enjoy!

XO,

Zoe

ACKNOWLEDGMENTS

Special thanks to Wicked Pen Editorial for editing and proofreading. I needed to find a place where my book baby would receive the attention it deserved. I couldn't be happier with the results of this book. Special thanks to my dedicated ARCS and to Jeanne, Mo, and Cheryl for early proofreading. Your encouragement and support make my day. I can't thank you enough.

# CHAPTER 1

## ROMAN

*I*f there's one thing I hate, it's a rat—particularly the two-legged kind.

The man behind the warehouse curls into the fetal position, clutching his belly with a groan. Crimson blood oozes from his mouth. My fist hurts from the connection it made with his ribs two minutes ago. One would think I'd be used to the pain by now.

I kick him in the head. It's not the first time I've treated a man's head like a football, nor will it be the last.

"Who took the shipment?" I growl in Russian.

As I watch, he spits out a tooth. Looks like my punch to his jaw had an impact.

Good.

We don't bother with security cameras. When it comes to contraband, cameras are more of a liability than a help. This place was once a factory where locals worked long hours churning out cement blocks. Nowadays, we use it to stash products.

A broken streetlight hangs overhead with bared wires dangling low enough to touch. After years of neglect, the place looks abandoned, but we maintain the chain-link fence topped with barbed wire to keep out those unfamiliar with the area. The locals know not to trespass.

"I can't say." The man sucks in a breath. "They'll kill me." His voice is barely audible.

I give him another swift kick in the gut. My boot connects with the thickness of his belly. He cries out in pain and gasps for air.

"I'll let you live if you tell me," I state calmly.

He's a dead man, which he'd already know if he were smart. He was dead the minute I discovered him sneaking away from the warehouse. He was hired to keep our gun shipment safe until we sold them on the black market.

Instead, he'd let someone steal them, costing us a considerable sum in lost revenue.

"I'll find out in the end," I warn him.

Reaching inside his thin jacket, Alex, my right-hand man, pulls out his Glock and racks it. "Let me finish him."

"No, we need the name," I reply. I almost want to chuckle at our routine.

"Fuck," Alex groans. He kicks the dirt with his boot.

"I'll give you a name, but wait a day so I can disappear," our once-trusted employee pleads, groveling at my feet. Interesting. Apparently, he's more afraid of someone else than he is of me. What's more, he actually believes I'm letting him go. My lips curl at the irony. We all tell ourselves lies to get through the day, but he'll learn the hard way that the Volkovs don't forgive or forget.

"Sure," I reply. "Who was it?"

"His name is Ratmim."

"Kozlov, the Belarusian?" I ask in surprise. *Who are the Kozlovs in bed with?* My mind races. The Belarusians have a reputation. They are cutthroats that come into Russia and plunder at will. It seems they have a safe haven in Belarus, and few Russians demand compensation. Our countries' politics are closely aligned. I'm at a loss when trying to decide which country is more benevolent.

"Where is he?" I demand. Hearing the impatience in my voice, Alex moves closer to me.

"I don't know," the man says. "He lies low. He has many enemies but also friends in high places, allies linked to the military and officials next to the President."

I let out a low whistle. Fuck. I've never met him, but I've heard Ratmim is a greedy bastard. Belarus is known to fan the flames of war in other countries under Russian directives. Years ago, the world slept as a struggling country was taken over by a corrupt election. The President now holds the title of the longest-sitting president in Europe.

However, Belarus is indebted to Russia, a debt that will be repaid no matter how many favors are given or how many years pass. This is what makes Belarus a thorn in everyone's side. They have an invisible cloak of protection and harbor many criminals from other countries, mercenaries who call Belarus home.

"Are you letting him live?" Alex murmurs, looking down at our former employee. The man cowers like a rat and moves his arms to protect his head from the expected shot.

"What do you think?" I ask with an indifferent shrug, pretending to consider the matter. Today, Alex and I play good cop, bad cop.

Maybe it's cruel, giving the man even a glimmer of hope that he might get out of this alive, but it's a cruel world, and this man has betrayed us.

There's only one solution.

"You can't trust this loser. He's been paid to screw us. He'll give you up to Ratmim. If anything happens to Ratmim, his organization will know it's you. You know this."

Alex is right. Our world is dark and unforgiving, and I don't want to kick the hornet's nest, but Ratmim took what's ours, and there is a price to be paid. Without retribution, we'll be viewed as weak. In our world, the weak don't last long. We'll be out of business or dead.

I have few rules in life, but blood and brotherhood come first.

I give Alex a quick nod, and a shot rings out in the cold night air. The man jerks and goes still. He betrayed us. A bullet to his head was merciful, as far as I'm concerned, but it's also less mess to clean up. Alex will call a "specialist" to sanitize the brain matter sprayed on the dirt. We drag the man by his ankles toward the riverbank. The dead grass crunches beneath our boots as we make our way to the Volga River. July has been a dry month, and we need rain.

We dump the body on the embankment, and Alex pokes around in the tall weeds until he finds what he's looking for. Bending, he picks up a cement block, half-hidden in the grass, carrying it easily with one hand. I find a rusty chain on the ground, and together, we run it through the block and wrap it around the traitor's waist.

We take turns nudging the lifeless body with our feet, moving it closer to the river's edge. With a final nudge, it rolls down the embankment, landing in the water with a splash.

We nod at each other: mission accomplished.

Despite the dry summer, the river isn't dangerously low, and we watch the bubbles rise to the surface as the body sinks to its final resting place. The traitor will spend eternity in a grave of muck… unless the river runs dry one day. It happens. According to the international news, an old lake near Las Vegas has dried up, and they've been recovering bodies ever since.

Not good, but that's a problem for another day. This is just another night of work for us. I turn and kick my military-style boots over the loose gravel as if to wipe away the memory of tonight. We walk in silence to my car. I dread calling my older brother, Nikolay. I'm embarrassed this happened on my watch. Granted, no matter who was here to run the family business, it would have happened. However, I take it particularly hard. It was my watch, and I hate mistakes. Any attack on us is personal. But in the wake of my father's death, I'm peeved like never before. Yeah, it's personal, all right.

Men who want to live don't make a bold move unless they know the consequences and are prepared for it. The reason we have wars is because someone acts without thinking. The Bratva leader has to think about moves on the ground as well as the repercussions that could hit from numerous directions. Knowing the players is important because every action has consequences. And I am in the mood to deliver consequences.

It's what I do for the family.

Alex doesn't speak until we reach my black Mercedes. He gives me a long, hard look across the roof. "What are we going to do about Ratmim?"

"I'll think of something. For starters, I'm going to check out Ratmim's neighborhood. He'll pay one way or another." I push the button on the key fob, and the doors click as they unlock.

Alex opens the passenger door. "You'll have to be careful. He's with powerful people inside and outside of Belarus to come into Russia that easily."

"Right." I slide behind the wheel.

Alex is the size of an American linebacker and barely fits in the seat. He has ten years on me, but I'm his boss. He's a man I'd trust with my life, and trust doesn't come easily in the mafia. I depend on my brothers and Alex. I've never been in love. Frankly, I doubt I'm capable of it. A woman would take time away from work, and I don't need the distraction. I might keep the company of women, but they are not locals. The women I associate with are the ones who live in luxury, the same luxury we buy with our ill-gotten gains.

I need to be vigilant to keep us all safe. The theft of our goods had to be planned. I wonder what gives Ratmim the balls to hit us. We're not close to their border, so what makes us so special?

I start the car, and when I've fastened my seatbelt, I put it in drive and head out of the city.

A tanking economy normally leads to opportunist groups, low-level organizations desperate for a payday. It's a nefarious way to make a living. We'll snuff out the wannabes who cross into our territory. But whoever pulled a stunt like this won't last long. We have a reputation to uphold.

"Why would Ratmim want our guns?" Alex asks.

Granted, guns are in short supply these days, but it means he is stockpiling them...or someone else is. Our business world is convoluted, many players on the board and not all of them known. Men like me lurk in the shadows in every organization and country. Political powers move us like pawns for their own enrichment, partnerships for violence and monetary gain that can't be associated with political figureheads, men just as sinister, if not more so, than we are. They are not to be undermined. But then again, neither am I.

# CHAPTER 2

## ROMAN

"We should find an indirect way to send a message. We don't want to be walking targets for Ratmim's allies in Belarus," I say, thinking out loud.

I continue to drive as anger swells in my chest. Risk is one thing. It comes with the job, but I hate being fucked over. There is no honor among thieves, and Ratmim is a lazy prick who would rather steal than obtain his own contraband.

It irks me to no end. He's under my skin and on my mind, two places I never allow anyone...not even women. Now that I think about it, especially women!

Especially women. Women have seized the hearts of my brothers, but their happiness is lost on me. The only light in my life comes in short spurts, stolen moments spent with family for special occasions and the infrequent vacation. We have enough money to buy anything we want. But there are parts of my soul that no amount of money can fix. I'm a sinful man. I take lives, acting as judge and jury. There is no doubt in my mind that I'm soulless.

The only good in me is my mother's doing. I have manners and can be a gentleman when required—highbrow society demands etiquette. She taught me how to schmooze with the billionaires. She has grace and good taste in men, but I possess certain qualities that allow me to slide into the jet-set world when needed, making contacts and moving products. Working in public is a great cover.

Women are readily available, but I view them as mere distractions and liabilities. They have no idea what I'm capable of. There might be rumors of what we do, but without proof, I'm golden, and the family is protected.

My brooding thoughts circle back to the events of the night. The situation is an affront too glaring to ignore.

"No one comes this far to fuck with anyone," Alex says. "They had to have intel to even know about the guns, and that's a scary thought."

"Right? Do we have a mole? Or did they get lucky? It could have been an innocuous event that led to us. Or it could be personal. My gut tells me this is exceptionally personal."

"They have protection in Belarus for sure." Alex lights a cigarette and cracks the window. "It makes them think their balls are bigger than they are because if we were to confront them on our own turf, we'd filet them."

He's right about that. I haven't been paying much attention to world events. I have no clue what's happening around me since Dad died, and that's not healthy for me or the family business. Nikolay knows the names of the players, as he's responsible for all of us. But I'm on the ground daily and should have a beat on what's happening.

"I think we should be paying more attention to our rivals, and not just those in our borders."

"Good idea, all things considered," Alex mocks me. He exhales toward the crack as if it will really help the shitty smell building inside my new car.

"You should give up smoking," I bark, venting some of my anger on him. It feels good. "This is a fucking new car. Show some respect."

Alex throws his shitty stick out the window.

"It's a bad habit. Maybe one day I will meet a woman who will make me give it up."

"You should do that on your own." I'm agitated. He smoked in my car, and I like to keep my shit tidy and clean. It's mine, and I protect what's mine. I work hard and make sacrifices. I'm always under pressure, most of which I put on myself, and it's been worse since Dad died.

I wonder if there was something I missed about his death. It's not like we have public information here. We're told what the government wants us to hear.

I peer through the windshield, searching the sky for answers. Clouds block the moon but keep in the warmth of the sunny day. Bad shit happens during full moons more often than not. The moon has to be full for a trusted employee of many years to turn on us and cost us a small fortune. We assume he was bought, but money does not always motivate people. For instance, fear for a loved one is just as powerful, if not more so.

We control businesses through threats and intimidation. Businesses pay for protection. In our country, it's a way of life. If you make money, you pay someone for the privilege.

I pull into a large development of apartments, scanning the horizon for interlopers, leery of the night ending well.

"Talk to you later," Alex says as he gets out.

The door slams, and I drive on, lost in no-man's-land. Periodically, I check my mirrors in case someone is following me. Tonight was a reminder that even the Volkovs aren't untouchable. Maybe we should have bribed officials to discover who was behind Dad's supposed accident. We assumed it was the government.

Maybe we were wrong.

I drive fifteen minutes to an upscale neighborhood where homes come with property. This is the location of our second childhood home, the one we were living in when Dad became the head of an organized crime family born out of Russia's turmoil. I used to spend most of my time in my mansion on the French Riviera, but things changed after Dad's funeral. I returned home to keep Mom from going stir-crazy. She was sitting home, alone with the ghosts and memories of the past.

I park in the driveway and head inside. Entering Dad's office, I have a sudden flashback. A few months ago, Dad told Nikolay he was to marry Anya, his best friend's daughter. It was an arranged marriage, and it was time for him to fulfill the family obligation. Our other brother, Dmitry, is the middle brother who managed to marry a love child of an illicit mafia love affair. Dmitry's union solidified our family with the Russians in New York City. I'm the only one left holding on to the single life.

I sit at his desk. It's just as he left it. There are some things we don't put on electronic devices, and information on Ratmim is one of those things. As much as Dmitry is our computer Geek, there are items we don't have on digital equipment. Dad liked keeping information off of devices, preferring to keep physical files.

There are numerous criminal organizations in Europe, especially in Russia. After the breakup of the Soviet Union, we quickly learned how to keep the elected officials happy: we pay them a percentage of our profits. It's a win-win. They use our money to remain in power and buy luxurious items that can't be traced. Those of us in organized crime launder their money and do their dirty work. In return, they look the other way. My world is filled with nefarious characters. We try to limit the players and remain under the radar, but there is a price to pay. Dad's life was one of those payments—retribution for not conceding to figureheads.

Did Ratmim act on his own, or was he asked to steal my shipment? I'm angry over Dad's untimely death. Life can change so quickly, and it haunts me. I will call Nikolay. He'll know what to do. He's the don and makes the decisions that keep us safe on the large chessboard. He knows more about international affairs than I care to admit.

I pull out my burner phone. Dmitry is the brother who is savvy with technology. He keeps us up to speed with the latest advancements in encrypted devices. He helps with research and he's in charge of our security systems.

I'm not keen on gadgets, but I follow his instructions to stay as safe as possible. Nowadays, everything can be tracked with a microscopic chip and a GPS location. I know a thing or two about sophisticated tracking devices.

"Brother, what's up?" Nikolay answers cheerfully. I suspect he and Anya were probably just finishing a resounding fuck. They're like rabbits. I can't be bothered with the fuss it takes to keep a woman happy. Women are fickle and expensive.

"Bad news." I pause, hating the fact that this indiscretion happened on my watch. "The guns are gone. The man who oversees the warehouse was compromised. I caught him. He told me Ratmim stole them."

"Fuck." He curses, and I can picture him looking for something to break or punch.

"I know. We can't let them get away with a score this easily."

"He knows powerful men," Nikolay warns me.

"So do we."

"There is more at stake than guns. Our buyer will be pissed."

"I know." This is a concern for my brother because this is how enemies are made. Men like us have a lot of enemies, and it's not always about a deal that's not completed. Our clients, more often than not, are irrational and impatient.

This is why we surround ourselves with bodyguards and live behind security gates. We take precautions, but we know we're still vulnerable. Anyone with enough motivation can get to us at any time.

Once in a while, life fucks us back. It happened to Dad and can happen to me or someone in our family.

Threats are ongoing. It's one reason we stick together. The tighter we are, the better. We stay close to make it difficult for assholes from other groups can't infiltrate us.

This country doesn't breed transparency. No country does. Those in power might make it look good, but it's a lie at the end of the day. The so-called "truth" is smoke and mirrors that have been perfected over time to manipulate people, rulers, and countries. It's been effective for centuries.

We live with lies. I see the world as it is with its messy underbelly. I can't afford to wear blinders. Freedom is an illusion. I have more privileges, but they come with risks that can't be taken lightly.

"Every politician needs someone to do their dirty work." Nikolay's voice is stern.

"True. We have to do shitty things for the government," I lament in a sullen tone.

"Yes, but this means there is a pissing contest going on at the state level."

"It's never pleasant." I think about Dad and Igor. Igor refused to sell shares of their company at a loss just to raise money for the men running the government. By the time the world outside Russia heard about it, it was too late for my father and his right-hand man, Boris.

"No, it's not. Keep your guard up," he warns. "They got what they wanted. I'll have to take the loss. We can't retaliate publicly."

"What? We can't sit for this!" My blood boils in my veins. This is preposterous. I want to kill Ratmim. Fuck him. He deserves death by torture, and I'd love to be the one to do it.

"Let me think about it." My brother's voice is calm and reasonable. It's one of the many reasons he makes a great leader.

"I want to find out more about him. I'm going to check him out. I've never seen him in person, but there is a picture here," I reply.

"Mm. You're sitting at Dad's desk?" He asks the question because we're not on a video call, and he's trying to figure out where I am. He knows me inside and out. We're brothers and often think alike.

"Yes." My hands hover over the sleek wooden desk. I'm in Dad's chair, flipping the picture between my fingers. Ratmim's face is committed to my memory. The intel says he has two sons. I could take the life of one of his sons without leaving a trace. Sure, they will wonder if it was us, but they will have no proof. The Kozlovs will be pissed but powerless to do anything. Their methodical hands will be tied, and the thought of this makes me extremely happy.

"I miss him." Nikolay's words surprise me. He hasn't talked about Dad since the night he was murdered. We've not had time to process our loss. Sometimes, I go to call Dad and remember he's not here.

"Me, too. How are you with that? You can't hold it in forever." Inwardly, I scoff. *As if I'm any better.* We're taught to keep our emotions inside. Nikolay doesn't share work with his wife, and I don't keep girlfriends. The less everyone knows, the safer it is for the family.

"True. I just need a moment to process it. I've been busy. Burying the loss by keeping the business going is easier. But now that things have calmed down, I will. Dmitry is settling in New York, and we're expanding, whether I like it or not. I miss us all living in the same city. We took that for granted," he says, his voice trailing off.

"I miss us hanging out here. Now that you're both married, I'm sure it will cut down on our time together," I add. "We're in different countries, and Dmitry is expecting a baby. Go figure." I put my lips together and give a low whistle. "I can't imagine what that will be like. I'm hoping I can wind up this gun thing and take my planned vacation."

"Yeah, you need to go. The vessel needs to be used. It costs a fortune every day to staff it, for fuck's sake. Family is family, we'll figure it out. I have the New York deal going through; that shipment is arriving this week as planned. Thankfully, Dmitry oversaw the deal and kept the Italians from getting a bigger cut. That was not going to go over well, so it's nice we kept the peace."

"It's not every day a man stumbles across an unknown mafia princess," I add. But Dmitry has been lucky in life, having survived a car crash meant to kill him with a fiery inferno. "Funny that the Italians lost their leverage years ago when they turned their back on one of their daughters."

He chuckles at the expense of the nasty old Italian don in New York, but the moment is short-lived. Nikolay takes a breath and is back to business.

"How is Mom?" he asks. "She looked great at the wedding, but I worry she'll never move on."

"She's doing better. The idea of having a grandbaby makes her very happy. Dad lives on with the next generation," I mumble. I feel a twinge of something like sorrow, or is it an emptiness inside me? Everyone in the family has someone except me.

"That means we all have to step up, brother." His pensive mood seems to have passed. At times, his mood can change so fast that I get whiplash.

"I'll step up, all right, when Ratmim is rotting in the shit soil he lives on."

"Don't do anything that will blow back on us. I have no desire to start a war." His stern voice reminds me of Dad.

Dad would let us fuck off, but when he used that stoic tone and was short with his words, we knew he meant business. That's when we snapped to attention like military men saluting a corporal.

"I won't, but I'm going to check out his operations. We need to send a message of some kind. It has to be done."

"I'm worried you're still too angry, but I know you'd never hurt us with your actions. You're normally disciplined and patient. But you're young, and when I least expect it, you're impetuous. Wait for the opportunity. It might not be resolved immediately. Don't let your anger trip you up."

"I won't." I'm flippant with my response. I'm not impetuous. I'm disciplined until I decide I want to fuck off, and then I become adventurous. Well, to me, it's my adventurous side. I'm a methodical man, a man of detail, but I have my limits. And this vacation is long overdue. I need to decompress. It's been an eventful year.

"I'll handle the shitshow here," Nikolay says. "Be careful."

"I will."

We hang up, and I sink back into the leather chair with wheels. Who is this Ratmim, and what is he hiding? Everyone has secrets, and secrets are power. Guns are in short supply. He made a bold move.

I wonder who he is connected to and what his sons are like. I hear they are brutal. When it comes to torturing their enemies, the Belarusian mafia has no loyalties. They come into Russia, but they're known to have an escape hatch in Belarus. Our countries used to be one, so we all speak Russian. They won't speak badly of Russia but have a veil of protection in Belarus. I look at them as cowards. They plunder and steal, and then they hide.

They are thieves with no moral code, which is where we're different. Our intel on them is subpar. I don't want to disturb Dmitry. I'm sure he would be useful, but he's a newlywed. I decide I'll handle this on my own.

I know I'm acting quickly when I should take my time. But as I twiddle the picture of Ratmim between my fingers, I wonder—how difficult can it be to get my boots on the ground? I can spy on him. We live every day knowing that we could meet untimely deaths with one wrong move and never see it coming. It happened to Dad, and it's a constant reminder to choose friends wisely and stick to your rules.

Our rules keep us safe. I keep my emotions in check, and my calm head remains attached.

I call Alex.

"We're going on a trip," I inform him.

"We have to be careful." He's my fucking work wife. The man can read my mind.

"Nikolay knows we're just looking for information."

"And…" He pauses. Alex has been known to reel me in on many occasions, all of them vodka-related. He's reserved and appears to have few emotions, but I see through him. No one knows Alex like I do.

"We're not breaking rules. If they don't know it's us, we'll all get what we want. I want to make them hurt. Ratmim took what he wanted, now I'm going to take something from him."

I sit pensively. We will go to Belarus and take out one of his sons. If it looks like an accident, there will be no war.

"Fine. I'll pack my gear," Alex says enthusiastically.

"Thanks. I'll charter a flight to Minsk."

"Text me the details. I'll pick you up tomorrow," Alex says. "You know I never go anywhere without enough firepower to blow ourselves out."

"That's what I'm afraid of, and you're there to keep me out of trouble," I reply with sarcasm.

I hang up the phone and think of Nikolay in London. He spends all his time there while I run operations locally under his direction. I couldn't care less about hobnobbing with business partners. I prefer to carry out hits on people. I carefully study my target and wait for the opportune moment to pull the trigger. Mission accomplished.

I've learned to be patient in order to be perfect. I'm not sure how to hurt this enemy, aside from taking a son, but I'll find something.

When I get to Minsk, I will weigh my options and make sure we don't attract a hit squad. Our country has a way of making moves that are never seen or anticipated. It's how I operate myself, using our government's playbook to our advantage.

I look at the family pictures still on the desk. In one, we're hunting in Alaska, all of us. It was a fun trip. I like the challenge of a perfect shot. Oddly, I didn't learn my profession from Dad. Artemy was my mentor and a lifelong friend of Dad's. I respected the fact that he knew how to live off the land. He taught me how to hunt and shoot. I wanted to learn more about the world in which I lived, so when I was older, I traveled with him and his friends.

We would sit in pubs and hotel rooms, devising unique ways to make our hits untraceable. I love researching, planning, and watching the pieces fall into place. It's like solving a puzzle. I have a keen sense of people. I can tell if they are empathetic, confident, or ruthless. Knowing what makes a person tick is easy when their desires are known.

I wish I knew what made women tick. Most women want me because of my cock and the fact that I look good on paper.

I shove the thought of women aside. A wife would be a liability.

I return Ratmim's picture to the file cabinet and notice a photo of Dad and a man at a political event. The man seems oddly familiar. I turn the picture over and see a date. I was too young then to remember, but Dad took Grandpa's business to new levels around that time. In hindsight, I wonder how Dad became so successful.

I toss the picture back into the file and walk to the door. Turning, I take one last look at the room, imagining us all here together with Dad. before I flip the light switch off.

Tomorrow is another day. I will find Ratmim's weakness and make him pay.

# CHAPTER 3

## DASHA

"**K**atsia, I can't make it tonight," I say loudly by my door. Moving deeper into my bedroom, I whisper, "Papa is home."

"Shit. What the hell is he up to now?" My friend senses the disappointment in my voice.

I'm upset that he's home, which means I won't be able to go out tonight as planned. I'm pissed that my father continues to order me around. He always finds a way to make my life revolve around him. He's in and out so much I'm dizzy.

"I don't know. I hate to let you down." I sit on my bed with my knees pulled to my chest and stare at my bare feet.

"It's fine. I have the others to hang out with, but I wish you could go. I even picked a dress for you to wear." I hear the sound of hangers sliding on a rod in the background and picture her putting something pretty back in her closet.

"I'm so sorry." I hate apologizing because my father won't let me have a social life. I make plans, but he cancels them. I want a job so I can get out of here. I want to make my own decisions and be an adult.

"Dasha, make dinner," my father bellows from the dining room. I bet he's sitting at the kitchen table, drinking brandy.

He never says please, and I gave up expecting to hear a "thank you" years ago. He barks orders. Unfortunately, I have to follow them.

"I've got to go. Have fun tonight, and text me pictures."

"I will. Later."

"Later."

I know better than to question the timing of our early dinner. It's only four in the afternoon, and he wants me to cook. That's nothing new. He expects me to do everything. He was away for a few days, the laundry piled up, and he'd never use the machine to do it himself. I have more clothes that need to be folded sitting in a basket next to Papa.

I walk down the short hall, glaring at the back of his head as I pass by. I clench my fists, my heart thumping in rage. He's a control freak. I can't wait for him to leave again. Maybe one day, he will leave and never come back. It might be my only way out of this hellhole.

I'm happy when he goes out of town with my brothers because I have the apartment to myself. We live on the outskirts of Minsk, where rent is cheap. The apartment is larger than most. I don't know why we must live here because my brothers live in the city, and it's expensive.

I'm convinced Papa wants to keep me hidden. It's the only logical explanation. I can't go anywhere without telling him. I can't hang out with men, and I have few friends because of his controlling ways. Most women my age are dating or getting engaged.

*I know English, but speaking it in the house would piss him off. I'd love to piss him off, but I don't want the consequences.*

I inform him in Russian that I'll make a potato casserole. I'd love to try recipes from other countries, but Papa is used to our food. He's overweight and never goes to the doctor. I begrudgingly love him, but I know he's holding me back. I could take classes and work in technology. A job in tech would pay enough for me to share a place with Katsia.

Papa has an excuse ready for me every time I bring up a job. He says I'll marry soon, and my husband will support me. I don't want a man to support me. I want to get out and be on my own. I want to go to a club and dance instead of dancing alone in my room. When it comes to my personal life, he instinctively ruins my plans time and time again. I'm beginning to wonder if he has cameras hidden in the apartment.

How am I expected to get married if I'm not allowed to date? When I ask him about it, he shrugs and changes the subject.

I peel potatoes and wait for them to boil. I fold the laundry I washed this morning and stack the shirts and pants on the table, where he sits slumped over his glass of brandy. He gives me a critical look, meaning I didn't fold them perfectly. No matter how hard I work, it's never good enough for him. He's never encouraged me to do anything besides graduate from school. I'm convinced he only let me stay in school because it kept me out of the way.

Why can't he help with the laundry? I stomp into the tiny kitchen without a word. His eyes follow me. I've lived with his scrutiny my entire life. I pull out a cast-iron skillet and think about hitting him upside the head with it. I dutifully set it on the gas stove instead.

I adjust the burner for the potatoes and soothe my simmering resentment by daydreaming of the day I can finally leave. When he's stressed, he's worse and gets snippy. He hits the brandy earlier in the day and sips it late into the night. His words are slurred by the time I escape to my room to read my smutty books.

My room isn't much, but it's my sanctuary. I have a small TV and watch programs without my father standing over my shoulder, criticizing my choices. He thinks TV shows and movies from America and anywhere else in the Western world are all garbage.

Papa does odd jobs for a living, working mostly at night. He makes secretive phone calls. Last week, I overheard him telling my brothers that he dislikes the Volkovs family. I want to know why but know better than to ask questions.

They always say the less I know, the better. Papa has connections with elected officials who have a reputation for taking bribes. Bribes for what, I don't know. Something nefarious is going on. I've always assumed he's part of organized crime. We don't discuss it, but I connected the dots before my seventh birthday.

Papa has an opinion on everything and tends to be a know-it-all. Even when he's wrong, he never admits it. I wouldn't be surprised if he tracks my computer and my search history. Preventing me from working outside the home is his way of keeping me under his thumb.

I only get a break when he's out of town. I wish he'd go more often. I wait on him hand and foot when he's here. He says my mother had a drug addiction and left us, but I don't believe it. One night, I heard him beating her and never saw her again. Did she run away, or did he dispose of her? I'm afraid to ask. I was only five at the time. He tells me kids don't have memories when they're that young. I disagree.

My family doesn't socialize outside Papa's group of friends. Friends? More like a band of thieves, really. They all dress in black, and what skin I see is covered in tattoos. I know they travel in and out of Russia. I know most of them by their first name. Some, like

Andrian, I know by his last name, too, because he loves to throw it around. There are rumors he deals in human trafficking. I avoid him as much as possible. My life is nowhere near normal, but it's all I know.

Papa treats me like a child even though I'm twenty-one. On the rare occasion I am allowed to leave, I have a curfew. Home by ten, or I'm in trouble. I live vicariously through foreign movies. I've seen pictures of the ocean and the Black Sea from friends who have traveled, and it sparked a fire in me to leave Minsk. There has to be more to life than being a subservient to a man. What will my future be if I stay here?

I was given an old cell phone to take calls from my brothers and Papa. My data usage is limited. I don't want Papa yelling at me if I go over my minutes, so I seldom use it. I do use the computer I have from school. I pleaded with him to buy me one. He believes in education and eventually bought me one. He also allows me to use the library and read anything I want. The selection of reading material is limited, but Katsia hooks me up with contraband. She has stashes of travel brochures. I yearn to experience other cultures one day. It would be a dream come true to get the fuck out of here.

I love to read romance books. The trashier, the better. Katsia has a connection who gets us "spicy" books. They're forbidden by the government, so I hide them under my mattress and dream about being ravished by a man who needs me more than the air he breathes.

We've all seen movies with homes the size of hotels and wonder what it would be like to live in such luxury. Me? I'd be happy to have a simple apartment with Katsia. She's going to the university to become a teacher, a profession that's acceptable for women. For now, all I have are dreams. Dreams that probably won't come to fruition. Without a job or money, I'm stuck.

I open the refrigerator that's probably been in this apartment since Stalin was in power and pull out the brisket left over from yesterday. I add it to the potatoes I've cooked and mashed. Papa has moved to his lounge chair in the living room to watch TV. He loves to watch football.

I'm always dressed in jeans and off-brand shirts. Papa makes sure my body is covered like a nun before I leave the house to go anywhere. Boyfriends are out of the question. He'd have a fit if a man so much as gave me a minute of attention. My friends who walked me home from school were afraid of his gruff greeting at the door and never came inside. Word of the incident passed through the school like wildfire. I was untouchable and became unnoticed overnight.

The casserole cooks in the oven while I finish the laundry. The timer on the stove goes off. Donning oven mitts, I pull dinner out of the oven and place the hot skillet on the table. Papa turns off the TV and returns to the table. I can smell the liquor he's been drinking from across the room, a scent that reminds me of lighter fluid.

"I have friends coming over tonight to play cards. I want you to make snacks for us."

It's not a request.

"Fine," I say with an edge to my voice to let him know I'm irritated, even if he doesn't care. He'll yell and take my phone away if I push too hard. I scoop the casserole onto his plate and try to think of something to say that's not confrontational.

"What are your plans this week?" I ask, wondering if he'll leave again.

"Why? Do you have plans?" he replies, and I wonder if he's baiting me. Maybe he knows I sneak out with Katsia. If he knows, he's never mentioned it.

"No, of course not."

"Don't forget your place. I put the roof over your head and food on the table." He's eating fast and takes a second helping before I've had two bites.

"I want to work. I can help," I implore him. I want to *do* something, to be useful.

"No, I can't have that," he says with a mouth full of food.

"Why? What's the big deal?" I push, wanting to know what he's thinking.

"I'm not a model citizen. I can't have you walking around." He points at me with his fork. "It's not safe for you."

"What do you mean? Are you in trouble?" I set my own fork down, my appetite gone.

"No. However, the less others know about you, the better it is for everyone."

"I can work for you. You don't have to pay me much," I suggest, not knowing what I can do but anxious to get him to concede something.

His open palm smacks the table and makes me jump as high as the salt and pepper shakers.

"I don't want you to bring it up again." Our eyes meet, and I wonder if he'll hit me. His cheeks are red, and the veins in his forehead are bulging. This is the first time I've seen him this agitated.

I advert my eyes and stare at my plate, hoping his foul mood will dissipate before morning.

* * *

KARAMBAMBULIA IS a national drink made of red wine mixed with liquor. It's popular, but tonight, Papa brings out an expensive bottle of cognac to show off. The men arrive, knocking on the door. When I open it, they all greet me warmly and make their way to the table.

"Ratmim." Andrian enthusiastically greets my father. They seem to be celebrating something, and I'm in the dark about what. The men clap each other on the back and gather around the table.

I made snacks for the night and set up a spread in the kitchen. I can't wait until it's after ten o'clock. I will pretend I'm tired and go to bed.

I like where my brothers live in downtown Minsk and enjoy visiting them, even though they don't value me. I'm occasionally allowed to tag along when Papa has unimportant meetings. I observe the murals on the side of the old pre-WWII-era buildings. The dreary buildings look better in the summer when the pretty flowers bloom. We only have a few months of the year when it's warm enough to plant things.

"Dasha, we need more pretzels," my father grumbles.

I move to the kitchen and grab a bowl.

"Don't touch the cards," Papa warns me, as if I didn't know his precious cards mean more to him than I do.

I set the bowl on the table. Andrian is fifteen years older than me with the manners of a billy goat. I doubt he cooks, as he eats everything in sight when he comes over. Now that he's older, his belly is so big that his shirt doesn't touch the top of his dress pants. Papa told me to always be nice to him because Andrian knows men who can toss us out of our apartment if we don't do what he wants, which makes me wonder if my father is paying rent. If he isn't, where is his money going? I know illegal gains are usually substantial. If so, where is his money? I've never figured out how much he makes for a living. We don't have flashy possessions.

"Thank you, Dasha," Andrian says with a suggestive undertone as I retreat from the table. I feel his eyes following me. I'm confused by this sudden change in him. He's never come on to me before. When I turn to look at him, his eyes linger on me longer than is necessary, making my skin crawl.

I shake my head enough for only him to notice and excuse myself for the evening. The men continue to play Durak and mutter among themselves. I choose to forget the awkwardness and head to my room.

I shower and change into nightclothes. My phone beeps with messages. I play the Snapchat videos Katsia messaged me. She's out with a group of friends and is having a blast.

I am a social outcast. Everyone has something to do tonight but me. I sit alone in the dark. My life isn't turning out the way I planned. I must have been crazy to think Papa would ever change. My mother and brothers have abandoned me, and my only future is being a glorified maid with no way out.

# CHAPTER 4

ROMAN

"What the hell are you doing?" I ask Alex as he loads every weapon imaginable onto the plane. It's like watching a woman pack for vacation, but instead of shoes, it's guns and ammo.

"Preparing for the unexpected." He gives me a serious look, and I realize he's done this so many times that I shouldn't second-guess him.

My goal is to plan this job and pull it off perfectly, not make it up as events unravel. Jobs can go sideways quickly, and I hate improvising. Everything we do in life is a risk, and I like to have control in all situations.

Alex piles more bags in the jet's luggage compartment, a lit cigarette dangling from his mouth. I look down to make sure we're not standing in a puddle of fuel. He knows smoking is not allowed on the tarmac, but he doesn't care. That applies to his clothes, too. His designer jeans are worn, and the soles of his boots are uneven. He loves watches and likes to wear his hair with a lived-in style worn by rockers in a band. He finishes loading the equipment and nods to his friend sitting in a waiting SUV. The driver acknowledges him with a wave of his hand before driving away.

Alex is not one to sweat the small things in life and has no qualms about shooting his way out of a situation. I often wonder if he cares whether he lives or dies. What he does care about is work. Once we have a target, he's like a bloodhound following a scent. He would rather go on adventures than have a personal life. He's methodical with his equipment but careless about everything else. I wouldn't be surprised to learn he has kids all over the world as a result of his carelessness.

I'm heartless. It's easy to get women. I have money. Even though I can be an asshole, women still line up for my approval and drink the expensive champagne my money buys.

"You have enough shit here to start a revolution," I tease, but we have that in common.

"Fuck you, Roman." He takes one last drag off his cigarette before he drops it, grinds it into the ground with his military-style shoe, and turns to board.

I follow him up the steps. I hate going to Belarus. I'd much rather be on the way to the Italian coast or the Greek islands. The family's huge yacht is at my disposal and ready to go. The weather is perfect for the open waters under sunny skies—no one tans in Russia. I plan to enjoy my freedom as soon as I resolve this current situation. The question is, who do I want on the yacht with me?

I buckle my seatbelt. Today is one more job of many. I'm sure Ratmim is a dirtbag, and his sons are just as dicey, growing up with the family business. Who's Ratmim in bed with, to get in and out of Russia so cleverly? I need to know. He's a low-level criminal, so the directive came from someone more powerful than him. Ratmim doesn't have a family tree peppered with public officials.

I keep my eyes on the ground and my ears open. Intel gathered in person is valuable. My peers consider me to be rather old-school for my age. They're all into technology, but I don't believe we should rely on one type of surveillance. There's no such thing as having too much information if you want to be successful. I can thank my mentor, Misha, for my attitude. Misha trained me to track the wind for long-range shooting, along with other skill sets needed to survive in the wild. Technology can be limited.

When it comes to guns, I'm proficient in most weapons but I love guns. I've worked with Alex for years, so we're like a finely oiled machine. In the field, once my gun is set up and dialed in for head-winds and tailwinds, Alex takes over. He's great at adjusting my shot for winds. I'm used to a scope for long-range shots.

I like to visualize water flowing to my target when I'm planning a long-range shot. Does the stream go over a hill, then dip down and stay true? What about wind stream and its effect on the bullet's trajectory? Alex and I have studied flags and wind to perfect our shooting techniques, honing our craft on numerous deer hunts over the years.

Normally, I'd call Dmitry for the information I want. He's an ace at hacking into systems, with an uncanny ability to get information that's never seen the light of day. They call it the dark web for a reason. If I asked, Dmitry would do a deep dive on Ratmim, but he's newly married with a gorgeous wife and a baby on the way. His life now is…complicated.

I'm happy for him, but in my opinion, love is for dreamers and masochists. My mom and dad loved one another, shared the same interests and passions, but they were lucky. They never tired of one another, but that kind of love is rare.

I prefer being single. I can do what I want, when I want. Nikolay says I'm spoiled, and that Mom coddled me too much as a baby.

Maybe so, but I have my own wing in the family house. It may reek of testosterone, but I don't have anyone telling me to get my boots off the coffee table, and that's fine by me.

There is a pecking order in the world of organized crime. We would not exist if we didn't provide services to men with political aspirations and power. We do what they cannot by using our street-savvy skills to make money through nefarious and morally gray methods. We capitalize on this, getting protection from them, and they, in turn, make other demands of us.

Most people don't realize it, but controlling something as simple as aluminum can destabilize the market supply chain and cause spikes in prices. When quantities are limited, we profit from the product, and the stock price increases. It's easy to manipulate the free-market system, and no one is the wiser. Aluminum is just one example of how we can make millions in a short amount of time. We create opportunities on Wall Street for our inside people to make deals that line our pockets. No one comes looking to see how much aluminum we have in stock.

We prefer currencies like the dollar and euro because they are more stable than the ruble. For now, I'm staying away from cyber currency. Let someone else get stuck holding a bag of worthless bitcoins. We've also invested in legitimate businesses. Buildings, land, and hotels. It's like a game of Monopoly.

I'm not sure where today's fishing expedition will lead. We will follow Ratmim, and somehow, I will extract what we need or seek my revenge without starting a war.

As the plane taxis down the runway to take off, I start to second-guess the mission. Maybe I'm being impetuous and seeking Niko-lay's approval. I failed my family and don't want to be seen as a fuckup. I'm the point man my brothers depend upon when the chips are down. I refuse to lose their respect over this.

The gun shipment was my responsibility. They were stolen on my watch, so I take Ratmim's theft as a personal attack. It's my job to make it right and negotiate compensation, but it won't be easy. We've all been hardened by real-life wars, and often, negotiation is considered a sign of weakness. If diplomacy fails, I have no choice but to give him consequences. In the end, I will find a way to make Ratmim pay for what he's done.

"I get that you're pissed, but do you have a plan?" Alex asks over the roar of the engines as we take off.

"Nope," I answer honestly.

He chuckles. "This is unlike you. I mean, you're the one who plans entire heists and has men trained to help. Why go it alone?"

"If we already know Ratmim took our weapons, he's not an adversary I need to worry about."

"Hm. They say pride comes before the fall. Isn't that a Bible verse or some fucking thing?" He gives me the side-eye and raises an eyebrow. He's older but not wiser. Between the two of us, I'm the one with the brains.

I chuckle. "Yeah, something like that."

Is he trying to say I fucked up? I scooch my butt further into the leather seat. This small plane is primitive compared to the family jet, but we don't use the jet for work. Don't want to risk losing it. The government would seize it in a flash if they suspected it was used during the commission of an unsanctioned crime

Alex clasps his hands behind his head, closes his eyes, and leans back against his seat.

Maybe tracking Ratmim on his home turf is a mistake. It would be better to wait until he's on vacation, relaxed and ripe for the picking. As hitmen, we find our targets and prey on them when they are vulnerable. Rarely do they have a home-field advantage. Then again, their routines are predictable at home and might give me a perfect opening. If not, I'll wait for the element of surprise and use it in my favor.

My phone vibrates in the pocket of my dark gray dress pants. I pull it out to read a text. It's from Nadia, the Russian model I'm currently fucking. She has one of those shapeless bodies that are perfect for fashion show runways.

She wants to know what I'm up to.

I don't reply. I turn my phone off and tuck it away. We can't risk being tracked.

"Woman trouble?" Alex asks without opening his eyes.

"Not yet. Models are so skinny. Sometimes it feels like I'm fucking a rack of ribs."

Alex laughs heartily and leans forward, clutching his gut. "I understand. I like my Russian women with big, bouncy breasts and an ass made for grabbing."

"I need to date someone who isn't constantly looking in the mirror or on their phone. Is it too much to ask? I feel like I never left school with these twenty-year-olds."

"I don't think you're asking for much. Be patient. Maybe you should try looking for someone with an imagination because you don't have one."

"That's harsh," I reply.

"It's the truth. You're too focused. You need to loosen up a bit. Maybe when you're not trying to be the perfect brother in the family, you'll find someone worthwhile."

"I'm fine. I'm comfortable with who I am."

"Comfortable can get you killed. Besides, all work and no play makes you a dull person."

If "play" means I have to attend fancy parties and drink overpriced champagne while making idle chitchat with dull people, I'd rather be home alone, working on the next heist.

"What of you? Who do you have?" I pretend to be offended as I cross my ankles and turn to see his face.

Alex grunts. When he delays going home after jobs, I know it means he's single and between women.

I've had crushes but never a long-term relationship. The women I date assume I'm wealthy because we meet at some billionaire's party. They don't know it's an illusion cultivated by my family to fit in. In reality, we all belong in prison. Our hands are dirty, and our souls are black.

It's tough living two lives. I hate making small talk at social gatherings. I have nothing to say and worry they see me for who I really am—a hitman who enjoys his job.

Honestly, I can do without the expensive toys and posh lifestyle. I'm getting older and have no business at these nightclubs late at night. The majority of people are younger than me, and I stick out like an old man at a bachelor party. Maybe it's a sign. Maybe I should be moving on to the next phase of my life. The role of an aging playboy is unoriginal.

We've been in the air for over an hour, so I unbuckle my seatbelt, stretch, and walk to the galley. We'll be landing soon. The first order of business is to find a hotel and pay cash for a few nights' stay. We'll follow up on the rumors we've heard among our contacts, rumors that I hope will lead us to the man who keeps his location a secret.

I take a bottle of water out of the minifridge and drain it. It chills my throat. I grab another for Alex and return to my seat to buckle up for the landing. I hate visiting Belarus. The thieves who come into Russia from here have no honor.

The landing is smooth. When the door opens, we exit the plane and find Alex's contact waiting to pick us up. Pavel is a Belarusian we've used in the past.

We open the cargo door and retrieve our duffel bags, Alex's stash of long-range weapons, and a gear bag. We load everything into a vehicle waiting for us on the tarmac. I shake hands with Pavel, a tall man in a long-sleeved dress shirt, black dress pants, and worn dress shoes. His dark hair is thinning prematurely. But I don't need him to have hair. I need him to do his job and do it well.

I need him not to double-cross us.

"How are you?" He's happy to see us. I wonder if he'd still be smiling if he knew what we wanted. The people here tend to turn away when things don't look right. They don't like trouble, and that's my middle name.

I take the back seat, letting Alex have the front. Pavel pulls onto a main road and heads into the city. The scenery reminds me of Russia, as it should, since this was once part of the motherland. Most of the states that fell away from the Kremlin remain close to Russia, and the borders are easy to cross. It's only in times of political turmoil that people may quietly dissent among themselves. For practical purposes, Belarusians and Russians are the same, with different leaders and slightly different cultures.

"So, Pavel, we haven't seen you in some time." I start a conversation while looking out the window. I want to be on the Mediterranean instead of in this landlocked country.

"No, you have not."

"How is business?"

"Slow. Very slow."

It's what I expected to hear. The economy is bad, and their homes are unimpressive. Many crops are grown here and traded to Russia for affordable energy.

"We're looking for Ratmim Kozlov. Do you know where we might find him?"

Is it my imagination, or does Pavel stiffen at the mention of his name?

Alex takes over telling him that we mean the man no harm. We have business with Ratmim and don't intend for Pavel to get caught in the middle.

"I don't know." Pavel hedges and grips the steering wheel harder.

"Pavel, it's more money. I will make it worth your while. We'll need your help to find him. No one will catch on if you don't spend all the money quickly. Be smart, and you'll be fine." As I coax him, his knuckles fade from pink to death-grip pale.

"I know you mean well, but he's not a man I want to cross. He makes raids inside Russia. His men are all over," Pavel says.

"Who is he aligned with for protection?"

"I'm not sure. There are so many lower-level officials. It's a maze. We are the mice in the fields. They are the cats."

His fear is real. Men like Ratmim don't like being bothered by anyone outside their network. If you passed him on the street and said, "Hello," he'd look at you with his ugly mug as if you were nothing to him. They freely switch their allegiances to whoever pays them the most. Greed is commonplace, especially when there is only enough money to meet people's basic needs. If you want anything extra, you'd better be willing to steal it or die for it.

Pavel pulls up in front of a local motel with four floors. Alex runs in and pays for a room while I continue to work on Pavel. I hand him hundreds of Belarusian rubles. "There's more where this came from."

"I'll see what I can find out," he murmurs, stuffing the money in his pocket. His knuckles return to normal as his hands relax on the steering wheel.

"Great. Alex will call you later," I tell him. Pavel nods.

Alex returns to the car and tells Pavel to drive around the back. We pull up to our room on the first floor and smuggle the bags inside. I'm not sure we'll need Alex's toys. On the other hand, it never hurts to have firepower. I just don't want to end up in prison here.

When Pavel leaves, I turn to Alex and say, "I think he'll help us. After we hide this shit, let's hit Pub 1999. Maybe we'll see or hear something that will help us locate Ratmim."

"Good idea," he says, kneeling on a threadbare carpet scarred with cigarette burns. Not exactly five-star accommodations, but we've stayed in worse.

I hand Alex one shotgun in a case and watch as he slides it under the bed. I repeat this again and again until all the weapons are stowed. Then Alex grabs his gear bag and shoves it under the bed. I plop our duffel bags on our beds.

"We're looking for a ghost," I say to Alex as we turn to leave our room and blend in with the locals.

The sun is going down, and it's quickly getting dark as we walk into town. Pub 1999 is in a small square in Minsk, where Ratmim was last seen six months ago. We suspect it might be his local hangout. We know the players in our backyard, but as we expand, it's imperative that we have intel on the crime families in neighboring countries. Belarus gets a pass from the officials in Russia because the men who run both countries have the same agenda: make money off the backs of people and let us be the bad guys and the clearing house for illegal gains.

It's not long before we see the sign for Pub 1999 hanging over a big wooden door covered in peeling red paint. I take a deep breath to calm my nerves as I enter the dimly lit establishment. It takes a minute for my eyes to adjust to my surroundings.

The people here are down to earth, but it feels like I've stepped back in time. Several men sit at the bar. They barely look up from their beer mugs to acknowledge our presence. Waitresses scurry about and definitely ignore us, which is a typical Eastern European attitude.

The décor is mid-century Soviet gray. I'm tired of seeing it everywhere. The aroma of roasting potatoes and onions confirms there's a kitchen in the back. My stomach growls, reminding me it's been a while since we ate.

A few couples sit at tables near the windows. Seeing the women in pretty dresses, I figure it must be date night. It's relatively inexpensive to eat out here. And as in every country I visit, the single crowd will be bar hopping further into town.

It's standing room only, but we get the bartender's attention and order two beers. We make light conversation as we thread our way to the back of the establishment, where we hope to overhear conversations. There's a bunch of rough-looking men gathered around the pool table. Some have removed their leather jackets to shoot pool, and I can see they're covered in gang tattoos.

Standing in a corner and using others as a cover, I can hear bits and pieces of conversation. Most of them are complaining about their women. I don't see Ratmim, so I'm not sure if these are his men.

Alex makes a face, and I can tell he's worried we might be on a fool's mission. We could return home with nothing, but I refuse to accept defeat. Patience is my virtue. We can wait this out.

"I doubt he's been here tonight," I say.

Alex shrugs. "It's early by their standards. We'll grab a table if one opens."

"Sure. Nothing looks out of the ordinary. It's a Saturday night, nothing much is happening. They don't take kindly to men who cause a ruckus. They're all locals."

"True, they always think they are better than us. It's because they can hide here," he mutters. There is a long-standing feud between Russians and members of other countries. The fact that the bartender was civil to us doesn't go unnoticed.

"We'll show them they can't do that anymore," I murmur, and Alex nods.

To pass the time, I fill him in on the details of Dmitry's wedding. Not too many weddings involve explosions.

"Shit, man, I had no idea. How is Izzy's father?"

"He'll make a full recovery, but Dmitry is living in New York now."

"So you're in Russia indefinitely?"

"It appears that way. That's why I was looking forward to getting away on the yacht. Now I can't go until this situation is resolved." I have earned my vacation; the sooner this is over, the better. I'm not sure where I'll go, but the yacht staff knows I'm coming.

We keep our voices low so we don't set off alarm bells and draw unwanted attention. We're not locals. How long can we hang out without becoming conspicuous?

I finish my beer and head to the bathroom, passing a group of men loudly celebrating on the way. One of them mentions a wedding. What wedding?

When I get back to Alex, he's been eavesdropping as he pretends to wait for a pool table. The men finish their game and return to their pitchers of beer. Toasts are made, and they clap one another on the back, one man in particular. He's vaguely familiar, but I looked at many pictures at my father's desk. I might have him confused with someone else. It's late, and we decide to return to the hotel. We don't know the players here. Maybe this was a wasted trip.

Alex's phone rings, and he answers it as soon as we get to our room.

# CHAPTER 5

## ROMAN

"Yes." Alex lifts his burner phone and begins to pace. "Great. Thank you so much."

He hangs up. I wait anxiously for intel on Ratmim. "So?"

"I'm told he'll be at a small wedding tomorrow." The right side of his mouth curls up mischievously.

My heart soars, and so does my adrenaline. Ratmim is within reach. There is no honor among thieves, but he must realize there will be a price to pay for stealing from us.

I'm not one to act on emotions. Smart men are patient and methodical. I prefer to sit back and watch situations evolve. The last thing I want to do is cause tensions to escalate between organized criminal factions. But today feels different. Today, I'm itching to start trouble as an outlet for my anger and frustration.

After my father's murder, it didn't matter that we consoled ourselves with the knowledge that he made a terrible business deal. His bad judgment put him and Igor on the list to be terminated.

This is what happens when men like us refuse political requests. They are never requests. They are orders. It's the price we pay to exist in a system full of corruption.

Sometimes I wonder if Dad refused to sell his stock short because it was a detriment to the oil company or because he was taking a stand against a broken system. Whatever the reason, his untimely death threw my need to be perfect into overdrive. It's part of the reason I'm tracking Ratmim. He's a loose end. There's no way of knowing whether he will target us again, and I don't want to leave it to chance.

"I suppose you have the name of the church. There are too many to search."

"Yes, of course." His tone indicates it's an absurd question.

I shrug. "It's Pavel. I mean, who knows?"

"Apparently, money talks. Let's get a rental car. We don't want to implicate Pavel."

My eyebrows raise. "Fine. Did he say who's getting married?"

"No idea. We suspected those were his men at the pub last night. Perhaps that was a bachelor party," Alex says as he puts a cigarette in his mouth.

"Could be."

The clubs have closed. We stand outside our hotel room, watching locals drive home.

Alex pulls a matchbook from his pocket and lights his cigarette. "How old do you think Ratmim is? From the picture, he must be in his fifties. Kind of late to be getting married."

"Who cares? We found him."

"Right." He takes a long drag on the cigarette. "What's the plan?"

"I have no plan. Which means this might not end well. For starters, we need to identify as many of his men as possible before they know we're here. We have the element of surprise, but I don't want to get in trouble with the law."

"Tell me about it." He exhales a smoke ring.

It's not like me to go into a mission without a plan. Before Dad died, I loved to micromanage every detail.

"Let's just focus on gaining intel. We'll follow him and find out where he's living. We'll track his associates, and maybe they will lead us to our guns. Then the next time Ratmim comes on our turf, we can make his death look like an accident."

"What do we do between now and then?" Alex asks.

"We make their lives miserable. They come to Russia to steal, then run back across the border to safety. If we find our guns, we steal them back." Leaning against a pillar, I smile at the thought of getting even.

He nods. "I didn't think about that." He inhales another drag and blows smoke.

"If we can find where they keep their stash, we can bring in more men. Take our guns back or steal something of theirs to hurt them financially."

"Mm. This could turn into something huge. I'm not sure Nikolay would want us to fuck them that hard."

"Right. Well, after Dad, I can't be too vigilant. Information is information. It doesn't hurt to keep our eyes on them going forward. New organizations pop up every year."

"True. I have to admit, being here sucks. Letting them come to us gives us the advantage." He takes another puff of his cigarette.

"That's my thought as well. If they weren't ballsy enough to intercept our weapons shipment, I'd be on vacation, cruising the Mediterranean."

# CHAPTER 6

## ROMAN

"Relaxing on a yacht sounds fun. Are you taking that skinny model with you?"

"Hell, no. I might go by myself. Not sure. You're free, aren't you?" I give Alex the side-eye and wait for him to spill the beans on his personal life.

"What fun is a huge yacht if you don't have enough people to party with while you're at sea?" he says without taking the bait.

"I'm bored with parties. It's always the same faces. All these women are getting hair extensions and breast implants and Brazilian butt lifts and lip fillers, and in the end, they all look alike. Is it too much to ask for a natural beauty?" I ask, shifting my weight from the pillar I'm leaning against back to my feet.

"I stick to women from my neighborhood. Trust me, that's not always the best idea, either," Alex says while grinding his cigarette butt under the heel of his boot.

I nod. He never says much about the women in his life, but I'm sure he's broken some hearts over the years.

"Ready to turn in?" I ask.

"Yeah, it's late. We'll get a car in the morning and arrive at the church early so we can watch everyone who walks in or out. Maybe we can figure out who's connected to whom."

"You read my mind." I open the hotel door, and we enter. The hum of the window-unit air conditioner greets us, but I'm used to roughing it when I'm tracking someone. I know how to infiltrate neighborhoods and get in and out without being noticed.

Once I make sure the room is secure, I use my burner phone and text Nikolay to inform him of our plan to run surveillance on Ratmim tomorrow. It's late, but he can read the text in the morning.

Life in the bratva has changed over the years. We know cybercrime is the easiest way to make money, and it can't be traced. We delve into many seedy practices to make our money, like extorting money from local businesses, running drugs, and selling weapons. Danger lurks around every corner. We have to watch our backs at all times, especially around our business associates and the powers that run our neighborhoods.

The upside to wealth is that it gives us things others don't have. I'm not going to complain about the nice home we live in or being able to afford the delicacies we eat and the alcohol we consume. In fact, it's very profitable to smuggle cognac into the country. There's a rising demand for it among the nouveau riche.

I have the freedom to travel. I can lease airplanes and afford a private jet.

I plug my phone into a charger and sit on the worn bed to pull off my boots, which I place neatly under the clothing rack. I packed a change of shirts and boxers because we're only going to be here a few days. I open my duffel bag, remove a bag of toiletries, and carry it into the bathroom.

"What do you want to watch?" Alex has the remote and is clicking channels.

"Nothing. Whatever you want."

I turn the shower on to warm the water. The tub has seen better days and seems to be held together with copious amounts of caulk and paint. I pull the white curtain aside and test the water. Deciding it's warm enough, I undress and step in. After washing my hair and body, I dry off with a thin, scratchy towel barely big enough to wrap around my waist. I rub the steam off the mirror and stare at my reflection.

I carry no extra weight, so it's easy to make out the muscles in my arms, chest, and abs. The ladies seem particularly attracted to the deep V muscles that point to my groin. I can thank the trainer who comes to the house a few times a week. I hate the pain of box jumps, but it's good for core strength training. I moan and groan during the workout, but I like the results.

The towel is still around my waist when I return to the room. I drop it on the floor, not giving a damn, as the carpet is old, threadbare, and stained. A floor is the least of my concerns. I slide into the cool, crisp sheets. The room is a dump, but the bed sheets are clean, even if the mattress is lumpy. We're off the radar in a hole that no one cares about. And that's how we do these undercover missions.

I stare absentmindedly at the box TV to pass the time. Everything broadcasted is garbage. It's ridiculous what passes as entertainment, and I hate the rating labels on shows and all the warnings of smoking and violence. Hell, even if you're lucky enough to stumble across an iconic show with lots of profanity, there's no movie left by the time they bleep out the saucy bits and make it "family-friendly." I don't have a family, and I say fuck that. Where do I get a say in how I want my movies delivered to me? I'm not a kid, for fuck's sake.

I can't stand recycled reality shows or comedies that aren't funny. The rest of the channels on this TV will have cheesy, predictable stories to warm the heart, and the international news will be depressing. It's totally written to manipulate voters.

"Ugh. It's all shit on TV. I can't wait to be home. This country sucks." Granted, our TV programs at home are only marginally better; many are censored and from our own country. This is why I had Dmitry set up an entire library of movies on a server that are accessible from anywhere, even the yacht. Our servers are encrypted, as is everything technological that we own. It's the same with our security camera. And we have staff that does nothing but monitor our houses and properties.

Except for the guns that are tucked away, we never want to give the impression that there is anything of value behind the concrete walls. I'm going to change that when I get home. I'll see to it that well-hidden infrared cameras are installed, along with weight sensors built into the floor to sound an alarm. If anyone but us moves our contraband, we'll know. And I'll make sure the staff doesn't know so the secret will never get out. Loose lips sink ships, and all that shit.

Alex heads to the bathroom to clean up and returns fifteen minutes later. "Anything new on TV?"

"Hell, no."

"It's late, morning will be here in no time." He makes his way to his bed, wearing only his boxers, and flops down.

"Is your mattress shit as well?"

"More like a bag of rocks." He punches his pillow a few times to fluff it before burying his head in it, then pulls the covers up to his chin.

"God knows when they last washed that thing. I always make sure the sheet is over the comforter. And you still cover every part of your body and pull that nasty thing up to your face," I tease him.

"And you still sleep naked and alone."

"Right, well, I'm turning off the light now." I reach for the lamp between us and flip the switch, hoping it works. It clicks, and the light goes out. I'd hate to have to get up and flip the switch by the wall because the floors are less than desirable without shoes.

I lie in the darkness, listening to Alex snore. He can fall asleep standing up. I'm envious of the fact that he's not an insomniac like me. My mind is like a wheel, always in motion. I wonder what tomorrow will bring.

I think about the model I could be fucking right now and wonder if I'll ever find a woman who would be content being with me and traveling with me. What's the point in being together when the women I date are always on a plane, heading for their next modeling job? It's great that they can have careers; the models make good money and see the world. But if I ever settle down, I'm not going to be her arm candy. I don't even care if the jet-setters, the millionaires and billionaires, know my name.

Strange that now that both of my brothers are married, the thought of getting married is on my mind. I've never had a desire to settle down. I'm the elusive brother. Only Mom can nail me down for the occasional family dinner and the holidays. I loved cognac and cigar time with my brothers, but those days were numbered, and we didn't even realize it. It all changed overnight. Now, we're lucky if we see each other a few times a year. We worked together, and I took our male bonding time for granted. Now?

My life has become as stale as three-day-old bread.

# CHAPTER 7

## DASHA

When I wake, the apartment is quiet. I stir and sit up, rubbing my eyes. A new dress is hanging on a hook on the back of the door. What is this? I don't normally get gifts unless it's my birthday or Christmas. My birthday isn't until August.

I throw the bed covers back and sprint to the dress, running my fingers over the gauzy material. Could this be a summer dress? It's rather fancy. The flowing sleeves have slits in the material so they will billow in a breeze. It's floor-length, but I can hem it if necessary. Why white, though? Papa knows I love to wear blue.

"Papa," I holler, opening the door and entering the living area.

"What?" he barks, clutching a coffee cup. His fingernails are dirty, and his knobby knuckles make his hands look more like claws.

"The dress, what's it for?"

Papa puts his cup down and takes my hands in his. The smell of last night's booze is still on him. He's hungover. I can tell by his bloodshot eyes.

"You're marrying Andrian today. It's been arranged for some time. I couldn't tell you before," he says without looking at me.

What a coward.

"No," I whisper in disbelief, pulling my hands free. I take a step back, then another.

"Dasha, it's necessary. I pulled an unsanctioned job, and Andrian is pissed at me. This will make it right. You don't want me to get hurt, do you?"

He sounds pathetic, but how are his problems suddenly mine? He can't take care of himself. A marriage to Andrian will mean a lifetime of this. I'll never be free, and the nightmare will never end. I won't be able to live on my own or fall in love or go to another country. Andrian will have me flat on my back, popping out kids. The thought of him between my legs makes me shiver.

Andrian's beady, reptilian eyes are creepy. He's a corrupt government official in bed with my father and others who do his dirty work. I hate him for keeping the status quo in our country. I want to leave here so badly, but I have no idea how to get out of Minsk, let alone Belarus.

I bolt from the room, slam my bedroom door, and call Katsia.

"Katsia, Papa has arranged for me to marry Andrian—today."

"No way. How can he even do that? What the hell is going on?"

"I don't know. He says he's in trouble, but honestly, it was just a matter of time before Andrian got something on him. The way he was leering at me last night made my skin crawl."

"What are you going to do? You can't marry him. Everyone knows he's mean and morally bankrupt, and he'll have you watched every second of every day. If you think your life is a prison now, it will only get worse. Plus, he surrounds himself with an unsavory group of men, and not just your family."

"I know. But what can I do? I have nowhere to go," I wail, feeling desperate and defeated. "Leaving the country is the only way I can get out of this." I slump onto my bed, clutching a pillow to my chest, and burst into tears.

Katsia's silence confirms my worst fears. There is no way around this. Andrian will look for me. He has the means to hunt me down. He has connections in other countries, and he knows powerful people. He can have my father thrown into prison on trumped-up charges.

I cry because I don't have a mother to protect me. I cry because my brothers helped Papa, and they would be implicated if Papa went down for a crime. It's no use calling them for help. They've been traveling to Russia and other countries for years, and I know they've moved illegal items around for our government. I hear them talk about guns, and they have numerous phones and secret meetings, though what about, I don't know.

Andrian is not involved in their daily operations, but he's connected to some degree. Never in public, but he comes to our house to socialize…or maybe to see me. How long has he had his eye on me?

The men in this family always put themselves first. The only thing they will miss when I'm gone is my cooking and cleaning. They're bullies, and even if they could help me, they won't.

"There must be something you can do," Katsia says. "I'm so sorry, Dasha. What can I do to help?"

"Nothing," is all I can say. We both know how this works. "Your family's life would be in jeopardy if you helped me. I can't do that to you." I sniffle and wipe my nose on the sleeve of my nightgown.

"Fuck!" she exclaims, surprising me.

I chuckle. "You've never cursed in your life."

"I know. But this is preposterous. I'm beside myself. I should be there with you."

"There's nothing anyone can do for me. I'm like a fatted calf going to the slaughter."

"He never said anything about this until today?"

"Right. He said he couldn't bring himself to tell me. No wonder Andrian was so smug last night. They've been working this deal out for some time."

"Ugh," Katsia groans. "Men."

"Right? All I wanted was to find an honest man who would treat me well. Instead, I get this knuckle-dragger who will want to stuff his slug of a dick in me." Fuck. I'll never know what it's like to fall in love. "I stood a chance of running away from Papa, but Andrian? Not even Houdini could escape this mess."

"Right. Shit, I wish we had contacts in another country, but with time running out, now you need a miracle. Maybe you can get the marriage annulled." She sighs. "Never mind. He has influence, so that's not going to happen."

"I'm doomed." I resign myself to the fact that I can't fight the men controlling my life. I thought I had time to get out. "Papa probably knew I'd make a run for it one day, and he kept me here as his insurance plan," I mutter, convinced that Andrian knew all along I'd be the sacrificial lamb.

"Maybe if you fuck Andrian, he'll give you privileges. Then you could use his contacts to get out of here, change your name, and hide somewhere."

"I appreciate your optimism, but I'm not smart enough to know how to do that, and it costs money that I don't have." In my world, I'm a fool for dreaming of a better life. I'm not asking for much. All I want is to be like the other people my age who work during the week and go to clubs on the weekend.

I jump when Papa pounds his fists on my bedroom door.

"Dasha, we need to talk," he calls.

"I have to go, Katsia."

"Text me what's happening. I'll be there for you."

"Thanks." I hang up and cross the room.

"I don't want to see you," I yell through the door.

"You can't say that. I have to give you away at the church."

"Church? You don't even know where it is. You're such a hypocrite!"

"Please, Dasha. I'm begging you, don't hate me."

"It's too late for that. I hate you. I hate you!" I scream.

"Well, the ceremony is at eleven o'clock. Small service. Just a few people."

"No doubt I'm saving you from a stretched neck!" I yell again. Papa's done it this time. My mind is racing as I try to think of alternatives.

I fling the door open. "Why couldn't you buy your way out of this? You all love money so much," I argue.

"He doesn't want money. He wants you."

"You don't see a problem with this? He's old enough to be my father!" My eyes bore into him. This is not happening, I tell myself. I'll wake up and discover this is a bad dream.

I pinch my arm. Ouch! That hurt. Fuck me, it's not a nightmare, it's my life.

"Leave," I command.

"You'll do it, right?" His eyes dart from me to the dress and back again.

"It seems my sole purpose in life is to throw myself on the mercy of men and hope they keep me fed and sheltered. Why would I have a problem with that?" I say with sarcasm, slamming the door in his face. Today, of all days, I can get away with this because in a few hours, I won't be beholden to him.

Instead, I'll have a new jailer, and something tells me it'll be a life sentence. Andrian can keep me in Belarus, take away my ID, and have me flagged at the border. I'm sure he has the money and powerful connections to pull it off.

I wonder if this was Papa's or Andrian's idea. I wouldn't put it past Papa to sell me to the devil if it made his problems disappear. Did he sell me for cash or barter my life to save his own skin?

I can't jump out a two-story window. I can't involve any friends. My options are fading faster than my hopes of marrying Prince Charming.

Shit. What if I pretend to go along with the plan and figure a way out later?

My chest is tight, and my breathing is labored. I feel dizzy and sit down at my desk, my heart pounding. I force myself to breathe more slowly, inhaling deeply and exhaling. I can do this. I can get to the next minute if I take it one second at a time.

I text Katsia, asking her to come over. I text Papa to let her in.

Ten minutes later, there is a light knock on my door, and Katsia quietly slips inside my room.

"Katsia!" I run to her and give her a hug.

She sets her purse on the dresser. "What are you going to do?"

"I don't know. You know Andrian. I can't imagine his hands on me. You've had sex. Tell me what it's like."

"It's better than doing it yourself if you're with the right man." She gives me a knowing smirk, and I get it. It must be like the romance novels I read.

"I wanted to lose my virginity to someone special…" My voice trails off.

"I know," she says quietly. Her face is drawn, and I know she's only holding herself together so I don't freak out again.

"Wait! What if he only wants me because I'm a virgin? If I give it to someone else, he might change his mind!" I grab her arms in excitement.

"Wow, you're right. Andrian's a pig. I bet he'd love to have a young virgin under him," she says, making a gagging noise.

I shake my head, trying to rid myself of the visual of Andrian on top of me. "I'd rather die than have that fat, hairy fuck put his dick in me."

"Right? I know. I'm with you. But how do we accomplish this in a few hours?"

I shrug. "How the hell do I know? Besides, what if I get pregnant? I don't have birth control."

"Oh, shit." She smacks her forehead with her palm and begins to pace. "Well, if we can get to my house, I could give you mine. Then all you'd have to do is find some dude to deflower you…" She peers into my green eyes with excitement in her voice. "It's worth a shot."

"Great, let's go. At least I'll be able to make one decision in my life," I exclaim. Finally, an opportunity to get out of this ridiculous and antiquated ritual of auctioning off daughters to pay their fathers' debts, and I'd love nothing more than to ruin their plans.

We race to the front door, but Papa steps in front of us. "Where are you going?" he demands.

"To Katsia's to get hair accessories," I fib.

"No, you're not. I don't trust you. You'll run off. It's time you woke up from your dreams and realize this is your life, your destiny." His voice is cruel, leaving me to wonder if he really hates me enough to condemn me to a life of servitude.

I shoot Katsia a look of defeat. She bows her head enough to confirm it's pointless.

"Katsia, you may go, but Dasha stays. She needs to get ready."

"I'll stay," she says, grabbing my hand, and dragging me back to the bedroom.

"Shit, now what?" I ask, shutting the door behind us.

"Okay, on your wedding night, grab tons of cold medicine or whatever and dump it in his drink. He'll be drinking at the luncheon afterward, but at night, he'll drink more." She sits on the bed beside me. "Drug him," she whispers.

And for the second time today, hope swells in my chest. It shouldn't be that difficult to carry out.

"It will buy you enough time to sneak out and meet up with a random man. Imagine you get pregnant and Andrian thinks the kid is his. Serves him right." She rises and walks to the door, running her hand down the wedding dress. "Your father finally gives you a new dress, and it may as well be for your funeral. What an ass."

"Welcome to my life. What else is new? I don't know how I missed him planning this. My only clue was yesterday, when Andrian was acting weird." I open a drawer and take out fresh panties and a bra.

I pull my hair up into a makeshift bun.

"I don't want to be pretty for him," I say. "It might be my final act of rebellion before I'm punished. I'm not wearing makeup."

She nods. "I'm so sorry, Dasha."

"I'm so lucky to have you as a friend." I hug her, and her arms fold around me. She holds me tight for a few seconds before we break apart.

I pull off my nightgown and put my undergarments on. Katsia takes the dress off the hanger and holds it high. I slip under it, and it falls onto my shoulders. I smooth it down with my hands, and Katsia zips the back.

"What does sex feel like? I hear it hurts the first time. Does it get better? I mean, I figure it does. Otherwise, why would everyone do it repeatedly, right?"

"Oh, yes. Much better." She snickers.

"Will I be able to get far enough, fast enough, to not get caught?" The conversation turns serious because I need to know I stand a chance of getting away.

"Okay, well, wear sneakers under your dress. The dress is long. I mean, nobody's going to be looking at your feet."

"Right, great idea." I open the small closet and pull out my sneakers. They were a Christmas gift I had begged for while in middle school. They are white and won't stand out too badly.

Katsia looks at her watch. "We don't have much time. It's getting late. Your dad will be banging down the door soon."

"This should be a happy day, but all I feel is dread," I murmur, letting out a long sigh. I stand in front of a mirror, let my light brown hair down, and rip a brush through it.

"You're going to be bald if you keep taking your anger out on your hair. Oh, no, I don't even have time to change." Katsia's face falls when she realizes she is dressed in jeans.

"Don't worry. If I'm lucky, you get another opportunity. Next time, I hope it will be to someone a lot younger and that we'll be in love."

"I want that for you, too, Dasha." She lowers her voice. "I want you to be happy. You deserve it."

I kiss her cheek. "Now, what can we do with my hair?"

"I'll braid it and stack it on top of your head like I did for my birthday last year."

"Oh. Yeah," I smile at the memory. "That was amazing."

Just as Katsia puts the last touches on my hair, as predicted, Papa comes to the door. "I hope you're ready, Dasha," he yells. "Don't keep me waiting. I can't have you embarrassing me."

"Fine, Papa." I practically sing the words to convince him I'm on board with his plan. He knows me too well, and if I don't play along, there will be consequences.

I open the door.

"You look great. Why no makeup?"

"I didn't want to smudge the dress." The lie rolls easily off my tongue. Katsia walks behind me, picking up her purse.

"Fine," Papa huffs. "Let's go."

We climb into his old VW four-door sedan. It smells of cigarettes and spilled beer. I roll down the window, thankful the drive to the church takes less than ten minutes.

"Are Vlad and Albert going to be there?" I ask.

"They said they would be."

This bit of information tells me that everyone knew this was happening except me and Katsia. Katsia rolls her eyes.

I stare at Papa's reflection in the rearview mirror and wonder how much he got paid to enslave me to Andrian. Papa is a pathological liar, and I trust nothing he tells me. It's hard to train myself to think in this fashion. It's not a normal or healthy way to live.

"We're here, and there are your brothers," Papa chimes in as he pulls the old car up in front of the neighborhood church.

Katsia and I exchange a look of panic. Vlad set the track record for the 800 meter races in secondary school six years ago. Hopefully, his late nights of drinking in pubs and a few extra pounds will slow him down.

But it doesn't keep the blood from draining out of my face.

This is where I hope Vlad trips over the short shoelaces in his dress shoes.

"Hi," I say, giving him an obligatory hug.

"Congrats." Vlad steps back, appraising me with his discerning eye.

"Dasha," Albert says, giving me an affectionate hug. I'm closer to him than to Vlad because we're not as far apart in age. Plus, Albert doesn't have Vlad's personality. Papa and Vlad are cut from the same cloth.

"Albert," I acknowledge him, standing on my tiptoes to place my arms around his neck.

"Congrats." He won't look me in the eye. He knows this isn't what I want, but he was probably forced to go along with this charade, just like I was. Did he speak up for me? It's doubtful I will ever know.

Katsia greets them both. They know each other from the rare occasions when Katsia hung out at our house in high school.

We chat as strangers stream past us. Who are these people? Finally, Papa says he'll stand inside the doors and wait for me.

Katsia takes my hand as I enter the hundred-year-old church with trepidation. The last time I was here was for my baptism. I have a picture of my mom holding me in her arms in front of the altar. I've never missed her more than I do right now.

I'm scared to run out the door but more scared to stay and seal my fate. I've wanted to run away for years, and it appears today is the day.

# CHAPTER 8

## ROMAN

*L*ight streams into our room between the crack in the pulled curtains, waking me. Alex is already up and dressed.

I check my Rolex. The time is seven-thirty.

I sit up and run my hand through my hair. "It's late."

"You looked comfortable," Alex says. "Pavel will meet us later for payment and drop us off for a rental. I'll text him when we're ready."

"Great, thank you." I toss the covers back and head to the bathroom to shave. My stomach is in knots. I have no plan other than to watch the wedding. If Pavel is right, I will see Ratmim for the first time there.

I return to the room and dress in jeans and a black T-shirt. I tug on my boots and tie them. It looks sunny outside, so I'm assuming it will be warm out.

"Breakfast?" I ask.

"Sure, the hotel has food, but I don't think we want to be on their cameras." Alex is looking at his phone. "There is a café around the corner where we can get coffee and eggs. It's a mom-and-pop joint, so I doubt there will be cameras."

"Great." I put my wallet in my pocket and grab my phone.

We walk for five minutes and come upon a small establishment, where we grab an empty table. A pretty Belarusian woman takes our order and returns with two cups of coffee.

I stir sugar into mine, lift it to my lips, and glance around, making sure we're not being recorded. Technology can work for and against us. The problem with cameras is that our enemies can pinpoint our locations at specific times. When that happens, we have to make videos disappear or torch a building to destroy the computer's hard drive.

We don't want any evidence of us being in Belarus. This is not a place we want to get caught doing anything illegal. It's even more corrupt than back home. But in our own homeland, we know the players.

"Good call on this place," I murmur, looking around.

I didn't realize I was so hungry until my over-easy eggs, sausage, and toast arrived. I look at Alex's plate and realize he has a double order of eggs to go with his meal. "Hungry?" I ask.

"Yeah, why not?" His gruff reply causes me to chuckle.

He might be older, but he's lean for his age.

We inhale our food and text Pavel when we're done. He pulls up out front, and we get in the car. We arrive at a rental car location within minutes.

"Thank you for your help, Pavel." I shove a roll of rubles into his hand.

"Thank you so much. Please don't mention my name. It would bring hardship on my family." His solemn voice doesn't go unnoticed.

I get out of Pavel's car and join Alex.

"Mm, what about this?" I say to him. "Do you have a fake ID?"

"Of course, you're going off half-cocked. I don't want to bust your chops, but for once, I'm the one with the plan."

"Right. I've been off my game since…"

"I know. It's fine. I get it."

He stands in line for a rental while I stay outside to enjoy the green scenery and the chirping of the birds. This is what vacations are for, to notice the simple things in life without being rushed. I rub my hand over my chin and decide that I do need female companionship on the yacht. I run faces through my head, trying to find a woman I can live with for a week or two on the water.

Oddly, no one comes to mind.

"Aw, man, they are waiting on a car to return," Alex says, interrupting my reverie.

"Can we walk it?"

"I don't like it. Too risky. We need a car. Besides, how are you getting to the airport if we have to leave quickly? No, we're doing this my way."

"Fine. What are we doing, then?"

"We go to another rental place, or we wait."

"Ugh."

Alex taps out a cigarette and places it in his mouth. He lights the tip and inhales.

"You really should stop smoking," I comment.

"I know. Women and cigarettes are vices, and they are both bad for me, but I can't give either up." He gives me a smirk and shrugs as he smokes.

"The women, I can understand."

He inhales again and blows circles in the air.

"How long are we waiting? What time is the wedding?" I'm getting nervous. What if we miss the opportunity? Our trip will have been wasted.

"Eleven. We have some time."

"I don't like this wait. Damn, if we were home, we would boost a car."

He snickers. "That was some time ago, brother."

"Mm." He's right. It was years ago. I survey the area and ask him to check the location of the church. I can run for ages. One way or the other, I'm going to get there.

"It's eight kilometers. What do you want to do?"

"I can run it. Why don't you wait for a car, and I'll meet you there?"

"You sure? It would be better if I were with you."

I lift my knee and grab my ankle, stretching one leg, then the other.

Alex observes me as he drops his cigarette on the ground. "You're crazy," he murmurs.

"You have any better ideas? I need the address."

I hand him my phone, and he pulls up the map, taps on the screen, and passes me the phone back. He points his chin in the direction of the church and says, "Get out of here."

"See you there." I start with a slow trot just to warm up, but I'm running at a good pace before long. I watch for cars at intersections, then glance at my phone to make sure I'm on the correct path. I run on sidewalks covered with leaves that never get swept. The only noise I hear is the chirping of birds and the hum of an occasional passing car. The sun feels good on my face, and I'm almost disappointed to reach the church and end my run.

There's nobody here. What the fuck? Did we have the right information? I double-check my phone. This is the place, and there are cars in the parking lot. I scan the area. Seeing as I'm the only one here, I seize the opportunity to take pictures of the license plates on the parked cars.

Organ music floats by on a breeze. Fuck, I've missed the part where everyone arrives.

I move to the side of the church and stand in the shade of trees. I text Alex: *I'm here and waiting.* I intend to wait until the ceremony ends, then take pictures of the men when they leave. I love this part, hiding in wait while my target has no idea that I'm on to them.

My phone vibrates, and I glance at the text. Alex is on his way.

I'm watching the building for signs of our nemesis and in a bored stupor when a wooden side door flies open, and a woman bolts across the dark green lawn. She hikes the plain wedding dress to her knees, and I notice with a chuckle that she's wearing sneakers.

My interest is piqued. Who is this woman, and what the fuck is going on?

Even in my surprised state, I take a picture of her. Her light brown hair is piled on her head, and she's not in heels as I expected. I'm mesmerized. Is she the one getting married?

I move in her direction. This is one woman I have to meet. Who the fuck wears a dress without heels to their wedding?

# CHAPTER 9

## DASHA

*I* did it! I can't believe it, but I did it! I was walking toward Papa when I spied a door to my right. While we were in the car, Katsia quietly reminded me that I'd pass a door to a room where religious studies are held. It has an access door to the outside, so now is the time for our plan.

I see the door and walk as if I'm on my way to my father. Katsia gives me a nod. She fakes a fall like she was tripped and fell on cue, creating a distraction. I rush through the door and find I'm alone in the room. I hiked up my dress and bolted out of the building.

This is my only chance to be free. I have no further plans. How many people will be near the church on a Saturday? Not many. Someone may give me a ride if I can get across the lawn and into the park.

I run as fast as I can and hope I don't trip over a root or twist an ankle. I'm making great progress, but as I'm nearing the children's playground, a hand grabs my wrist.

"Ahh," I scream, my heart in my throat. Did Andrian put men around the perimeter of the church?

I look up to meet my warden's eyes. They are cerulean blue, beautiful but cold and remote. His chiseled jaw and furrowed brow are unforgiving. He reminds me of one of those gargoyles perched atop a building, guarding what is theirs.

No, I don't think he's here to help me. So why has he stopped me?

"Where are you going?" he asks, speaking Russian. We speak the same language, but his accent is different.

"I'm on a walk," I blurt out. What are the odds that he's just a random dude hanging out alone in the woods between a church and a playground? Only pedophiles do shit like that.

His eyes dart from the church and back to me. I hear shouting. My freedom is in jeopardy and will be over at any minute.

Fuck. The clock is ticking.

"They're after you," he says with confidence. This realization pleases him as a smile flickers and fades like a shooting star.

I have a choice to make. Do I place my fate in the hands of a dashing stranger or relinquish it to my abusive father? It's my life, my decision. I choose the stranger. I'd rather face an unknown future with an unknown man than return to what I left behind.

"I need to get out of here. Quickly," I add, knowing my brother can run fast. Maybe he'll be helpful today and develop a torn ligament.

"Fine. Follow me," he says with a glint of mischief in his eye. Taking my hand in his, he leads me into the park and behind a pavilion. Nearly out of breath, we stumble into an alley filled with trash cans and the stench of rotting garbage.

"Where are we going?" I ask. "Where's your car? How are we going to get away?" My voice reaches an unflattering pitch. I look up and down the street like a cartoon meme. What the hell is going on?

The stranger doesn't seem fazed by our lack of a getaway car. He glances at his phone, puts it in his pocket, and flashes me a wicked smile that makes my stomach flutter.

"Oh, we're getting away," he says with confidence. I'm impressed by his calm demeanor and wish it were contagious. I'd love to be swimming in a sea of tranquility right about now.

"We can go anywhere, trust me," he says with a wink.

I melt under his gaze. Is he flirting with me? I must be imagining it. I must be delusional. I blame it on the crazy circumstances. There is no way this hunk of a handsome man is interested in me. My hair is all over the place, I'm wearing no makeup, and I'm sweating like a whore in church.

On the other hand, he looks as fresh as a daisy and smells good, too. His face is ruggedly handsome, and his muscular arms are covered in tattoos. I look for ones associated with a local drug ring because Albert pointed them out to me years ago and told me never to speak to them. Some criminals would shoot you on sight rather than have you look at them. Anonymity is big in the underworld. I catalog his tattoo, no skulls or crossbones, so our meeting isn't unfortunate.

"Those men are getting closer. We need to get out of here." My voice rises in panic. I've embarrassed Andrain and Papa, and if I'm caught, there will be repercussions—and I don't mean taking my phone away. They would leave bruises or worse.

Time is running out as I hear shouts in the forest. I turn to see if my brothers are among them. All I see are middle-aged men stumbling through the trees, most of them overweight and out of breath. It's almost comical. This will be to my advantage and give me more time to make a clean getaway.

"You need to ditch this dress. It makes it impossible for you to blend in with the crowd," he says, as if I didn't already know I look like the bride of Frankenstein in this hideous gown.

Tires screech, and I glance up as a car careens down the street. I jump back, anticipating the worst. The driver might be having a heart attack at the wheel and hit us. The stranger grabs me around the waist and pulls me to his broad chest.

"This is our ride."

Mother of God, the man drips sex appeal like taffy made with honey. The feel of his chest against my back has my juices flowing. The aroma of bergamot and citrus tantalizes my nose.

He releases my waist as quickly as he grabbed it, breaking the spell. With a flick of his hand, he opens the vehicle's back door, and I sail headfirst into the seat like a sack of potatoes. He lunges in behind me, slamming the door shut.

"Go, go," he yells. The car peels out on the asphalt.

Hearing the tires squeal, I cover my ears and find that I can't move. His hands are on my hips, and his body partially covers mine. I assume it's a protective measure. I wonder if Papa's men had guns on them today.

"I'm not going to hurt you," he says. He releases me, and I struggle to sit on the seat. The length of the dress hampers me as I move my legs to the floor.

"All men say that shit, then do whatever they want," I say. I speak from experience. It's a lesson I've learned in my short life—people lie.

"Not me," he replies. He sits beside me and cocks his head to look behind us.

I find myself in an upright position and fasten the seatbelt over my lap.

"Are they following us?" I ask.

"No," the driver says, and I get my first good look at him. He appears to be older and probably Russian. I'm not sure where he fits in this puzzle, but I rule him out as an Uber driver.

"Where are we going?" I ask my fellow passenger.

"To find you decent clothes, for starters."

"Who are you?" My eyes examine him. He's devastatingly handsome, with a large frame and broad shoulders. Most men would kill to look like him. Unless he's genetically gifted or juicing with steroids, he spends a lot of time working out.

"Roman is all you need to know."

He doesn't seem at all fazed to be running from a bunch of unknown men for an unknown reason. Maybe he's in on the whole thing, and my father set this all up. How else would his driver know to pick us up?

"Okay, Roman, who's your driver? Are you friends of the Belarusian mafia?"

"Hardly." He chuckles. "That's Alex," he says, and nods to the man behind the wheel.

I examine Roman's profile and try to discern if he's telling the truth. Hard to know for sure, but seeing as how I need his help, I'm willing to rely on the kindness of strangers until I'm safe.

We travel along in awkward silence until Alex pulls up in front of a women's clothing store.

"Wait here, I'll be back," Roman says, getting out of the car and leaving me alone with Alex.

"Fancy driving, Alex. Who's your friend?" I ask.

"Roman, like he told you." Alex's piercing eyes meet mine in the review mirror. "He has resources. You could have wound up in worse hands. Since we're getting to know each other, what's your name?"

"Dasha."

"Do you have a last name, Dasha?"

I need to come up with something quick. I can't use Katsia's last name. It would be too easy for my family to locate me. Until I know what's going on, I need to play along with a false name and a fake story. If I can pull this off, maybe the story will have a fairytale ending.

"Dasha Varona," I answer as confidently as possible to cover my deceit. It's a common name, and I hope it will keep me off the radar when Papa tries to look for me.

"Well, Dasha, today is your lucky day."

"Why do you say that?" As far as I'm concerned, I'm still in danger. I can't rely on luck to save me. I have to save myself, but it's impossible to do without friends who can help, and I need money.

"Look, you're pretty, even if your dress is not. But pretty will only get you so far."

I cross my arms defensively. "Thanks for the compliment."

"You're in luck. Roman is a wealthy man who can get you out of whatever trouble you are in. His family has a plane and a yacht."

"I'm not in trouble. I just don't want to marry that pig," I say in my own defense.

"Who's the pig?" He twists in his seat to look at me, giving me his full attention. "Ratmim?"

"Yeah," I blurt, flustered by his sharp tone. "Ratmim."

I can't tell him that Ratmim is my father. Knowledge is power, and I don't know him. It might not be safe.

"Is that where we're headed, to Roman's yacht?" I ask.

"Yes."

The car door opens, and Roman gets in. He drops a huge shopping bag on my lap. "What did I miss?" Roman looks at me, then at Alex.

"Her name is Dasha," Alex says, then turns back around and drives the car. "And she was supposed to marry Ratmim."

"Ratmim?" Roman's voice is silky. "Really?"

"Wow, look at all these clothes," I exclaim to change the subject, opening the bag and rooting through the contents. The bag is full. I've never had so many new clothes.

"Lose the wedding dress and put something else on," Roman barks.

"What? In the car?" I stare into his eyes, and my gut tells me he's serious.

"Yes, and quickly. I'll help," he says while fumbling to find the zipper.

I unbuckle my seatbelt as he brushes the hair that fell out of my updo to the side. His hand finds the zipper without fumbling around. I hear the zipper as it glides down my back. Normally, I'd be afraid of a man's hands near my body, given how many times Papa has slapped me over stupid stuff.

Roman doesn't invoke fear in me, and there's something kind of sexy about the moment. If Alex weren't here and we weren't being chased like rabbits, I could picture him pulling my dress off and making out with me in the back seat of a parked car.

Instead, my hair gets caught in the zipper, and he carefully untangles it before he yanks the dress to my shoulders.

"Oh," I murmur in surprise. I fumble inside the bag and find a blouse and jeans. I rip off the tags, and Roman holds the wedding dress up like a tent to give me privacy. I slip into the shirt, buttoning all but the top two buttons. Papa would disapprove of me changing in front of a strange man. Fuck him. Papa is in my rearview mirror for the time being.

I bend forward to untie my trusty sneakers. I leave them where they fall on the car floor. I shake out the jeans, holding them by the waist, and shimmy into them. When I'm finished, I push the dress off me, and Roman grabs it, balls it up, and places it on the seat between us.

I straighten myself out and click the seatbelt into place. Alex is driving at breakneck speeds and making lots of turns. I assume he's staying off the main roads to avoid being seen.

"Who do you work for, the government?" I ask Roman.

"No, just the opposite. All you need to know is that I can help you if you want to get away from here."

I try to hide my internal panic. My mind is racing, and every one of my senses is on high alert. I regret not thinking this far ahead. The truth is, I never thought I'd make it past the church's lawn. Papa keeps a thumb on me and has had me thinking I can't do anything on my own for so long that I am in shock.

I acted on impulse and took advantage of an opportunity to run. Now what?

I hear the car shift into a higher gear and notice we're moving faster. This is good. I'd rather keep moving and put as many kilometers as possible between me and my past.

I can't believe I pulled it off, but I'm afraid to celebrate, as I don't want to jinx myself. The day is young, and my life is filled with disappointments. Why wouldn't this just be one more to add to the list of many?

My heart races as I twist my torso to look out the back window.

"Relax, we're not being followed," Alex says, reading my mind. He's calm and constantly checking the mirrors. Clearly, he's done this before.

"Did you know I was at the church?" I ask Roman as he's tapping away on his phone.

"Not at all," he murmurs without looking up. "Were you expecting someone?"

"No."

There's no way he knows the danger we're in, nor the magnitude of what just happened. He must think I'm a runaway bride, and this is just a lark—a rich guy looking to fill a boring afternoon by saving a damsel in distress. If I'm to pull this off, I need to let him believe that's my story.

"Who were you running away from back there?" he asks, looking at me with suspicion.

Ah, let the games begin.

"Someone I don't like."

"You liked him enough to want to marry him," he states as he puts down his phone and turns to face me.

The accusation could not be further from the truth and makes me angry enough to scratch his eyes out, but I swallow my rage and try to think of a response. I'm tempted to tell him the truth, but I run the risk of him turning me over if Papa or Andrian offer a reward.

Would Roman even believe me if I told him the truth? I prefer not to lie, but it's a given in my world that everyone lies and is out for themselves. It's a matter of survival.

I've never been in a situation like this, alone with two virile men, and I have no clue what to expect. Anything could happen. They could sell me into a prostitution ring, or worse.

"Why were you in the park?" I ask. "Where are you from?"

"Why were you there?" he counters.

I realize I have no leverage in the situation. I need them.

"I was supposed to marry someone." I shrug and look out the window.

"I thought as much." He nods as if he understands. "We were passing through," he says, finally answering my question. "Now we're returning home."

That makes sense. They're both Russian, and we have lots of Russian living in our country. I wonder why he picked Minsk, of all places, but I decide it's better not to push my luck by asking too many questions.

I have a flashback to the church and hope Katsia will be okay. She knows not to trust anything my father and brothers say.

I shut my eyes and lean my head back against the seat, taking deep breaths. I'm still trying to relax when the car comes to a sudden stop. I open my eyes. We're in front of a hotel.

Oh, fuck! Are these men going to rape me and murder me?

I have five seconds to decide my next move. I don't know these men, but anything's better than marrying Andrian. I know what he's capable of.

Roman opens the door, and I get out.

Fuck, fuck, fuck.

I could be raped or killed, chopped up in trash bags, or found in a ditch somewhere if this all goes to shit. I'll fight until I can't breathe.

"We need to grab our stuff." Roman's voice is gruff and businesslike, and he seems preoccupied as he texts someone.

He slides his key card into the door. Alex follows.

Fuck.

The hotel room is not what I expected. It's a dive, even by my standards.

"Let me grab my shit out of the bathroom, and you can use it," Roman states.

I stand uncertainly in the middle of the room. What have I gotten myself into?

# CHAPTER 10

## ROMAN

We enter the hotel room, and I go into the bathroom to retrieve my stuff, a shaving kit and a few personal items. We travel light.

When I come back out, Dasha is still standing. She seems scared and tense. Probably has a million worst-case scenarios running through her mind.

"We're not going to hurt you," I tell her. "I'm a man of my word. I won't let anything bad happen to you. We're just making a quick stop. Use the bathroom—we're flying out soon."

"Flying? Where are you taking me?"

"You look like you can use a vacation. Am I wrong?" I ask, even though I already know the answer.

"No, but..."

Her hesitation makes me wonder if she's been mistreated. I'm suddenly distracted by her perfectly rounded breasts rising and falling with each breath. I long to pull off her T-shirt, unclasp her bra and let her mounds tumble into my hands. She may be young and naïve, but there's a temptress in there, itching to be unleashed. I'm sure of it.

As far as I'm concerned, having her is a stroke of luck, an opportunity too good to pass up. I can't help but smile. Alex feared I'd start a war. Instead, I'm rescuing a woman in distress. If she really belongs to Ratmim, he'll come looking for her. It's best if we hightail it to the yacht.

She slips past me and goes inside the bathroom. As soon as the door shuts, I nod at Alex, and he kneels and pulls a gun case from under the bed, then another and another. He steps back outside and stows the weapons in the trunk of the car as I hold vigil at the bathroom door. Dasha doesn't need to know about the weapons. She might panic.

I don't blame her. Hell, I would, too.

The guns secure in the car, Alex lights a cigarette and smokes outside while I grab our bags and throw them in the trunk. As I'm shutting the trunk, Dasha emerges from the bathroom and joins us. Taking the bag with her ugly, ill-fitting wedding dress off the back seat, I toss it in the parking lot dumpster. It lands in the container with a satisfying thud. Any evidence that we were here will never be found. We had fake IDs coming in Belarus and have remained off cameras.

"Get in. We have a long way to go," I say, opening the car door.

"Where are we going?" Dasha asks.

I join her in the back seat. "Where do you want to go?"

"There are so many places. Anywhere."

"Do you like the water? Here's the plan. We're going to drive into Russia. From there, we'll catch a plane and board a yacht. I think the sea air will be relaxing."

"I don't know. I've never been. What's it like?"

"I think you'll love it."

"I don't have any money," she says. "I can't go home."

"That's fine. I have more than enough money, and I can get you away from here."

"But will I be able to leave once we reach a destination?"

Her voice is pensive, and there's something in her sadness that enhances her natural beauty. Her alabaster skin and emerald eyes take my breath away. I don't want to break her spirit. I'm impressed with and intrigued by Dasha. She's definitely not like any woman I've met before, but that doesn't mean I'm falling in love. Not a chance. Instead, she's going to fall in love with me. I want Ratmim to know for the rest of his life that his wife was with me first.

Nothing could be more fitting for that arrogant prick. Exacting my revenge will be sweet. I'll sink my cock in her and enjoy every minute of it.

Alex starts the car.

"What about Alex?" she asks. "Is he going with us on the yacht?"

"Alex is my right-hand man. He goes where I go."

She nods as if she understands.

I have a lot to do and get busy. I grab my burner phone and send the church parking lot pictures to Dmitry so he can run checks on the license plates. I arrange to have a jet waiting for us in Russia. I verify the yacht is stocked and ready to go. Dasha needs identification and a passport. I text a contact in my phone. I'll have Dmitry create other documentation later. She'll have a new life if I let her go. But for now, she's my leverage over Ratmim. The only thing we're missing is another woman on board. I want Dasha to feel safe.

"So, Dasha, Alex has a friend who will be joining us on this trip. Is that okay? I think you'll like her."

Her face lights up. "Who is she?"

"Her name is Irina."

I meet Alex's gaze in the mirror, and he nods at my unspoken message. Alex is loyal to the family. This is all going according to plan. We'll go over the border tonight, and in the morning, we'll meet my contact and go from there.

I wonder how long it will be before Dasha makes a move. Once she has a passport, she could go almost anywhere. Unless she's a mermaid, it will be easier to hold on to her if she's on a yacht in the middle of the ocean.

My goal is to keep this feud with Ratmim out of Russia and to keep him on defense, not offense.

I can use Dasha as a pawn until I tire of her. Then I'll let her go.

Alex drives out of the hotel parking lot, and Dasha glances nervously behind us.

"We're not being tailed. I have my eye on it," Alex reassures her.

Her shoulders relax in relief, and she sinks more comfortably into the seat.

"I'm with you now, but I won't be staying," she says a little defiantly.

"And where will you go?" My tone is mocking. "You have no money, no phone. What are you going to do?"

"You don't know," she counters. "I could have a stash somewhere. Young kids today are savvy."

She's goading me, and I find it amusing.

"I doubt that, judging from your dress and old sneakers," I say, calling her bluff. "Have you been to Russia?"

"A few times on short trips," she says. "I think Papa had business meetings there." She shrugs. "The change of scenery was nice. At home, all I do is stare at the walls and keep house."

# CHAPTER 11

## DASHA

It's a long drive to the border but, the car is comfortable. I've done it a few times with Papa. The trip is monotonous, nothing but farmland and boring as hell.

I glance at Roman. The lines in his brow tell me that he's stressed, and I don't want to cross him. Not now, anyway. He's been reluctant to give me his last name. I wonder what he does for a living and what they were doing in Minsk.

He senses my scrutiny and looks at me. I turn my head and stare out the window to avoid his gaze. We're playing a game of questions to obtain an advantage over each other.

We have many Russians who freely come and go over our border, but these two pique my interest.

I breathe a sigh of relief when we make it out of Minsk. The more distance I put between myself and my family, the better. But what have I gotten myself into? Who are these men? Can they be trusted? What choice do I have?

If they are telling me the truth about planes and yachts, that means they are involved in some illegal activity. No one in this country, or in Russia, owns or has access to lavish things unless they are connected, like Andrian.

My father is just one of many mafia bosses, and he breathes because Andrian allows it. Something must've happened in order for Papa to marry me off to him. I know Papa travels to Russia occasionally and that my brothers go with him. When they were teenagers, they whined for a more significant share of the profits, and by the time they graduated secondary school, they were on the payroll. They never disclosed what they did when they left the house abruptly in the middle of the night and disappeared for days.

I didn't ask, but voices carry in our apartment, and I've overheard phone calls and snippets of conversations during game night. I pretend not to pay attention, but I've heard them mention the Volkov family over the years. Andrian blames them for being kicked out of Russia, and Papa helps Andrian with his dirty work. They never have anything good to say about the Volkovs, and I think they hate them.

My thoughts return to my predicament. My biggest fear is that Roman makes his money off of human trafficking, like Andrian. If that's the case, I'm in real danger. Sex trafficking has become a massive problem with all the turmoil in neighboring countries.

We drive for hours and stop for a break. Alex stands guard while I use the bathroom, and Roman grab sandwiches from a small shop carrying souvenirs, magazines, and sundries for travelers.

We stand by a picnic bench to eat. I scarf down the turkey sandwich as if I'm homeless and hungry. The irony is that I'm both.

Alex finishes his food and tosses me a bottle of water. He lights a cigarette, and Roman paces. He's talking on his phone, but he's smart enough to stay out of my range. I wish I were a fly on a wall and could hear what he's saying.

I finish my bag of chips and toss my garbage in the bin like a model citizen. I remain standing and pull my foot to my butt to stretch my cramped legs.

A car with a family drives by and parks. I contemplate taking my chances with them, but Roman would be on me in a hot minute, and I want to keep on his good side. Besides, I could end up with the wrong crowd.

I'm comforted by the fact that another woman will be on the yacht. If there is a yacht, but so far, I haven't caught Roman or Alex in a lie.

I took a big chance when I followed him through the woods. I was at the end of my rope and didn't care what happened to me at that point. It's been a while since Papa hit me, but it's never far from my mind. Andrian would have been the same way or worse. I may as well take my chances with the handsome stranger and see how this plays out.

Have I traded one cage for another? Maybe.

Roman's sultry blue eyes and deep voice make me feel things I've never experienced. When he's near, a tingling sensation between my legs leaves me longing for his touch.

I'm curious what it would feel like to have his lips on mine. This attraction is different from the crush I had in secondary school. That was just puppy love, it flamed out when our personalities weren't a good match. I had to keep too many secrets from him. Papa's reputation got around to him as well.

Katsia is the only person I share secrets with, and never anything that can be used against my family. I miss her and wish she were here. Papa let me keep her around as a friend to pacify me. He considers all women who challenge the status quo in our country a threat to national security.

In other countries, women have careers and a choice about having children. In this country, I am treated as a servant by my family, something to barter and use to their advantage. My life has been forfeited, and I'm tired of accepting my role.

If I run from Roman, I'll have to keep running, and life on the run sounds like another prison sentence. I will keep lying to get to the next step. At some point, though, I will have to escape, and I will. I've done it once, and I can do it again.

"So, you've never been outside of Minsk?" Roman asks once we're back in the car.

"I've been to Russia a few times, but I mostly stay at home," I say, thinking of my controlling father.

"I find that hard to believe. Young women your age go to clubs and make friends and date. Don't you have friends?"

"I've been out a few times," I say defensively.

Why does it matter? For all I know, he plans to lock me in a windowless cabin on his yacht.

Roman can assume whatever he wants. Who am I to correct him? I will give him as little information as possible and watch for subtle clues that tell me who he is.

I'm staring out the window at the passing countryside when I see a sign in Cyrillic letters that reads RUSSIA. People told me the border is open, and they're right. There's no checkpoint or guard.

I will need a passport eventually, and Roman claims he can get me one with my new name. I'm not stupid. I know he will expect something in return. Will he force himself on me, or will it be consensual?

I would prefer it to be consensual. I'm curious about seeing his naked body, and the thought of having it pressed up against me is exciting. But when it comes to the particulars, I'm terrified.

Sex, according to my trashy novels, is like soaring on a wave of euphoria. It's about time I rode that wave, if for no other reason than to lose my virginity so that Andrian loses interest.

The whole idea of virginity seems like much fuss about nothing. What's so special about being the first man to put his dick inside me? Plus, the last thing I need is to get pregnant. I've got enough problems.

"So, where are we going on your fancy yacht?" My voice is challenging. I'm waiting to see if there really is a huge boat or if he's nothing but talk, like Papa.

"You'll see." He gives me a devilish grin that makes me wonder if he's had this trip planned all along. He doesn't impress me as someone who leaves much to chance. Was he asking me where I wanted to go to test me? Did he change his plans to accommodate me?

Roman assumes I was at the church to marry Ratmim. He doesn't know Ratmim is my father. As long as I'm worth more to him as Ratmim's fiancée, let him believe it. For the first time in my life, I have leverage.

"How do you know Ratmim?" I ask.

"Business." Roman shrugs as if a one-word answer should suffice.

It doesn't.

"Did he do something to you?"

Roman's face turns dark. "What's with all the questions?"

"No reason."

I sigh. I must've exceeded my quota for the day.

It's getting dark outside. I close my eyes and pretend to sleep while I sneak a look at Roman as we move under streetlights. Sex appeal clings to him like the tailored shirts he wears.

What is he up to? Men in the mafia don't do anything unless there's something in it for them. Why are these two risking their lives for me? They know Papa. They know what he's capable of, and yet they don't seem scared of him.

I doze off, jolting awake when the car bounces over speed bumps. I sit up and look out the window. I stretch. My muscles are stiff from the long ride. "Where are we?"

"Where do you think?" Roman chuckles and waves a hand at a small airplane. "The airport."

The planes are small, not big enough for commercial flights, so we must be at a private airport. Alex parks next to one of the airplanes.

We exit the car, and I stare at the jet, marveling at the sleek lines of the aircraft and wondering how much it cost. Such luxurious travel is a perk only the rich and powerful enjoy. I'm both curious and anxious to fly in style. In all my daydreams of visiting exotic places, I never pictured this.

While the men load the plane, I take a short stroll to stretch my legs. Several rifle cases are loaded into the hold. Why do they have so many, and what were they up to? Were they planning to kill Papa? A risky move in my country. Much smarter to have waited for him to come to Russia.

A tall man wearing a trench coat crosses the tarmac, approaching Roman. They shake hands, and the guy hands him something in an envelope. Roman slips it into his pocket. The man in the trench coat strides off, and Alex calls me to stand beside him.

He lights a cigarette, and I fan the smoke away from my face. "You know smoking is bad for you."

"Yeah, that and a few other habits. How can I pick just one?" His lips curl, showing his teeth, but it's not a smile. There's something menacing about his expression, so I drop the subject.

Roman's eyes zero in on me. I blush under the intensity of his gaze.

"I have your passport," he says. "We can board now."

Holy cow, he got me a fake passport. What else can he do with a snap of his fingers? He's like James Bond, for Christ's sake.

I hang back, waiting for Roman to board first, but he slips behind me. "Let's go," he says, calling out to Alex.

Alex nods and drops his cigarette.

I tenuously walk up the steps. This is the first time I've ever flown, and my stomach is in knots with anticipation. I glance down to make sure I don't miss a step and notice my sneakers. I'm no fashionista, but I've seen enough movies to know I'm underdressed for a private jet.

Katsia and I would watch American movies and dream of a better life. We planned our wedding day down to the last detail: designer dress, fresh flowers, and gourmet appetizers, with a seated dinner following the reception. Our hair and makeup would be done professionally, just like a Hollywood starlet prepping for the red carpet. Of course, we were only kidding ourselves, but our fantasies temporarily alleviated the monotony of our dismal lives, mine more than Katsias's.

Once inside the plane, I see four recliner-size leather chairs. I sit in one by the window, and Roman buckles the seatbelt over my lap. His closeness takes my breath away. Even though he's no longer in my personal space, his cologne lingers in the air, teasing me and triggering a now familiar throb and slickness between my legs.

We've been on the road for so long that the dark stubble on his chiseled jaw has grown in, giving him a rugged look. If anything, it makes him even more appealing. I gaze at his profile, transfixed, my heart racing. I quickly avert my eyes in case he turns to look at me, not wanting to get caught staring at him.

"Is Irina still coming?" I ask Alex when he plops down in the seat across the aisle. There's safety in numbers. I'll feel better knowing I'm not alone with two men if she's on the yacht.

"Yes. I hate cell phones," he grumbles while angrily poking the screen with his finger.

The plane starts to roll, and Roman buckles himself into the seat beside me.

"Yachts come in different sizes. How big is this one?" I ask him to get a feel for the sleeping arrangements.

"It's big, big enough to sail across the ocean. Don't worry, my little dove. You'll be safe. I don't take women against their will."

It's like he can read my mind.

# CHAPTER 12

## ROAMN

How did I manage to pick the perfect pair of jeans for Dasha? I motion for her to board the plane ahead of me, my gaze on her curvy ass as she climbs the steep steps. The sight fills my mind with salacious thoughts. I'm such a bastard.

I'm greeted by the pilot. Overhead lights illuminate the spacious cabin. Dasha glances around and selects the leather seat closest to her.

"I'll help you." Leaning over, I buckle her seatbelt. My mouth hovers near her face, and electricity crackles between us.

I move away abruptly. I can't let my guard down. She's the enemy. However, I feel for her being alone and away from home, so I sit beside her. Alex enters last and sits to my left on the other side of the aisle.

I fasten my seatbelt for takeoff. Dasha tucks her long tresses behind her right ear and folds her hands in her lap. Nope, she's never flown before. Fear rolls off her like sweat on a humid day. She nervously taps one foot on the carpeted floor.

She let her hair down hours ago. I quietly observe her with hooded eyes, so she won't know I am watching her. I sit silently and pretend to be preoccupied with my phone, watching her shove bobby pins in her pocket. Maybe she thinks she might need to use them at some point on this journey. I imagine her handcuffed to my headboard, and my cock jerks. Why not? She is a willing captive. She was looking for a way out of her wedding, and I was looking for a way to exact revenge on her soon-to-be husband.

Arranged marriages are used to forge alliances, and the women are usually tucked away until needed. Dasha's naïveté makes me believe she's never been with a man before, and the fact that her eyes rove over me as if I'm the last man on a deserted island tells me she finds me attractive. She was shy when she changed clothes under her hideous wedding dress. A woman who'd been with more than one man wouldn't be so modest. Hell, most of the women I've been with flaunt it, walking around in skimpy shorts and halter tops on foreign vacations. To them, their youth and toned bodies are meant to be enjoyed and appreciated. Their behavior is a respite from their everyday life, where they would be shunned for such transgressions.

Dasha is beautiful. Her high cheekbones and full lips are model quality. She should be dripping in diamonds—no, emeralds—to enhance her gorgeous green eyes.

The wedding dress she was wearing when we met hung off her. I assume she's always dressed modestly. She wore socks and sneakers on her wedding day. Doesn't she have a mother to help her dress? She's all of twenty, if that. A mafia princess is usually pampered and sheltered from the prying eyes of enemies. The glimpse of her voluptuous white breasts gave me a hard-on. I doubt she's ever had a tan, and I can't wait to see her in a bikini. I imagine what it would be like to run my hand down her taut back and over her curvy ass.

The thought brings to mind that it's been a month since I've fucked anyone, and I'm long overdue. My cock twitches as I plan to deflower my enemy's bride. She was sheltered and there is no way her father would let her have a boyfriend. I've been around women long enough to read the innocence in her eyes. She's not used to sitting close to a man who isn't a family member because her body language speaks volumes. She sneaks looks at me with hooded eyes.

I shouldn't touch her. She's been saved for my enemy, but fuck Ratmim. He took something that was mine, and I will take something of his. Besides, I can't trust her. She's not Russian. I remind myself that she's a means to an end.

The captain interrupts to announce safety features. The overhead lights dim, the engines rumble, and the floor vibrates as we taxi down the runway.

Dasha grabs my hand, which is resting on the armrest between us. My breath catches in my throat. Her petite hand squeezes mine, causing me to look at her. Her once-rosy lips are pursed, and they are the color of a pale slice of watermelon. She wasn't lying. It's obvious she's never flown.

"It will be fine," I reassure her.

"That's easy for you to say," she replies, looking at me for reassurance as the plane jerks and moves ahead. With a powerful thrust, the plane's nose is off the ground.

"There," I say, "how was that?"

"My tummy tickled a bit, like driving over a road with an unexpected dip. It might have scared me more in daylight. I can't imagine what it's like to look at the world from up here."

I chuckle. "I think you would enjoy it. There will be more opportunities."

I'm surprised by my remark. I'm talking to her as if we've known each other for years. Why am I so at ease with her?

Seeing the world through her eyes amuses me. I was a child the first time I flew, and I am reliving that experience. The whole family was on an Aeroflot flight to England. My father acted as if it was nothing and told us boys never to show fear.

Back then, there was no service on an Aeroflot plane. If you smelled food cooking, it was the crew heating their meals. Nothing for the passengers. I remember an older man tried to bring his rooster on board, and when the crew said no live animals were allowed, he killed it and brought it anyway. Maybe that's what I smelled cooking in the aft galley.

Dad acted as if it were nothing to board a commercial airliner to England.

Dasha nervously returns her hand to her lap. I liked holding her hand, and I didn't mind reassuring her. Strangely, I'm used to these adventures. Now, I realize that I've taken them for granted.

We own many luxurious cars, and we have personal staff. We also own homes in foreign countries. We've managed to amass our billions steadily over the years. It takes a healthy chunk of rubles and Euros to keep it all going, another reason the stolen guns piss me off.

I never stop to think about how far the family has come from the little farmhouse in Úglich. Grandpa started the family business selling items to tourists in the big cities, magnets and nesting dolls and the like. He expanded his reach beyond our borders when the country changed. His connections afforded him the ability to join others who were selected to align with newly elected officials. Shortly after that, Dad took over the business and entered the real estate market, competing against his rival, Andrian Abramov.

Dad knew how to corner the market on luxury homes and gained more connections, and Andrian was stuck in Belarus with family when the world changed and wasn't allowed back in. Igor rubbed elbows with new contacts in London and acquired shares in gas companies. Eventually, he brought Dad into the mix.

Dad was swayed by the incredible profits. He had no way of knowing that Igor had refused those company stocks at a loss to raise money for his cronies when called upon. He knew better than to refuse but was greedy when he should have been complicit.

We don't know who set up the hit that came in the form of a deadly car accident. Dad never trusted large companies due to government involvement, and ultimately, he proved himself right. We divested ourselves of the stock after his death, and the rest is history, as they say. However, the money Dad made off that deal wasn't worth his life. He and Igor should have given the government what it wanted. We can't fight those above us. They own us like everyone else.

"It's weird," Dasha says, interrupting my thoughts. Her focus on the darkness outside the plane seems to calm her. "It's night, and we're flying through the sky.

"I don't think about it much."

The drone of the engines provides a backdrop, and I'm just grateful there's no turbulence. The last thing she needs is a bumpy flight.

"Do you travel a lot?" She averts her eyes to her hands in her lap. "It feels odd not to have a purse or a phone on me."

I imagine she feels naked without a tether to humanity.

"I can imagine. Do you have anyone back home you need to contact?"

She's pensive for a minute, and I can't tell if she's hiding something from me or considering whether she should reach out to someone. I don't believe for a minute she doesn't have one, if not two, girlfriends. Even a captive bird manages to find life within a cage.

"No, I'm fine. Thank you."

Alex chimes in with, "I need a fucking cigarette," and we both chuckle at his predictability.

I'm sure that when Alex is not smoking, he will enjoy all the amenities the yacht offers. There are swimming pools, hot tubs, wave runners, water slides, and scuba gear. What we don't have, we can get. There's a small sailboat and a motorboat stored in the hull that we can use to go ashore, go sailing or water skiing, snorkel, or just fuck off. Hell, I can even fuck someone on the bow if I want.

I love the water, so for me, this trip is an entire vacation packed into a steel hull. I have my best friend, the sun, water, spas, and many things to do and places to go. It's liberating to be at sea.

But such luxury comes at a high price. It takes an extraordinary number of rubles and euros to maintain our lifestyle, and that's another reason the stolen guns piss me off. We're all expected to bring in money, and the shipment was worth one million USD on the black market.

Alex finally gets his cell phone connected to the Wi-Fi and confirms Irina will be waiting for us. I haven't seen her in months. It will be nice to catch up with her. She's the one woman I think Alex should marry. Maybe we're friends because we're the same age. Plus, she's no stranger to our world, which makes her feel like family.

"Now that I'm on the plane, can you tell me exactly where we are going?" Dasha asks.

She's brave to bring it up. She must be concerned about her safety, and it doesn't take much to be courteous to her. It's not her fault she's not on her honeymoon like she should have been.

"We're traveling to France," I volunteer. Who is she going to tell, anyway?

"Alex mentioned the yacht. Do you sail?"

"Yes."

I wonder if she's running through *The Kidnapped Handbook* and got to the chapter entitled *Get to Know Your Captor*. I dismiss the notion. She's a babe in the woods surrounded by wolves.

At this point, I realize we've been up for hours.

My stomach growls, reminding me that we also haven't eaten in a long time, so I unbuckle my seatbelt and head to the galley. "I'm getting a drink. Would you like something to eat?" I ask, looking at Dasha. "I can heat something up."

"Yes, please, something to eat and water to drink."

"Sure. Feel free to move around. There's a bathroom toward the back. I'm not concerned you'll throw yourself out the door," I add with a sardonic tone.

Her eyebrows rise, as if to question my sanity. It's great to know she's keeping her wits about her. Some women would be hysterical by now. We've been confined in a car for a long time and now we're on a plane, and I haven't managed to piss her off. It's a new record for me.

Alex follows me. "You're in a good mood. What are you so happy about, the girl?"

"Of course not," I say. "I'm just happy we made it out of Minsk undetected."

"I hope to hell you have a bottle of vodka on this plane," Alex says with a grunt.

"Of course. When have I never had liquor?"

I glance back at Dasha, but she's not in her seat. Probably in the bathroom. We've been in the air for an hour.

"You're not your usual stoic and dour self," Alex says. "Don't tell me the girl is getting to you."

"I've got my eye on the prize," I say, defending myself. "I can't decide whether to hold her for ransom money, which could get messy, or send her back to Ratmim without her virginity."

"If she's been raised to marry Ratmim, I wonder who her parents are. He is such a rat."

We both chuckle.

"I'm thinking I can ride her long and hard and send her back to him broken," I say. "One million for her virginity. Who could complain about that?"

"I don't know." Alex shakes his head. "We're getting involved in shit that stinks. We never checked her out with your brother. Maybe we should take her fingerprints when we get to the boat and find out who she is. She has no identification."

"Good idea," I agree, "but fingerprints will only come back with a name if she has a record. She doesn't strike me as someone who would steal a hymnal, let alone guns."

I pull meals out of the refrigerator and stare at the containers. I have servants to cook for me.

"She was too scared and jumpy for her to be there voluntarily." I pick up a sealed box of food. "She said as much herself. However, we'll go on our vacation and see what happens. I mean, no one knows we were in Belarus. Dasha disappeared on their watch, and it isn't our mess to clean up."

I place the prepared dinners in the microwave. "Damn, does the cellophane stay on or come off?"

I'm a man with two left thumbs when it comes to the kitchen. Mom cooked and did housework until we hired a personal chef.

"Read the instructions. Too bad we don't have someone to service us on this bird," he grouses.

"Fewer eyes on us. That's what I was thinking when I had you book this flight."

I read the card with directions. It says to take the wrappers off the food and punch the number 5 on the machine before I push start.

"Right, well, I hope you didn't cut staff on the yacht," Alex replies sarcastically. For a man who grew up with nothing until my father took him under his command, he sure likes the entitlements he receives when he's traveling with me. Premium liquor is one of those perks, and he knows where to find it. He opens the bottle of Zyr, a domestic vodka, and drinks straight from the bottle.

"Good stuff. God, I needed this," Alex groans, wiping his mouth with the back of his hand. He puts the bottle down and selects a beef tenderloin dinner to heat up.

The microwave dings, and I pull my meals out with oven mitts. I'm an ace with a rifle, but give me burning food, and I'm nervous. I manage to get the meals on the special serving trays. I grab two bottled waters and return to the cabin, leaving Alex to fend for himself.

Dasha has returned to her chair, her hair in a long braid that drapes over her voluptuous boobs. Damn, I got her a tight blouse on purpose. Her hair is gorgeous, and with it tidied, it accentuates her long neck and high cheekbones. She doesn't need an ounce of makeup to look beautiful, and she's infinitely more appealing than the gourmet dinner in my hands. My mouth slackens as I take her in. Even when she sleeps and slightly snores, I find her adorable.

"A tray on the right side of your chair comes out."

Dasha peers over the arm of her chair and flips the tray open. I set her food and drink on it and settle in the seat beside her.

"Not the best, but it will do," I mumble as I open the bottle in my hand. "The food is scorching."

She watches me drink water before she opens hers and gulps. She puts it down and ravishes the lobster ravioli purchased from a private restaurant.

"This is amazing. What is it?" she asks.

"Lobster and sauce."

"Italian food, right?"

"Mostly, or American, I'm not sure." I dig into my chicken parmesan and find it satisfying. I flip my wrist to look at my watch and check the time. It's been a long-ass day, and it will be a long as fuck night.

Alex sits down with his dinner. I have to admit that his concerns are valid. I should have done more research before going after Ratmim. Instead, I reacted to the stolen gun shipment angrily, still fuming over Dad's death and the fear that I'd let my brother down.

Damn. Alex is right. I let personal loss and worry make me act out of character, and that is a cause for concern. At least I have Alex with me. He's like an all-star goalie, always there to cover me when I fuck up.

I blame myself for my father's death, and it's clouding my judgment. My actions certainly have nothing to do with the intoxicating woman beside me.

I eat my dinner. It's been a long fifteen hours. The drive to the border was grueling, and I still haven't learned much about my hostage.

Alex has every reason to be concerned with our situation.

I feel Dasha's eyes on me and glance at her. She gives me a questioning look. Her eyes have turned a deeper green, but there are circles under them.

"If you're tired, go have a nap on the bed. We have two more hours to go."

She lifts her dinner tray, stands, and collects mine as I finish eating.

"There's a kitchen area?" she asks.

"Up front."

She nods and walks toward the kitchen. Alex catches me staring at her behind and busts my ass about it.

Dasha busies herself in the kitchen and returns to pick up after Alex. She disappears again, and Alex and I give each other a questioning look.

"I thought she was a principessa," he whispers. "Why is she acting like a scullery maid?"

"I don't know, but we need to find out."

Things are not adding up. Her behavior is not what one would expect from a mafia princess. She doesn't wear the clothes and jewelry, for one thing. Her only ring is a thin gold band with a peridot, lighter than her eyes. The dress and sneakers she wore to her wedding were more appropriate for a picnic.

Perplexing. Mafia queens are drenched in finery. The dress she was wearing when I found her was disappointing, even by my standards. I'm no fashionista, but I know a designer dress when I see one, and hers was not couture by any stretch of the imagination.

Ratmim's bride is unexpected, to say the least. Her sneakers indicate she's a woman who either likes to rebel or is very practical. Things are still not adding up.

I assumed her family was wealthy and powerful if she was promised to Ratmim. Could I have been wrong? Could this be some elaborate trap? Is she playing us?

I don't think so. I think back to our first encounter. I stumbled upon the church at the exact moment she was making her getaway. That wasn't a trap. This is a coincidence. She didn't seek us out.

Who is Dasha, and how did she wind up at the church of my enemy?

# CHAPTER 13

DASHA

I return to Alex, who's sitting in his seat. He's wiping his fingers on the little towelettes that came with the silverware packet on the serving tray. He raises his eyebrows in surprise when I dutifully reach for his tray and an empty soda can.

Alex murmurs his thanks, but he doesn't seem pleased by my consideration. I return to the tiny kitchen. It reminds me of the kind little kids might play with in a daycare center.

I'm comforted by the small space nonetheless. The kitchen is where I feel at home and safe from scrutinizing eyes. Alone with my ingredients, I can make creative meals without men harping at me. Papa and my brothers can't cook, and they don't bother me when I'm in the kitchen. To me, an afternoon making dough and putting together a pot pie was a mini vacation.

I wash the trays in the little sink with a sponge and soap from a tiny dispenser and dry them with a linen towel. From the light smell of bleach embedded in the cotton fibers, they are professionally cleaned by a service.

I open the cute little cubbies, find the compartment with other trays, and stack the three I washed inside. I look around the tiny area and notice not one, but two mini fridges. I open one and peer inside. It's stocked with drinks and liquor. I have no idea what Prosecco is, but there is also a bottle of champagne, soft drinks, and bottled water. I close the door and open the other refrigerator. It is loaded with more food. How much are we to eat? There are cold-cut sandwiches on French bread and a tray of cut cheeses, meat, and fruit. I've never been to a fancy party, but I know that the tray of meat and mixed delicacies is called a charcuterie board. These men are obviously incredibly wealthy and versed in the ways of the world and don't think twice about blowing tons of money on fancy stuff. I'm having one hell of an adventure. I find Roman interesting, and if I can befriend this Irina or Alex on the boat, maybe one of them will help me get away. I close the fridge door with a soft click.

"Everything okay, Dasha?" Roman calls over the whistling of the plane.

"Just fine." I quickly pull a bottle of water out of the electric cooler to buy more time. I'm also thirsty. It must be the altitude. I remember hearing my brothers talking about how to hydrate when they fly. I open it, drink some, then peek my head around the thin wall into the cabin area. The men are whispering to one another, but I can't make out the words. They peer back at me with the inquisitiveness of a kitten.

I stand in the aisle, where they can see me. What do they think I'm going to do, overtake them with my bobby pins? I down my drink and slide the empty bottle into the garbage can on the wall. I clear my throat and return to my seat. I reach for my seatbelt, and a large hand covers mine, startling me.

Tingles run up my arm at Roman's touch. My eyes lock with his, which are now a dark shade of blue.

My heart pumps faster. He's not pale like many Russians. He's different, and I find him attractive. My cheeks must be turning fifty shades of pink.

"You don't need to fasten that. The captain will tell us if we need it due to bumpy weather or upon landing. You can go to the back and sleep. I promise, you'll be safe."

"I am tired," I admit. He removes his warm hand, and I suddenly feel cold. Must be a draft in the plane.

"Okay, I'll rest." I stand and tug my blouse over the top of my jeans to have something to do with my hands. He makes me nervous. I've never been around a man close to my age for this many hours, and certainly not without supervision. Hell, I don't even know if Roman is married. My heart skips a beat. If he's taken, then…

I glance down at his large hands. He's genetically gifted, a tall man, over a meter tall and then some. I'm short, and if I didn't know how to swim, my butt would be an anchor.

I go to the back of the plane and enter the room. It has the same yellowish lights, a TV, cupboards, a built-in desk, a large bed, and nightstands. I am shocked but delighted. The bed does look inviting. There's no reason I can't lock the door and get an hour of sleep. I flip the lock on the door with a smile on my face. I've had more independence being a captive than living at home.

I sit on the plush mattress and untie my old Converse sneakers, setting them neatly in front of the nightstand. The carpet is new and smells fresh. Wow, it's like a mini house inside this plane, and to think it can fly. I pull back the comforter and crawl in. The pillow is the softest feather pillow I've ever laid my head on. The thin duvet is enough to be comforting, as sleeping without something covering my shoulders is difficult. I pull it to my chin and smile. I'm safe, warm, and fed. It feels pretty fucking good.

I have this window of time that is all mine. I'm safe for the moment, but I don't know what awaits me in France. I wonder if Papa is looking for me. Andrian will be furious. I stood him up, and my flight will be a major embarrassment for him and my father. The wedding was small and had few attendants. Even so, the nuptials would be in the press. It's only a matter of time before I have to answer one or both of them. Word will get out that I ran away. Maybe they will make an excuse that I was sick. At any rate, my father will have to make it right. I don't know how unless he gets me back. For some reason, Andrian wants me.

Are there men looking for me? Roman and Alex are crafty. They converse without the need for words. Papa and my brothers talk too much to be good criminals. Quiet, broody men like Roman are the ones who make the important decisions.

I close my eyes and listen to the hum of the plane. I'll worry about home and what awaits me there if I'm caught tomorrow.

* * *

SOMEONE KNOCKS ON THE DOOR. I'm slow to wake up. It takes a minute for me to realize I'm not in my own bed, and then the past twenty hours come flooding back. I didn't know traveling was so exhausting.

"I'm coming." Quickly, I scramble from the bed and unlock the door, wearing my socks. Roman is standing in the aisle.

"Time to get in your seat, Princess," he announces. Is it my imagination, or is there a spark in his eye? I wish Katsia were here. She would know all the social cues of dating.

The flash in his eye disappears, and he returns to the main cabin.

I grab my shoes and trot behind him. I sit down and slide a white sneaker with tiny, embroidered red hearts on my left foot, then its twin on my right. Once they are on, I tie them in the same order.

"You've had those a long time?" He's eyeing my sneakers as if they are relics.

"Sure, some things are tough to let go of." I shrug and wonder what his point is.

"I imagine it's unusual to wear something like that on your wedding day. If I were to get married, which I'm never going to do, I would want my bride to wear heels and the most gorgeous dress with a diamond necklace and matching earrings."

"That's nice." Is he for real?

"So, why sneakers?"

He's not letting this go.

"They're never out of fashion, are they? I thought the hearts were appropriate. I mean, getting married means you're in love, right?"

Who am I, right now? This man can end me at any point, and I'm being evasive. I suppress a smirk, pursing my lips and running my tongue to moisten the parts inside my mouth.

"Are you in love?"

Stalemate. Shit. *I don't know what love is.* I only know the feeling of puppy love, teenage hormonal stuff. We had a secret crush during school hours. A note and a smile were all it took to make me believe I'd found my prince charming. I thought we'd date, fall in love, and get married. It was the solution to all my problems, a way out of my miserable life. But my father would have none of it.

It lasted for a week before he moved on to another girl, and that's when I learned a hard lesson: all men are the same. I won't fall for Roman's pretty blue eyes and perfect chin because it would make me vulnerable, and nothing good happens to me when I let someone in.

It will be difficult to seduce him when I have no clue what to do. However, Katsia was right. I need to lose my virginity so Andrian won't want me anymore if I'm caught. I've heard my brothers bragging, and they both deflowered many girls before they were eighteen. Like it was a competition.

"Why do you ask?" I'm being evasive, and I know it.

He moves his hands outward, palms up. "Why not answer the question?"

"Well," I stammer, "there are many kinds of love."

He twists his body around and slides his strong fingers under my chin, making me look him in the eye. "Answer my question, Dasha," he demands.

His deep baritone voice has a different tone to it, the style that means business, and I remind myself that despite all their flashy toys, these two are dangerous men who travel with weapons.

"No. I didn't love him."

Roman releases me and gently caresses my face with the back of his hand. I forget to breathe, choking on my saliva in my surprise. I'm such a dolt. I cover my mouth with my hand and act like I'm coughing as I recover.

Alex is speaking to Roman. I'm unsure what he's saying because I'm gripping the arms of my chair so tightly that my fingers are numb. The plane dips, and then it skips once on the runway. The wings are lit, and I notice the rudders are up. The noise increases as the plane shudders. Fear engulfs me. My breathing is rushed. Then it's over, and we're moving along as if nothing happened.

I glance at Alex. He's on his phone. Roman turns to me, and I offer him a half smile. I don't want him to guess how scared I was. I have to act like I belong.

"So, how was your first plane ride?" Roman asks as the aircraft rolls to a stop.

"Great." I fake a smile as I push the annoying belt I forgot to fasten aside and stand. I shift from leg to leg to warm up my muscles. I assume we'll be walking.

The men seem happy we've landed. Alex grins at Roman before he steps off the plane. Roman goes next, and I see another vehicle waiting for us.

Where the hell are we going now?

I follow the guys, and they load the car. I'm wondering if a yacht exists at this point. But I play along and get in the car, watching the men load it with their gear, and then we're whisked off by the driver to God knows where.

I assume we're in France because the driver greets them in French, not that I'm an expert. The hills surrounding us are beautiful. Wherever we are, the scenery is breathtaking, and daylight is approaching, the horizon lighter than the rest of the sky.

Roman notices me looking around. "If you think this is pretty, you won't be disappointed when we get to the helipad," he says.

Heli what?

The car travels along curvy roads. A sign states MONACO in large letters. We continue for five more minutes, passing more signs which are in French. I don't know what they mean. *What does an H stand for, a hospital?* I assumed we were going on a boat or yacht.

"I'm glad you did so well on the flight. I'd hate for you to get sick on this." Roman flashes me an impish grin.

The car stops, and I'm looking at a helicopter. It's gigantic and intimidating.

Oh, my goodness, what is happening? I wanted adventure, but this is the equivalent of skydiving, something I'd be too afraid to ever try.

"Let's go," Alex says as he opens the door. I wait by the car as the men load the helicopter.

I feel like a criminal. I've been in a car and then on a plane for over a day. I can't wait to shower and wash the road dirt off. An SUV pulls up. The helicopter lights shine brightly. I stay close to the vehicle we arrived in. The SUV's headlights are still on, even though it's parked. Two men get out and methodically walk to the trunk, unload luggage, and load it in the helicopter. The helicopter's lights illuminate the bags. They are brown, with gold lettering and tanned leather straps. Holy crap.

I observe the situation with fascination. Everyone moves precisely and in unison, as though this were rehearsed, but I know that's ridiculous. The men shake Roman's hand, and he motions for me to enter the helicopter.

I can do this. I run the mantra through my head on repeat.

I take a firm step in his direction. The helicopter blades are rotating, making a whop-whop noise that disrupts the quiet morning. I'm terrified the blade will chop my head off. It's silly. I'm not that tall, but I duck my head anyway, just to be sure.

"Step up," Roman says, taking my hand and helping me into the helicopter. He climbs behind me, sits beside me, and hands me noise-canceling headphones. I fasten my seatbelt. I'm never taking it off, but it's not comforting to think we're probably flying over the water. Monaco is on the French Rivera, famous worldwide for its prestige, ambiance, and notable people. Not to mention the museums, history, and food. I know enough about every country to be considered "well-read," as Katsia puts it.

I can't wait to meet Irina. I miss Katsia. Having another woman around will be a refreshing break from the two men. They don't talk much. Every time Roman opens his mouth, I know he wants information from me. It's only a matter of time before he finds out the truth, and then what will happen to me?

This is a game where the winner takes all. I'm not good at games, and Katsia says I wear my heart on my sleeve. I need to change that. I need to seduce Roman and not fall in love. He must have women throwing themselves at his feet. He has money, which buys men's silence and power, at least where I come from. Men who run their mouths or don't comply with orders end up missing and presumed dead.

I don't want to die a virgin. I want to know what it's like to be with a man. If I can make Roman fall for me, maybe he'll set me free when this is over.

ROMAN

The helicopter lands on the helipad of the yacht *Severnoye Siyaniye*. In Russian, it means "Northern Lights." Seeing the aurora borealis never ceases to amaze me, so I named the yacht after one of nature's most magnificent spectacles.

Dasha falls into that category as well, but she doesn't know it. I love watching her experience life outside of Belarus for the first time. It's like watching a kid in a candy store, in awe of everything.

The boat is a haven for me and one I don't get to enjoy often. My original plan was to stay two weeks, but it might be shorter with the recent turn of events.

The Mediterranean Sea is warmer than the Black Sea, twenty-one degrees Celsius this time of year, balmy by European standards. It will be warmer next month. I hope Dasha can swim. I can't wait to teach her how to ski, assuming she's never been on the water.

I want to win Dasha's trust. There are no apparent signs of abuse, but my gut tells me she's been mistreated. I need to convince her that not all men are assholes.

While deckhands unload our possessions, I lead the way, and Dasha follows me down to the sun deck with the infinity pool. The morning sun is glistening on the sea like an aquatic welcome mat. I extend my arms over my head and stretch, inhaling the salty air. Closing my eyes, I commit this moment to memory. Living in the moment is important, and we often forget to enjoy the beauty around us.

"This is home for a week or two."

Dasha is quiet, and I turn to check on her. She is staring straight ahead, mesmerized by the view of the hills on one side and the sea on the other. She slowly turns and looks at me. "This is amazing. I mean, I never could have dreamed of something so beautiful."

"Well, get used to it. Follow me. I'll give you a tour of the place." I still need answers, but this isn't the time to press her. I don't want to spoil the moment.

I lead Dasha up a flight of stairs. At the top, glass sliders curve to fit the shape of the yacht, extending to the entrance to my room.

"This is the master suite," I announce as I let her into my sanctuary. Our feet sink into the plush cream carpet, even in our shoes. We pass through a sitting room with a marble coffee table and a leather sectional couch that can accommodate eight. A big bouquet of fresh flowers sits on the coffee table. When I want to watch TV, I press a button on the remote, and the monitor will rise from inside the cabinet where it's housed.

"Everything on this vessel is top of the line," I state.

"It is always so perfect?"

I turn and snap, "Yes."

Her eyes flinch, and I feel bad for being territorial. Maybe I'll get used to having her in my space with time. I've never lived with a woman, so we're in uncharted territory.

We continue the tour, passing two large walk-in closets, and enter the bathroom. The oversized shower is equipped with dual shower heads. The double-sink vanity is spotless, and the mirror is lined with Hollywood makeup lights. In the middle of all this is the focal point, a jacuzzi tub.

"Wow," Dasha gasps. I'm glad she finally said something. I was beginning to worry that she was offended by my gratuitous display of wealth.

"Mind-blowing, huh?" I still remember the first time I toured this vessel, and I'm still impressed. "I have several crew members—men and women—who run the boat. The deckhands take care of the outside. The stewards take care of the interior. The chef takes care of the food. You are not to lift a plate. You will be served. There is only one thing I require from you."

I stare at her until she turns her doe eyes to mine. "What?" she asks.

"I need to know more about you."

"You mean Ratmim. Your enemy?"

"That, too, but I want to get to know you." I approach the king-sized bed. "You will sleep here." After I bought the boat, I installed a Murano glass skylight that can be opened and closed with a remote. "With me," I add, "so I don't have to worry about you running off."

This cabin has total privacy and is the safest and most protected from intruders. We have security guards, but you never know what your enemies are capable of or how far they will go to get what they want.

Dasha is staring at me with wide green eyes, and I try to smile. "Don't worry. I'm not the type of man who forces himself on a woman. Quite the opposite." I wave at our surroundings. "This cabin offers a panoramic view and a deck with a sunken hot tub. The tub has built-in loungers so you can recline and gaze at the stars at night. It's sublime."

I decide I want to fuck Dasha under the night sky. She's too good for Ratmim. I want her for myself, and it's only a matter of time before I fuck her long and hard.

Dasha walks up to the glass doors leading to the deck. The door has a motion sensor and automatically opens. She steps onto the teak flooring and walks to the railing.

"I take it you like it here?" I ask.

"Who wouldn't?" She looks around at the couches and loungers positioned around a gas-powered fire pit.

"Good. We'll be pulling up anchor soon. I'm going to shower." I unbutton my shirt. It exceeded its expiration hours ago, and I can't wait to don a fresh one. "You should check out your closet," I call on my way to the shower.

I'm taking off my pants when I hear her open the door to her closet. I smile when she gasps. The closet is outfitted with every-thing she needs and more. I made sure my staff bought only the best. She doesn't have much, if her sneakers are any indication.

I turn on the faucet, strip off my boxers, and step into the water. I duck my head under the shower and reach for shampoo.

My phone rings, and I turn to look for the source. Damn it, I left it in my pants on the floor, and Dasha is standing over them.

Fuck.

I picture her running off with it and me chasing after her with a washcloth over my junk. Fuck! I jump out of the shower with no time to grab a gold monogrammed towel and get to her just as she pulls the phone from my pants pocket. She drops my pants and hands me the phone. I didn't have to ask, and she didn't run.

"Mm," I growl, and snatch the phone from her. To my delight, she's checking me out. Water drips from my hair and down my torso. "You've never seen a man naked before, have you?"

She shakes her head slowly.

"Well, I have a few nasty scars and a tattoo on my chest and some on my arms. I can be an ass at times, but no woman's ever complained about my performance."

I expect her to bolt. Instead, she pulls a towel off the rack and hands it to me. I wonder when she'll stop surprising me. I wipe the phone dry and toss it in my shoe temporarily. I need to keep her busy with bullshit until I can lock up her passport and the phone in the safe hidden in my closet.

"Would you like a shower? The faucets are tricky."

She nods and slides out of her sneakers. She puts a hand on the vanity and peels off her socks. She unbuttons her blouse but keeps her eyes on me, as if she's putting on a show.

This woman is a moving target when it comes to contradiction. One moment, she's virginal and naïve, and the next, she's bold, brazenly baring herself before me. What happened to the shy girl who changed her clothes while hiding under a wedding dress?

My breathing increases when she drops her top, unfastens her bra, and frees her voluptuous breasts. Her pink nipples immediately harden, and I try to resist the urge to nibble them.

She demurely unfastens her jeans and shimmies out of them, exposing her toned legs. I catch the enticing swivel of her hips and can't wait to dip my fingers in her hard round butt cheeks. Stepping out of her jeans, she leaves them on the floor and stands in front of me, unabashed by her nakedness.

My cock goes up like a flag on a national holiday. She accesses my physique with curious eyes, and I'm doing the same to her. Her hair color is natural, matching the triangle between her thighs. She grabs a washcloth off the stand and enters the shower. Son of a bitch, she's ballsy. I follow her, closing the door behind us.

"Shampoo." I point to a unit on the wall. "Conditioner and body soap." She steps to the other side of the shower and stands in the stream, wetting her body. She moves around so the jet hits her back. No doubt she's stiff from the long trip.

I can't look away. She's facing me with her head tilted back, her eyes closed. Her breasts are ample white pillows beckoning me to caress them. I wonder if she would like my teeth to nip them. It usually heightens the intensity of a woman's orgasm when it's done at the peak of climax.

She opens her eyes just enough to catch me looking at her, then opens them the rest of the way and checks me out from head to toe. My cock twitches when her gaze lingers on my groin.

Fuck. I'd hate to scare her with my huge cock. I'm at a loss for words. Maybe there are no words. Do I make a move or wait? I decide to be patient and wait for the right moment. I can't let her manipulate me into sex. I need to keep my distance until I figure out what I will do with her. Since we're confined in close proximity for the foreseeable future, it's easier if I don't have a clingy woman following me around.

As difficult as it is, I tear myself away and rinse off again. I wait for her to finish before I turn off the faucets. I step out and grab the towel that I left on the floor. I walk to the stack on the wall and hand her another without making eye contact.

"Thank you," she says as she begins to dry herself. I towel off quickly and wrap the large bath sheet around my waist.

"Let me get your back," I suggest. She turns, and I take my time blotting the droplets off her delicate shoulders and back.

I shake my head in annoyance. I'm going soft. For Christ's sake, I'm a mafia hitman. I'm not supposed to care about drying some woman's back. She's driving me crazy.

Seeing her naked is a vision I won't soon forget. I could have easily kissed her in the shower. She gave me all the go-ahead signals, but I'm glad I didn't take the bait. I can't exactly send her back to Ratmim if she's pregnant with my child.

This reminds me, I need to get her checked out by one of our doctors. It's the one thing I insist my women do for me to prevent any accidents. Plus, I always use protection. I wouldn't put it past a woman to intentionally get pregnant to trap me into marriage. In a nutshell, I trust no one except Alex and my family.

Dasha has flipped the switch from immodest, wrapping the bath towel around her gorgeous body. Her wet hair clings to her shoulders. Her toes are adorable as she curls them under my scrutiny.

She asks, "The clothes, are they for me?"

"No. They're for me," I say with a wink. She laughs. "Yes, they are yours to keep. I hope they fit. We'll go shopping when we reach a port with stores."

"It's more than enough clothing," she replies. I suspect she's never owned more than two dresses, one to wear and one to wash. Most women have a closet full of shit and shoes to match. Dasha is not one of them.

"I will leave you to it. That sink area is yours. You'll find everything you need, and if you don't, let me know, and I'll have it delivered."

I shut the bathroom door behind me, take a deep breath, and focus on making my boner go down.

Hidden behind a cabinet in the closet is my safe. I open it and put my extra phone and our passports inside. I close the door and make sure it's locked. I need to figure out a game plan. I text Alex to meet me at the pool bar.

I slide on a dry-fit T-shirt that hugs my biceps and run my fingers through my damp hair. I need to shave, but that can wait until tomorrow. I slip into fitted jeans and loafers before exiting my closet. I peek in Dasha's closet and the bathroom, but she's not there. Panic floods my brain until I find her peacefully sleeping in the bed.

I pause to gaze at her angelic face before leaving to meet up with Alex and Irina.

# CHAPTER 15

## DASHA

$\mathcal{I}$ wake up, and my first thought is of Roman. He's on my mind more than I care to admit. It must be a crush because I have butterflies in my stomach every time he comes near. The man unnerves me, and not just because the chips are in his favor. He has the body of a man who's genetically gifted in every area, and I mean every part. My lady parts yearn to be with him physically. I imagine his hands on my breasts and wonder what it feels like to have him fondle and kiss them. My nipples pebble at the thought.

I shake away my erotic thoughts. What's the point in dreaming about something that may not even happen? He had an opening, and he didn't take it. I'm miffed. Was it because he doesn't want me? Is he having second thoughts about using me for his revenge?

I lay awake, silently waiting for something to befall me, because the past twenty-four hours have been full of surprises. The plane's low whistle was stuck in my mind, but now it's gone. I've been driven in a car for a day, flown, and now helicoptered. The shower was the first I've had in days and much needed. I never knew a shower could be so therapeutic. By the time I was finished, I could not keep my eyes open and slipped into the bed.

I wonder what Roman is doing now. Is he with Irina? Is that why he didn't make love to me in the shower? There are moments when I see desire in his eyes, but he seems intent on holding himself in check. I need to speed this up if I'm to lose my virginity before I'm sent back home.

My God, this bed feels delicious. The cool cotton sheets caress my skin as I wiggle around to feel them on my naked body. We don't have nice things like this in our stores back home. I have no idea how he acquires such luxuries, but if Roman picked all this, he has impeccable taste.

I sit up, pulling the duvet to my chest as I enjoy the panoramic view in front of me. I'm gobsmacked, watching the warm sun kiss the coastline and make it sparkle. The blue sky is dotted with puffy cumulus clouds, and the sea is dancing with waves that look like small snow-capped mountains. This could be a movie or a dream. I'm afraid to pinch myself and wake up.

How did I know there was so much more to see and experience beyond my dreary life? Everyone at home is content to do the same routine every day. I don't want it to end if this is a sample of what lies ahead. I take a deep breath and exhale. I'm on a roller coaster of highs and lows as I delight in the new and worry about the old catching up to me.

I throw the covers off and stand, my bare feet sinking into the plush carpet. I curl my toes into it, grounding myself in my new surroundings. The urge to make the bed hits me, but Roman said I'm not to lift a finger or do the crew's work. The urge to pee overwhelms the urge to tidy up, so I head to the bathroom.

Sitting on the toilet, my mind wanders to the shower with Roman. It was the closest thing to a sexual experience I've ever had, and sadly, it ended too soon. The only other erect penis I've seen was attached to my oldest brother. It happened years ago when I walked into his room and caught him watching porn on his phone. He threw a blanket over his lap, but not before I realized he was pleasuring himself. He cursed at me, and I ran out of the room.

Thoughts of my family make me wonder what they are doing back home and if Papa is looking for me. I will pay the price for my defiance at some point, but until then, I'm going to live my life. I'll start by unpacking the new clothes.

I amble into the closet, and I'm stunned to find the luggage gone and all the clothes put away or hanging perfectly spaced seven centimeters apart, as if a ruler had been used to precisely set the distance between each garment. Wow, I'm impressed with the invisible staff.

I sit on the padded stool in the closet and look around. There is so much to pick from that I'm overwhelmed. What will I wear? I have zero experience putting together a look that fits my surroundings.

I want to make a good impression on Irina. I'm getting anxious and hope we hit it off. If I get tossed overboard, maybe she'll let my family know where they can look for my body. I push thoughts of my demise down like a bad case of heartburn. I have too much to live for now that I've gotten a taste of something more.

I choose a blue sundress with a lemon print. The bright yellow fruit reminds me of travel brochures I've seen for Sorrento and Capri. The dress has built-in support, which means I don't have to wear a strapless bra.

I can skip the bra, but I can't skip the panties. The first drawer I open holds bikinis, the next holds silky lingerie, and the last one holds intimate wear. I pull out a black thong and hold it up to the light. How am I supposed to wear it? It looks like a slingshot.

I slide the dress over my head, tug on the skimpy panties, and enter the bathroom. My hair is a fright. I slept on it wet. I find a hairbrush and methodically run it through one section at a time until it's free of knots. I grab a can of mousse and spray it in my hand, but it hits the mirror instead.

Shit!

I use a towel to clean up the mouse. I don't care what Roman says. If I muck up the place, I'm not leaving it for someone else to clean. Moments like this make me feel like an imposter. I have no business being on this incredible yacht. I try spraying the product in my hand again, and this time, it works. I run the product through my hair and find a hair dryer while I use the brush to add volume.

It's not half bad when I'm done, but I need my bobby pins. I return to the closet to find my jeans and discover they're gone. They must be in the laundry. What about my sneakers? I look around. To my relief, they are on a shelf next to a pretty pair of white sandals. I decide to wear the sandals today and save my sneakers for later.

I return to the bathroom and open drawers until I locate hair accessories but no bobby pins. I pull my hair up and tie it into a ponytail in case it's windy outside. I don't want to deal with another mess of knots.

Finished with my hair, I move on to my face. I've never mastered the art of makeup. The jars of cream, tubes of foundation, compacts of bronzer, and the myriad of brushes intimidate me. I peruse the basket and find a tube of tinted foundation with sunscreen added. I figure it can't hurt. I've never been in the sun much, but I know it can damage my skin. I squirt the product onto my fingers and gently rub it in. I open a bronzer and use the brush to apply some to my cheekbones. There are tubes of lipstick in every color. I select one with a hint of red and apply it. It makes my lips pop, and I smile. I take a step back and look at myself in the mirror. I wish I had a phone so I could send Katsia a selfie. Maybe I can pull this off after all.

Now, where do I find everyone?

I slip on the sandals and leave the most comfortable place I've been in for two days. I can't recall whether the ship has four or five decks, but I know Roman's suite is on top so I have to walk down steps to get anywhere. I've got this.

I'm not positive, but I think the crew deck is below the main deck, and the engine and machinery to keep this beast going are below sea level. I decide to check the main deck first and slip down a set of carpeted steps.

"You must be Dasha."

I turn and find a woman who looks a few years older than me. That, or she looks more worldly. I can't decide. We must be the same height because she's at eye level. Her soft brown eyes immediately put me at ease. Her dark hair is cut into a bob that frames her face perfectly.

"Are you Irina?" I ask, assuming a crew member would not wear a crocheted cover-up over a white one-piece swimsuit.

"Yes, I've been waiting to meet you. I heard you were tired." She smiles, and I see two rows of snow-white teeth, the kind you see in toothpaste commercials.

"Are you with the others?"

"Yes, follow me." She beckons with her hand, and I notice she's wearing the same sandals. Fueled by confidence, I follow her with a bounce in my step, anxious to see what today offers.

Roman is at a table with the remains of what looks like breakfast. His eyes meet mine briefly before they travel down my body. I hope he approves of my dress. I can't go wrong if his staff hand-picked my wardrobe.

A breeze glides over the vessel's bow, and I look around to see a lounge area with a bar, couches in the shade, and chairs in the sun. A buffet table overflowing with fresh fruits and baked goods tempts me, along with the smells of sausage, eggs, and warm maple syrup.

"Have something to eat," Irina instructs. "The Bloody Marys are rather spicy if you like that kind of thing. I'm having another mimosa." She raises a finger, and without a word, a young woman in a pressed uniform brings her an orange drink in a champagne flute. Wow, that's service.

I head to the buffet and grab a plate out of the plate warmer. The male server is dressed in a crisp white outfit that reminds me of the dress uniform Tom Cruise wore in *Top Gun: Maverick*. He smiles and asks if I want eggs.

"Yes, please."

He carefully scoops a generous portion of scrambled eggs onto my plate. I nod yes for the sausage and a croissant. With my plate full of more food than I can eat, I approach the bar, where a woman fills pitchers with fresh-squeezed orange juice. I ask for the same thing Irina is drinking and watch her pour champagne into a tall glass and add a generous splash of orange juice. She hands me the drink, and I take a sip. It's a slice of paradise, fizz, and orange juice. I take another sip and remind myself to go slow. If I'm thirsty, there's always water.

A different woman in uniform takes my plate, carries it to the large round table, and sets it next to Roman. I'm beginning to think the crew members outnumber the guests and wonder if they know my situation. I bet they all had to sign documents of confidentiality.

Such precautions make sense to avoid having your personal life in the headlines. That might bring enemies to your front door.

The scenery around us is relaxing, but the strict protocols and rules of etiquette leave me feeling a little uptight. I constantly worry that I'm going to say or do something wrong.

I sit next to Roman, and Alex looks up from his phone and asks how I slept.

"Like a baby." I smile. "I didn't realize I was so tired."

"Well, hopefully, you've caught up. We'll have to get you out on deck for fresh air." Roman's deep voice softens, causing me to blush.

I have a flashback to the shower and his naked body, water cascading down his muscular torso and ginormous erection. It's enough to make me drop my fork.

I'm so distracted that I can barely eat. It's as if Roman cast a spell on me. I can't help but breathe in his scent—hints of citrus mixed with clean, fresh air that tickles my nose.

I force myself to take delicate bites of egg and sausage, then try the croissant. I know France is known to have the best pastries. When I bite into the buttery, flaky bread, I almost moan.

Everyone's eyes are on me. Did I moan out loud?

"What? Did I do something wrong?"

Roman chuckles. "No, not at all. Eat, and be careful with that orange juice. It has alcohol in it."

No wonder I don't have a care in the world. A few sips of the orange elixir and I forget my troubles.

Irina and I exchange knowing looks. Is my lust for Roman written on my face?

"Where are you from, Irina?" It's a safe question.

"All over, but I live mostly here in France."

"You speak French as well?"

She holds the stem of her mimosa by her fingertips as she perches on the arm of Alex's chair, diva-like. "Many languages, you?"

"Oh, not me. Russian and some versions of it and English."

"Roman, you?"

"English and Russian, a bit of others when I need to get around." He drains his tomato juice drink, leans back in his chair, and laces his fingers behind his head.

"What happens today?" I ask, taking another sip of my drink.

"Today, we will go out in the boat." Alex smiles, and he and Irina chuckle.

"You'd better not tip the sailboat over again," she says, but something tells me she's not mad at him. I have a feeling she enjoyed their watery sailing trip.

"You're taking out all the fun," Alex protests, to which she rolls her eyes, but her lips tell a different story. I wonder what their history is and suspect she may be more than just a friend.

I want to ask Irina what she does for a living, but it seems no one talks about work. I don't want to be rude, so I'll wait and pick her brain when we're alone. She's so gorgeous. If she told me she's a Bond girl, I would be tempted to believe her. She does everything effortlessly and looks good doing it, though she's aloof and somewhat guarded. How can I be friends with someone so out of my league?

# CHAPTER 16

## ROMAN

The princess has joined us. Alex and I called for men to be at my house. We'd be fools not to anticipate Ratmim finding us. I want to enjoy being at sea, but revenge comes with stress and unknown factors.

I take solace in the fact that Dasha is interested in me. She's never been with a man. That's obvious. The curiosity in her eyes gives her away. That and her shyness confirm my suspicion. I want to make love to her, and I want her first time to be special.

Why do I care so much? Other men would fuck her and sell her.

My thoughts drift from her to business. I have a text from Dmitry in New York. The cocaine will arrive in Russia this week. I text the man who will be in charge of the exchange when it comes in. I should call Nikolay, and yet, I delay the inevitable. I'd rather contact him when I have the guns or the money to replace them.

"Alex, I'm not sure how to handle this. I have men at my compound, and Mom's protected in case Ratmim has a stupid idea to make more trouble."

He smokes his cigarette. "It's better to be prepared and not need men and guns than to be caught without them. Have you fucked her yet?"

"No." My voice is low. I'm still at war with myself. A woman in a club is a one-and-done. They know what they signed up for, but Dasha is something different.

"Well, tap that and get her out of your system. Being this far away is a great idea, but he's going to find her eventually. We need to call with demands. Keep the call short so it can't be traced."

"I agree. He owes us a million dollars. We also need to make sure no one finds our coke. I'll put more men on it. You may have to head back early. I don't trust anyone more than I trust you."

Alex nods and blows a smoke ring. "Sure. Whatever you need."

"Let's take the women out on the boat to ski in the Côte d'Azur. We can have some fun. It's turned into a working vacation, but we're entitled to one day off."

"Sounds great. I'll drive the boat." Alex's face perks up. He loves to be in a boat more than he loves land. I'm surprised he still lives in Russia. He should buy himself a house on an island. He can easily afford it.

Irina joins us, and we exchange hugs.

"Thank you for coming," I say.

"I hope you won't need me. Are you expecting trouble, Roman?" Her voice is filled with contempt as she drops the questions.

"Aww, you only think the worst of me," I chide her.

"I know you. And you have trouble written all over your face." She waves her finger in the air. "It's rare you call me to hang out unless you need something." She turns away to hit the buffet table and obtains a plate of food she won't eat and a drink she'll love. She returns to sit beside Alex, predictably picking at her food like a bird.

"Well, we might have incoming. Hard to tell. I'm weighing my options at the moment."

"It's never good to take a captive. You open yourself up for more trouble." Her eyes scan me. "Ah, she's more than just some girl, right?"

"Mm."

"No, this one is special. Who is she?"

"The fiancée of the man who stole from me."

"You should have just put a hole in his head," she says. "You've exposed yourself. It's not like you to take risks like this. Something about this young woman enthralls you."

"Perhaps."

"Don't say I didn't warn you. And if I get hurt, you'll pay for it."

I lean back in my chair and meet her eyes. "I'm sure of it. Nothing about you is inexpensive." I slip her a smile to let her know I don't hold it against her. We're excellent friends, and I want to keep it that way. She has contacts and expertise that are second to none. And as a woman, she can access some areas more easily than my men can. She can be invaluable and comes with a pipeline to contacts in other countries.

"Well, make sure I get my share of the product you have coming in, and I'll be sure to do my part so that no harm comes to this precious princess you have lost your mind over."

I nod. How do I remain objective when I only want to feel Dasha's body, fondle her breasts, and show her what an attentive lover I can be? I can't control my cock forever, but my instinct tells me that once I sink myself into her pussy, I may never be sane again. I'm not myself as it is. It's not like me to behave this way.

We catch up on the past six months, and Irina leaves to check on dolphins swimming alongside the boat. When she returns, Dasha is behind her.

The women will get along, and Irina's loyalty is to me. It's not a bad idea to have another hand on deck. My eyes follow Dasha when no one is looking, and my pulse races when she sits next to me. I remember her in the shower and know that I can't delay the inevitable.

I will dazzle her with a fun afternoon, then a private dinner, just the two of us. The night will be clear enough to gaze at the stars. How difficult can it be to fuck a willing captive?

After brunch, we retire to our room to change for the trip.

"You know, Ratmim will eventually find me," she states. Is it fear in her voice or concern?

"I know. I'll be ready. Tell me, what is he like?"

I slip out of my shoes and watch her face for details that are left unspoken.

"He's coldhearted, has no regard for women, and might have killed people."

"On his own or for someone else?"

"Both, but I'm not sure. I'm not in the loop on the details. He goes into Russia frequently and other countries."

She slips her shoes off and sits on the bed, wringing her hands.

"You'll need a one-piece swimsuit. And a cover to wear over it to keep the sun off. The sun and sea will tire you out. I'm glad you had a nap," I add as I enter my closet. I'm learning about Ratmim, but what details is she not sharing? That's the larger question looming in my head. Dmitry is running the license plates.

I strip, removing my jeans and shirt in favor of swim trunks and a dry-fit swim shirt. I find sunglasses and put my boat shoes back on.

We meet in the middle of the spacious room. The swimsuit fits her well, and I can make out her figure underneath it. I groan. I'd love to throw her on the bed and thrust my cock in her. I wonder why she was so willing to bed me earlier. Does she think I will let her go if she complies?

"Do you have a family?" she asks.

"Yes, two brothers. A mother. You?"

"Brothers and my father."

"Are they friends with Ratmim's sons?"

"Not really." However, she's a terrible liar.

"I assume your last name is fake. Is your first name fake as well?"

"Why should I tell you?"

"Why not unless you have something to hide? You don't want to marry Ratmim. Why not sell him out? It's better for you to be on our side—he stole weapons from me. I can't let it go. Nor should I be expected to forgive him."

"I know the penalty for that is death. Are you going to kill him?" Her eyes have an unexplained look of concern. Why does she seem to care if she doesn't want to marry the man, and he's such a pig?

"I'm not sure he can make restitution."

"Not sure how that would work," she murmurs.

"Me, either." We both understand that neither of us will back down. And the truth is, neither of us can blink.

"Well, let's not worry over it now," I add to break the intense vibe. "We can share the day, no?"

"Yes," she replies, clearly relieved that the question-and-answer session is over.

We make our way to the bottom of the yacht, and one of my men pulls the boat up. We embark, and I notice a cooler. I'm sure it is filled with drinks. We have towels and sunscreen. I sit next to Alex in the front, and our guard is in the back with the women.

Alex floors it, and I hear Dasha let out a scream of excitement. I look back. Her eyes are wide, but she has the largest grin on her face. I'm happy she's capable of such excitement, as I want her screaming my name when I make her come for the first time.

We fly over the light chop and make our way closer to shore. Alex drops anchor. I surf the horizon, looking for trouble, and check on our guard to make sure he's got his eye on our surroundings and not the pretty woman next to him.

Irina is right. It's stressful being responsible for someone else. It's not just the responsibility of Dasha—we've opened a door, and who knows who might walk through it? I flick the morbid thoughts from my head, reminding myself that Ratmim stepped on our turf first.

Alex and Irina get the skis out. I pull out the life vests from a cabinet in the boat.

Dash pulls her cover-up over her head. I'm unprepared to be greeted by pert nipples making an impression in her suit. My cock is rising to the occasion. Damn, I might have to make an unplanned dive into the water.

I put the life vest on Dasha and zipped it. I'll wait for my go at the water. It's too hot. The area is populated—it's the time of year to be here. Alex jumps over the side of the boat with skis on his feet. I drive the boat, easing him up and then hitting it hard.

He jumps some waves, getting in his groove, and the women hang at the back of the boat to watch. I take in Dasha's cute ass and immediately put my mind back on driving. Alex wipes out. Irina swims to him and adjusts the skis, and Alex puts them on her feet. Alex climbs aboard. Then I ease Irina up as she gracefully stands on the water. She's a natural. Alex yells in excitement as she jumps some waves, and when she's tired, she lets herself down.

I stop the boat. "Your turn, Dasha."

"Oh, no. I can't do that."

"Yes, you can. I'll help you."

"I've never done anything like this."

"Come on." I give her my hand. "It's easy. Let the boat pull you up, and you stand in the skis. It might take a few tries, but if Alex can do it"—I shrug—"anyone can."

Alex nods at her, and she stands. We kick off our shoes. Giggling, she holds my hand as we walk to the side of the motorboat.

"On the count of three, we jump in."

She nods.

"One, two." I give her a mischievous grin as I let go of her hand. "Three."

We both sink under the water and bob to the top.

"Swim to the tow line."

We reach it at the same time. I hold her foot and adjust the skis to it. Then I slip them on both of her feet.

"I don't know about this," she says, but I can tell she's excited, even though she's apprehensive.

"You can do it. Remember what I told you."

She nods.

I climb back into the boat and stand beside Irina as Alex eases on the gas pedal.

Dasha is pulled through the water.

"Hit it," I yell to Alex.

Dasha is halfway up.

I motion for her to stand. She's going to fall if she doesn't.

Her eyes are glued to me, and I'm enjoying the attention.

Dasha nods and stands. She's holding on her own as she glides over the waves, and then I see it. She smiles, a smile brighter than any summer day.

I'm beaming. Alex maneuvers the boat around others. We maintain a clear path. A boat passes us, creating a wake. There is no way to escape the rough water, and Dasha falls. But she's still holding on to the rope.

Irina and I notice this and start yelling, "Drop the rope."

Dasha cannot understand what we're saying or what she should be doing. She'll run out of air eventually and drop it out of necessity. Finally, she drops the rope, and Alex circles to pick her up.

I jump in and feel the coolness of the water. I swim to her as Alex mans the boat.

"You did great. I forgot to tell you to drop the rope when you go down."

"Right. Well, I needed air," she gasps, floating bravely in the water. Her breathing slowly returns to normal. "I don't know why I thought I had to hang on to it."

I chuckle. She's tenacious and has guts.

I help her back in the boat.

"My legs feel weak," Dasha gasps. "Wow, what a workout."

"You get used to it," Irina replies. She helps Dasha out of the vest, and they sit together.

"What do you say we drive around and dry off before returning?"

"Yes," Irina shouts with a smile as she hands me a drink. Dasha pulls a hard lemonade from the cooler. Funny, her sundress had lemons on it this morning.

I turn the boat over to Alex despite the gang's protests that I should ski. I wanted to come and give Dasha a new experience. I can ski whenever I want. Today wasn't about me.

Alex speeds around, and we return to *Severnoye Siyaniye* an hour later.

We all head to our showers. I'm wondering what today's shower will be like.

When we enter our room, it looks like we were never there.

"That was awesome." Dasha's cheeks are pink from the sun.

"You got some sun. Do you feel okay?"

"Yeah, fine. Why?"

"You're not used to the sun, and it's hotter than you would think. The sun and glare off the water can cause issues with the heat."

She moves to the bathroom.

"Shower?" I ask.

She nods and slips past me, not so shy today.

She undresses in front of me. I can't get out of my wet clothes fast enough.

I turn on the water, and she steps in first. She pulls her hair down and lets the water flow through it.

She's a nymph, and my cock springs to life.

I join her under the water. I groan as I take her in my arms with the water running over her. She lifts her chin. Her lips are perfectly poised for mine. I place a hand on the wall over her and forcefully kiss her. I'm filled with an aching need that's gone unmet for so many years. I'm thirsty, and she's the only one to quench my desire.

She kisses me back, and we grapple like crazed teenagers eager to get more of each other. I push my tongue into her mouth. She pushes back. She sparks something in me, a desire to be more, do better, and be more than what I've become.

Desire fills every fiber of my being.

I push her up against the wall, using my free hand to cup her ass. In my excitement, my nails dig into her youthful flesh. She gasps for air as our kiss deepens. I feel her arms around my neck. Her petite hand runs from the top of my head and slides through my thick hair.

I devour her lips, nipping, teasing. My chest flexes, keeping pace with faster breathing as my heartbeat increases. Adrenaline flows through my veins like oil in a pump.

My cock is wedged between us. She reaches a hand down and grabs me.

I moan. God, she makes me feel incredible. I never want this to end. I lift her on the wall, cupping her ass. She pulls me tightly to her. Her nipples are rubbing on my chest and turning hard. The water flowing over us adds to the ambiance, but it isn't ideal for me to fuck her against the wall on her first go. No, I'm going to do this right.

I turn off the water, grab a towel, and wrap it around her shoulders to keep a draft off her as I carry her to my bed. This is the new me. This will be a night she'll never forget.

# CHAPTER 17

## DASHA

Kissing in the shower leaves me hungry for more. His lips cover mine, and I never want this to end. He doesn't mind that we're soaking wet and lying on the expensive mattress. The water beads on our bodies, making them slick. The sensation of his hairy chest rubbing against my skin is delectable, and my nipples tighten.

He leans over me and looks into my eyes. I stare back at him.

"You are mine. You'll never be with another man. You'll never look at another man the way you look at me. If any man touches you, he will die."

I nod, knowing he would kill for me.

"Say it."

"I'll never look at another man the way I look at you." My words are not hollow. I can't tell him he captivates my thoughts. When he walks into a room, my heart soars.

I'll never have these feelings for another man. It's not because he's my first. More importantly, when he smiles, I know he's happy. He rarely smiles, so sharing it with me is meaningful. He validates my existence as being worthy or more than what I've become under my father. Roman doesn't treat me differently because I'm not as worldly or sophisticated as his friends.

We can sit together in silence and not be uncomfortable. He provides the finest things in life, but I don't need grandeur or the life of a rock star, although it is rather nice, I'll admit. He's opened my eyes, showing me a world I have only ever seen in magazines and travel brochures.

It was always a pipe dream to leave Minsk, but Roman made it happen. When he holds me, I'm not scared of anything, and I love it. He believes in me when I don't believe in myself.

His lips ravage mine, and he kisses and sucks on my neck. I feel his hands in my hair as he threads it through my thick tresses. Making a fist, he tugs on it, and I gasp. My head tilts back, giving him more access to my neck.

My back arches, and he buries his face between my breasts and groans. He caresses one with his hand, then sucks the nipple into his mouth. He plays with it, flicking his tongue over it before gently nipping it with his teeth. It's like strumming a chord that leads to my vagina, and my body has an awakening of lust I've never known before.

I'm wet between my legs and not from the shower. Pressure builds inside me, and I'm afraid my ovaries will explode if I don't find a release. I grind my hips against him as he lies prone over me.

I close my eyes and run my hands through his dark hair, over his shoulders and biceps, and down his back, exploring his toned body with touch instead of vision. Sweet mother of God, I can't get enough of him.

My pussy longs for him to fill me. He moves his attention to my other breast, pushing it into his mouth and eliciting a moan.

"You like that, don't you?" he murmurs.

"Yes," I gasp, surprising myself.

His lips work their way over my ribs, down my abs, and when he reaches my lower belly, I squeal. My eyes fly open, and my hands go to the area to defend myself. His lips tickle and delight me at the same time.

He moves my hands away. "You're beautiful. Now be a good girl and spread your legs for me, Dasha."

I feel vulnerable but comply, wondering what he will do next.

The mattress dips as he shifts his weight. I lift my head and see him kneeling on the floor. He grabs my legs and pulls me to the edge.

His fingers move to the triangle between my legs. I stiffen when his fingers part my lips, then relax when his tongue licks me in places no one has ever touched. He flicks his tongue over my clit, then massages it with his thumb.

"Ah," I moan loudly.

I squirm on the bed as he drives me crazy. The feeling is delicious, but protecting my inner sanctum is second nature. I move my knees together. I can't be vulnerable. He's worming his way into my heart. What will happen when I willingly give myself to him?

Roman places his hands on my knees and parts them. "Relax. Trust me."

This is sex, nothing more, I remind myself.

He spreads my legs wide, and I feel his hot breath on my private parts. I want to cover myself but don't want him to think I'm a prude. I'm naked physically and emotionally.

His warm tongue touches my clit, brushing over it gently, then becoming more demanding, flicking it with more pressure than before. My desire increases. Pleasure reverberates through my body. The stimulation causes my blood to rush to the area. My lips swell in response. He sucks my clit and then slides his tongue into me.

"Oh," I gasp as his tongue moves in and out. He massages my clit with a finger before sliding it inside of me. I lift my butt off the bed, grinding into his hand to get my fill. He surprises me when he pulls his finger out. I'm crushed. Is that it?

He adjusts himself slightly before thrusting two fingers inside me and massaging my nub with his thumb. I inhale in surprise and roll slightly to one side, writhing in pleasure.

My wetness gushes over his fingers. Ripples of pleasure spread over my body, and goosebumps pepper my arms. I have never experienced anything like this. It's intoxicating how he pleasures my body. A tear slips from my eye. I'm overwhelmed with emotion, the very thing I told myself to fight. I'm his willing captive, held and spellbound, waiting for whatever comes next. My body betrays me.

I hear him open the drawer to the nightstand. Then he puts a shiny packet in his mouth and rips it with his teeth. A condom. He quickly rolls it over his hard cock.

I'm captured by the sight of his cock suspended over my pussy. He's much larger than I imagined.

"It will hurt at first, but then it will feel good," he assures me as he slides me into the middle of the bed and leans over to kiss me. I clasp his head between my hands.

He caresses my face and looks adoringly into my eyes. He must be a man capable of emotion because his eyes are filled with something other than contempt. I can't hide my lust for him. He cups my neck and moves over me as I return his kisses. A fire of desire engulfs me as his fingers move down my body and slip into me. I'm immobilized, frozen. There's no release for the desire that swells in every cell of my body. My mind is spinning, devoid of thought.

He pulls his fingers out, and something thicker takes their place. He gently pushes the head of his cock inside me.

"This part will hurt," he warns as he breaks through the only barrier between us. I cry out as my walls stretch to accommodate his girth. My eyes sprout tears of pleasure or pain. I'm not sure which.

He cups my butt cheeks and slowly pushes his way in, so deep that I gasp. I'm full inside. I close my eyes and let my body take over. He pulls out and plunges back again, this time easily, and we start to move together naturally as he slides his thick cock into me repeatedly.

He changes position and moves in a methodical rhythm. I relax as the pleasure builds. Instinctively, I wrap my legs around him, hugging him as we move together. We're just the two of us on a wave, and it's nirvana.

He lifts his head, his neck strains, and his back arches. I move a hand to his chest and grab his chest hair, pulling on it. He pumps me again and again as my pleasure rises to new heights. He fills me. My walls constrict around him. Blood thumps so loudly in my ears that I'm afraid I will die of a heart attack if I don't get a release soon.

I'm ready to explode, and with one final thrust, he pushes me over the edge and into sweet oblivion.

"Ahhhh." I cry out for as long as the euphoria lasts. I'm in another world, suspended in time. My nails dig into his shoulders. My insides feel slick as I squirt juices over the head of his cock.

It doesn't take long for Roman's moans to fill the room. His body shudders, and he buries his head in my neck. When he's finished, he holds me before rolling to the side and slipping the condom off. He stands and disappears to dispose of it.

I watch him as he returns to me. His face is tan from our day on the water, and the tattoo on his collarbone is prominent.

"How do you feel?" he asks as he lays beside me and drapes an arm over my hips.

"Good. It hurt."

"Sorry about that. There's no way around it. And the good part?"

"Oh." My face flushes with embarrassment. "It was incredible. I never knew it could be that way."

"Hm, it gets even better. There are endless possibilities, and every time you come, it feels different."

"Really?"

He nods, tracing a circle around my navel with his finger. "As long as you have an attentive lover, it will always be an adventure."

"It's like taking a trip and never leaving the bedroom."

"Kind of. And I hope you never lose your adventurous spirit."

"Am I adventurous? I've never been anywhere. How can I be adventurous?"

"Because you take chances even if they scare you. Not everyone can do that. How many people dare to run away on their wedding day and leave the groom standing at the altar with his dick in his hand?"

I chuckle. The image of Andrian with his dick in his hand amuses me. Roman is right, it was scary, but I did it anyway. I never stopped to consider that it took courage.

"Hm. But what if he finds me?"

"We'll deal with it when it happens," he says as he stands.

He pulls me up, and I notice I've made a mess of the bed.

"The cabin steward will take care of it. Let's rinse and see what the others are up to."

I nod.

We shower and dress. When I walk, I feel that it's somehow different. I'm afraid everyone will read my face and know what we did.

"Ratmim will find us," I warn him. "He won't care what happens to me."

"I disagree. I'm betting on the fact that he does care. Why would you say that?" His blue eyes turn dark like a storm brewing on the horizon.

"I'm just saying he doesn't like women."

"He likes men?"

"No, he treats women terribly."

He grabs my arm, no longer the sweet, tender lover he was only minutes ago.

"What aren't you telling me?" he growls.

"Nothing," I answer quickly, pushing his hand off. "You're hurting me."

He drops my arm and storms out of the room.

Shit. He's going to be so pissed when he figures out the truth.

# CHAPTER 18

## ROMAN

We're cruising at a leisurely ten knots along the French coast. Next week, Monte Carlo has an annual gala, and we will attend. A number of other wealthy people will be at the half-masked event, and it's my cover for illicit business. Deals. What could be more exciting than holding criminal conversations under the watchful eye of the public? It's the way of things. Few billionaires rise to the top without fucking over someone. I'd rather be the one doing the fucking and not the one getting fucked.

This is another reason the stolen guns mean so much to me. As Nikolay insinuated, I don't make mistakes unless I'm being impetuous. I rip my mind away from my personal issues to take in the woman before me.

Dasha is beautiful in a one-piece halter-top jumper with wide pant legs. The top ties around her swanlike neck. I like keeping her to myself and protecting her from an uncertain fate. Having her around makes me want to be a better person, but how can we have a normal life since our beginning was based on dubious consent?

We leave our cabin and find the others lounging and enjoying cocktails on the main deck. Alex's eyebrows furrow when he notices our arrival.

I give him a questioning look, and he pulls me to the side. "We need to go to your office right away."

Fuck. If we can't talk in the open, we have a problem. A litany of possible scenarios comes to mind, and I have a sinking feeling Dasha is one of them. She's the result of a madcap adventure that wasn't planned in advance, leaving plenty of room for error.

I need to call Nikolay. I don't want my brother to think that I've gone rogue and stirred up trouble. Unfortunately, I have a suspicion that's what happened.

Dasha's green eyes question me. "Is everything okay?"

"It will be," I answer and feign confidence. There's no need to worry her unnecessarily.

"How did you and Irina meet and become friends? She's awesome."

"Irina and I met by chance at a party years ago. She was looking for information on Russian and Belarusian organizations, and I helped her with what I knew of Russian groups. She was looking for the man who murdered her mother at the time. She had just joined the DGSE, France's counterintelligence and secret intelligence agency."

"Wow, that's quite the story."

"It is, she's great. So enjoy your time together," I add.

I watch as Dasha joins Irina on a canvas sofa in the shade. A light breeze is blowing. I glance at the horizon and see dark clouds gathering over the ocean. We may be in for some rough seas later.

Alex leads the way to my office on the next deck and closes the door behind us. I sit behind the desk and tap the keyboard. The monitor springs to life.

"Pavel called."

"That can't be good." My heart sinks. I'm not ready to return Dasha.

"He said that Ratmim's daughter has run off. *Daughter*," he emphasizes to make a point. "Dasha is not his bride." Alex paces, a cigarette in his hand. He knows better than to smoke it here, so he jams it between his lips without lighting it.

"What?" My eyes grow wide. "Daughter? Was she getting married?"

"To someone named Andrian," he says, angrily throwing his arms in the air.

"Who is this Andrian?"

"The last name is immaterial, no?" Alex growls, clearly annoyed.

"Maybe not. There was another picture in the file that looked vaguely familiar. I can't recall who it was or why Dmitry would be tracking him for Dad."

"Your Dasha is Dasha Kozlov—Ratmim's hidden gem. Not many even know of her existence. Rumor has it their organization is gearing up to head out of town quickly. They reportedly packed for a week or more. Did you get the license plates back from Dmitry?"

"I've been meaning to call him about that. I didn't tell him it was urgent, but he's had enough time."

"It's urgent. Damn it!" Alex slams a fist on the desk. "I'm to keep you from starting a war. Somehow, your little misadventure stirred up a hornet's nest."

"Fuck!"

My fingers fly over the keyboard, dialing Dmitry for a video call on our encrypted VPN network. He answers immediately, his face appearing on the big screen on the wall. "Brother, what the hell are you up to? You send me pictures of foreign license plates, then I don't hear from you for days. You had me worried. These are bad people."

"How bad?" I ask ominously.

"The late-model BMW belongs to Andrian Abramov. You might be too young to remember, but there was bad blood between him and Dad. I wouldn't trust him if he were the last man alive. He's moved up in the world, seeking riches he lost when he was kicked out of Russia."

"And why did he hate Dad?"

"Dad got the riches he wanted. Andrian was cheating the system, and the powers that be didn't take kindly to it. The problem is, he's still connected to nefarious men inside Belarus, and it's rumored that he's storing weapons to destabilize a neighboring country."

"Fuck. That must be why he stole our guns." I turn to Alex. "What else do you want to tell me?"

He hesitates before blurting out, "I wouldn't be surprised if the girl has a tracker on her."

"What? What girl? Roman, what girl?" Dmitry demands.

"The one running from the church in a wedding dress. She was escaping on her own. We made it easy for her to get away." I run my hand over my chin, absentmindedly scratching the three-day growth.

"Well, Nikolay needs to be informed. It'd be better if he heard it from you. You're dealing with an unsavory lot, Roman. They don't take kindly to others sticking their noses in their business."

"Well, they started it when they came on our turf and put their hands in our pocket. Those guns are hard to come by, and I want the million dollars he cost us."

"I'm here if you need me. But we need to figure a way out of this. Fill me in when you know more. I'll try to track their license plates and see if they are moving."

"I'm with you, brother. Let me see what I can find." We ring off.

I look from the black screen to Alex, who is nervously flipping the cigarette over his fingers.

"Dasha lied to me," I say in disbelief, staring blankly at Alex. "How could she deceive me?"

"Did she, or did you deceive her? Look, she's in survival mode. She figured out that if she was Ratmim's bride, she was valuable to you. It improved the odds of her getting out of this alive." Alex shrugs. "You can't blame the girl."

I sit pensively. I'm not happy with what he's telling me, but it makes sense. Even though I want to be upset with Dasha, this is my own doing.

Now, I have to figure a way out of this mess without starting a war that would cost men lives or eliminate us entirely. The weight of this is almost too much to bear. We have to assume that Andrian wants us dead, and now I've given him justification to come after us. He's probably been sneaking into our territory for years, and we had no idea the danger we were in until now.

"If I hadn't stumbled into this mess, we'd never know Andrian targeted us."

"True, but if we had more information, we'd be better prepared to make educated decisions. This is why we don't rush in."

My blood boils. Granted, I was impulsive. I need to fix this, and I'm not sure how. I'll need my brother's help.

I stand abruptly, tipping the chair backward, and storm toward the door.

"Where are you going?" Alex asks.

"To get answers," I snap, shooting him a look that could stop a charging elephant.

Using long strides, I walk through the passageways, my fists clenched at my sides. How dare she not tell me the truth? I'm still fuming when I reach the girls.

Alex follows closely behind, carrying a wand designed to detect tracking devices in his hand.

I grab Dasha's wrist and pull her from the couch. Her eyes are wide with confusion and fear. "What?" she asks defensively.

"Why didn't you tell me your father is Ratmim, not your fiancé?"

"You never asked, you assumed. And you seemed content with your assumptions. I thought it was safer being his daughter," she yells back at me. "You made the assumption. I didn't correct you at the time.

Alex hands me the wand. I scan her body, starting with her head. I move the device down her body and try to forget how incredible she looks naked and out of these clothes. The wand makes a beeping sound near her hand.

"The ring. Who gave it to you?"

"My father. He said it belonged to my mother."

"When did he give it to you?"

"When I was thirteen. I'm twenty-one, so that was eight years ago. Why?"

"You were a teenager."

"Yes. Why?"

"Give me the ring."

"No. It's the only thing I have of my mother."

How dare she say no to me?

"You are not to talk back to me. I need the ring. Now!"

"No." Tears fill her eyes. "It's important to me."

"You will give it to me if you want to stay alive." My eyes narrow in anger because she won't obey me. "That ring is a tracking device. Your father's been tracking you since you were a teenager."

Her face turns pale as the blood drains from it. She said her father didn't treat women well, and now, she learns he's been tracking her like human chattel.

"My father tracked me?"

"Yes. That ring never belonged to your mother. Back then, we didn't have the technology to make microchips. It would have cost a fortune to make a tracking device. Think about it. Your father gave it to you when you were a rebellious teenager to keep tabs on you."

Her eyes flash at the revelation. "So, he knew every time I sneaked out when he was away and never said anything that would show his hand…"

I nod.

She pulls the ring off her finger and hands it to me.

I drop it to the deck, crush it with the heel of my shoe, and pick it up, tossing it overboard.

"While on the plane, the helicopter, and this vessel, the GPS isn't trackable. But I'm not that trusting. Your father and Andrian will know our approximate vicinity if they got the last ping off the coast of France."

"You know Andrian?" Her eyes grow wide, and she bites her lower lip nervously.

"I know of him. What do you know?"

"He's very powerful and evil. He carries out hits in our country."

"Does he freelance in Russia?"

"Probably, but I can't be sure. He makes the deals, and my father and brother carry them out. Andrian can get to targets. He's known worldwide. I know that much."

I look to Irina. She nods, confirming she has heard of him, too.

"Why is this the first I'm hearing of him?" I turn to Alex.

"He's not part of our circle. We focus on gathering intel on Russian competition, not that of other countries. It's usually not a concern for us."

"Except when someone is getting their hands dirty by stirring up international events." I look back to Dasha. "Did they do a hit in Russia this year?"

"It was May, early. My older brother went there and came home with a broken leg and some minor injuries. Why?"

"I have to go," I inform the women. I turn to Alex as we walk back to my office. "Let's call Nikolay and Dmitry. I want to know if Ratmim and Andrian were possibly involved in the hit on Dad."

"Damn, I didn't think about that. We assumed it was our government."

"What better way to camouflage a vendetta than to kill your enemy when you know someone else has them on their kill list?" I ask. "It's fucking ingenious."

"Fuck. I never thought of that." We enter my office. "It is brilliant," he concedes.

I pace, too agitated to sit. "It is a brilliant plan that would have worked had it not been for our chance encounter. Ratmim kills off my dad, and now he steals our guns. If we hadn't made that trip, we might never have known there was more to Dad's car accident. Andrian wants to ruin us. We are still a target. But if he knew where we were, he would have already left Belarus. And they are still there."

"We're safe for now, but they could be waiting for us when we return to France. We need more men and time to figure this out," Alex murmurs. "Maybe we can do an exchange at the gala in Monte Carlo. It will be public. There will be cameras everywhere."

"We need a plan. I could call Andrian and arrange a swap. He can give me the money he owes, and we'll give him Dasha." I mull it over in my head.

Alex is staring out the port window. He turns with a glare that tells me he's not okay with that idea. "You'd give her back? You know she's mistreated. It's clear you finally fucked her. Don't tell me you've lost your mind. She reeks of you now. Andrian will sell or kill her if she returns to him. Have you gone daft?"

"No, I haven't. I have no intention of giving her back. I have an idea. Sit."

Alex takes a seat. I call Nikolay and Dmitry. We need an exchange in Monaco. We formulate a plan for a risky trade. Dmitry will delve deeper into data to see if we can pinpoint Andrian's and Ratmim's locations when my father and his friend were killed. Knowing the person responsible doesn't ease the pain of losing them. Hate doesn't begin to express my emotions when it comes to Andrian and Ratmim.

Business for the day had been concluded. Dmitry is checking European license plate scanners to track the men to see if they are coming for Dasha. Alex is in touch with updates from Pavel.

"Why did Ratmim let her escape when he can track her?"

Alex shrugs. "Maybe it wasn't working, or he wanted her to have a few days of freedom before he made her marry Andrian. Nice guy, eh?"

A shiver runs up my back. What Dasha's family does is morally wrong. Nothing can change that fact, but there's no way I'm giving them Dasha. Human trafficking is one way to make problems disappear, and she's an innocent.

My feelings are torn. I care about her, but I'm pissed she didn't tell me about her father. Alex and I join Irina and Dasha on the deck. I feel sticky from the humidity and predict rain is imminent.

Dasha's eyes are hard to read when I sit next to her. I put my hand on her leg, and her body stiffens.

"How long have you known about the ring?" she asks.

"I should have checked you when we left the church, but I had other things on my mind. We missed some protocols in our rush to get out quickly."

"Why didn't they track me and pick me up immediately?"

"I don't know." I rub my hand on her leg possessively. "I can only guess your father may not have told Andrian immediately. Maybe he wanted to give you a week to get this out of your system." I shrug. "I can't read his mind. I know that he or Andrain will come for you."

"You know this for a fact?" Her voice quivers.

"Yes. They're on a mission to take down the Volkov family."

"Your last name is Volkov?"

"Yes. Why?"

"I've heard them talk about you. They say you lie, and I know they lie as well. I never understood what the feud was about. Why do you hate each other?"

"Years ago, my father found success where Andrian failed, and ever since, Andrian has sought revenge. We think he may have had something to do with my father's death. And more recently, we had a gun shipment stolen from us, and I think he had a hand in that, too. It won't ruin us, but it cost us a lot in lost profits."

"Are you giving me back to him?" She's playing it cool, sipping her iced tea, but the ice cubes rattle in the glass, even though her hand isn't visibly shaking.

"No. He thinks I am, but we're working on a solution." I lean over and kiss the top of her head.

I slide my arm around her shoulders and feel her relax. I pull her into my chest, and she rests her head on me.

"What about some appetizers?" I say to change the subject.

The dark clouds I saw earlier gather overhead, reminding me that my enemies will be gathering along the shore, waiting for our arrival at some point in time. I need to figure out a way to keep us all alive.

# CHAPTER 19

## DASHA

"Do you think Andrian and my family killed your father?" I bite my lower lip. Oh, my God. What if it's true and my family did the unthinkable? As time passed, and I saw the malevolent side of my father and his cronies, I developed questions I was not allowed to ask.

"Yes, I do." His face falls, and he suddenly looks like a man who has lived too many years in a short life.

It hurts to know my family killed my lover's father. I've often wondered what they were capable of doing while they were away on these unexplained trips. Today, the blinders were torn off like duct tape to reveal murder and human trafficking. They were associated with the man who made money from it, even if they didn't physically round up people to be trafficked. And that alone tells me that my family is no better than Andrian.

"I'm sorry, Roman. I didn't know." My stomach lurches. I'm nauseated; my worst nightmare has come true. My father has groomed my brothers to be killers.

"It's not your fault, Dasha. I'm still waiting for conclusive evidence. Can I ask what happened to your mother?" I see his pain, and yet he's asking about my loss.

"I don't know. I have her name. My father is a habitual liar, so I'm not sure it's really her name." I lean forward and put my empty glass on the coffee table. "She left when I was very young. I have a few pictures. They're old, and that ring obviously wasn't hers."

"I'll get you a new ring, a real emerald."

"I don't need it," I quickly reply as my face heats up. Am I blushing? He's offering to buy me jewelry, which is sweet of him, but all I ever wanted—and still want—is my freedom.

The air is as heavy as the conversation.

I lift my chin and push my shoulders back. Katsia says it conveys confidence. I've never felt it until today. Roman was so mad at me for misleading him and about the tracker in the ring, but I stood my ground. Katsia would be proud of me. I miss her and wonder how she's faring.

Roman dips his head and kisses me, a warm, tender caress. I return his kiss willingly. It reminds me of earlier, and the tingling sensations return between my legs. The hair on the back of my neck stands up as if lightning is nearby. From the look of the darkening sky, it's either the weather or the man who's hotter than hell sitting next to me. Roman's presence cannot be ignored.

"I'm sorry about earlier," he says, his eyes soft, his voice even softer. This is a first. I've never had anyone apologize to me before.

"It's okay. I understand. I had no idea about the ring. I feel so stupid." I take the palm of my hand and smack my forehead. "I should have thought about it a long time ago. I had no idea he was savvy with that kind of technology."

"It's not your fault. Your father has been lying and cheating his entire life. As much as I tell myself you are the enemy, you're not like him."

His hand still lays possessively on my thigh. I place my hand over his and give it a squeeze.

"My older brother, Vlad, is like him. My younger brother, Albert, is more like me. He's with them because he has no choice. I'm sure my father would make life difficult for him if he weren't complicit. I'm lucky my father kept me away from their criminal activities, but I wasn't allowed to do anything else. I have one friend. Her name is Katsia."

Why am I telling him so much and blabbering on like we're besties? It's almost as if I trust him. Do I trust him? Can he be different from all the other men I've known?

Can Roman be different from my father and Vlad? If Roman has another side to him, then I hope Albert does, too. I wish I could get Albert out. I'm in no position to barter with Roman until there is an agreement with Andrian.

"I'm sure what you say about your brother is true. You're not as silly as I thought you were when I first laid eyes on you jogging through that field in a wedding dress." He sounds amused, and his mouth twitches at the corners.

"What? That look on your face…" I laugh and slap his thigh in jest. "You're laughing at me!"

"No, I'm not." Then he bursts out laughing.

"What?" I can't remember the last time I laughed or even cracked a smile. I laugh harder because it feels liberating.

"You were a sight, all right. I was there on a reconnaissance mission taking pictures of the cars in the parking lot so we could trace them. All of a sudden, bam!" He claps his hands together, and I jump.

"What?" I giggle, wanting to know more about his first impression of me.

"Well, you were this vision in white sprinting across a very green lawn. I thought you were pretty, your hair piled on top of your head, and…your sneakers." He laughs. "Those were…comical. I'm like, either she has this planned, or it was a last-minute decision. Either way, I had to intercept you. I was intrigued." He calms himself and gives me a reassuring smile.

"Intrigued. Hm." I put an elbow on my knee and place my chin on my palm. I tilt my head to look at him. "Okay. The truth is, I was forced to marry Andrian. My father sprung it on me that morning. Maybe he wagered my ass in a poker game and lost. Anyway, Andrian is gross, lecherous, and disgusting. I can't think of enough repulsive adjectives to describe him." I lower my arm, sit up straight, and take a deep breath. "I decided I'd rather take my chances at getting away than be stuck with him forever."

It feels good to tell someone what happened that day. I glance over to Alex and Irina, who are playing cards. They seem content with their game as Roman and I carry on our conversation.

"I can't imagine what you went through and probably would have done the same." Roman shakes his head as if it's too crazy to be true. "It sounds like your father kept you on a short leash. You were so well hidden that your name didn't even come up on a background check into your family."

I slip my shoes off, pull my feet under me, and lean against the oversized couch. The wind is picking up, so I gather my hair and braid it to keep it from flying around. I look to the horizon and notice that both the sky and the water have changed from blue to menacing gray.

"How did you survive the tyranny of your father?" Roman asks.

His voice draws my attention back to him. He's wearing a dry-fit gray shirt that shows off his muscles. I remember how solid they felt under my fingers when I stroked his abs during sex. The memory makes my body tingle. He looks at my face intensely, causing me to blush.

"I read books. I love reading. What we can get is limited, but Katsia has a source for banned books." I chuckle. "Those are the best ones. Now that I've been with a man, the things I read make more sense." I sigh. "I'm a book nerd. I wasn't allowed to attend university and rarely got a chance to go out and party with Katsia and her friends. My father scared off everyone with his harsh words. He's the type to systematically go around the table at holiday dinners and cut down everyone with his criticism. He's such a killjoy. I'm surprised I have any optimism left. The man sucks the life out of people with his depressive thoughts and biting words. Needless to say, I don't have many friends. Most people my age are afraid of him, and maybe they have a right to be."

"Really? I guess I'm lucky. My parents had a wonderful marriage. The holidays were always at our house, and Mom would set the table with our best china and her mother's silver. She put so much effort into how it looked, from the fresh flower centerpiece to the handwritten place cards. She has an eye for decorating and redid my brother's house before he got married." He takes a breath. "It didn't matter if we had money or not. We loved being together. I guess that's part of why it hurts so much that my father is no longer here, because we'll never have an opportunity for all of us to be together again." He's quiet for a moment. Hopefully, talking about his loss has been cathartic. "I'm still adjusting to life without him," he muses.

"I think we've been ignoring Alex and Irina," I say to bring Roman back to the present.

Roman glances at the gold watch on his wrist. "You're right. It's time for appetizers and drinks."

"I am getting hungry."

We stand just as lightning cracks and thunder claps nearby.

"Oh!" I scream, startled, my hands flying to my mouth.

Roman wraps his arms around me as an alarm blares. "That's the lightning warning," he teases. "It doesn't count if the first strike hits you."

"Why do you say that?"

"Because the first strike activates the alarm. If the first strike hits you, it doesn't really matter, does it?" He smirks and shrugs his shoulders. I can't tell if he's pulling my leg or not.

"Let's go in," Alex says as he stands and escorts Irina inside. He gives me a brief nod of acknowledgment. We follow them, and the sky opens up when we reach the bar.

I stand at the window and watch the monsoon, knowing I'm safe. The others are talking, but I can't hear the conversation over the sounds of the storm. The high winds blow sheets of water against the windows, and waves wash over the deck. I'm mesmerized and slightly petrified. I've never been on a boat, let alone a boat in a storm.

Roman slips a funny-shaped glass into my hand.

"It's called a lemon drop martini. I notice you like lemons, but be careful," he warns. "It's mostly vodka."

I take a sip. "Oh, my," I say, licking my lips. "It's delicious. I can see how this can be dangerous."

"Martinis are known as liquid panty-droppers," Irina chimes in. "Be leery of men bringing you alcohol," she warns, and then she winks at me. She's wearing a white sundress, which contrasts nicely with her dark hair. Her flawless skin has tanned overnight. I wish I knew more about her. I don't know how or when she got here. And I don't know what she does for a living. I'm guessing she is more than friends with Alex.

"Come. Have a seat." Alex says, putting his shot of chilled vodka on the bar and pulling out a chair for me. The chairs are white leather and feel as soft as glove leather when I sit. I rest my heels on the silver footrest.

"Oh, my, I forgot my shoes!"

"They will be there later," Alex assures me.

I love having a collection of shoes in my closet. I have no idea where I'll wear the red-bottomed ones. They are so tall, I should practice walking in them. Heck, Roman has a shoe collection as well. I notice he's wearing a different watch today and assume he collects them.

"It's not a big deal," he says, and doesn't seem concerned. "There is no way you are going out to get them in this storm, so don't even think about it." I know not to argue with him when he uses that serious tone.

I wonder how long he's planning on keeping me. I'm nervous about the exchange. Of course, Andrian would want me back. The fact that I'm no longer a virgin makes me smile. Mission accomplished.

I need to plan an escape before the exchange because my body wants Roman, but I can't trust him with my future.

He takes a sip of his drink and sets the rock glass on the bar. Then he lays his hand on mine. I cover my surprise by taking another sip of the martini. Does Roman know that I still want to escape?

He rubs a thumb across my knuckles, cradles my hand, brings it to his lips, and kisses it. He treats me as if I'm a delicate flower.

I relax. It's silly to think he can read my mind. If that's the case, why do I feel guilty for wanting to get away from him?

If I'm being honest with myself, my issue is that I want him. I would love nothing more than for him to carry me to the couch in the next room and fuck me. Every cell in my body yearns for his touch. He smells of salty air and musk. I inhale him and wonder how many more days we have together.

Thoughts of his hard cock dampen my panties. I'm so turned on that if he put his fingers in me right now, I'd come on them. The way he makes me feel physically and emotionally is an experience I want to repeat over and over.

"Oh, here come the appetizers," he says, and snags a huge shrimp off a serving tray as it goes by.

A charcuterie board shows up with fresh fruit, nuts, olives, crackers, and a gooey chunk of cheese with a small utensil to spread it. I sample the green grapes without knowing how to eat the cheese properly.

Irina scoops some of the white cheese on a cracker and nibbles it, holding a paper cocktail napkin in her other hand. Alex chuckles when she suggestively licks cheese off her upper lip.

I take a shrimp. It's so large, it takes three bites to finish. I've never had much seafood, and it's delicious. Alex dips his shrimp in something that looks like ketchup. I try it and decide I prefer my shrimp naked.

"I hope you like seafood," Roman says, leaning into me as he holds a drink of amber liquid with a floating ball for an ice cube.

"Why?"

"We're having lobster for dinner."

"Um, I've never eaten one. You'll have to show me how to do that."

Alex chuckles. "You'll love it. They were flown in from Alaska."

"Irina, your dress is beautiful," I say to divert the conversation from me.

"Thank you. I treated myself to some shopping for the summer."

"I haven't asked anything about you, but I understand you live in France?"

"Oh, yes. I love it here."

"Don't let her fool you. She knows seven languages, and she's an incredible asset to us," Alex brags.

"Alex." Roman's voice warns him not to say more.

"Well," Alex says with a shrug, sipping his vodka, "she is. We team up for work from time to time."

Dinner is announced, and we leisurely stroll to the dining area. Roman motions for me to sit first. I slide easily over the cream-colored leather.

The chef, wearing a white coat, comes to the table and describes what he's prepared for us. It all sounds foreign and delicious. The chief steward places a dinner plate in front of me. The lobster takes up the entire plate. It's huge and intimidating.

"You eat it like this," Roman says. He uses what looks like a nutcracker to crack open the claw. "This is the sweetest, most tender meat." He pulls meat out of the claw with his fingers. "And you dip it in butter like this." He dips the white meat into a ramekin of butter.

He lifts his fingers to my lips. I lean in and open my mouth. He feeds it to me. This feels so sexual that I'm almost embarrassed. The lobster meat is sweet, and the butter coats my tongue.

"Oh, my," I exclaim after I've chewed and swallowed the meat. "That was so amazing."

"Well, if you like this, you might want to try oysters," Irina adds as she skillfully cracks her lobster and eats.

We have fingerling potatoes and creamed spinach as side dishes. I've almost finished eating my lobster when I notice we all have a chilled plate of Caesar salad next to our dinner plates. I grew up with dumplings and boiled potatoes all my life, never knowing these delicacies existed.

"This is a great trip, Roman." Irina smiles at him. "I'm glad I came." The way in which she says that last bit leaves me to wonder why she, specifically, is here. I have a feeling there is more to her than meets the eye.

# CHAPTER 20

## ROMAN

*I* enjoy introducing Dasha to new foods and watching her eat to her heart's content. She needs to gain a few pounds. Dinner conversation flows well, and I get a chance to catch up with Irina on things that aren't work-related. She's observant and hasn't missed the fact that I'm infatuated with the little bird next to me. And yet, she's discreet enough not to bring it up at the table.

After dessert, we adjourn to the movie theater, which also functions as a library. I watch Dasha's face light up when she sees all the books, a personal collection the family has accumulated over the years.

I fire up the big-screen TV and surround-sound speakers. Irina insists on watching *The Accountant* for the umpteenth time, no doubt because she thinks Ben Affleck is hot. Alex and I like the movie because it's about a guy laundering money for the mob. Dasha has never seen it and hides her eyes when the boys suffer physical and mental abuse from their father. We're in a recliner for two, so I lean over and tell her it all comes together at the end. She nods, and I slide my arm around her to protect her from reliving past trauma.

We enjoy the movie, and afterward, we make our excuses and head upstairs to our cabin.

"Thank you for a wonderful evening," she says as we climb the stairs.

"My pleasure. I hope it stopped raining."

We enter the bedroom, and I walk to the sliding doors, peering out into the darkness. No rain. It wouldn't matter, anyway. This part of the deck is covered. I open the doors, kick off my loafers, and step outside. A crisp breeze blows in off the water, and I turn to say something to Dasha.

She's gone. Damn it! I could have sworn she was behind me a second ago. I panic, fearing we have intruders, until I realize the cameras haven't sent an alert to my watch.

I remind myself that the likelihood of Andrian finding our location is slim. The ring with the tracker has been destroyed, and the last possible ping would have been when we were waterskiing. There is no way Andrian is giving up so quickly, and I wish we could stay at sea indefinitely.

Dasha walks toward me in a black, lacy, see-through teddy.

"There you are," I say, relieved to see she's okay.

"I thought you'd want to be outside now that the rain has stopped," she coos.

Damn, she takes my breath away. My staff deserves a bonus.

I reach out and pull her into my arms. "You're so beautiful. I can't wait to buy you jewels and more sexy clothes. This is a great beginning," I add, touching the silky material that barely covers her nipple. I kiss her lips, at first gently, then with need and urgency as I ravage her mouth with my tongue.

I feel her hand on my cock and groan against her mouth.

My cock is restrained by my jeans, and she unfastens the zipper. I let the jeans fall and step out of them as we hurry toward the huge sofa lounger on the deck. She pulls my shirt over my head and tosses it into the salty air as we tumble onto the sofa.

She moans as I place my hand over her pussy and massage it through the fabric. My cock twitches in response. I bend my head, licking her nipple, and the texture of the lace makes me want to thrust my cock in her and take her hard and fast.

This is still new to her. I need to take it slow. She scoots back on the furniture, and I slip my head between her legs.

She spreads her legs, anticipating my next move.

"Good girl," I murmur.

I kneel on the deck and lick her pussy. She's wet for me, and I'm not surprised. I am surprised by her taking the initiative. I like her boldness and want to show her my appreciation.

I lick her clit through the fabric until her back buckles, and I hear her moan.

"You like it like this, Dasha?"

"Mm."

I push the material out of the way and flick my tongue over her again. "Do you want more?"

She answers by raising her pussy in the air and riding my face as I eat her and drink her juice like it's the nectar of the gods. She makes me feel invincible.

Dasha squirms, and her moans grow louder. If I let her, she would come right now, but this is only the beginning. I unsnap the crotch and pull the teddy off her. Her skin glows in the moonlight.

I start at her ankles and trail kisses up her toned thighs, flat stomach, and gravity-defying breasts. God, they are marvelous. She squirms, moans, and clutches at the fabric cushion as I kiss, nibble, and lick her all over, consumed with a need to have every inch of her.

This is not a one-and-done. No, Dasha is the real deal. Twice is not enough. I want forever with her. There's no way I'm letting her go. She is the key to unlocking something better in my life. She's the one I've been waiting for, she is the light to my darkness. She has lived with men who break the law. She might not know all the details, but she's connected some of the dots over the years. She knows her father has to lie about what he does for work and that he leaves out details. I know from experience she has to cover for her families illicit business practices.

Her boobs are large enough to be fake but definitely are not. Believe me. I know the difference. They fill my hands perfectly as I knead them and enjoy their fullness. In my excitement, I grab one too hard, and she yelps.

I back off and lie by her side, my weight supported on one elbow. Her face in the moonlight is more mesmerizing than even the aurora borealis. I nuzzle her neck and massage her nipple with the palm of my hand until it hardens.

Her hand moves from the back of my neck down my back and grabs my ass, digging her nails into me and prompting me to fuck her. My cock practically points in the direction of the bed. I'm getting excited, but still, I wait.

I cup her other boob, lift it, roll it around, and take the nipple into my mouth and play with it like it's candy. She gasps and grinds her pelvis into mine.

"Tell me what you want," I prompt her, already knowing the answer.

"You." Her breath is uneven. She'll learn that delaying gratification will make the orgasms more intense.

I drag my fingers down her belly to her clit, slowly circling her nub and increasing the pressure. When she can't take it anymore, I hear her say, "Fuck me. Fuck me, Roman."

I tug at her nipple again. It's like a release valve, and she takes a deep breath. I lick two fingers and slide them in and out of her pussy to make sure she's ready for the next part.

I roll on top of her, placing the tip of my cock in her pussy. I gently push into her silky warmth and feel her nails dig into my back. If the level of pain she's inflicting with her nails is an indication of her pleasure, I'm all in.

"You are mine, Dasha. Never forget it," I murmur in her ear.

Her walls are tight, and I take long strokes, giving her my full girth and length. The heat is building with each thrust.

I reach under her and flip her so she's on top. Her expression is one of shock and awe as she adjusts her knees into the cushion.

"Ride me. Ride me hard," I coax.

She moves her hips and tilts her head back as I grab her boobs and brush my thumbs across her nipples. They harden immediately.

She places her hands on my chest and finds her rhythm riding my shaft.

I feel her hungry pussy constrict around my cock, and I groan.

She whimpers and closes her eyes. Her upper body stiffens. Her clit is hard on my cock, and her muscles squeeze me. I raise my pelvis to give her more, and she screams as her body convulses. I hold on until she finishes. Then an incredible wave of euphoria comes over me. My cock is bathed in her cum. I flip her onto her back and pound her pussy until I can't hold out anymore. With a beastly growl, I pull out and come on her belly.

I almost didn't pull out in time. That's never happened before. It's not the perfect form of birth control.

Fuck.

I caress the side of her face, and our eyes meet. A tear rolls down her cheek.

"That was intense," she says with a smile. I grab the closest article of clothing and clean us, then toss it on the deck.

I pull her to me. We lie together under the stars. Neither of us speaks.

I'm buzzed with euphoria and look at the night sky with its millions of stars. "Have you ever looked for constellations in the sky?"

"Not really. But I know that's the Big Dipper," She points to three stars in a row. "And if it's there, the Little Dipper has to be close."

"Yes, it is. There." I point to the other constellation.

"Have you studied all of them?"

"There isn't enough time to do that. It's never-ending. I often wonder what it would be like to live on another planet. I read a lot of sci-fi when I was a kid."

"No way," she gasps. "You like to read?"

"Most of the books in the library were read by me or my mother."

"Your mom must be amazing."

"She is."

"So, what will happen to me, Roman?" She circles my nipple with a finger and asks the one question I've been avoiding.

DASHA

We're looking up at the stars, pointing out constellations, when Roman declares out of the blue, "I'll come up with a plan. There's no way I'm turning you over to our enemy."

"How? I don't see why Andrian would agree to a deal. Surely he values the guns more than he does me."

Roman doesn't answer. I stare at the night sky and hope for a shooting star to wish upon. If I saw one, I'd wish all our problems would go away.

Finally, he says, "It's not just about money. Andrian has a vendetta against my family. He's been hiding in Belarus for years, plotting for the day he can take us down. None of us are safe. My father took over a job that he felt belonged to him, and since then, he has held a grudge. Dad probably knew he was in Belarus but didn't know he was barred from returning to Russia. I guess that's where your family comes into the picture. Andrian needs them to carry out missions inside Russia."

"Like pull off a hit on your dad and steal from you?"

"Yes. He took from me, so I took you from him. I didn't know it at the time, but he won't see it as a mistake or a coincidence. Andrain will stop at nothing to get even. We're basically two gladiators in an arena, and only one can win."

A shiver runs down my spine. "You can beat him, can't you?"

Here, I finally get to enjoy life, and these few days with Roman could end up being the highlight of my miserable existence if the Volkovs don't beat him.

"I plan to. If I don't, none of us will ever be safe again. And I shudder at what he will do to you to get back at me should I walk away."

"And Irina? Who is she?"

"She's a contact for us. She's skilled in languages, hacking, and weapons. She's very good with knives and guns."

"Like the ones you brought with you?"

"Yes, and handguns. Alex and I are long-range shooters—snipers. I like the challenge of the environment. Wind, rain, temperature— everything has to be taken into consideration."

"So, you're into science?"

"Yes, I need to know a bit of science to achieve my desired results. And Alex is very skilled as well."

Out of nowhere, a cool breeze blows in off the water. Goosebumps sprout on my arms, and I hug myself to keep warm. Roman places a hand on my legs.

"You're cold. Let's go inside."

I nod and stand up. The situation is worse than I had imagined. I thought that if I went home, I'd be punished, but I could end up dead, a pawn in a game between two families. My luck couldn't get any worse. Why did Roman have to be at the church on that fateful day?

We step into our room. It's like I'm in a fairy tale. Everything is spotless, and the bedcovers have been turned down for the night. It's wonderful to be pampered after so many years of caring for my father. I almost wish he were here so I could ask him why he didn't use the tracker to intercept me in Belarus. We drove for hours. Did he want me to get away? Or am I part of some plan to push these two enemies into a confrontation?

I dismiss the idea. My father didn't allow me to escape. The man is incapable of doing anything nice. He's a thief, and he took the guns to stockpile them for one of Andrian's nefarious government missions. We all know he outsources jobs that are political suicide for him.

Andrian holds all the cards. I bet he put my brothers in a bad situation and blackmailed them into agreeing to the marriage. The only way this nightmare ends for us is to beat Andrian at his own game.

I brush my teeth and grab one of Roman's shirts from his closet. I put it on and roll up the sleeves.

"You must be exhausted," I say as I crawl into the soft bed.

Roman's eyes are half closed as he slides in next to me. He rolls over and drapes his arm across my body. "Good night, little bird."

"Good night," I reply, wiped out, too. Maybe this is what people call jet lag. There's only a one-hour time difference, but the events of the past few days are starting to catch up with me.

Outside the porthole, I can make out the distant lights of the French coastline. Roman mentioned we're in no hurry to get to Monte Carlo. He still needs time to formulate a plan. Even with all the Volkov money, it's impossible to hide forever when you have a powerful enemy.

We need more than a plan. We need a miracle.

* * *

WHEN I WAKE UP, I'm alone. Roman walks out of the bathroom wearing only a towel around his waist. I'm surprised to see he shaved. It makes him look so much younger.

I sit up. "How old are you?"

"Twenty-six. Why?"

"Curious. I like you better without the scruff, but it felt good…"

He chuckles. "Yeah, it feels good down there. A bit of friction goes a long way, eh?"

His intimate teasing embarrasses me, and I resist the urge to dive under the covers.

"I was thinking this morning," he says, "is it safe for you to call Katsia?"

"I imagine. Why?"

"I think she'd like to know you are okay, don't you?"

Is this a ploy? Am I too jaded to give him credit for being chivalrous?

"Actually, I'd love to speak to her."

"You can't give her much information. They might try to trace the phone. It's a burner, and we run it through various encryptions."

"Right. That's good, right?"

"Of course. We'll have breakfast like we did yesterday. You're okay to meet me there in an hour?" He ducks inside his closet.

"Sure." I'm relieved that I'll have time to shower and fix my hair. The humidity has made my hair frizzy.

He steps from the closet fully dressed for the day in a long-sleeved fishing shirt, jeans, and loafers. I doubt he's wearing underwear. "See you at breakfast." And with that, he's out the door.

I need caffeine and press the intercom on the wall.

"Yes, madam?"

"Can I have coffee delivered to me?"

"Yes, madam. It will be delivered to your cabin shortly."

"Thank you."

A girl could get used to this. I decide to start with a shower first and peel off Roman's shirt. The air in the bathroom smells of his cologne. Is it possible to miss him when he's only been gone a few minutes?

I wash my hair with shampoo that smells like coconuts. The conditioner makes my hair feel so soft that I use it to shave my legs. I may as well smell like coconuts all over. I never cared so much about how I smelled before.

When I finish and leave the bathroom, my caffeine fix has arrived, and the bed has been made. I swear, if I got up to pee in the middle of the night, I would come back to find the cabin steward had made my bed. The staff are that efficient.

I was expecting a paper cup of lukewarm coffee. Instead, there's a silver tray with a ceramic pot of fresh coffee, two china cups, and an assortment of sugars and flavored creamers. I decide to save my calories for dessert and pour myself a cup of plain coffee. The first sip tastes like blueberries and doesn't need cream or sugar. Yesterday, the coffee tasted like hazelnuts. The chief steward must rotate the coffee flavors.

I'm getting into a routine: breakfast, fun, and sun, then cocktails and appetizers, followed by a late dinner. And the best part is that everything runs seamlessly. It's amazing how the mostly invisible crew anticipates and meets our every want and need. There has to be a huge staff working behind the scenes to make this trip magical.

With all this time on my hands, I find myself preoccupied with Roman and his incredible body. Ugh. He's as addictive as caffeine. I never want to leave the bubble of tranquility onboard this floating hotel, spa, and restaurant. But I'm sensible enough to know we're on borrowed time if the Volkovs don't figure a way out of this crisis. I'm sure it's not the first time they've had an enemy. Their world is full of them. What is that line? The enemy of my enemy is my friend.

I try to blow out my hair, still clutching the towel, and decide to screw it. It's easier to be naked. I drop the towel, finish drying my hair, and look for accessories to keep my tresses up and tidy for the day.

I'm getting used to life at sea. Here's hoping Andrian doesn't find me and drown me in it. I need to keep Roman close to protect me. Alex, too. He's competent and loyal to Roman, despite his cigarette addiction and thirst for vodka. They work together and are obviously good friends. I wonder if they have guards protecting them when they are living their normal lives in Russia.

I choose a blue sundress with matching sandals from the selection in my closet and toss them on the bed. It crosses my mind that my passport is somewhere in Roman's belongings. I quickly look around the room to ensure I'm still alone before stepping into his closet. I stop and stare at all his suits and shirts, perfectly lined up and color coordinated. I touch the creamy fabrics and wonder at the cost. How many tailor-made suits does a man really need?

Below the clothes is a pullout tray of silk ties and matching hand-kerchiefs, all neatly folded. Rows of cuff links, tie clips, and tie bars remind me of tongue studs, just longer. I have no doubt they are made of silver and gold.

Rows of shoes are perfectly lined up with the toes pointed forward. I feel like I'm in a high-end department store, surrounded by designer clothes and shoes. I've never set foot in one, but I see the ads in Katsia's fashion magazines. *GQ* always has the hottest guys—that is, until I met Roman.

I run my hand over the smooth surface of the dresser until I feel a crack. I look closer. It's not a crack. It's a seam. I follow the line and find a button. Jackpot! Maybe this is the safe I've been looking for. I push the button and hold my breath in anticipation of setting off an alarm.

The top of the dresser rises, revealing rows of watches, bracelets, and rings nestled inside a velvet lining. A hidden compartment—ingenious.

Where is the safe with my passport? When we entered the yacht Roman walked into the closet and I'm sure he locked up his hand gun and our passports. It has to be in here somewhere. I hit the button again, and the dresser lowers. I run my fingers over the doors and drawers, trying to find the hidden safe. I'm probably wasting my time if Roman designed this closet. He's the smartest man I have ever met.

Just yesterday, I learned that aluminum and steel block GPS signals, as on planes and ships. To keep from being tracked, I should have wrapped aluminum foil around the ring to block the signal, but who knew?

Papa knew, no doubt. That's probably why he rarely let me out of his sight and checked up on me all the time, dropping in on my school study groups to see if I was there. Had he done it to control me, or was it because he didn't trust Andrian? It would be nice to know.

I give up on the closet, pour myself another cup of coffee, and stand at the windows. Gazing at the view, I realize the coastline has changed and looks nothing like the French Riviera. We must've sailed through the night. Gone are the palatial estates and hundred-meter yachts. Instead, I'm looking at a rural coastline dotted with terracotta-colored tiled roofs. The water is a vibrant blue you only see in posters of Italy. Wait, are we off the coast of Italy?

Italy! I put down my cup and do a naked happy dance. It's time to get dressed and find Roman.

Being alone is overrated. I'm not the type of person who enjoys solitude. I've had a lifetime of it. I can't wait to see if we are in another country. This is like getting a gift for Christmas. Only better.

# CHAPTER 22

## DASHA

I stand at the railing, gazing at the shoreline. The marble Duomo is centuries old, a marked contrast to our sleek modern vessel. If I had a camera, I would capture the juxtaposition of the old world meeting the new.

I look for Roman but don't find him. My heart sinks like coins tossed in a wishing well. I don't see Alex, either. What are they up to? Delicious smells are coming from the breakfast area, so I follow my nose.

Irina is already there, looking badass in a swimsuit that leaves little to the imagination. Sunglasses shield her eyes from the bright sun reflecting off the placid water. She encapsulates a modern-day woman.

Damn. Will I ever feel like I fit in?

I'm overdressed. I wish I'd get the memo on activities for the day, so I don't stand out like an American tourist. I like Irina and wonder if she'll ever share anything about her personal life. If she's used to the billionaire lifestyle, I'm sure there are tales to tell. I'd dearly love to pick her brain for information about Roman.

"Good morning," I greet Irina, trying to sound as perky as possible. "How did you sleep?" Besides the weather, I have nothing else to talk to her about. I suck at making small talk, especially with a woman like her. She is so out of my league. I'm afraid to ask her about her work life. Roman claims they're friends, but I'm still suspicious. It wouldn't be the first time a man has lied to me to manipulate the situation.

"Like a baby. I usually do."

Lucky for her, she doesn't have a price on her head. I keep my thoughts to myself. Growing up with my douchebag of a father, I learned how to quell my sarcasm, and if Irina is here to help Roman, she's helping me. I need her as my ally.

How long will this mafia feud continue? The timeline and plan of action have not been shared with me. Roman doesn't appear to be overly stressed. If anything, he's too calm. Is he telling me everything?

The threat of imminent violence or even death is never far from my mind. I'm only functioning from the adrenaline rush of the stud sharing my bed. I woke up last night and found him curled around me. I held my breath and prayed it would never end.

I wonder how much Irina knows about me. She knows my father's name, which I find strange. I've never heard him mention the name Irina, and I can't imagine their paths crossing. She knows several languages, which is unusual but not unheard of. In fact, most adults my age know English as a second language. In Belarus, most of us choose English over German in school.

I'd like to be friends with Irina. She seems to know me without me having to say much. If she's familiar with the players in the criminal world, maybe she's an undercover agent who's gone rogue or is part of Roman's organization.

I've never had the opportunity to live on my terms, and these few days on the yacht have shown me what I've been missing. Freedom is not about drinking and dancing all night. It's about having a choice in deciding who you spend your time with. I want to share my life with someone I care about. A life where we both work, come home, share our day, and eat dinner together. We can enjoy each other's company and take a vacation every year. Maybe there is a family, maybe there isn't. This romance with Roman has taught me so much. Not just the sex. Although making love under the moon, on the deck, in the bed…who knows where next, is nothing to complain about.

Alex joins us, looking refreshed in a polo shirt and jeans. He's wearing flip-flops again. I imagine he loves being in a country with hot summer days. I doubt he ever gets a chance to wear sandals or flip-flops in Russia. "What's it going to be today, girls?" he asks, accepting a Bloody Mary from the steward who appears out of nowhere. I'm beginning to think this deck has trap doors and secret passageways.

"I have no clue," I reply in all honesty. "Are we off the coast of Italy?"

"We are indeed." Alex sips his drink. "What you see out there is called the Tuscan Archipelago, which comprises seven islands."

"Seven?" My interest is piqued. "I've heard about Eastern Europeans and Russians traveling to the Black Sea in the summer for its nice beaches. I never thought about islands off the Italian coast."

"Then you're in for a treat. The beaches and sunny weather are amazing, and the food is out of this world. Everything is fresh, the pasta, the bread, the vegetables, and fruit, and it's all served with bottles of wine." Alex grins.

"You mean you drink wine in Italy, not vodka?" I tease.

"Italy and France have very good wines, but France is the only country that makes Bordeaux."

"What is Bordeaux?"

"A specific red wine. There is a variety of other Bordeaux's and they can be red, white, or sparking wine," Irina answers. "Other countries and wineries make merlots and other reds, but France is known for Bordeaux. It's stronger tasting than a Chianti, which is made from Tuscan grapes. Just look for a rooster on the label around the neck of the bottle. It ensures the wine is from Tuscan grapes."

A handsome steward shows up with a tray of bellinis, and Irina helps herself to one. I pass on the bellini and ask him to bring me a mimosa. As he leaves to fetch my drink, I notice Irina checking out his ass. I really can't blame her. He looks Russian and has a nice athletic build.

I follow Irina to the buffet. Today, there is an assortment of breakfast meats, cheeses, made-to-order omelets, and Belgian waffles. The smell of cinnamon French toast makes my mouth water.

"Don't feel bad if you're overwhelmed by wines," Irina reassures me. "A person can spend their entire life learning about them and still not know everything. We pick up information from others, and I've visited numerous wineries. Most wineries offer tours that are both educational and fun. I happen to know some owners of Italian vineyards. Their estates are massive. I spent a night in one of the mansions in Tuscany. I love speaking Italian."

"I wish I knew half of what you know. I can't possibly keep up with you. The way you speak and dress and carry yourself. Hell, you're even fluent in a number of languages. It's enough to make me dizzy," I confess without admitting that she makes me feel like the ugly duckling standing next to a swan. "There are heels in my closet that I'm afraid to walk in. I'll probably never wear them."

"Oh, well, I can help you with that. I'm good at fitting into any social setting. My mother worked undercover for the French government. I picked up many tricks of the trade from her. I can teach you anything you want to know. We should hang out for an afternoon. It would be fun."

"I'd like that very much. I could use the help."

"Women who are secure aren't afraid to share what they know with other women." Her knowing smile makes me wonder if she's referring to clothes, makeup, or sexual positions.

Irina orders a simple breakfast of turkey sausage and an egg white omelet, and I'm tempted to do the same if it will give me her body. She must work out with weights because her arms are extremely toned. I need to find the gym on this vessel and the motivation. Maybe there's a personal trainer who will kick my ass in gear.

I ask, "Do you see your mother much?"

"Sadly, my mother was killed in the line of duty a few years ago. I miss her terribly. She was so much fun to be around."

"I'm so sorry. I never knew my mother. I wish I did. I wonder what we have in common regarding personality traits and what things we both like."

"Dasha, take my word for it, you're nothing like your father," she says, sipping her bellini.

"Do you know him?"

"I've known of him for years. He runs with a bad crowd, but I don't see you as a follower. You're an independent thinker with a moral compass."

"Hm, well, I'm not so sure about that. I stayed home way too long. It was only by luck that I got out at all."

"We all need luck now and again, don't we?"

The chef is looking at me, and I realize he's waiting for me to tell him what I want to eat. I recall how much I loved the lobster last night and want more of the same. I ask if it's possible to have a lobster omelet. The chef says it's not a problem, and he'll make it with hollandaise sauce. I have no idea what that is, but I'm willing to try. I've loved all the food he's made me, so I'm throwing caution to the wind. I pass on the mouth-watering pastries, choose a small bowl of fresh fruit instead, and follow Irina to the table.

We leave Alex to bullshit with the chef while he sips his second Bloody Mary.

The table is draped in a white linen tablecloth and has a Napoleonic bicorn hat as the centerpiece. The blue plates are perfectly aligned, and each holds a blue and white striped napkin with a silver shell-shaped napkin ring. The napkin is artfully scrunched to cover the plate like a flower. A pitcher of orange juice adds a splash of color to the otherwise blue-and-white theme. I'm beginning to associate the colors blue and white with anything nautical.

The table is in the shade, so Irina pushes her sunglasses to the top of her head. I notice her long eyelashes and wish I looked more like her.

The sun is different here. It's warmer, and the houses on the coast look straight out of a painting with their pale yellow exteriors, barrel-tiled roofs, and green shutters. The view reminds me of fragrance ads I used to tear out of magazines.

Irina lifts her glass and nods to mine. I pick up my drink, and we tap glasses. "To new friends. May our journey be long."

"Zdorov'ye, to your health," Alex says, coming up behind us. He reaches between us and puts his glass into the mix.

"To new friends," I say as we clink glasses again.

Alex takes a gulp of his drink and says, "Let's enjoy this change of scenery before we return to Monaco. I feel more at home in Italy. The weather and the people are warm, and I don't have to have billions in the bank to fit in with the locals."

I wonder if he feels like he lives in Roman's shadow.

As if our host can hear my thoughts, he appears on deck. And as though he were the world's largest magnet, all eyes are drawn to him. What drives me nuts is that he doesn't have to work for it.

Roman's eyes find me, and his face breaks into a broad smile.

"Well, this time, I'm the one who's late." I inhale his clean scent mixed with the salty air as he kisses me warmly. "Little bird," he whispers into my ear.

My guess is that he calls me "little bird" because I'm the bird who flew the coup. The endearment is sweet. No one has ever given me a pet name before.

As soon as Roman sits down, the chief steward brings him a Bloody Mary without being asked. I guess it's her job to know what he likes and when he likes it. She tells him what the chef has prepared for breakfast, and he requests an omelet with veggies.

While the chef prepares his order, she returns with the omelets for Irina and me. I pick up my fork to skewer a Cremini mushroom, and Roman steals it.

"Ah, it's so good," he teases, then chews it before swallowing.

"You think that's funny?" I reply.

"Maybe a tiny bit." He holds his thumb and finger a centimeter apart and winks.

"Now that's the size of Roman's cock," Alex adds, making jokes at his friend's expense. A plate overflowing with enough breakfast food to feed three people is placed in front of him.

I snicker and cover my mouth.

"You're not going to defend me?" Roman jests and acts like he's wounded. I don't know if that's possible. The man is as guarded as a medieval knight in full battle armor. "Just for that," he adds, leaning over my plate to steal another mushroom from my omelet before I've eaten a bite. "I'm taking another mushroom."

"I love mushrooms. You stole it."

"All's fair in love and war. Besides, I take what I want," he says, and his face turns serious.

"Don't I know that," Alex chimes. Skewering a sausage with his fork, he bites it in half.

Is Roman capable of love? In bed, he shows a tender side that he doesn't reveal publicly. He's Bratva, trained to keep a lid on his emotions. I know this, so why does my chest hurt when he doesn't communicate his feelings with words?

He's not the don. Surely he can bend a few rules. I have a flashback to Andrian and the look on his face the last time I saw him at our house. He's not a man to cross.

But neither is Roman if the weapons on board are any indication.

"Eat up. We'll be docking soon in the Port of Portoferraio. There are shops there, and we can walk to Napoleon's Fortress," says Roman.

"Really?" I ask before leaning into him. "Is the fortress as formidable as the one around your heart?"

"You'll have to find out," he replies as he sips his drink. The chief steward brings him a plate of food, and I steal a mushroom off his plate and pop it in my mouth.

"This is the most fantastic, juicy mushroom I've ever eaten," I bait him, tilting my head back as if it's orgasmic and clutching the edge of the table.

He sits back in surprise, then breaks into a smile. The sound of his hearty laugh warms my heart.

"Et tu, Brute?" he replies.

I give him a saucy grin and hear Irina and Alex snickering in the background. By the amused look on Roman's face, he's not often challenged. I teased the lion, pulled his tail, and got away with it. This is a first. It feels good to be bold, and I sit taller in my chair. My confidence is growing.

Roman scoots his chair closer to the table and gives me the side eye, which I ignore. Katsia said men don't like easy women. Every day away from my father has shown me how repressed and stifled my life has been. It's with Roman that I feel most comfortable. He said he wouldn't turn me over to Andrian, but he hasn't explained how he plans to make that happen. I want to be optimistic and believe him, but life has taught me that it's more realistic to be pessimistic.

I sip my drink, and as soon as I set the glass down, the chief steward replaces it with a fresh mimosa. I'm going to be sloshed if I continue to drink.

"Eat up," Roman implores me as he cuts into his omelet.

"I'm so full," I complain, pushing my plate away.

"I'll have that worked off of you in no time," he says low enough so that only I can hear.

"I love this island," Alex announces while lighting his first of many cigarettes and gazing at the shoreline.

"Me, too. I haven't been here in years," Irina says. "I'm going to get ready to go ashore. I'll be down in a few."

Hell, I thought she was already dressed to go ashore. She'll probably come back looking like she stepped out of *Vogue Italia.*

With everyone in such a good mood, I seize the opportunity and say, "Roman, I've been thinking."

"Yes?" He finishes eating and wipes his mouth with a linen napkin.

"Can I call Katsia now?"

Roman reaches for his drink and sips, contemplating what? I have no idea. "I planned on it later this evening." He sets the glass on the table and stands. "You look incredible," he says. He pulls my chair out, and I stand beside him. "I think it's time for you to have an Italian handbag, and I know just where to get one."

I glance up in time to catch a smile on his face. My stomach does flip-flops like a Russian gymnast on steroids.

Roman takes my hand and suggests we climb to the crow's nest so we can watch the docking process. From this vantage point, we can see how close the boat comes to buoys and other boats without hitting anything. The deckhands scurry around, throwing lines ashore and tying them off. It's a tight squeeze with such a big boat, but we are safely tied up to a concrete dock in no time.

While all this is going on, Roman is pointing out some landmarks, recounting the island's history in an animated voice. The fullness I feel inside is not from breakfast. I'm happy and content for the first time in my life. It occurs to me that the quiet conversations and noisy lovemaking we've shared the past few days have made me vulnerable. He's lit a fire in me, fanning it with caresses and kisses, making me feel worthy of his attention.

Damn, why does he have to be so devastatingly handsome? I'm supposed to be looking for a way out when this affair ends. Instead, I'm realizing all too late that I've fallen in love with my captor.

# CHAPTER 23

## ROMAB

Docking goes smoothly, and once all the ropes are tied, we cross the gangway to the concrete pier. I've been to Elba before and know the town square is within walking distance. Taking Dasha by the hand, I lead her in that direction. This would feel like a first date if Alex and Irina weren't tagging along.

"Walking on solid ground might feel different after days at sea," I warn her.

"Thanks, I didn't know," she says while looking back at *Severnoye Siyaniye.* "Wow! Your boat is the biggest one in the harbor. Why does it look bigger from shore?"

"Because you've only seen half the ship. The bridge, crew area, engine room, and other guest cabins remain, plus other rooms. By the way, how do you like it so far?"

"It beats being at home. I'm just not used to being waited on. Having someone else wash my panties feels weird. Everything else is great, the food, the fresh air, the activities. I could go on and on." She talks rapidly, and I hear the genuine happiness in her voice.

We walk past local fishing boats unloading their early-morning catch. A flock of seagulls lands, looking for scraps from fishermen. We cross the street to avoid getting pecked or pooped on.

Dasha is always on my mind. I won't soon forget the scorching hot sex we enjoyed outside on the deck. Between her responsive body and the way her pussy clenched around my cock, I almost didn't pull out in time.

Sometimes, the mishaps in life bring the greatest rewards. We were two lost souls when we met. I was looking for revenge, and she was looking for an escape. Unbeknownst to me, I found my enemy's daughter, who happens to be promised to the man we suspect of killing my father. That's the silver lining: two birds, one stone.

I'm smitten with Dasha. She is mine to hold, mine to fuck, and my property.

Her presence, her smile, and her humor are entertaining. She doesn't look at me like I'm a murderer. She's not afraid to tease me. Before Dasha came along, there was an emptiness inside me. I never wanted to be seen as weak and focused on work instead of relationships. My heart was small. I would sacrifice myself for my brothers and my mother. Yes, they are family. However the thought of what Andrian would or could do to her is unacceptable. I'd give my life to save hers. She didn't ask for this life.

I had to have her again when I woke her up last night. I can't get my fill of her. Even now, just holding her hand, I'm turned on by the thought of her red-painted lips around my cock. The thoughts of her under me, over me, beside me, well, it's sublime. She's coming out of her shell, and I love her sense of humor. She's becoming her own person. She's not afraid of me. If anything, she desires our physical contact as much as I do.

Dasha is different from the women I've been linked with in the past. Women like Nadia are used to flying first class and vacationing on yachts. If not me, some other billionaire will pick them up. Men with money like having pretty things. It just so happens those pretty girls like the lifestyle. They spend their youth surrounded by people who cater to them and their every whim. Unfortunately, those one-dimensional creatures are as boring as dry toast. They have nothing to say. They never enjoy eating food. They subsist on ice chips and champagne.

My shallow arrangement with them worked primarily because I'm a commitment-phobe, and I was fine with a string of one-night stands. When I'm horny, I show up at some society party, where I find plenty of beautiful women looking for an opportunity. The rules are set. I know what they will say, and that they will do whatever it takes to ride my cock. But it's redundant. I use condoms so that I won't be trapped by pregnancy.

Women, even the ones I'm fucking, are not allowed to spend the night at my house. I like to be in control of my environment. I have secrets I can't share. But with Dasha, I see the potential of a life partner.

But this is a critical time in my life and in that of my family, and that's a problem. I have to remain focused for us to all come out of this ordeal alive. I've never had so much at stake and hinging on one hit. Andrian has to die. Ratmim, too, but Dasha may never forgive me if I take out her father. I hope he won't be with Andrian when I strike.

This is how love changes us. I would never second-guess taking his life if it weren't for Dasha. My feelings for her complicate the situation. I'm a monster, and yet Dasha seems to like me. Will she still feel the same if I kill her father or brothers?

The odds of us meeting were never great. I've gone from being a stone-cold loner, never caring if a woman was in my bed, to holding her all night in my arms. When she touches me, I burn with desire. She's in my mind, in my heart, and in my soul. I'm obsessed.

"The port is full," she comments, and I focus on finding the direction we need to walk.

The streets are crawling with large groups of tourists speaking German, French, and English, all of whom are here for the day. They stroll leisurely through the streets without a care in the world. Children carry cones of gelato melting over their hands.

This could be an extremely dangerous situation if anyone here intends to harm us. My heart rate increases, and I realize I've been holding my breath. Now I know what my brothers go through when they are out with their wives.

I pause at a street corner. Our joined hands prevent Dasha from crossing the street. She wasn't willing to drop my hand to continue without me. I take this as a sign that she cares for me.

"What is it?" she asks.

I look around, scanning the streets, the port, and the horizon until my unease passes. "That ferry is coming here from the mainland. We'll have to visit Florence one day. I think you'd love it."

"You talk of things in the future as if you know we'll survive Andrian." She begins the conversation I've been avoiding. Is she concerned for my safety?

"This is what I do, Dasha. I'm not a nice man. I worry you won't like me when you learn what I'm capable of. I'm not much different from the men you've grown up with. I'm not good with words—I'm good with weapons. I protect my family and our interests."

We walk on. She's quiet, and it worries me.

"All I care about is the man you are when you're with me," she says finally. "I don't want you hurting women and children. But if you hurt men who deserve it, I understand."

I stop walking and pull her into my arms, kissing her full on the mouth in the middle of the sidewalk in front of my friends. I claim her as mine, and I've never been happier.

Her lips are warm. My kiss deepens, and my tongue dances with hers until I pull away, breathless. I turn to walk, taking hold of her hand. I tell myself it's to keep her safe. However, she's mine; now every man knows not to touch her.

The midmorning sun reflects off the azure water and dances off the buildings around us. The atmosphere is alive with a festive buzz.

"This island is so beautiful. Have you ever seen anything prettier?" Dasha asks.

I stop to wait for the others to catch up to us. My guard is behind us.

I look down into her eyes, dark and drowsy from my kiss. I slip a finger under her chin, gently tilting her head so her eyes have no choice but to meet mine. "Nothing is as beautiful as you, my love."

Alex and Irina finally catch up to us.

"Ah, I have to say, I never saw you as a romantic," Irina teases.

"You didn't," I snap.

"Right," she replies, taking my gruffness in stride.

"Way to go, Roman," Alex says, getting a jab in.

"We have a fortress to see," I say, changing the subject.

We pass a shop with a tourist center sign for people with questions. Other storefronts offer services for underwater excursions. The island is great for snorkeling, and there are numerous beaches. These aren't the typical stores found in a mall, but rather privately owned businesses. The island is run by Italians who live here and only speak Italian. I hope it never changes.

We stay to the right and follow the street as it wraps around the curve of the port. The other side of the harbor has two restaurants, both known for their seafood and pasta. Seafood is best when it's fresh from the sea. I hope my little bird will like seafood. I mentally note the time, as most things on the Elba close for the afternoon *controra.*

"Well, I am looking forward to pasta, seafood, and vino this afternoon," Alex adds.

Irina cheerfully breezes pass us in a wide-brimmed straw hat, palazzo pants, and a matching white top that comes to a bow at her belly button. She's a pretty girl, but I've never been physically attracted to her.

"Oh, my, I see a gelato sign." Irina points out the street vendor as we round the corner. Italian ices and gelato are requisite in warm climates, and today is going to be brutally hot.

The island is made up of hills. Most are steep. I scan the horizon out of habit. I know what's it like to be a killer and where I'd sit and wait to get my shot. I've been known to hit my target when they are on vacation, and now is not the time to be lax. I can't let Andrian and his men get a jump on us.

Monaco makes more sense than Elba for what Alex has in mind for an exchange. Regardless, Andrian will be dealt with sooner rather than later. If he is behind the hit on my father, my brothers will also want their revenge.

We have two guards with us, one for the girls, and one with us. We all wear a gun clip under our button-down shirts. I'm not expecting trouble, but I have the playbook in my head. It's taken me years to find a woman who understands me and can tease me without fear of retribution, and I'll be damned if I ever let any man touch Dasha.

Alex walks up from behind and flanks me on my left. We scan our surroundings. I doubt that Dasha's father could have tracked our location during the short window we were vulnerable. It would be nearly impossible to pick my vessel out of all the boats off the coast of France the first day we arrived. Naturally, Ratmim would assume the ring was defective when he lost track of her the first time.

I hate assumptions.

Alex and I leave the girls with the guards as they wait in line for gelato. No matter how many countries try duplicating the recipe, it's not the same as Italian gelato.

Even away from the crowd, we remain vigilant. I'm looking past Alex, and he's looking past me as we stand next to one another.

"Roman, I've been thinking. This mess with Andrian is coming to a head soon. Have you considered giving Dasha to him?"

My head snaps like a whip, quick and deadly. My eyes narrow on his. "She's mine," I growl. "Anyone who fucking touches her dies. I'll protect her with my life. We've muddied the waters. Andrian hates us, and if he learns I've fucked her, he'll kill her. I can't live with that. Can you?" I stare into my friend's eyes.

"No, I'm just trying to be your advisor and make sure you've considered all the options. She lifts your spirits and makes you smile. You deserve to be happy. She's your light to the real riches in life, the things money can't buy," he finishes, and nods toward the girls.

We watch the vendor hand them cups of lemon gelato and two spoons. I step forward and pay him before returning to Alex.

"What I'd like to do is frame Andrian with drugs. We know it's one of his vices. He's been tagged as an international supplier of fentanyl and heroin. I'm sure Irina can be of assistance." She not only has connections in criminal circles, but she also has them inside the government.

"She will. She has friends who can help, too." Alex nods.

"Yes." I pause. "She does." Planning a hit while standing in the middle of the town square feels odd. The tourists walking past haven't a clue.

"Do you have a plan?" he asks.

"Not definitive, but I'm thinking about it. I need to reach out to Andrian with my demands. Pavel will keep an eye on him and let us know what transpires after that. I will send some men. We need more information. Andrian has been one step ahead of us."

"Once you set the terms of the exchange, we have to end this, once and for all."

"We will," I promise, kicking the small white stones at my feet.

"We'll pull it off," Alex replies. "I might not be in love, but I want to live long enough to find it one day."

"We know Monaco. How difficult would it be to set up the meeting before the gala this weekend? We can take care of his guards and him. Then we attend the gala as a cover. No one would ever know. Talk about sinful pleasures. Taking that scum off the streets is long overdue."

"You're right," he replies nonchalantly.

We follow the girls to a bench under a juniper tree. It's the only shade around, and even at that, it's not much. Juniper trees are synonymous with the Mediterranean but are not known to give one respite from the blazing summer sun.

This makes me think of vantage points. Monaco is on a hill. I can't help but smile. Monaco is my second home. Membership has its privileges, and I've had invitations to the gala for months.

"Have you heard anything from Pavel?" I ask Alex.

"No, he's been doing twenty-four-hour surveillance but has heard no formal plans. I like the idea of hitting them before the gala. We have a few days to prepare for it."

I nod. It sounds about right.

"Irina is champing at the bit to get Andrian. What are the odds she was with us when we discovered he was the mastermind behind the gun shipment heist?" Alex asks. "Call that a stroke of good luck for her."

"I don't like it that Dasha is at the center of this," I reply sharply. "Maybe Andrian anticipated we'd travel to Minsk for revenge. It's a stretch, but maybe he left my man alive to tell us who took the guns." *Fuck.* "He might be setting us up. It was all too easy," I say with a burst of anger at myself. "It never occurred to me there might be a larger play at hand."

Alex lights a cigarette. "Slow down. We don't know that's what happened, and Andrian is too stupid to think that far ahead. Nothing has changed. We have to strategically plan his"—he lowers his voice as a couple of tourists pass by—"you know."

"We will. All we have at this point is conjecture. We don't have much to worry about until we return to France. Then we need to move like the wind and set a perfect plan. Whether they are there or not when we arrive, we need to be careful."

"I wish we could sail into the sunset and leave this behind." Alex takes a long drag on his cigarette and blows it out slowly. "You need to call Andrian with demands."

"I will. But first, let's enjoy the day. Come to think of it, Dasha plans to call her friend Katsia today. Maybe we'll learn more. Call it a hunch, but women stick together."

# CHAPTER 24

## DASHA

*I* notice two extra men in our shore party. Bodyguards, I presume. One was with us on the afternoon we went water skiing. The other guy, I don't recognize. The familiar bulge under their shirts tells me the men are carrying guns. A chill runs down my spine. We are never out of danger.

Now I know what it's like to be Roman. I was curious about his life in the real world, and today, I'm getting a sneak peek. It's an eye-opener. This is what my life would have been had I been raised with all the entitlements of a pampered princess.

Looking back at my daily life, it was boring and miserable. But living in obscurity all these years may have been my best chance at survival and a normal life. Did my father have a plan all along? Did he care about me but never show it?

Growing up knowing I had a target on my back would have been unbearable. I'm sure my father has pissed off plenty of men over the years, all of them fully capable of murder.

I was denied the opportunity to live independently. I was raised to be dependent on a man to provide for me. But now I realize that even freedom has a price and its limits.

Is this the life I want? Did I jump from one cage to another?

Irina and I find a bench in the shade to sit on.

"This lemon gelato is amazing." My eyes drift to Roman. His height and bearing make him stand out in a crowd. My heart flutters. It's as if he's the other half of me. My chest swells. He might like me. He held my hand before his friends and kissed me in public. Public displays of affection are rarely seen in my country. You'd think it was a national crime to do anything other than hold hands.

Deep-throat kisses are only seen in the movies, like the ones on the jump drive Katsia keeps hidden. The last one we watched together had graphic sex scenes. It's the only reason I knew what to expect when Roman took my virginity.

"He loves you," Irina blurts. Just like that, she drops it on me.

"No." I shake my head in denial, but my eyes are glued to her face.

"Oh, yes. I've known him for years. He never spends all night with a woman, and you look like a woman who has had her brains fucked out."

"Pfftt," I spit out in disbelief. We did the deed twice yesterday, and I still want more. He fills me with his cock every chance he gets, and I'm not complaining. When he leaves a room, I want him. It's like pickleball. We ping back and forth. He goes, I miss him. He comes back, fills my pussy, and then my heart expands with joy. Then we repeat it all over again. Sex, food, fun, and more sex.

"I bet it was hot after he found out you were Andrian's bride, not Ratmim's," she chuckles.

"Why is that?"

"Make-up sex. When you have an argument and make up, you have sex. Some women do it intentionally to ensure their husbands pay attention to them."

"You're joking."

"Oh, trust me, Parisian women can be very calculating." She raises her eyebrows to fend off a challenge. At this point, I'll take her word for it. Irina knows things, and I'm anxious to learn more.

"Interesting," I reply. "I'm not into playing games. I'm not very good at them, and I hate losing." I'm worried my emotions are easily read, and I need to change the subject. "This gelato is addictive. I could eat it every day." I take the last spoonful of the creamy goodness and lick the spoon with my tongue.

"Leave it to the Italians. They have great wine and incredible food, and the men know how to fuck."

I choke on my gelato, coughing as it melts down my throat.

"What? I shocked you?" She chuckles. "Well, I've been watching you, and I like you. You're the right woman for Roman. He needs to give up the silly models he hangs out with."

"Models, as in fashion models?"

"Yes. They want to live glamorous lives, but most are washed up and broke by thirty. If they date Roman, they don't know Roman. They can't know the real him. You, however, understand. He lives in two very different worlds. I, too, play many parts in life. Sometimes I act, sometimes I spy." She shrugs her shoulders and takes another scoop of her dessert.

I try not to think about all the beautiful models Roman has been with. I worry that I won't be able to keep him interested when he's been with women more experienced and worldly than me. How can I compete with them?

Dying to know more, I ask Irina, "What else do you do?" She is a woman of mystery, and I'm fascinated by everything about her.

"Hm, you'll find out in time. For now, enjoy life."

My mind is reeling. Does Roman love me? Does he still want to date models? He's never mentioned other women. Is he still in touch with any of them? Is he using Alex to relay messages to other women? Or worse, does he have a woman waiting for him at home?

I notice Roman and Alex walking toward us. The sun is at their backs. What are they talking about? I feel they are doing something under my nose, and I can't say I like it.

I stand and find a trash can for my spoon and empty cup. I toss it in, and Irina does the same.

"You know," Roman says as he stands close to me and looks over my shoulder. His voice makes my pussy drip when he seductively lowers it. "I can think of better uses for that lovely mouth of yours after seeing you lick that spoon." His breath fans my ear as he makes a *tsk-tsk* sound, like I'm a bad girl. "I promise I'll be better than the gelato."

I pretend to be unexcited by his promise. "Mm. I don't know. The gelato was killer."

"I'll show you tonight."

Fuck me. I want him so badly that it hurts. He's teasing me, knowing I long for him.

"The fortress," Alex barks energetically.

"Yes." Roman glances around, his eyes surveying our immediate area. Once satisfied, he reaches for my hand, and we begin to walk. "It's straight ahead."

We take our time climbing the steep hill. The homes we walk past are stacked beside each other on the hillside. There are no air conditioning units in the windows. Instead, the windows are open, and clean laundry hangs from the clotheslines, drying in the sun.

A warm sea breeze stirs the air. I take in my surroundings and savor the moment. The smell of Roman mixes with musk and citrus and tantalizes my senses. I can't tell if my heart is racing due to the exercise or from his proximity. Either way, my pussy is wet with anticipation of what we'll do later.

I can no longer deny my feelings for Roman. I love how he touches me and the way he smiles when I catch his eye. I'm in love with him.

And I'm a fool for wanting him. He's dangerous. If I come out of this exchange alive, I need to get as far away as possible.

Roman said he wouldn't return me to Andrian, but what else does he have to barter with other than me? And this brings up the issue of trust. I'd be insane to trust him, wouldn't I?

My thighs and calves are in full revolt when we reach the fortress at the top of the hill. Roman takes care of the tickets, and we climb the narrow steps to a plateau. There's not much up here besides a grass courtyard and a defensive wall. A small building on the left has its door open.

I cross the courtyard with Roman and lean against the wall overlooking the sea. It's hot enough to soft-boil an egg, so when a breeze blows through my hair and cools my neck, I love it.

"Wow. What a view," I exclaim. The fortress isn't much to look at, but the view is worth the hike. Distant islands dot the horizon, and under a cloudless sky, the Mediterranean is spectacular. The water color can best be described as somewhere between blue and teal.

"The sea is gorgeous," Irina says, standing beside us.

"To think this was Napoleon's exile. If that's the case, exile me anytime," Alex jokes.

I chuckle. I'm sure the emperor missed Paris and being in power.

Before leaving, we visit the museum. The gardeners initially used the building. Now it's filled with a collection of Napoleon's personal artifacts and family pictures.

The wood floor creaks as I walk around, viewing historical relics on the wall and inside glass displays. I try to imagine what it was like to live here back then. Alex is right. The quaint island with an incredible sea view is not even close to life behind bars.

We finish exploring the fortress and head down the hill to the house where Napoleon stayed. It's a museum now and full of loud, sweaty tourists. A tour guide walks around, sharing facts and pointing out items of interest. I feel out of place inside a home built so long ago. The beds are too small, and the family portraits are too big. It's obvious how much we've changed over the years. A time-travel story about Napoleon appearing in the modern world would be fascinating.

When Roman notices me fanning my face, he suggests we all go outside and cool off. Looking down the hillside, I stifle a groan of dismay, knowing we have to go back the way we came. Each narrow street is lined with parked cars, but aside from bustling tourists, it's quiet.

A delivery truck rolls up and stops. I can't imagine taking the ferry daily from the mainland to this island to make deliveries. I see no American fast-food chains or coffee shops here, and it's lovely. Corporate America has changed the landscape in so many European cities, and now they are all starting to look alike.

We stop by a small shop filled with Italian leather purses. Roman says they are made locally and branded with a logo for the island.

Irina *oohs* and *ahhs* over the styles and colors.

"Pick one," Roman says.

I'm overwhelmed by the number of choices, but I like one that's pink. I have no clue if it will go with anything, but it's so pretty that I don't care. "This one, I think."

We make our purchases and head into the quieting streets that were crowded fifteen minutes ago.

"It's time to take a break. I say we walk back to the ship for the *controra* and return later tonight for dinner. Sound good?" Roman asks, but I doubt there's much choice.

"I'm meeting a friend, and we'll join you on the boat later," Irina says. "Want to tag along, Alex?"

He shrugs. "I'll come with you. I have a hunch Roman's going to be busy."

We leave Alex and Irina and walk back to *Severnoye Siyaniye,* our bodyguards trailing at a safe distance.

* * *

A LIGHT LUNCH is prepared and waiting for us on the deck. A crew member appears, offering us each a chilled washcloth and a cold water bottle. I make a beeline for the shade and kick off my sandals.

"The tops of my feet are hot," I exclaim.

"That's not all that's hot on you." Roman eyes me, making his lascivious intentions clear.

"Mm," I purr.

"Maybe we should shower to cool off," he suggests.

"How can I refuse? It's too hot to be outside this time of day. I can see why the locals take naps."

"You'll want one when I'm finished with you," Roman teases. He turns to make his way back to the cabin. I swipe my shoes off the deck and chase after him, giggling.

I love watching his ass in his fitted jeans. I love grabbing it even more. Roman is shucking off his clothes as he walks toward the shower.

"Is it rude to leave our clothes all over the floor?" I ask.

"Don't worry about it. The crew is paid to pick up after us. Now get your ass over here," he demands. I hear the shower running and drop my shoes. I'm still fully dressed, but I dutifully walk into the bathroom.

He's in the shower. He grabs me around my waist and pulls me into his rock-hard chest. His arms hold me so tightly that I can't move.

"Oh," I squeal as water soaks my dress.

His lips are warm on my neck. He unzips the dress, peels it off, and throws it into the corner. He kisses my breasts and rubs the nipples through my lacy bra. I enjoy the friction, and my nipples stiffen.

He slides the strap off my shoulder, baring my breast. He sucks my nipple into his delectable mouth. I moan and place my hand on his head. I fist his hair and tug it as he drives me wild with a desire evident from the puddle in my panties.

I moan as he plays with my breasts, and then, with a flick of his hand, rips my undies off and slides two fingers inside me. I gasp. He fucks me with his fingers as the warm water cascades over us.

Fuck me.

I'm find myself wanting him. He turns the water off, grabs a towel, and wraps it around me, carrying me to the bed. Using one hand, he yanks the bedding back.

He lays me in the bed and quickly makes a pass over me and himself with the towel. I look at him, and I can't take my eyes off his engorged cock.

"I want to feel myself in your mouth," he says.

He stands, and I move to the floor, kneeling before him.

"Stroke me and wrap those cherry-red lips around my cock," he commands.

I run my hand up and down his swollen shaft. I bend my head over him and part my lips. He moves gently into my waiting mouth. I wrap my lips around him like I'm eating a banana. I need to breathe and open my mouth wider to suck air.

"Ah," he groans. "Mm."

Great. I didn't hurt him.

He puts his hand on my head and shows me what he likes until I get the hang of it. As I find a rhythm, he drives his cock to the back of my throat, and he's fucking my mouth. From the guttural noises he's making, I think he's about to come, but he pulls back.

"I have to be inside you. I want to fuck you and feel your pussy clenching my cock."

He grabs something off the side table and adjusts himself, and I see the condom on him "Get on the bed," he says. I comply. I'm wet for him and can't wait to feel him in me.

He kisses and squeezes my breasts with one hand while he massages my clit with the other. I moan and writhe on the bed, grabbing at his hair, his back, anything I can tug on to keep myself grounded. This type of pleasure is not of this world.

Our eyes meet, and his lips part as he takes hold of his stiff cock and guides the tip into my pussy. He adjusts himself into a prone position above me with an elbow on each side of my head. I slide my arms around his waist. He thrusts into me, taking me by surprise. His abs flex and I run my hands over them. He pumps the hell out of me like he's lost control. My clit hardens, I feel myself soaring, and I cry out, shouting his name as I experience an intense orgasm, followed by another.

My nails dig into his back. I'm fatigued from sexual release. My arms and legs feel like limp noodles. I can't move as he continues to ride me.

His strokes quicken, and then he stops. His body shudders, and he roars. When his orgasm subsides, he clutches me, pulling me to him in an embrace.

"I love being with you," he murmurs.

That was unexpected.

"Me, too," I reply.

It looks like Irina was right after all. He has feelings for me. What else can she tell me about Roman?

He rolls off me, disposes of the condom, and grabs my hand, pulling me with him to the shower.

Afterward, we sit in the living quarters of our room. I have a towel wrapped around me. Roman joins me, a towel around his waist, his washerboard abs can't be overlooked. His dark hair is tousled. He's sexy as hell and even though he is part of a mafia family, I want him. I long for him to make love to me again.

I study him as he enters the room, I decide to inquire about one of his tattoos.

"What is the meaning of that?" I asked, nodding to his chest. I sit on the sofa.

"This?" He puts his fingertips on the tattoo on his collarbone.

"Yes," I implore him.

"Sinful Promise. We have secrets. I'm a sinner because it's what I do. I hurt people. It's my promise to the brotherhood, which means I can't share all the details of my life with someone like you."

"Oh." I sit perch on the edge of the couch. "Do they deserve to be hurt?"

"Yes, most of the time. Can you live with that, my little bird?"

I contemplate what he said. It's like Irina told me: he lives two lives. There's a difference between me and the women in his past. I know the real Roman. I understand the darkness that lives in him.

"Yes, I get that you can't share everything with me." I stand. "And to be honest, I'm not sure I want to know everything."

This lightens his mood. He leaves the room, then returns from his closet. "Here, this is a burner phone with your app on it. You can log in and call Katsia…if you want."

I jump and hug him. I've missed Katsia.

"Remember," he cautions, "there may be someone with her, so be careful."

I step outside with the phone, and Roman follows. We sit on the sofa. I type in her number. It's ringing.

"Hello?"

"Katsia," I exclaim.

"Wow, it's you."

"Yes, are you safe?"

"Your family asked if I knew your whereabouts, but you didn't tell me anything. Your brothers didn't seem motivated to chase after you. How are you?" she asks.

"Fine."

"Your dad mentioned he had to get a computer to find you, but all he saw was a blip off the coast of France. That was it."

"Are you okay?"

I have her on speakerphone. Roman listens with a blank expression on his face.

"Yes, yes. What is going on?" she asks.

"I called to let you know I'm fine. I can't talk long."

"Wait. Albert has been over. He said if you call, he needs to hear from you."

"What about?" My eyebrows furrow together with concern.

"He said they killed a man named Volkov and that Andrian used it to blackmail them into giving you to him."

Roman claps a hand to his mouth.

"Why did he tell you?" I'm leery of my family.

"He's not cut out for this life. He wants out, Dasha. Albert wants to get away from Vlad and your dad." There's a sense of urgency in her last statement.

"I don't know if that's possible. What am I to do?"

"Well, Andrian is trying to locate you, and they are checking places near the border. I imagine they will have something soon."

"What does Albert need?"

"A safe exit. I don't know where you are or who you are with, but if you can find a way to help him, you might be saving his life. He's not cut out for that stuff, Dasha. We both know it."

I nod. "I'll see what I can do. Don't let anyone know you heard from me, and hide that phone."

"I will. When can you call again?"

"I'll call as soon as I have something."

"Okay, I miss you."

"I miss you, too." I hang up and stare into space, flabbergasted. "I can't believe my brother wants out," I mumble. "But how can I help him?"

Roman runs a hand through his damp hair as he paces. "Do you trust him?"

I take a few seconds to think about it. "Yes, I do. I doubt Dad would manipulate him to get to me. We haven't been close since he moved out a few years ago. I think it was my father's way of keeping the business away from me. It also isolated me."

Without looking at me, Roman nods in agreement. He stands and begins to pace. "This might help us."

"How?"

"He could be our man on the inside to give us intel. I'll figure it out. For now, we need to meet with the others."

I do trust Albert. He doesn't have the ruthless personality the others have, and if he can't cut it, well…I worry he'll come home with injuries or worse. There is nowhere for him to go. He'll be trapped. Andrian will want him to work for him and try to mold him. There's only one way out of the mafia: in a casket. I have to help my brother.

"I can't let them hurt him, Roman." I wring my hands and look at him with tears in my eyes. "I've lost my mom. I don't want to lose a brother." I miss Katsia and wish she were here. I'm away from home, and the superyacht is incredible, but these people are not my family. A tear rolls down my face. I have to help my brother get out safety. I need Roman to do it.

"I know. But nothing will happen overnight. Let's enjoy the afternoon. We will have an incredible evening with our friends."

Enjoy the day? I want to do something, hit something, cry, scream, anything but enjoy the evening. How can Roman be this cold? He's so fucking calm. Does he have feelings for anyone or anything? He's a light switch, on one second and off the next.

"What are the plans with Andrian? You haven't said much, and we can't sail around the world forever."

"We're taking a break while the pieces fall into place. I have a contact in Belarus, and your brother might be useful. As long as they don't find us first, I like our odds."

"What does that mean for me?"

"That you'll be fine, and when this is over, you can do whatever you want. Now, come," he says as he pulls me into his arms and uses his thumb to wipe my tears. "It will work out. You'll see."

# CHAPTER 25

## DASHA

*I*'m emotionally drained. Roman takes my hands in his, and pulls me to my feet. We walk to the bed. The sun and stress has taken a toll. I lie in bed, Roman is beside me staring at the sky at the clouds over us. I drift off. When I wake, I enjoy the clean crisp sheets under me and it's heavenly. I reach for Roman and discover I'm alone. What the fuck is up with that? He's like Houdini, always disappearing.

I grab his pillow, hoping for another whiff of him, and my hand hits something. I quickly sit up and see a small box and an envelope. I open the envelope and pull out a note written on heavyweight paper.

*These are for tonight.*

That's it? No signature? I check the back of the card. He didn't sign his name. There's no Roman, no *Love, Roman*. Nothing, nada.

I pick up the elongated box and carefully untie the red ribbon. Then I close my eyes and take a deep breath as I lift the lid.

What! Diamond earrings! I gasp in disbelief. I've never had authentic jewelry. They are hoop earrings with rows of brilliant diamonds set in white gold, platinum, or silver. All of which are expensive.

I leap from the bed and sprint to the bathroom mirror. I hold an earring up to my ear. Stunning!

I remove my imitation diamond studs and slip the new earrings into place. I can't help but chuckle. I'm naked, wearing diamonds, as if I'm so important. Who would have dreamed I'd be walking around on a yacht, sipping champagne and eating caviar?

I can't help but feel giddy about my gift. Katsia gets excited if a man sends her flowers. Roman must like me to go to all the trouble. And how did he pull this off when we've been at sea for days? Like I said, Houdini.

Is this what they mean when they say gilded cage? It's not gold, but it's pricey. I might not know much, but I make the connection. He called me a principessa when we were on the airplane. Is this how a principessa lives?

Does his gift mean anything at all?

I reluctantly take off the earrings and return them to the box. I open the narrow drawer in my closet designed to hold jewelry and place the box safely inside. There's a lock, but I don't have the key.

It's late in the afternoon and a few hours before dinner. They never eat before seven. Plenty of time to lounge around the yacht.

I open the drawer holding all my swimsuits and pull out a skimpy bikini, one of many. This one is hand-crocheted and looks amazing. I've never been outside my bedroom with so little on, but it's not like we're at a public beach. We're on the yacht. No one will mind.

I check my reflection in the mirror. I look pale in a white bikini. The sun will be good for me. I love the swimsuit, even if it's revealing. I smile, remembering Irina in hers. Now, I'm beginning to feel like I belong. My father would disapprove, and I smile again. I relish that he's not here to tell me what to do.

I pull a matching cover-up off a hanger. It opens in the front, and I loosely tie the fabric belt. I feel naked, but it's time I step outside of my comfort zone. I brush my hair out and pull it up into a messy bun. I'll have to do something special with it when I wear those earrings.

I make my way down to the main deck, where I expect to find Roman. Instead, I'm the only one there. There are bowls of shrimp on ice set up on the bar, but oddly, no crew. I'm getting nervous. My heartbeat and breathing quicken.

Except for the lapping of the water, it's quiet, too quiet. I've never felt so utterly alone as I do at this moment. It doesn't matter what I have or where I am if there is no one beside me to watch the sunset or talk to at the end of the day.

I hope everything is okay. I step behind the bar and find a bottle of Italian red wine. It has the rooster logo on it, so according to Irina, it must be good.

I find the bottle opener, and after a short struggle, the cork comes out with a pop. I pour the liquid courage into a wine glass and lift the glass to my nose, inhaling deeply. Picturing myself, I chuckle because I have no idea why people sniff wine. I'm merely copying what I've seen others do. The wine smells nice. I take a sip. It's very good. Not too dry, not too sweet.

I take another sip and help myself to a shrimp cocktail. I slowly chew, stare at the rugged coastline, and wonder what Alex and Irina are doing.

"You're awake."

Startled, I turn to find Roman in his swimsuit, dripping wet. Water beads on his buff torso. He has a towel slung over his shoulder. He must have been sunning because he's tanned and looks sinfully roughish with a day's growth of beard. His hungry eyes devour me as he approaches. I've seen men look at Katsia like that and never dreamed a man would look at me the same way.

I nervously swallow the shrimp in one gulp. I'm paralyzed and can't take my eyes off him. Within two long strides, he's in my space. I take another sip of wine.

"I can see you're making yourself at home."

"I didn't know what to do. I…"

"I'm teasing you, little bird. I want you to spread those wings." He unties the belt to my cover-up and opens it to gaze at my body. My nipples harden, and I know he sees them through the suit made of yarn. He slowly pushes the cover off my shoulders and lets it float to the ground.

"I didn't know what to wear," I begin, but his kiss cut off my explanation.

I part my lips and allow his tongue into my mouth. He takes the towel off his shoulder and wraps it around my hips to pull me against his hard body. The friction of my nipples against his hairy chest makes my pussy slick. I want him. I need him. I return his kiss, enjoying the coolness of his mouth and the heat of his body.

Running my fingers through his damp hair, I fist and tug it as my hips grind against his pelvis, and feel his cock come alive. I slide my hand inside his swim trunks and grab his cock because he likes me to touch him. When I hear the sharp inhalation of his breath, all I want is to make him gasp again.

"You look amazing, Dasha." His hands travel down my back and grab my buttocks so hard, they lift me an inch off the ground. "I want you."

"What if the others return?"

"We're meeting them in town."

My knees buckle, and I moan when his fingers slip into my pussy.

"Just as I thought. You're wet for me. Dasha, what am I to do with you?" The growl he uses turns me on.

"I'm sure you can think of something," I reply, so excited I can barely breathe. Did I just say that?

"That I can." And with that, he unties my bikini top and snags the bottoms. Both pieces fall to the deck.

He shucks his swimming trunks.

"What about the crew?"

"I sent everyone ashore. They'll be gone for hours."

He scoops me up into his arms, carries me to a cushion used for sunbathing, and places me on it. "I think you need some sun," he teases as he spreads my legs.

"Someone will see," I protest.

"It's my yacht, my rules."

I admit that having sex with the risk of getting caught increases the intensity of everything, especially the orgasms. Afterward, we lay there, letting the warm sun bake us. Then Roman strides buck naked to gather our swimsuits. I catch mine when he tosses it to me.

"Let's go," he says.

"Go? Go where?"

"Swimming?" His sun-kissed face has a happy glow.

"Sure." Thankfully, our family had a membership to the city recreational center when I was a child. I learned to swim in an indoor pool. But the ocean?

"It looks deep," I reply as I tie the top around my neck and back. I slip into the bottoms and reluctantly pull them up. It was fun being naked on deck.

"Follow me."

He leads me through passageways I haven't been in and opens the door to a room with a large pool. The water is a deep teal. We're in the back of the yacht, and there's a deck if we want to hang out or jump in the ocean. It would be a great spot to enjoy a sunset.

"This is incredible. Do you swim in the ocean?" I ask.

"Sometimes, but there's always a risk the wind or current could carry us too far from the yacht, so it's best to wait until we have a boat in the water."

I will file this away for future reference. What am I thinking? We don't have a future. I need to remember this is all temporary, and all we have is now.

"This is the deep end. Jump," he says as he splashes me and jumps in. What the hell? I hold my nose and jump in, too. The cool water is exhilarating, and when I surface, my hair is slicked back, and my eyes pop open.

"Do you like it?"

"Like it? I love it."

He swims some laps, and I do, too. Then I swim to him. He takes me in his arms. I drape my arms around his neck. We're in the deep end, so my feet don't touch the bottom.

"I've been wondering where you spend your time," I say. "This is your hiding spot."

"The last thing I want to do is hide from you. To have you in my arms, on this superyacht, visiting this beautiful island, is a dream come true."

I'm speechless. What is he inferring?

"I like it here, too, but I was a bit freaked out by the guards with us today."

"Really? That was just a precaution. I can protect you, but we're being hunted right now," he explains.

"You're so calm. I don't know how you do it. I'm freaking out. I don't think you realize what Andrian is capable of."

"Don't worry. I've done my research. I do better when I'm prepared. The trip to Belarus was a last-minute impulsive idea. I rushed in and stole a woman I thought belonged to my enemy, and here we are. Now I have two enemies. One wants to eradicate us from this world, and the other is just a soldier carrying out orders. I need to know how you would feel if your family members died in the bloodshed that's likely to happen in the days ahead."

"What do you mean?" My family is no prize, but they're still family.

"There will be a meet. People will die. The only way this feud ends is with Andrian dead. You are smart enough to know he will come after all of us when he learns that I have you."

"What do you mean?" I ask again.

"Andrian is barred from Russia. He's not barred from France.

There's nothing to stop him from attacking us there. Your father and brothers may be with him."

"You're saying they will be killed, too?"

"It's a possibility. If Albert is on our side and helps, we will do our best to spare him. As for your older brother…"

"Vlad."

"I can spare Vlad's life as long as he no longer interferes with our business."

My heart stops. I don't want to see my brother hurt. However, it is better than being dead.

"Will you get Albert out if he helps you?"

"Yes, I will do my best. I mean him no harm. However, there is a score to settle older than you."

"Right." I need to focus more on the now and less on the future. This brief interlude of stolen moments with Roman is something I will cherish forever.

"Now," he says, and kisses my nose, "did you get the box?"

"Oh, yes. Thank you so much. The earrings are incredible. I'm afraid to wear them."

"Why?"

"Someone might want to steal them."

"I'm with you, no one would dare touch you, or I would kill them." His tone is void of emotion, and I pull back enough to look into his face. He's serious.

The thought scares me and excites me at the same time.

His eyes turn a darker blue, reminding me of the color of the sea before the storm hit us off the coast of France.

"Fine. I'll wear them." I quickly agree. "They're beautiful."

"Great. Let's lie in the sun again before we meet everyone for dinner."

I nod.

We make our way to the sun deck and collapse on the loungers. Roman rubs suntan oil over my back and legs, covering every inch. When he massages the oil between my thighs, I'm aroused, and from the bulge in his swim trunks, so is he.

I'm glad he's taken the time to ask me about my brothers. Roman may kill people, but he cares about my feelings and thoughts for some reason. I was never extended the same courtesy or concern at home. My family only asked for my opinion regarding dinner options and snow predictions.

From what he's telling me, there will be a resolution to my situation, and our lives depend on a favorable outcome to the meeting with Andrian. As much as Roman wants revenge, he's thinking about long-term consequences.

I remind myself that no matter how much I love him, I have to leave in the end. It's too easy for me to give in to the temptation of his body. Sure, he can provide me with a life of luxury, but I'll always be his property.

I must get my head out of the clouds and back in the game. Roman might be manipulating me, baiting the hook with this illusion of freedom. He knows it's what I want more than anything, so he could be using it to gain my trust. Trust is a powerful weapon, and my survival depends on not trusting everything he says.

What is he planning? What does he plan on doing with that cache of guns, other than starting a revolution?

"Dasha," Roman calls, interrupting my thoughts.

"Yes?"

"It's time to get ready for dinner."

# CHAPTER 26

## DASHA

"**W**hy do I have to dress all fancy when it's just us?" I complain, stepping into a silk dress with baroque motifs in light floral colors.

The dress is mid-length and drapes over my shapely hips. The ruffles on the bodice run down the front, making the garment appear seamless. The rouleau straps imply no bra. I glance in the full-length mirror and twirl, watching the dress swirl around my legs. I love the way it shows off my cleavage. Whatever this dress cost, it's worth every Euro because I feel pretty in it.

Roman buttons his starched dress shirt and rolls up the sleeves. The tattoos on his arms are vibrant, contrasting with his tanned skin. One forearm is covered with a large snake; the ink on the other arm consists of unfamiliar symbols. I assume one might be for the Bratva. "You're with me," he says shortly. "You represent my family."

"That's a job for your wife," I mutter as I walk around the end of the bed with sandals dangling in my hand.

He crosses the room so fast that I fear he's about to hit me. I usually don't get hangry, so why am I being mean? He grabs my arm, forcing me to face him.

"I don't take sex to family functions." His eyes bore into mine. "These people are an extension of my family."

"I know."

"Then act like it," he warns.

"I'm sorry."

"You are mine. Make no mistake about it. No other man will ever know what it's like to have his cock inside you."

I inhale. Fuck. His words frighten and excite me simultaneously, like a lightning storm.

He releases my arm and walks away to retrieve his watch on the nightstand.

I sit on the bench at the end of the bed with my sandals. I slip my foot into one and tie the cloth bow around my ankle. I do the same with the other foot and glance at him as he fixes the watch on his wrist and looks out the glass doors. He tucks his shirt in. He's not armed. I look at his reflection in the door. His eyes are guarded. I can't read his mood. Did I deliver a punch he can't stomach?

The truth often hurts the ones we love. Does he plan to make me his woman forever? From my experience, women don't flourish in this kind of life. They are made to stay home and only get trotted out on special occasions. Their men come and go as they please and keep to themselves.

"Are you ready?"

I slip into the closet and return with the earrings. "Almost," I answer as I thread the posts through my earlobes.

I try not to look at him. I don't want him to read my expression. Katsia said she could read me like a book. I refuse to give Roman any more leverage.

"You're beautiful and deserve to have beautiful things, starting with those earrings."

"I think they're too much," I caress one with my fingertips.

"Nonsense. You set the tone for the room."

"Irina does that already," I counter.

"Well, Irina is Irina. You, however, are the jewel. Remember that. She has worldly experience, so what if yours has only begun? Isn't this what you wanted? To be out and seeing the world?"

"Yes."

'Then be happy with it. Don't look to someone else to make you happy. Make yourself happy, and it will all fall into place."

He leads me down passageways and stairs until we reach a door that a bodyguard opens for us.

Should I believe him? Considering that the words come from a man who appears to have everything, I have to wonder.

We walk ashore, followed by the guard. Roman places his arm around my waist and directs me to the side of the port we've not yet seen.

There are only a few restaurants, and we stop at the last one, which has three sides overlooking the harbor. Right away, I spot Irina, Alex, and...another woman? She's beautiful, with honey-blonde highlights, the kind you get at expensive salons. She's wearing a yellow sundress that shows off her toned body, a body you only get from working out. The gym must be a full-time job because she looks amazing.

"Ah, there you are." Alex waves and raises a glass of red wine. "Roman, this is my friend Francesca."

"Hello." Roman lifts her hand to his mouth and kisses it politely. "Ah, congratulations are in order, I hear."

"Yes," she beams, her smile lighting up the room.

Do women always surround this man? I can't help but get jealous when he gives them attention.

"Pleasure to meet you. Yes, we finally got married. As you can imagine, it was an extravagant wedding," she says with a slight Italian accent. I notice everyone is speaking English.

"Yes, I can only begin to imagine two, um…corporations merging." And Roman gives her a knowing smirk.

It's as if they are playing a game of international espionage full of subtle hints and innuendos. They're all in on a joke I know nothing about, and I'm beginning to feel left out.

"Ah." Irina also has a glass of red wine in her hand. "This is Dasha. Dasha, Francesca, my friend from Italy."

"Pleasure to meet you." I manage a tight smile.

"Dasha." Francesca surprises me with a hug. I put my arms around her to play along with the charade of immediate friendship.

She does smell nice, like vanilla crème brûlée. Let's hope she's just as sweet as she smells. If I had to guess her age, I'd say she is close to thirty.

Francesca pulls back and stares at my earrings. "Those are stunning. Someone has good taste."

I notice the ice on her earlobes and suspect they are the real deal, too.

We're interrupted by a hostess carrying menus and follow her to a table near the water. Soft overhead lights make it feel more like an evening garden party than a restaurant. Maybe that's because we're off the Italian coast with the most magnificent unobstructed view of the Mediterranean Sea. Light waves lap against the nearby shoreline, and a cool breeze blows off the water. Irina hands me her wrap for my shoulders and promises I will warm up after some wine.

The wine flows around the table like water. I sip mine. It's not sweet and has hints of licorice. It coats my lips, and I can't help but take another sip. Warm ciabatta in a basket lined with a cloth napkin is placed on the table. The waitress pours olive oil into a saucer next to the basket.

Francesca takes a slice of the bread, breaks off a piece, and dips it into the oil. Interesting.

I follow the conversation. It flies around the table more quickly than I can keep up. Irina and Francesca are two peas in a pod. They sit close to one another, laughing at inside jokes. They remind me of the way Katsia and I act when we're together.

I can't miss the ring on Francesca's finger. The diamond is so bright that it may as well be a lightbulb. Who and where is her husband? Alex said her home is in Florence, and I love listening to her when she speaks Italian. I'm curious as to how she fits into this cast of characters.

The waitress speaks English well, moving with alacrity as she drops off seafood appetizers.

"These are sea scallops." Roman spears one and places it on my plate. "I think you will like them."

"I'll try." I decide it's too large for my mouth and choose to cut it with the butter knife. I'd rather go hungry than be seen eating like a farm animal.

The waitress brings another bottle of wine, and Roman refills our glasses. She also brings containers of fizzy water. Roman explains that it's carbonated and famous in Italy.

Stuffed mussels are passed around, and Roman puts two on my plate. I'm beginning to worry I'll be full by the time the main course is served.

I wait for Roman to eat one first. He picks up the shell, unties the string, and dumps the contents into his mouth. He chews and swallows.

I pick up a shell and inspect the inside. It's meat and finely chopped tomatoes. I tentatively slide the contents into my mouth, mindful not to drip any on my dress. The flavor is heavenly. I chew and find the mussel. It's meaty, not chewy. I swallow.

"It's good, right?" Alex has been watching me. Roman, too, as they await my verdict.

"Yes, it is. Delicious! It's going to be tough to go back to eating my boring potato dishes." I wipe my mouth with a cloth napkin. I'd like another but need to save room for the next course.

"Yeah, you're not getting food like this in Minsk," Roman says, and Alex chuckles.

The waitress arrives to take our order for the main meal. We all order seafood dishes.

I glance around the room. All the tables are filled, and people are waiting outside. I feel guilty for taking so long to eat dinner. This multi-course meal takes hours. I hope the people in line get to eat before the restaurant closes.

I sip more wine, or as they call it, *vino*. I'm getting better at detecting the layers of flavor and enjoying the complexities of the wine. "I love Italy."

"What's there not to love?" Roman adds with a smirk, "I love it, too. I can't wait to show you more places."

Does that mean we have a future? The more Roman teaches me about sex and feeds me seafood delicacies, the harder it will be to leave him when this is over.

My dish of linguine with clams shows up. I stare at the purple octopus on Alex's plate and decide I made the better choice. No way could I eat those scary-looking tentacles with all the suction cups.

I hear the words *gala* and *Monaco*. From what I can tell, we're still going. I have no idea how Roman plans to attend such a public event when we're on a kill list.

For dessert, we share a chocolate ganache torte. After dinner, we leave with several bottles of wine. I hear the waitress tell Roman it's made from grapes grown on the island.

We all walk back to the boat, including Francesca. Nobody tells me if she's joining us for the rest of the journey or staying the night. As the outsider, I'm always the last to know what's happening.

Once we're back on board, the chief steward opens a bottle from the restaurant, and the drinking continues as she pours everyone a fresh glass. By the time she opens a second bottle, the room and my head are spinning. My stomach is in my throat.

"I think I need to help you to bed," Roman says.

"I feel dizzy." I'm not sure if my voice is too loud, but he helps me stand. The boat feels like it's rocking when it's not. This can't be good.

Francesca chuckles. "Ah, I forgot to warn you, Italian wines sneak up on you." "Really? I think I've had too much."

"It will pass," Irina says as she kicks off her shoes and curls her legs under her.

Roman escorts me to bed. He undresses me, taking off my dress and helps me to the bed. I sit on the side and sink into the mattress.

"Don't lay down yet." Roman shoves a bottle of cold water into my hand. "Drink."

I chug the water and hope to God I don't throw up. So, this is how Katsia feels when she parties too much.

"Good girl. Sleep. Call me on the intercom if you need anything."

"Okay," I mumble. Closing my eyes, I lay my head on the pillow.

It's dark when I wake. I reach over, and Roman's not there. He must still be downstairs. I need something to wear and walk to the closet. I pull on a cream-colored negligée and matching sheer robe. It's for looks, not coverage, because you can see my pink areoles through the fabric. I find my way back to where I left everyone.

It's dark, and the running lights are the only lights on deck. I freeze when I see the glowing ember of Alex's cigarette. Who else is here?

"I don't know if I can trust her. The video shows she was snooping in my closet." Roman's voice gives me a clue as to where he's sitting. Wow, he must have hidden cameras everywhere. Is he making a sex tape of us, too?

"I don't know if we can trust her or her brother," he continues. "I'm counting on him to provide us with the location of the guards Andrian will have placed at the meeting place. We'd better be prepared for a double-cross. There's too much at stake."

"I agree," Francesca chimes in. My eyes are adjusting, and I have a better idea of where everyone is sitting.

Finally, Irina defends me. "I've talked with Dasha enough to know she's not one to trust a man readily. But she trusts you and Alex.

"Furthermore, why would Dasha not want to find her passport?" says Francesca. "She has to know there's a chance she will be caught in the crossfire once we come under attack from Andrian. She needs a backup plan, Roman. You'd do the same thing."

"That's a fair point," Roman admits.

"Do you trust Dasha?" Alex asks him.

"For the most part. She hasn't tried to murder me in my sleep." His tone is one of veiled amusement.

I hide behind a small credenza. Everything is bolted down, so I don't have to worry about knocking it over as I crouch. It's dark, and they can't see me. But is there a camera on me? If so, it's too late. I'm finally getting enough information to fill in the blanks.

"Let me tell you what I think." Irina sounds serious. "I've known you for years, and you never let a woman sleep over. She's in your bed every night, and you're not complaining. This is totally out of character, so she must mean something to you. She's special."

"I agree with Irina. You're smitten with her. I think you might even be in love with her," Alex chimes in.

"Maybe?" Roman replies.

"You're daft. How do you not see it?" Alex scoffs.

"I thought I couldn't love. I'm a killer, not a lover. I stay detached for a reason. I was always afraid attachments would distract me from my job, so I never looked for love."

"Yes, but it found you." Irina chuckles. Alex puts out his cigarette and claps Roman on the back, and they all share a laugh.

"Hey, I deliver deadly blows, and my marriage works," Francesca chimes in. "See, there's still hope for you. We know it's the Volkovs or Andrian in the end. Andrian is malicious scum. He stirs shit up just because he can. He creates chaos and makes money off of it. I hear there is a plan to destabilize a European country. How long before he's in our country doing that shit?" If Francesca were a cat, she'd have her claws out. "I'm down for wherever you need me to do," she adds.

Now I understand why Francesca is here. Everyone has a part to play in the showdown.

"So we kill him for the greater good," Roman says, thinking aloud.

"For all we know, he's behind the kill order on your dad," Alex tells him.

"If that's the case, it's an all-out war, and we win by cutting the head off the snake," Irina says. "I've wanted his head on a platter for years. We can do this together."

"Yes, we can," Roman says.

I hear the clink of glasses as they make a toast. The meeting is about to adjourn. I need to be back in bed, and if Roman arrives, I have to pretend to be asleep.

# CHAPTER 27

## ROMAN

The afternoon of sun, swimming, and sex has taken its toll. I'm buzzed on the incredible evening, the food, wine, and friendships. Exhausted, I stumble into my cabin and drag my ass to the edge of the bed. I barely have the energy to kick off my shoes and unbutton my shirt. I drop it with my pants, belt, and boxers to the floor.

The room has a soft glow from the low lights I left on earlier. I crawl under the sheet and lean over, checking on Dasha. She's breathing comfortably. I feel bad for letting her get drunk on my watch. The glow of the moon illuminates her long eyelashes resting against her cheek. Something shiny on the nightstand catches my eye. It's her new earrings. I guess she woke up at some point and took them off.

I roll onto my back and stare out the skylight.

Fuck me.

Leave it to Irina to call me out on my bullshit. I do love Dasha. I didn't think I was capable of loving another person. I built a wall around my heart. No one has ever been able to get past my defenses. But Dasha.

Alex is my compass, and if he believes I'm in love, I'm in trouble. Alex has been pushing me to call Andrian. Because I've been dragging my feet, he must think I don't want to give Dasha up. There's some truth to that, but honestly, the idea of vacationing on the yacht and fucking Dasha appeals to me. Why would I want it to end?

Love is supposed to be a huge distraction, but I've never been so focused. I've had time to think, and now that we have Francesca on board, we can pull off the ultimate showdown. For this mission, I'm not relying on my brothers. They are far away, and this is what I do for the family. If they come, great, but I will be fine with a few well-trained men strategically positioned in France.

I'm counting on Pavel and Albert to provide the intel necessary to locate Andrian and take him out. How many others meet the same fate remains to be determined.

There is the question of why Dasha was in my closet. My gut tells me Dasha still wants her freedom and she needs the passport. It's the only thing she needs to start over. Am I guilty of trying to buy her love? Are the clothes and earrings bait to lure her into my gilded cage?

Why else would she stay with me? I'm a killer who could be killed at any time. Dad was taken out, and we have yet to avenge his death. We may be getting closer to the truth, thanks to my incredible friends. They are putting their lives on the line to help me against a formidable foe.

What would a future with Dasha look like? I don't know what she wants other than to escape her past. If I can help Albert get out safely, will that be enough? It's hard to know what she's thinking.

Sometimes, she looks content. Sometimes, her thoughts are far away.

Dasha has no guarantee I'll hold up my end of the deal, so of course she's looking for a backup plan. If I were in her position, I wouldn't be trusting of me, either. She's had nothing but bad experiences with the men in her life. She's told me how her home life was less than ideal. How can I convince her I will not give her to Andrian?

Dasha is in a precarious position; now I'm in one as well. I smile in the dark. Oh, the webs we weave. In my defense, I only lie to those who betray me.

For a mission to be successful, we must trust one another, all of us. Can I trust her brother Albert? Can we trust her friend Katsia? Or is Andrian using them to manipulate whoever has Dasha?

For now, he doesn't know that someone is me. Otherwise, Andrian would have tracked *Severnoye Siyaniye* and had men waiting on the island. There is no evidence our cover has been blown, so time is on our side.

Andrian has been watching us in Russia for some time and knows what he'll be up against, but we've also been doing our homework. Dmitry has been feeding me information, and I'm making sure we have the intel we need.

We will head back to Monaco tomorrow. We'll have two days on the water, but we'll need a few days to obtain supplies, coordinate our plan, and prepare for what I hope will be a successful mission.

For now, I'm going to focus on enjoying Dasha's softness against me and accept that I am indeed in love with her. I can't imagine a day without her in it. She is a survivor, spontaneous and adventurous. I enjoy watching her blossom with each new experience. She picks up on things quickly and will have no problem fitting into our world.

She is the opposite of me in many ways, and I find it refreshing. But if she's to remain in my world, she'll have to accept the limitations that come with it. She might resist exchanging one cage for another. The freedom she experienced on this remote island and growing up in anonymity is over.

Once we're on French soil, her life will change, and she may not be as compliant. Will she sign up for a lifetime of the gilded cage I can give her? Does she want children? Would she knowingly bring them into our world?

My mind drifts. My body is warm with alcohol, but I prefer that my body be warmed by Dasha. I roll onto my side and pull her to me. She stirs briefly. I bury my face in her hair and breathe in her essence. My cock twitches, but the rest of me only wants sleep.

* * *

I SMELL coffee and hear liquid being poured. The mattress dips as someone sits on the edge. I open my eyes.

"You're a sight for sore eyes," Dasha greets me.

"I'm sure." I sit up, taking the coffee cup from her petite hands. She bends down to drop a quick kiss on my cheek.

I raise an eyebrow. What did I do to deserve her affection?

"Thank you for last night. Your friends are very nice. By the way, what does Francesca do? She and Irina seem very tight, like best friends tight." She pauses and gets that far-away look. She must be thinking of her friend Katsia.

"They are, actually. They have a lot in common."

"Such as?"

"What's with all the questions so early in the morning?"

"No reason. Girl stuff, that's all."

Dasha is dressed in a swimsuit, and her sheer coverlet clings to her shoulders. I sip my coffee and check out her curves. All I want to do is grab her boobs and fuck her until she comes on my cock.

I down the coffee and notice we're moving. The Italian coast is on my right, indicating we're heading home. Given the position of the sun, it's later than I expected.

"We're hanging out on deck. I hear we're returning to Monaco, so we've decided to make it a day of drinking mimosas and relaxing under the summer sun," says Dasha.

"Sounds great to me. I have some work to handle today, so I'll join you later." I fling the sheet back.

Dasha pretends to be drinking from her cup, but I know she's staring at my morning wood through her eyelashes. She inhales sharply and fumbles, placing her cup on the nightstand beside mine.

I growl as I leap from the bed and grab her around the waist.

She shrieks.

"I'm going to bend you over the bed and fuck you."

I let her go, quickly grab a condom from the nightstand, and slide it over my rock-hard cock.

She escapes me, which only fuels my desire to make her submit.

I let out a hearty chuckle as I catch her in the bathroom. She squeals, but she's laughing.

I hold her close. Picking her up, I carry her to the bedroom and toss her on the bed.

She smiles up at me. "And what are your intentions, Roman Volkov?"

"To make you mine and to fuck you until you scream my name when you come."

"Mm." She slips off her bottoms and unties her top, letting her boobs tumble out.

She shimmies across the bed, and I tackle her and kiss her hard. She kisses me back. She's feisty today and flips me onto my back. She's lost her shyness and wants to be on top. I love letting her take control of her desire as she slowly lowers herself onto my cock. The pleasure is exquisite.

I grab her boobs, playing with her nipples and rubbing them until they are hard. She grips my shoulders and rocks her hips, grinding against me. When I feel her quicken, I arch my back, giving her more of my shaft. She cries my name when she comes.

I flip her over, thrusting with long strokes as I lose myself, suspended somewhere between peace and euphoria. It's a state of mind and pleasure I wish I could hold onto longer, but it evaporates almost as quickly as it came. I cling to her. She's my goddess of all things good in the world. I groan as I fill the condom, shuddering under the intensity of a quick, excitable fuck. The fact that she yelled my name pleases me.

Now, I need to shower, and it is with regret that I have to speak to Andrian.

* * *

ALEX and I are in my office. I use the computer with an encrypted VPN to call Andrian. Undoubtedly, my enemy has sophisticated technology and is eager to pinpoint my location.

He answers in Russian.

Without preamble, I say, "You have something of mine, and I want compensation."

"Who is this?"

"Roman Volkov. You stole something from me and need to make amends to the tune of one million euros, not rubles."

"Is that all, eh? You are stupid, all of you. I took more than your guns. I took out your father. It was so easy to kill him, and it will be easy to kill you, too." His words drip with hatred.

I look to Alex, who puts his palms together, signaling for me to remain calm.

"The weaponse are gone?" Andrian barks.


"Great, then you have my money."

"What makes you think I would give in to your demands?" His surly voice makes my skin crawl. "I'm the one with the advantage."

"I propose we make an exchange in Monaco. It's one country you can still get into."

"Why would I come?"

"I have what you want."

"There is no way you have anything I want," he bluffs, but I can tell I have his attention. "What is it? More guns?" He laughs, and I want to strip him of is arrogance.

"Maybe you're missing a woman, maybe not."

"No!" I can tell he's pissed. He still wants her, judging from the level of anger in his voice. I give Alex a nod. We're back in the game.

"Yes, I do. She's a pretty girl. Easy to see why you picked her. We were on to you," I lie, wanting to unnerve him and keep him guessing. "Dasha is with me, and I think she's worth a million."

"What makes you think I will pay for her? She isn't worth that much. You'd be better off selling her at auction to some sadist with a fetish for virgins."

"Don't you want your dignity back? You can use her as an example for those who have disappointed you." I hate saying this about Dasha, but he'll never get his hands on her. I need him to take the bait and come to me. "I propose an exchange: your virgin for my money, and we'll call it even."

"You put a hand on her, I'll kill you," he threatens.

"Fine. Monaco, Saturday. I'll call with the time and place."

"Good. I can't wait to kill you and your family."

"Don't forget to bring the money, asshole."

I hang up.

"Ugh," I say to Alex. "I need a shower after talking to him."

"Good thing Dasha ran, and we were there. I don't trust him. She may still end up on the auction block." Alex adds, "Or worse."

"He admitted killing Dad. I have to call my brothers. We all have a target on our backs, thanks to my impetuosity."

"You never would have learned the truth behind your father's murder otherwise. Andrian is cunning. We can't underestimate him. You take him out, or he will systematically hunt each of you down. Now that he knows you have her, the clock is ticking."

"I'm calling my brothers." I type in their phone numbers on the keyboard, and within seconds, their faces appear on the monitor.

"Bad news," I tell them. "From what we've been able to piece together, Ratmim was hired to steal our weapons, but his boss, Andrian, set everything up. He needs the guns to stir up unrest in another country. Dasha can't go back to him."

Nikolay groans and puts the palm of his hand to his forehead. "Roman, I told you not to start a war."

"Women and children are to be off limits. But Andrian has no code. He's a trafficker. What are her chances without us?"

"Sounds to me like you're pussy-whipped," Dmitry interjects.

"Andrian bragged about sending Ratmim's sons to kill Dad. He is coming for us no matter what, brother. He has been lurking in the shadows for years to get revenge. Dad was broadsided. He dismissed Andrian as a threat, and look what happened. Andrian had the perfect cover to eliminate Dad without suspicion falling on him. We have a source inside, and Dasha tells us the same thing. Their details support the allegation that the deaths of Dad and Boris were no accident. They were cold-blooded hits orchestrated by Andrian."

"You should have led with that," Nikolay says.

I ignore his comment. "Andrian is very good at games. We can't take this lightly. He will pursue us no matter where we go or what we do, so I'll have Mom go to the safe house. He'll be watching. He wants us dead."

"Okay," Nikolay replies. "But it's not worth starting a war if we can't win it. Do you have a plan, Roman?"

"Yes, I do."

Nikolay stares at me, reading my face. "Are you focused now?"

"Don't worry. I can love a woman and still do my job."

"We're coming," Dmitry says.

"Thanks, but I can do this. I have a team I trust. I need you both to stay safe."

Nikolay sits back in his leather chair and looks me in the eye. "What's the plan?"

"I'll lure him to Monaco. I have a skilled team in place. We'll make it look like a drug deal gone wrong so we won't have to worry about others coming. There is unrest in his country. It will be a huge win for more than just us if we eliminate him."

"I'm coming," Dmitry insists.

"No need. I've got this. It's my job. I'm the one who rushed into this."

"We would have never known otherwise, silver lining and all that shit." Nikolay chuckles nervously. "No, he's coming after all of us. We need to get our revenge because the opportunity is here now."

"I call dibs on the kill shot," I say.

"Fine," Dmitry says.

"We need to get Mom and our wives in safe houses. Do we know if he's infiltrated our ranks?" Nikolay asks with concern.

"He doesn't have to. He knows men in high places who provide him with intel. I've been giving this a lot of thought. I suspect that when Andrian sent Ratmim and his sons to carry out the hit, he had them inject Dad and Boris with something. Their injuries from the crash were not considered lethal, but no one bothered to test for drugs or poison," I murmur. "Andrian has been linked to men who do these things. It's all starting to make sense."

I realize with horror that Dad never stood a chance.

"Where are you now?" Nikolay asks.

"On board *Severnoye Siyaniye* off the coast of Italy. We'll get to Monaco first. I'll get what we need. If you make it, fine. If not, I can handle it."

"This is too important. The more men, the better. We all have a role to play," Dmitry says. "Besides, I can't have this piece of shit breathing when I have a wife with a child on the way. He dies, one way or another."

"I agree," Nikolay says. "And here I thought we were going to war over a woman, but now I see there's a lot more to it."

"It's complicated," I reply, "but without Dasha, we'd never know her father was hired to kill Dad and steal our weapons. I'll see you both soon."

# CHAPTER 28

DASHA

"Let's get massages and enjoy the jacuzzi. I hear there is an infrared red-light sauna," Irina suggests.

I sip chilled water. I went overboard on the wine last night, and Roman says it will rehydrate me. "What is this sauna?"

"It's healthy for you. You'll love it. We can get a massage, too. Can you believe that?" Irina adjusts her sun hat and reclines on her cushioned lounge chair.

Francesca looks up from her book, "The Micheli's need to get a yacht like this. I've never been one to spend much time on the water, but I fell in love with Elba. I could easily spend a year or more cruising from one new place in Italy to the next, enjoying the food and ambiance. I hear the islands further down the coast are to die for, with hot thermal baths fed from underground springs. If only I didn't work all the time." She's wearing a white bikini and looks like a bodybuilder, minus the fake tan and fake boobs.

I try not to stare and use the water bottle to hide my face.

I comment, "Either you're training for a bodybuilding competition, or you're on steroids." I pull a lounger closer to her and sit down, removing my coverup to reveal my bright pink bikini. The color is a reminder that I'm the youngest one in the group.

"Thank you, you're a dear. I love to work out with weights and practice martial arts. Krav Maga is my favorite. I cherry-pick my favorite moves from each fighting discipline and combine them to create my own style. I used to box, too." She shrugs her shoulders and sips her champagne as if everyone can kill someone with their bare hands.

"Maybe you can show me some stuff in the weight room. I've been meaning to get to it."

"I'd love to." She hangs on to her straw hat as a gust of wind cuts across the bow. "It's a gorgeous day to catch some rays."

Like Irina, she's wearing dark sunglasses, so it's hard to tell if she's for real or if she's giving me lip service, but she impresses me as someone who means what they say. I tug on a ball cap a crew member gave me and lay back on the lounger. The cap is more my style, and sunbathing is new to me. The closest I ever came to being a lady of leisure was when I was sick in bed with the flu or bronchitis.

I'm counting on these ladies to show me how it's done.

"We need some music," Francesca says, closing her book.

"I'll handle it." Irina gets the attention of a deckhand, and less than a minute later, European pop streams from surround-sound speakers.

"That's perfect," Francesca sighs.

"I take it you just got married," I say, curious but trying not to sound too nosy.

"Oh, yes. We've been together for some time. It was a matter of getting around to it. I stay very busy with a number of businesses in southern Italy—not Sicily, mind you. And my husband, Sal, well, his family business is in Tuscany."

"You're so lucky. If Tuscany is anything like Elba, sign me up," I reply.

She and Irina chuckle.

It's beginning to look more and more like she's part of a family business, and so are the Volkovs. Is this an international convention of mafias? What better way to escape detection than to float on a yacht that can't be traced to a holding company with their names on it? She said *Sicily* like it's a dirty word, so she's not connected to them. Everyone knows Sicily is notorious for the Cosa Nostra.

Irina shares very little about her personal life. It's hard to tell if she's part of a mafia or a private contractor. I'm still trying to figure out her role with these friends.

We lounge, drifting in and out of casual conversation.

"Tell me, Dasha, how is Roman in the sack?" Francesca asks.

"I don't have anyone to compare him to, but he's been very generous."

"I heard you ran away from your wedding. That took some balls. There might be hope for you yet." Her smile conveys acceptance.

Hope of what, I wonder.

"I'm not one to get involved with the men my father is in bed with, and I knew I had to get out. The fear of Andrian outweighed everything."

"I agree. You did the right thing, Dasha." Irina sits up and pushes her sunglasses to the top of her head. "Andrian is a bad man. You did the right thing listening to your gut instinct. Those instincts are there to protect you. Never ignore them."

"You've had that feeling before?" I turn to face her, sitting cross-legged on the lounger.

"Absolutely, more times than I can count. Andrian is responsible for my mother's death. I want to look him in the eye and get justice for her."

"He killed your mother when she was undercover?"

"Yes. I've spent years waiting for the opportunity to get close to him. He sticks to his own, and they protect him. He rarely lets any outsider near him. It's kept him safe all these years. He's like that drug kingpin in the show *Ferry*, moving ecstasy and heroin through Europe like it's candy."

"I had no idea."

"We didn't realize you were indirectly connected to him. I was coming along on Roman's vacation as a friend. We've not seen each other in some time."

Alex and Roman are friends, and I've never seen anything but affection between them, like the siblings they are. "Roman's with Alex now, I presume?"

"Yes, I'm sure of it."

"He seemed preoccupied when I left. Is it about the upcoming meeting and exchange in Monaco?" I ask.

"Yes."

"And Francesca, you impress me as a person who kicks ass and takes names later. I assume you both bring something to the table?"

"We do." She smiles as she adjusts her lounger. "I'm along to guard you."

"Roman has guards," I point out.

"Mm. Well, how do I say this? He doesn't have any men who can do what I do." She snickers, and her full lips, perfectly colored a brilliant shade of red to match her nails, curl into a confident smile.

"You're a killer?"

"For being so young and naïve, you catch on quickly. I think there's hope for you yet, Dasha."

"This life, is it worth it if you have to look over your shoulder constantly? I know you both can take care of yourselves, but my only skill is running fast."

Francesca chuckles. "You can learn anything you put your mind to. In fact, let's head to the sauna, and after we've sweated out the alcohol, we'll change and take you to the gym. I'll show you some fight maneuvers and how to use the weight machines. Would you like that?"

"Anything I need to do to be prepared in case that pig comes for me again, consider me in."

My new friends laugh, and I hope they are laughing with me, not at me. I have so much to learn, but I need to start somewhere. I feel better knowing Francesca is so qualified. Roman has been working the entire time I've been in his possession.

"Does anyone know the plan for me?" I ask.

"You'll be fine." Francesca gently pats my leg. "Let's get massages and hit the jacuzzi and sauna."

I follow their lead. As soon as we're inside, I look back to see the deckhands scurrying around, picking up our towels and putting the loungers back in place.

I try the red-light sauna. I don't know how it works, but my body feels invigorated afterward. Irina is getting a massage, and Francesca and I sit in the jacuzzi. Francesca pours me a cup of cucumber water.

"Why cucumber?" I ask.

"It's a great antioxidant."

I drink from the cup she hands me. "How do you know all this?"

"I'm older, and I've had great mentors."

Mentors. Interesting.

"I wonder what the guys are doing," I murmur.

"Working. Enjoy the last leg of this trip, because until Andrian is taken out, your life is in danger," Francesca states without emotion.

I take it Roman was raised to live in this world as well. It comes with the territory—kill or be killed.

I finish drinking the water, and it's my turn to have a massage. The masseur leads me to a dimly lit room with soothing music and relaxing smells of aromatherapy oils. He instructs me to get undressed while he leaves. I toss my wet suit into the sink and quickly sit on the table with the sheet covering my nakedness.

He knocks, and I reply, "Come in."

"You can lay on your back for now," he says. "Have you had a massage before?"

"No."

"Fine. Do you hurt anywhere or have tight areas that I need to work on?"

"I'm good."

I lay back on the padded table, and he puts something under my knees to relieve the pressure on my lower back, arranging the sheet to cover my torso.

"Close your eyes and concentrate on your breathing. Inhale deeply, hold it, and exhale slowly. I will start with a light massage. If the pressure is too much, let me know."

"Fine."

He puts oil on his hands, then rubs them together. He touches my shoulders and runs his hands down my arms. I close my eyes. If I imagine it's Roman, I'll get turned on. I shift my thoughts, remembering watching the stars at night from our deck. The masseur moves to my legs. When he gets to my calves, he remarks that they're tight. It must be from walking up and down steps daily or the gym.

"I'll have you turn over in a minute so I can work on your back," he murmurs.

Suddenly, I hear a large bang and sit bolt upright in time to see the door hit the wall for the second time.

"What is going on it here?" Roman is standing in the doorway. His eyes narrow on me. He is pissed.

"What? We're all getting massages," I say in my defense as the masseur cowers in a corner with his hands clasped in front of him. His eyes are fixed on the floor, and he is shaking.

"No man touches you, Dasha. No one. Do I make myself clear?"

"It's not sexual, Roman. Are you going to dictate every moment of my life? I'm not doing anything wrong."

"I said no one touches you," he repeats, and from his scowl, I know he's not going to let this go.

"Fine. Have it your way." I clutch the sheet around me and hop off the table. Walking like a geisha in the sheet, I grab my wet swimsuit and storm past him.

"I am the only man who will touch you," he says, following on my heels.

"How did you know where I was?"

"I know everything that happens on this vessel and in your life. Get used to it."

"You think you can always tell me what to do?"

I wish I could run, but the sheet is wrapped around me like a mummy. When we get to our cabin, I head straight to the bathroom and toss my suit on the shower floor.

"My rules are meant to keep you safe." His voice is lower, but he hasn't calmed down. "Don't you understand? I love you. I need to know you are safe all the time."

"And what are you going to do after Andrian is gone? Make up some other excuse to keep me locked up?"

"It's for your protection."

Wait. *He said he loved me.*

"Well, when this ordeal is over, there will be some modifications to your rules. I'll wear a watch so you'll know where I am, but I won't have you barging into my personal space and embarrassing me like that again. That poor man was terrified."

"I'll apologize to him."

Satisfied, I nod and drop the sheet. I need to find something suitable to wear to the gym.

He grabs my wrists, pulls me close, and crushes his lips to mine.

"I was so jealous seeing his hands on you."

"I appreciate your protection, but he's harmless."

"That's not the point. You are mine, and I will see to all your needs."

His cock is hard against my naked flesh.

"I'm meeting the girls at the gym."

He nuzzles my neck before he releases me. "Fine. I have to go, anyway."

He turns abruptly and is gone.

I slump against the closest wall, shaking. Roman can be intense. I breathe and pull myself together because I have to meet the girls. Everyone here is tougher than me, and that needs to end.

I find workout clothes in my closet and tug on socks and sneakers. I see a crew member and ask her the location of the gym, and she leads me to it. I open the glass door and step inside. Techno music is blaring.

Francesca punches a long bag suspended in the air, then spins and kicks it with her foot, sending the bag flying. Holy shit. If that were a person, they'd have cracked ribs or worse.

Irina sits on a bench, working her back muscles by pulling on a bar with a lot of weight attached. She smiles when she notices me. "I see you survived Roman's possessive fit."

"Yeah. I didn't know he literally meant no man touches me."

"He's hard-core with his rules, for sure. Most of them are." Francesca winks. "Come over here. I'll show you some warmups on the mats."

After a quick warmup, Francesca demonstrates some of her favorite moves. The first one surprises me when she drops to the mat and sweeps my legs out from under me. I'm on my back, staring at the ceiling, wondering what just happened.

"Plant your feet, be aware of your surroundings."

I do as she instructs and dive out of the way the next time she comes toward me.

"Good. Let's try yoga moves to loosen your muscles before I teach you how to jab the bag."

"That bag?" I warily eye the equipment, which reminds me of a side of beef.

"Sure, you'll be fine."

Irina joins us on the mat, and I follow their lead as I stretch my back and legs. After twenty minutes of stretching, we move to the bag, and she puts boxing gloves on my hands, the Velcro making a zippy noise as she adjusts it.

"These are huge," I comment.

"You'll get used to it. Come." She puts her hands on my hips and positions my feet before she shows me what to do. We start with a simple jab. "One, two," she says each time I hit the bag.

I like the workout. We spend over an hour at the gym, and for the first time in days, I'm not missing Katsia.

We head back to our rooms to shower and change before meeting for a late lunch of finger sandwiches and iced tea on the main deck.

"You did very well today, Dasha. You should be proud," Francesca says.

"Thanks. I didn't do much." I bite into a cucumber sandwich and wonder how this is considered food.

"We'll do more tomorrow before we reach France. You never know when you'll need to defend yourself."

"Spend enough time with Roman, and you'll need it eventually," Irina says, chuckling.

Irina is skilled at martial arts as well, and I marvel at the fact that I'm sitting with not one, but two women with lethal hands. We all wear many faces. They look normal, but their eyes tell me they have lived more than most. I'm sure they've both been through their share of rough times, yet they are independent and fit in well with the criminal elements surrounding them. I would have thought they were powerful CEOs if I didn't know any better.

"How do you two live this life and the one I don't see?" My eyes ping between the two of them.

"I grew up this way, so it came naturally. I made my place in my father's life." Francesca refills her tea glass and nibbles on a carrot stick.

Irina nods and says, "When I lost my mother, I took that pain to the streets. I learned there were ways to get even when laws are flawed."

"Both of you are so determined, so strong and worldly. I'd love for some of that to rub off on me." I hungrily stab at my Cobb salad with my fork and try not to eat too quickly. The workout has made me hungry.

"Trust me, it will happen if you stick around long enough," Francesca says.

Roman and Alex show up and polish off the rest of the sandwiches. They must be finished with their war games because now they want to watch football. Alex is naming teams and players I've never heard of, so he must be a super fan. Personally, I couldn't care less.

After working out, I'm tired and sore and want to curl up on the couch.

Roman sits beside me. His eyes fixate on the large-screen TV and the game. He talks about the players, but he may as well be speaking a foreign language. When their team scores, he and Alex jump to their feet, shouting and slapping each other on the back.

This is our last night at sea. When the chief steward offers to pour me a glass of wine, I accept. We'll be confronting the man I ran away from in Belarus sooner than I had hoped, and the wine will help me to forget.

# CHAPTER 29

## DASHA

Tonight is formal night on the yacht, and we're all dressing up, so I select a shiny black metallic gown with a deep V in the back and a revealing slit up the side to show off my tanned legs. I'm wearing the heels with the red bottoms for the first time. I have no idea how Roman filled the closet with designer shoes and clothes so quickly, but I'm glad he was so thoughtful.

As we make our way to the main deck, Roman's hand rests comfortably on the small of my back. I enjoy having him beside me and focus on putting one foot in front of another without twisting an ankle.

The opulence takes my breath away when we enter the formal dining room. The table appears to be made of green and blue glass that reminds me of quartz and is big enough to seat sixteen people comfortably. Above the table hangs a chandelier fashioned of hand-blown glass. Sinatra crooner music plays softly in the background.

Francesca breezes in wearing a free-flowing caftan dress. The vibrant red and blue colors make her tanned skin glow. She's wearing cute sandals that look a lot more comfortable than my sky-high heels. Gold hoop earrings lined with diamonds and sapphires hang from her ears. Movie stars borrow expensive jewelry for the red carpet, but I don't think Francesca has to borrow anything.

"I love your dress," I tell her.

"Oh, thank you, Dasha. I've been dying to wear this again. I wore it more than a year ago to the opening of an art gallery."

"That's right. I remember having too much free wine at that party," Irina says, walking in behind her with a big smile.

Irina's hair is straightened to perfection, framing her heart-shaped face. The knee-length fringe dress and the long strands of pearls she's wearing remind me of a Gatsby-era flapper girl, and the creamy color complements her sun-kissed complexion.

I listen as Irina tells us about her latest trip to Asia. She says the hotels in Japan compete for business by hiring the best chefs for their restaurants, and the food we're getting on the yacht is just as good as anything she's eaten in a Michelin-star restaurant.

"Oh, and everything in Japan is expensive," she adds, rattling off a list of countries she's visited. After hearing about her experiences with some of the toilets in these places, I'll be crossing them off my bucket list.

Alex shows up wearing a black suit like Roman's. Neither man is wearing a tie, and both have the top buttons of their dress shirts open. And why not? It's just us. Call it casual formal.

Francesca stops and stares at the chandelier. "Magnificent," she says.

"It was made in Turkey. Each tube of glass was hand-blown. My mother has quite a knack for finding unique items from around the world to use in her decorating." Roman picks up a remote and points it at the chandelier. "Tonight, we dine by candlelight."

"That's amazing," I gasp as the lighting dims.

"Yeah, we can't have open flames on a ship. Too risky. The last thing you want is a fire at sea."

He puts the remote away as a crew member approaches with a tray of cocktails. Roman picks up two and hands me one.

"What's this?" I ask cautiously, not wanting to overindulge again.

"A vodka martini made with pears and elderflower liquor," Alex says. "You'll love it."

To demonstrate, he finishes his in one gulp.

I'm not surprised. Vodka is like mother's milk to these guys. I take a sip of the pale green drink. It's not too sweet. In fact, it might be my favorite drink to date.

"I don't know how I'm going to eat again. I say, patting my stomach.

I've tried so many new and incredible seafood dishes this week. How am I ever going back to eating simpler fare?

"I know. The diet starts as soon as I step off this boat. But I must say, the past few days have been worth the extra kilos," Irina says. "It's the vacation I needed."

"Thanks for including me," Francesca pipes up. "I could do this every day."

"I'm glad you ladies had a nice time. That's the point, isn't it? Enjoy today, for we never know what tomorrow will bring," Alex says.

Roman approaches the table first and pulls a chair out for me. I smooth my dress behind my buttocks and try to look elegant as I sit. He takes his place at the head of the table to my left, and Alex sits beside me. Irina and Francesca seat themselves across from me.

The place settings are exquisite. Each plate has the initials RV monogrammed in gold. The number of different utensils is mind-boggling. I'll need to watch the others to see what to use with each course.

Now that I've had a taste of the good life, why would I ever flee? I don't want to go home, and life alone would not be easy. What would I do for a living? How would I pay for basic necessities like rent, food, and utilities? That's a struggle for most couples, and I'm one person. A passport is my ticket to a fresh start, but where would I go, and how would I go about starting over in a new country?

Roman still has not mentioned anything about seeing me on camera snooping in his closet. How many other cameras are hidden, and how much is recorded?

When our martini glasses are empty, they are replaced by wine glasses. The chief steward opens a chilled bottle of white wine and pours some into each glass as she explains how it will pair well with the seafood.

The first course is brought out, and a bowl of black shells is placed in front of each of us.

"Mussels in lemon butter sauce," Roman states for my benefit after seeing the befuddled look on my face.

I place the gold-colored cloth napkin in my lap and watch Irina extract the mussel from the shell. I pick up the same tiny fork she's using and do the same. It's delicious. The buttery sauce is so good, I could lick the bowl.

Our empty plates are whisked away, and wine glasses are topped off without asking.

"So, what's new, Roman?" Francesca asks, leaning back in her chair.

"I spoke to Andrian, and he bragged about having my father killed. Now my brothers are taking precautions to protect the rest of the family."

"Don't worry, we'll get him," Irina states with confidence as she lifts a wine glass to her lips. "Make no mistake about it. I've waited years for this." She sips and puts the glass down.

Roman leans back and drapes his arm over the back of his chair. "I never dreamed it would come to this. However, it's a stroke of luck we happened upon him and his plan to systematically pick off each member of my family."

"He's a scourge that needs to be eliminated from the planet," Francesca says, reaching for her water glass.

I get the feeling that Andrian irks her. More importantly, she's supporting Irina. I would, too. Katsia is my ride-or-die, and I'd have her back. In fact, I need to ask Roman if I can call her again. There might be an update.

Andrian deserves to die. He's profited from selling innocent women and children. There is no way I would ever let him touch me. Roman said that whoever touches me, dies. Well, this is one man *I* want to burn.

The next course is a salad made of arugula, goat cheese, and pistachios with a balsamic vinaigrette.

I listen to Irina and Francesca converse in Italian and wish I knew what they were saying. It's a pretty language. They must not be spilling secrets because the crew can hear them, and some of them speak Italian.

I glance at Roman. He's pensive, which doesn't surprise me. Talking about Andrian is ruining my appetite.

Roman looks into my eyes. "Let's save the unsavory aspects of our enemy until after dinner," he says, as if reading my mind.

"Great idea," Alex says. "I hate to think of that cocksucker while we have all these beautiful women and delicious food around us." He lifts his glass. "A toast! May we be brave, strong, and conquer all."

We all lift our wine glasses and tap each other's stemware. "To our health," we say unanimously.

"I, for one, want to thank you, Roman, for this trip." Francesca raises her glass in another toast. "I've had fun for the first time in a long time, and I'm going to miss you all."

"I don't know if you'll have time to miss us." Irina gives Roman an inquisitive look that he ignores. "We tend to find a way to see each other." She looks at me. "When we get to Monaco, our work will be just beginning. We're making the world safer."

Her smile takes some of the edge off her words.

Roman clears his throat and drinks water like he's swallowing words he can't express. What is his deal tonight? He seems jumpy. No way is he afraid of Andrian. Roman is realistic, yes. But fearful? I don't think so. What else could be bothering him?

Following Francesca's lead, I lift the smaller of the two forks and pierce the finely chopped arugula. Something soft touches my leg. I flinch and look around the table to see if anyone noticed.

My eyes land on Roman. His hand is on my leg. A warm sensation builds between my thighs as he caresses me, inching his hand toward my panties.

I clamp my knees together, and Roman leans forward, fixing his gaze on me as he forces his hand between my legs. I can't deny him. His fingers dip into my wetness. I stifle a moan and bite my lip, hoping no one notices. Damn him for putting me in this position.

"When will we be in Monaco?" I ask.

Roman quickly pulls his hand away as if I touched him with a hot poker.

I can't have him fingering me under the table in the middle of dinner. What's next, sweep everything off the table so he can fuck me on the tabletop? Now that I picture it, it is pretty hot. But not tonight.

"In the morning," he says. "Actually, we'll go ashore while it's still dark. *Severnoye Siyaniye* will set sail after we leave. I don't want anyone to know what ship we arrived on."

"Great idea. Do we know if the port will be busy? It's easier to get lost in the crowd," Alex comments.

"I'm sure there will be cruise ships this time of year. You know Monaco." Roman rolls his eyes and shakes his head. His thick dark hair glistens under the light of the chandelier.

I didn't believe it was possible for him to look sexier, but the tan makes his teeth look whiter and his eyes bluer, a color that reminds me of the turquoise sky off the coast of Italy on a sunny day. He leans back in his chair, watching me as the crew clears our salad plates. Why, I have no clue.

What does he intend to do with me once we are in Monaco? Will I be held in a room with no windows? Will I be a prisoner or his lover?

I sip from my water glass, giving him no emotional response. It's better left in the bedroom. There, I can let my walls down. I'm a fool to think I mean anything to a man who dates models.

Five servers parade in with plates and set the main course in front of us. The chef describes the dish as a filet mignon with lobster smothered in hollandaise sauce with a side of asparagus.

Everyone claps, and I join in to show the chef my appreciation.

"Ah yes, Steak Oscar, one of my favorites," Alex announces, cutting into the meat. "Medium rare." His voice is jubilant. "Perfectly cooked."

I've never eaten filet mignon. I lift my utensils and cut into the meat, finding little resistance. I'll save the lobster for later. My first bite of the beef melts in my mouth, as soft as butter and just as rich. I lift the cloth napkin to my mouth and stifle a moan as I blot my lips.

Roman leans in close. "I see you're a fan of the meat," he whispers in my ear. "Save some of that moaning for tonight."

His voice drips with anticipation. Dropping my napkin, I look at him, and his eyes flash, getting that stormy look I've seen before.

"The asparagus is just the way I like it, not too hard and not too soft," I reply softly.

"What are you two carrying on about?" Alex huffs.

"Dessert," I lie.

"Instead of dessert, let's have them bring us more of those martinis we had before dinner," Irina suggests.

"Hear, hear. Amazing crew and vessel you have, Roman," Francesca says.

Roman stands and lifts his wine glass. "Thank you, Irina. And thank you to everyone here tonight. I consider you to be my closest friends." He nods to Francesca. "We've only met, but I'm happy you're with us. Your reputation precedes you."

Francesca inclines her head cordially. "No problem." She looks to Irina, and they nod in solidarity. They have the kind of sisterhood I have with Katsia, only Katsia isn't able to follow me into the fray.

These two women look like they were raised in it, gave it hell, and came out stronger than ever.

I hope I come out of this stronger, too. I've made progress in asserting myself, but I have a long way to go if I ever want to hold my own with this crowd.

# CHAPTER 30

## ROMAN

After dinner, I lead everyone to the entertainment room and lower the large viewing screen mounted above the fireplace with the press of a button on a remote. I stream the latest *Mission Impossible* movie using Wi-Fi and satellite.

"I can't get over the surround sound," Dasha comments. "It's better than the movie theaters in Minsk." She adds, "Not that I ever got to go there much."

A steward brings caramel popcorn and sodas while we push buttons to make the theater chairs recline. I show the girls how to turn on the heat and massage. I can't tell what they like more, the massaging chairs or the movie. By midnight, we all head to our cabins. I have someone I want to fuck until dawn.

By the time we make it to our master suite, my lips are on hers. I need a release after toying with my hand on her leg during the movie. She kisses me back and nips at my lower lip.

I grab her wrist and twirl her around like a dance move. As I pull her against my naked chest, her tits press against me. I grab one voluptuous boob and squeeze it.

"You drive me crazy," I murmur in her ear.

"Mm," she moans, grabbing my shoulders. I play with her nipple, rolling it between my thumb and first finger until it's a hard nub.

She's putty in my hands as her pelvis grinds against my solid thigh. I can tell she wants me. I put my lips on her nipple, playing with it as I slip my hand between her legs.

"You're wet for me. Tell me what you want, my little dove."

"Mm," she murmurs, her lips moving against my chest as her hand rubs my nipple.

I slip two fingers inside her and finger fuck her, gently stroking her clit.

She moves her hips, and my fingers move in deeper. "Oh," she gasps when I find her G-spot.

I don't want her to come this soon, so I pull my fingers out and toss her on the bed. I grab a condom from the drawer and a piece of black fabric that I throw on the bed. I rip the foil with my teeth and roll it over my hard cock.

I pull her by her ankles until her ass is on the edge of the bed.

"Turn over," I command.

She complies. She trusts me.

"I'm fucking you hard."

I slam my cock into her wetness and close my eyes, lost in the euphoria that claims me, my body, and my soul. I have to have her. I think about her night and day. I want to fill her with my cum.

I thrust into her again, and the deep breath she takes tells me I've hit my mark. I want more, so I take more. I slam into her harder, holding her hips firmly, fucking her harder as she clutches the bedcovers. My balls slap against her, and her wetness seeps and baths them.

I'm so fucking turned on that I want to explode, but I wait. I bend over her, grab a tit with one hand, and massage her clit with the other as I pump into her.

She's on the brink of coming. I can feel it, and with one final thrust, we explode together. I fill the condom, and after my release, I'm still stiff and give her another thrust. She comes again, her body quivering under me.

I clutch her to me, holding her chest and her pussy as my arms are still wrapped around her. My orgasm is intense and satisfying. My calves are fatigued. I pumped her pussy so hard I was standing on my toes, and now they ache.

Fuck me.

*What am I going to do?* I know she longs for her freedom. I've done my best to give it to her and keep her safe. But will it be enough for her to stay?

I pull out of her and dispose of the condom. I return, and she waits for me in the bed. I crawl in beside her, and she curls into me, her head on my chest.

We gaze through the skylight above us. Clouds pass over the moon. Neither of us says a word. What can I say?

I run my fingers through her silken hair. When my fingers brush her shoulder, I'm hard again.

Fuck.

I lean my head toward her neck and give her a gruff growl before I flip her on her back.

"Whoa," she gasps in surprise.

"I have to have you again."

"You…"

I cover her mouth with mine, muffling her words. My fingers brush against the black lace fabric on the bed.

"I'm tying your hands." I straddle her naked body as she lies splayed beneath me.

She gives me her wrists, and I wrap them, then pull her hands over her head and tie her to a metal loop secured behind the bed and out of sight.

I kiss her body, licking her neck and nipping her nipples. I pause, watching her respond to me. She squirms and draws her knees together protectively. I kneel, raking my hands over her boobs and her taut abdomen. I gently graze her flesh with my fingertips and run them over her curvy hips.

I attempt to pull her legs apart, and she fights me, jamming them together and using her legs muscles to fend off my advances.

I enjoy a challenge and let her have a brief respite before I kiss her belly and force my fingers between her legs. I dip into her wetness. Her moans fuel my fire.

I lower my head between her legs and put my hands on her knees, holding them wide. I lick her pussy, and she twists, moaning with every lick. The pleasure I feel at her sounds of delight is almost painful. I suckle her and bring her to the brink of orgasm, knowing neither of us will ever be satiated until I sink my cock into her.

I grab another condom and sheath myself, pushing the enormous tip of my cock into her. She arches her back and cries out.

"What do you want?" I ask.

She raises her hips for more but says nothing.

"I need to hear you say it."

"Mm," she murmurs.

"Dasha." My voice cuts through the cool air. "Tell me you want me to fuck you."

"No." She bites her lower lip and twists her waist, clamping her knees together.

I pull out and stand.

She immediately pleads. "Yesss."

That's all I needed to hear.

I quickly untie her wrists and flip her onto her knees. My cock nudges her opening. I run the head inside her lips, dipping in to tease her, and pulling out. I lift her at her waist until her ass is in the air and my palm is on her back, holding her in place. I give her buttocks a resounding slap and am rewarded when she gasps.

Why is she being so stubborn?

Her hands clench the rumpled blanket under her, and her back arches. She pushes her ass against my cock.

"Fuck me. Please, fuck me, Roman," she pleads.

I slam into her so hard that she slides on the bed. My balls are tight. Her muscles constrict around my cock, and when I hear her scream, I come so hard I'm winded.

My arms are fatigued. I don't know if I can move. I hold my right leg and physically move it to get out of my position.

Fuck me.

I roll onto my back, gasping for air.

I glance at Dasha. She's lying on her stomach, totally spent.

"I didn't know I could be this exhausted. Hell, I'm young," she sighs.

"I know. Me, either." I kiss her forehead as she moves to the pillow. I can tell she's on her side, and I feel her eyes on my face. I can't look at her, I'm afraid for her to see me in this emotional state. It's new to me.

"I love you, Dasha. Get some sleep. Morning will be here soon."

I drift off to sleep. I'm in a dream, and my phone is ringing. I thought it would stop, but it continues. It's so annoying that I wake up to make it go away.

What the hell is it? I hear it again and glance at the nightstand. My phone is lit. Fuck, it's my phone that's ringing. Lightning cracks overhead. What the fuck is going on?

"Hello?"

"Roman, be careful," Nikolay says. "Our warehouse outside London is on fire. I'm moving Anya to the safe house. I've alerted Dmitry. Be on guard. Andrian is an animal."

"Got it. Stay safe."

"What's the matter?" Dasha asks, her eyes groggy from sleep.

"Trouble in London. Everyone is fine, but Andrian is stirring shit up."

She sits up. "What does that mean?"

"It means I'm waking everyone for a meeting. I have a plan."

"What can I do?"

"Join us. You have a stake in this as well."

As lightning snaps and cracks overhead, I roll out of bed and dress in lounging clothes. Flashes of white light fill the room, and Dasha's eyes grow wide with fright. Thunder booms and echoes around us.

I have men on the ground, and we're working hard to even the final playing field for the showdown. I have to figure out a way to end Andrian. I never want to see the look of fear in her eyes again.

# CHAPTER 31

## DASHA

*E*veryone gathers in the conference room with three large windows. The wooden floor is covered with an ornate blue and white rug. There is a sofa that seats four comfortably. A square skylight is in the center of the ceiling. The only wall in the room is a long bookcase with four sections. Each section has three wooden shelves. Under the shelves is storage. A round railing, standing four inches above the shelf, keeps the books from tumbling out when the sea is rough. Sometimes, I forget I'm on a boat.

A crew member quietly enters the room carrying a tray laden with a large white carafe, numerous cups, tea bags, and an assortment of condiments for the coffee and tea. He sets the tray down and leaves quietly.

Francesca is wearing a designer sweatsuit of thin, light blue fabric. Matching ballet-type shoes cover her feet. Her hair is piled high, and she has a chic scarf woven through it.

Irina stands at the doorway, pausing to yawn. Her white knit tank top shows off her perfectly symmetrical breasts and the shirt

278

covers the top of her drawstring lounging knit pants. The matching knit sweater extends to her knees. She screams *sexy* and *Braun* at the same time. She's the ultimate *femme fatal,*

Alex has on jogging pants, a white wife beater, and a jacket. It's as if he's going out on a run in a city. He's even wearing sneakers.

"What the fuck is up?" His eyes dart around, reading the room.

I'm sitting on the overstuffed sofa. I pull my feet, warmed by socks, under me. I found a knit lounging outfit with long drawstring pants suitable to wear to the meeting. I pull the matching three-quarter-length sweater over my chest and fold my arms.

Irina and Francesca sit beside me on the sofa.

"All right." Roman claps his hands, then turns to face us. "Bad news: one of our warehouses in London is on fire. Good news: everyone is fine. Aside from damages and an insurance claim, we'll rebuild. We assume Andrian's men are responsible."

"Fuck, yeah," Alex says. "Who the fuck else is going to be gallivanting around at night after he knows you have Dasha? It's another brick in his wall, is what it is."

"Right, makes sense. Hit you here and there to keep you off balance and wondering where he will strike next," Francesca says.

"Yeah, it's what I would do, too," Irina says. She's sitting on the edge of the sofa cushion, her hands clasped between her legs. "He wants to get in your head. He's playing offense."

"Fuck that." Roman pours himself a cup of coffee. He straightens, his shoulders tight. "I've been thinking about this and talking to Alex, and…" He stops as another phone goes off.

Alex pulls the phone out of his jacket pocket. "Mm. Yes, Yes.," he answers. He hangs up. "That was Pavel. Andrian's posse left town in four huge SUVs."

"How many men are in those vehicles? Did Pavel say?" Roman asks.

"He thinks twelve. That would be about right, four to a vehicle plus weapons."

"I'm sure he's carrying a small army, and we'll be prepared for them in Monaco."

"Wait, what time is it?" I ask.

"It's two-thirty. Why?" Roman asks.

"I can call Katsia in the morning. Maybe my brother will have more information for us."

"Sounds good."

I shudder. How can my brothers live with themselves, knowing they are being used to kill others indiscriminately?

Roman is the leader of this mission, and he's sure to have doubts about my brother's loyalties. I would as well, but I've known Albert all my life. This past year, the business with our father and Andrian seems to have hit an extreme. Papa isn't a low-level criminal. He's in league with Andrian, and Andrian is at the top. With that comes more money and deadly decisions.

Albert could be setting us up. But what if he's not? He could be our mole on the inside. In the end, we'll both have a new name and life. I believe he confided in Katsia to get out. I'm hoping we'll be able to help each other. My fate rests on the Volkovs killing Andrian. If Andrian lives, Albert and I will die, one way or another. I shudder at the thought.

Roman moves to the conference table. A square in the middle of the table lights up. Curiosity draws us in. There is a screen on the glass surface. It looks like a computer-generated map.

He puts one hand on the table, and with his other, he points to a building. I stand with the others at the conference table. My legs are shaking. The bad men are on their way. A dark cloud is approaching. Dangerous men will be at our doorstep soon.

Fuckity fuck.

I try to suppress the anxiety in my chest, but the tightness isn't going away. I look at Roman. He's calm and in control, a leader. I trust him. He has as much riding on this as I do, if not more.

"This is an old warehouse near the sea," he says. "It's abandoned, and we have the advantage because hills surround it. If Dasha's brother can tell us how many men are in the group, and his information matches Pavel's, we can assume the intel is reliable. And if that's the case, we'll know when we have all of Andrian's men. We'll screen them for weapons at the warehouse entrance. I assume he'll want to pick us off there, take Dasha, and escape. I also assume they will have men posted in the area. If we take out one of their point men and get his coms, we can find the others before they know they are compromised."

"That's brilliant," Francesca purrs as she shifts in her chair. She places an elbow on the table, using her palm to prop her chin up. "It's so John Wick."

"We're trained killers, we can take them. We need to be smart about it. Dasha, you'll be at my house with Francesca. I'll have my regular men on the outside, waiting for them. I have to assume that Saturday, Andrian's men will have narrowed down the numerous homes I own. They will, in all probability, have kicked in some doors."

"We'll meet at dusk," Alex says, "and try to locate his men. As darkness falls, we'll be able to use the infrared scopes on our weapons. We'll take the men outside. The only question is, how do we kill Andrian and whoever is with him once they have you inside the building?"

There is silence in the room. I hear the air circulating in the vent above the table, but it's the thought of putting Andrian down like a rabid dog that is chilling.

"We'll think about it," Irina says. "We have time. We need to stake out the area as soon as we can."

"Yes," Roman concedes.

"What about me?" I ask. "Andrian wants me. Don't I have to be there?"

"That's where Irina comes in. She's going to dress as you. You are not to tell a soul. She's your body double."

Irina turns to me. "Don't worry, I'm great at disguise. I will make a mask of your face, use a wig and makeup. That will get him in the door and to the table. By the time he realizes I'm not you, it won't matter. He won't know until it's too late."

"What? I can't let you do that." I turn to her, "You're my friend. He's my enemy. I can't let you do that," I repeat.

This is not what I wanted. I don't want others to put themselves in danger for me. I ran away. I have to face the consequences.

"He's my enemy more than he is yours, Dasha. Don't take that away from me." She stares me down, and I realize she's not going to change her mind. None of them are. It appears the others have been talking about this for days.

I sit quietly, my hands clasped on the table. I lower them to my lap. My palms are damp. I'm sweating with fear.

"Also, we need to make sure Dasha's brothers survive," Roman says. "We don't know if one of them will help us or not." He flicks the screen. "These are pictures of Dasha's father, Ratmim, and her brothers, Vlad and Albert. We suspect Albert might be trying to help our cause, but there's no definite way to know. I assume Vlad is being groomed to be a group leader and will move up the ranks over Ratmim in a few years when he's older. We will hold the boys, if possible, and question them. Our best bet is to take Andrian out quickly. We'll save more than we've lost in the long run, so I'm fine with that."

"If we take out the men aimed at you and Dasha, Alex should just take out Ratmim before he enters the warehouse," Francesca says. "It will be clean, and you will be in less danger that way."

She moves her arm off the table and uses it to balance herself as she stands. The early morning has drained us all.

"I want to be the one who kills him," Roman says.

"Well, I don't know how that will occur," she states matter-of-factly.

"I don't, either. We have good men to help us spot the enemies we expect to be around the area, but when Ratmim notices his men didn't take you two out, the jig will be up," Alex says.

"We're not sure that is his plan," Roman replies. "This is how I would do it." He shrugs and looks at me. "Dasha, we'll get in touch with Katsia and Albert and find out if he knows what they are planning."

I nod. "It's worth a try. I don't know how much they tell him. Vlad is higher up. He's older."

"Right, well, we have a strategy with lots of moving pieces. I'm sure these will likely change in the next forty-eight hours."

"We'll hide in the hills," Alex says. "Using the rifles will keep the noise level low. I will work with our men to take out the guards on the perimeter. Roman and Irina, posing as Dasha, will be at the door."

"She'll pretend to be my prisoner, so I'll hold her like one," Roman interjects.

"Where will I be?" I timidly ask.

"My house it's guarded, and no information on it comes back to my name specifically," Roman says. "I'll have men there. Things can change if my brothers arrive. We're not sure who will get here in time right now."

I understand the situation, but I don't like the idea of being alone with guards. I'd feel better if one of the four people in this room were with me, but I know the objective is to kill Andrian. With him gone, it will save my family and all the Volkovs. If they don't make it out alive, I'll die knowing it's a win for society as long as Andrian is wiped off the planet.

"And we're still attending the half-mask gala in Monte Carlo afterward?" Irina asks for confirmation.

"Yes. Dasha, you'll be dressed. I'll pick you up, and my tux will be with you at the house. We'll arrive at the house, change, and use two vehicles to deliver us to the gala. The three of you will be together." Roman nods to Irina and Francesca. "We need to buy our formalwear later today. After we do that and check out the warehouse, we'll be in lockdown so we don't run into any of Andrian's men. Getting from the scene to my house takes ten minutes. The gala is a perfect cover and takes five minutes by car."

"When the police get to the warehouse, it will look like a drug deal gone bad." Irina's smile is so bright, it hurts my eyes.

"We'll be transported by helicopter to the airport in an hour. My men will pick us up, and after we are settled in the house, we'll do our recon. We'll scope out the warehouse and lie low. It would be better if my brothers were here, but we can do it either way." Roman flips a switch, and the table goes dark.

"I think we have a plan. Let's get ready to be picked up," Alex says.

And with that, the meeting is adjourned.

My stomach feels tight. Nerves, I'm sure.

"Do we need to pack?" I ask Roman when we return to our room.

I notice the rain has stopped because there are only pools of static water on the skylight over the bed. The rain has moved out to sea.

"No, you'll have everything you need."

"Okay," I reply. Who am I to question him? He might be the youngest brother, but I'm impressed with his plan. There are wrinkles for sure. However, he's a good leader.

It doesn't sound like his brothers will be able to make it in time to help us with the uncertainty of the situation.

I wear a Lycra outfit to travel in and new black sneakers. I find the big purse in my closet and zip my old sneakers inside. They are all that's left that was mine, and I like the feeling of owning something.

It's still dark, but we're all on deck before dawn. As instructed, I crawl into the helicopter, and Roman gets on last, taking the seat beside me.

We wear ear protection, and within fifteen minutes, we're on land, and two SUVS pull up. Men in suits wearing earpieces speak, telling me when to move as they escort me into a waiting vehicle.

Now I'm beginning to feel like a hostage.

# CHAPTER 31

## ROMAN

*I* wonder if my brothers will come, even though I told them I'm handling the situation. It's not safe for them to travel, but Dad's death has uncovered a personal vendetta that affects us all.

Part of me hopes they can't get here in time. Dmitry is going to be a father, and the child will need him. It's a long flight from New York City, and I don't want to be responsible for him or Nikolay should the meeting not go according to plan.

The fact is, I went to Belarus. I found our father's nemesis, and I will end him. That's all there is to it. I have friends who are equipped to help me.

My vehicles follow the winding, tree-lined roads. At times, I catch a glimpse of the picturesque view of the Mediterranean on my left. I'm anxious to get home and get Dasha settled.

"Where do you live?" Dasha asks.

"You'll see," I reply. I wanted to surprise her, take the boat in from the yacht and act like I was trespassing on someone else's property, but today is not a day for practical jokes or romantic overtures.

The country of Monaco is only for the wealthy. We roll down the long driveway and come upon a huge house the color of burnt sienna. Cream shutters adorn the windows. Here, everything is a mixture of French and Mediterranean styles. The lawn is manicured, and a cottage sits on the back of the property for the housekeeper, Sofia, and her husband, who oversees house repairs and landscaping.

Within twenty minutes, we pull up to the gate. It opens, and I hear the distinct chatter of muffled voices as the men communicate, treating our arrival like a presidential detail.

My mansion overlooks the sea. The vehicle proceeds to the house and stops. Two guards are waiting and step forward to open our doors. Dasha gets out on her side, and I exit on mine. The guards survey the property and speak into their coms. They are dressed in black suits, and one of them nods to me that the coast is clear. I begin to walk, and Dasha follows. It's a familiar protocol, these precautions, though this is slightly different. We've just never had to live our life as if we were under the surveillance of a madman.

We join Alex, Irina, and Francesca, who follow us through the back door of the house.

"Where are we?" Dasha asks, scanning the estate.

"Home."

"Right. You're a billionaire. Why not have a home on the French Riviera suitable for a king?"

I decide to overlook her sarcastic remark for now. We go through the kitchen, where the staff is busily cooking breakfast meats and omelets. Coffee permeates the air. The espresso machine groans.

Ah, home. I love the water, but this is my true home. Russia is my motherland, and I know I'll live there most of the time, but vacations make what I do bearable. I don't kill women or children, and we don't traffic them, either. I hope the codes we live by will never be tested.

Sofia takes a break from overseeing the kitchen staff, facing me as I walk by. I give her a nod, and she nods back before returning to work. We have an understanding that requires little conversation. She's the best cook. She runs the house efficiently and anticipates what I need. I don't give her grief and pay her well.

The commotion of the kitchen is music to my ears. I am pulled out of my thoughts by a familiar voice yelling my name, and I rush into the formal living room.

"Brother," I exclaim, grabbing him in a hug. "I thought you were in a safe house."

"I'm the don, and no one fucks with me." Nikolay slaps me on the back. "I want to take Andrian out." He observes me for a minute. "You look well," he says finally.

"I am."

He looks to my left. "You must be Dasha." He extends his hand to her, and Dasha nervously accepts it. They shake. "I hear you've been at the center of all the excitement."

"It's not how I would have liked for us to meet," she replies with hooded eyes. "I'm sorry about your father."

"Thank you. However, we'll make it right," Nikolay replies confidently.

"Nikolay!" Alex's boisterous voice can't be missed as he enters the room.

"Alex, nice to see you." Nikolay greets him with a hearty slap on his back, and Alex engulfs him with his large arms to fuck with him. We share a warm chuckle. We're like a pop band getting reacquainted after a break.

"These are our friends, Irina and Francesca." I introduce the women, who are casually dressed in a jumper and capri pants with a matching tank, respectively.

Nikolay murmurs a greeting. "Thank you for coming. How is your husband, Francesca?"

"Great, he's hanging out with his brothers. Dante conveniently arranged for a guys' weekend in Greece, so here I am." She smiles and shrugs as if she doesn't mind putting her life on the line.

Her reputation precedes her. She was diabolical enough to take out her own brothers when they aligned with traffickers, so it's not inconceivable that she's here to help us get rid of one more.

"Lucky guys," Irina says, extending a hand to Nikolay.

"Thank you for joining us, Irina. Roman has mentioned you over the years."

"Nothing but clean stories, I hope," she teases.

"Absolutely," my brother replies with a wink.

"Any word from Dmitry?" I ask Nikolay.

"I'm not sure. He is trying to get out of New York and traveling under an alias." Nikolay shrugs. "Your guess is as good as mine."

I nod. It's to be expected in times of war. The playing field is treacherous, and I'm not used to him being so far away.

"It's probably time for me to call Katsia," Dasha murmurs.

"Oh, right," I say. "Let me show you to our room, and we'll call her."

As Nikolay converses with Alex, I excuse myself, and the women wander to the backyard overlooking the sea to take in the view.

I lead Dasha to the belly of the house. "This is similar to but much smaller than my brother's house in London, which has nine bedrooms and ten bathrooms. I gave up a larger house because it didn't have the view," I tell her.

We take the circular floating staircase with wooden steps, and Dasha slides her hand along the metal railing as we climb to the second floor.

The house has many windows and a more modern floor plan with more open spaces than other houses. The furniture is modern, Scandinavian in design. The sleek curves of the sofas blend in with the Persian area rugs and chrome-framed coffee tables with glass tops. Simple but elegant furniture provides continuity throughout the house. The walls are painted light gray, providing a backdrop to highlight the numerous and colorful pieces of art that adorn the walls.

"I didn't know you liked art," she says. "I noticed some on the yacht. Are you a collector?"

"Somewhat. Some come as payments for things. Others, I buy."

I lead Dasha to my room overlooking an infinity pool in the backyard and beyond that, the sea. Along the coastline, colorful houses punctuate the fact that I'm no longer in Italy. My room has an oversized bed made perfectly with throw pillows. At the end is a soft gray bench with armrests. A long, curvy chaise faces the window.

"This is beautiful," Dasha murmurs, walking around the room to take in the panoramic view. She yawns and politely covers her mouth with her hand. "I'm sorry, it was a short night."

"Mm, it was," I reply, knowing I've skipped sleep to fuck on more than one occasion.

I pull my phone out and open the app. The phone rings on the speaker.

"Dasha?" asks a young woman's voice.

"Yes, Katsia. How are you?"

"Fine. Your brothers have left. They are headed to France."

"How many men are in the group?" I ask.

She's quiet.

"It's okay, Katsia. He's helping me," says Dasha.

"He wasn't sure. He thought six or seven."

I put a finger to my lips in silent warning. I don't want Dasha to mention anything about the disparity in numbers.

"Thank you, Katsia. Do you have a number where we can reach Albert?"

"Albert may not be able to answer when you call. He's afraid of getting caught."

"That makes sense. Message him this number, and we'll wait to hear from him."

"All right. Dasha, are you okay?"

"Yes, fine. And you?"

"Yes. I can't wait to see you. I heard your father is not with the group."

"Really?"

I find this weird. I thought Ratmim would want to be in on the action. However, using younger men makes more sense. The fact that Albert's number doesn't match Pavel's concerns me. Alex has known Pavel for years, and he makes good money with us. Albert has nothing to lose and something to gain if he sells us out.

I rub my hand over my five o'clock shadow.

"I don't know. All I know is that he's home."

"That's fine. I have to go. I'll see you soon, Katsia," Dasha replies.

I hang up.

"What is going on?" she asks. The concern over the conflicting information is written on her face, and her green eyes turn a shade lighter.

"I'm not sure. Katsia is your friend. Is she fucking Albert?"

"Not that I'm aware of. I think she would have told me if she were seeing him when I was still home. She's not one to hang out with thugs. She likes a good time in the clubs, and she might have a boyfriend here or there, but most of them go to university with her."

"I'm not sure we can trust his information."

"But we need to know where their guards are going to be," Dasha frets.

"We have time. They don't know where we're meeting yet."

"Right. I don't understand…"

I drop a kiss on her ruby lips. "Don't worry. Let's join the others. You need to eat."

We walk into the formal dining room. The centerpiece of the room is a wine refrigerator, but it's not a traditional appliance by any means. The wall is cooled behind the glass doors, and each bottle of decadent wine is cradled horizontally to prevent the corks from drying out. Additionally, I can see labels on the wine.

"That's an amazing…wine bottle…" Dasha stutters a little over her words, and it's plain that she's never seen something so elaborate for wine storage.

The others fill their plates from a buffet before moving to the circular marble dining room table. A woman dressed in a stiff white shirt and black pants fills cups with coffee.

Before we make it to the buffet Dmitry enters.

We hug each other and Nikolay joins us.

"I didn't know if you would make it," I say.

"We are stronger together. We all want that man dead," he replies.

"Good, we're together. We need to show strength and that no one fucks with the Volkovs," Nikolay adds stating, "Dad would be proud."

"He would," I agree."

Nikolay and Dmitry talk as we walk to the buffet. "I'm sure you're hungry Dmitry," I say as I hand Dasha a plate. She's suddenly shy when we take our seats. She's around new people, and my brothers are handsome.

"Starving, I think I'm gaining weight with my wife, it's early in her pregnancy but she craves pickles."

Nikolay chuckles. "I can't believe you're going to be a dad. She's safely tucked away in New York City, I presume."

"Yes, we have many resources. I'm confident she's safe or I would have never left her. It doesn't hurt that her father is still the Don."

Dmitry is being groomed to take over for the Don ever since he married his daughter, which is a long and bizarre story I'll have to tell Dasha one day.

Dasha drops her napkin in her lap and eats tiny bites of food as she cautiously observes my brothers. We've started a war, but it's not her fault. I'm not sure she'll see it that way. Her family was complicit in killing our father.

Nikolay glances across the expansive table at us. "So, Dasha, how did you like the yacht?"

"It was incredible." She meets his eyes, then looks back down at her plate.

"She must take to it. She didn't get sick," I say.

"That's good. You either love it or you hate it," he replies, trying to make her comfortable.

"I've never been out of my country, so it was surreal to me," she murmurs.

"You fit right in," Irina says. Lifting her coffee cup, she nods to Dasha, who smiles.

"After breakfast, we'll go check out the warehouse," I say. "The women need outfits for the gala."

"Man, Anya is going to hate that she's missed this." Nikolay pushes his plate away and sits back in his chair, rubbing his chin.

"Well, you'll be happy she's somewhere safe when this all goes down," Alex adds.

"Francesca, would you mind protecting Dasha while we hunt Andrian ?" I ask. "I can use my brother's help. I doubt anything will happen, but I need to make sure Dasha is safe, and I trust you. Irina has talked to me about your skills. I appreciate you helping Dasha with defensive drills while we were on the yacht."

Dasha glances at Francesca, who pauses with her mimosa in midair. She meets my gaze. "I'd be happy to help any way I can, Roman."

"Thank you."

Francesca's eyes drift to Dasha, and she nods. I'm used to doing my own thing and working alone or with Alex. This is a large group effort. I have to be prepared to live with the consequences of my actions on all fronts. It's what leaders do, and Nikolay is giving me the opportunity to do what I do best.

Kill.

# CHAPTER 32

## DASHA

*I* was hungry, but the eggs move at a glacial pace down my throat and sit like grease in a trap, pooling in my stomach. My father and brothers killed the father of these men, and it shames me.

I tilt my head to take in Roman's profile. His face is roughish looking, the beginnings of a beard on his cheeks and chiseled jaw. I admire his confidence. I'm surprised that he hasn't lied to me. He's different from the men in my family. These are attractive qualities.

If I hadn't had the guts to run from the church, I never would have discovered who I am. I'm still learning what I like and don't like. I wish I were competent like Irina and Francesca. The manner in which Roman speaks to them shows that he holds them in respect. Respect is something I knew nothing about until I met him, and the knowledge that I'll have to leave after Andrian is killed pains me.

I'm beginning to get to know myself, but I have no clue what I'll do for a living or where I'll live. I'm also clueless about Roman. What am I to him? I don't know, but I'm relieved I won't have to see Andrian again. Maybe that's enough.

Dmitry's eyes bore into me, and I turn my head to meet his gaze. He searches my eyes. "Dasha, how did you like Italy?"

"I loved it. I ate a ton of seafood, and I loved it all." I give him a nervous smile.

"That's what you do when you're near the water. It's the best seafood and so fresh. I love living in New York. My wife is starting her career on Broadway, and she loves being a designer there. However, it takes so long to get to Europe."

"It's nice that she knows what she wants to do for a career. My country doesn't have many jobs like that. I was never allowed to further my studies."

"Well, maybe you can now." He gives me an encouraging nod, and I take that as a sign of acceptance. Strong men don't need to beat women. They have confidence. It's insecure men who berate and beat women. The men in this room are sure of themselves, and for that, I'm grateful. They have a score to settle, and I wonder if it will cost my brothers their lives.

I finish my coffee and take a breath. The men stand, and I join the women hovering at the table.

Roman double backs and slides a black card in my hand.

"What is this?"

"Use it like money. It will pay for everything today." He slips his hand on my lower back, leans in, and kisses me. "Don't run off anywhere, or Francesca will have to hurt you," he murmurs.

Goosebumps cover my arms. I shoot a look at Francesca. I would never put her to the test. She excludes confidence as well and has an eye for detail. Like Irina, her presence commands attention without being showy. I imagine she's a perfectionist.

Francesca glances over as if she knows Roman gave me the rules for the day. Maybe he did. He tends to get things done without me observing anything other than a text or the meeting last night. I assume they will solidify a plan today.

Roman leans close, his mouth hovering over my lips, and nuzzles my neck.

"Roman, leave the woman alone." Francesca winks at me.

My face must be a thousand different shades of red. I put a hand to my cheek to see if it's warm as Roman pulls away.

"She's so addictive," he replies, "but I must work. Irina, I'll fill you in when I get back. Please show Dasha how to enjoy a town filled with billionaires."

"Oh, we will, all right, and on your credit card," Irina banters.

"It would be my pleasure. You'll have two guards with you today. We'll meet here this afternoon and review tomorrow night's final plan."

"Great, boss." Irina salutes him with a chuckle.

"I like the way you say that," Roman teases as he saunters off to meet up with his brothers.

"What is a gala?" I ask. "I've heard the word, and I know it's a fancy affair, but why do people do it?"

"To work business deals, parade the family jewels on their women...and the ones in their pants." Francesca's flippant reply stuns me.

"Relax, it's a fancy name for a fancy party," Irina calmly states. "However, I need to get supplies for tomorrow, and you, Dasha, will need to sit for me when we return so I can make a mold of your face." She slips her arm through mine.

"A mold?"

"Yes, so I will look exactly like you. But first, we're going to have our hair done. Mine's a mess from the water. And we have to buy dresses for tomorrow night. You and Roman need to make an impression so that everyone will remember you being there."

"I don't know if I can do that," I reply, walking with them.

"Do what, exactly?" Francesca looks concerned. Her eyebrows draw together.

"You will make an impression." Irina's pretty eyes narrow on mine. "You are Roman's cover. Now go grab a purse for that black credit card and meet us in the kitchen in ten. We have work to do."

She claps her hands twice, and I'm surprised I don't jump out of my form-fitting sportswear. I'm tense, too tense.

I wonder how everyone goes about life as normal, knowing we might all be dead tomorrow. Am I the only one who's obsessed with living?

I walk to the bedroom upstairs but go the wrong way and have to double back. Shit. I'm trying to remember a familiar centerpiece in a hallway when I overhear two women talking.

"He seems to like her more than that model. His eyes light up when he sees her. I wish I were so lucky to have a man fall for me like that."

"True, but will she be good to us if she lives here?"

"We get a paycheck either way."

"I guess. I like our annual bonuses."

I'm guilty of eavesdropping. I retrace my steps, finding the way to the bedroom. Is it possible Roman loves me because he's always getting laid? Why would he want someone who has nothing when the women he normally dates have money and success?

I walk into the bedroom closet and find it filled with clothes, just like the one on the yacht. I select an outfit more suitable for shopping, quickly changing into jeans, a fitted top, and my new sneakers. I've never had clothes tailored to my large boobs before, and whoever picked out my wardrobe has impeccable taste. I can't go wrong with the choices in front of me. I catch a glimpse of myself in the full-length mirror. My hair is unruly. I zip into the ensuite, brush it, and pile it on top of my head like Francesca's last night, sans scarf.

I flip through a drawer and use a makeup brush to apply bronzer to add a healthy glow to my face. The sea air and sun have accentuated my high cheekbones, and my green eyes sparkle against my tanned skin. I'm beginning to like how I look.

I glance around and find a different purse, and hide the one that contains my sneakers in a drawer so they don't get thrown out. I'm sure the staff here operates around the clock as well.

I meet Irina and Francesca in the kitchen and notice they have changed, too.

"Let's do this," Irina announces, and two men in suits open the doors for us, speaking into coms in their ears.

"Is it always like this?" I ask.

"The men with us? I can protect myself, but it's nice to have extra eyes on the ground, especially in times like these," Irina says as we climb into a large SUV with dark-tinted windows. "I'm undercover and change my appearance on a regular basis for jobs."

"Isn't it dangerous?"

"Sure, but I'm an adrenaline junkie. Which reminds me, I need to make a call so the drugs will arrive in time for tomorrow."

She lifts her phone and speaks in French.

"Life in the fast lane," Francesca murmurs. "So, Dasha, tell me, are you in love with Roman?"

"Um."

"It's fine, everyone falls for him. He's a magnet. I'd be more surprised if you weren't into him."

I remember hearing them talk about me on the yacht. They'd debated whether they could trust me and wondered if I would try to escape. I can't go anywhere as long as Andrian breaths. He'll hunt me down, and I don't have the resources money buys.

"Be good to him," she warns.

"I have no ill will with him. He saved me."

"What do you want in the long run?"

I gaze out the window, taking in the beautiful view as we drive down the mountain. We come into the main city. It is vibrant, with stores and people everywhere. I've never seen crowds this large. We're not allowed to congregate in groups back home.

"To be happy," I murmur at last, turning to meet her gaze.

"An admirable goal. You're welcome to stay with me after this is over. I know you love Italy, and it will give you time to figure out what you want."

I'm overwhelmed by her generosity. "Thank you, Francesca. I appreciate that."

Irina finishes her phone call, and the vehicle stops in front of an exclusive shop, judging from the expensive cars in the parking lot. I peer at the storefront. The sign hanging over the door has gold script lettering, and the window display features an assortment of sexy-looking full-length dresses, purses, and shoes. This is convenient.

"Won't everything be sold out, considering it's such a popular event?" I ask.

"These shops are prepared. It's a smaller group than the Oscars. I think we can handle it," Irina says, then chuckles as her door opens.

The shop is filled with women who are older, and there are guards at the doors.

I look around and see a case of jewels by the register.

"Oh, the bling," Francesca says as she slips her arm through mine and pulls me to the back of the store. "Dresses first, then shoes, purse, and jewels. You would look incredible in a dark green dress."

I'm escorted to a rack of gowns. I touch the fabric and run my hand over the bodices of the dresses. Some are heavier and have the texture of velvet. Others are light and fluid. There are sleek gowns that remind me of an hourglass. I decide they must be similar to mermaid-style wedding dresses, and I'm afraid my large ass would look peculiar in them. I frown. How do I decide?

Irina and Francesca scour other sections of dresses. Soft, soothing music plays as we shop. Assistants seem to be all the rage, and it appears they've assigned themselves to the customers. I'm learning that exclusivity implies incredible service, and the fact that we have two guards and a woman who wants to assist us isn't lost on me.

I hear women whispering and turn to the front door of the store. A woman stands there. Approximately my age, she has long, shiny brown hair, light blue eyes, and perfect cheeks. She's beautiful, with a face that stops me in my tracks. Her legs are longer than the day, and she has four gorgeous women with her, all glammed up in skimpy but tasteful outfits. The woman with the long legs appears to be the leader of the group, and she's wearing a white camisole with an open black blazer. The white shows off her perfect tan. Her lips are full, and she walks with the loose-limbed grace of a model.

Irina is suddenly beside me. "Oh, fuck. That's Nadia."

"Nadia?" Is this the model I heard them talking about on the boat?

"Mm, yeah. She was on the cover of *Sports Illustrated*. She's from an impoverished coal mining town in Russia, but she's living the dream now. Rags to riches, right there."

"Are she and Roman are a thing?"

"I can't deny it. They've fucked like bunnies, but he's into you."

I decide I can't compete with Nadia. I'm learning to fight for what I want, but I'm not fighting over a man. It's beneath me. I have more important things to do with my time.

I observe her for a minute. She is stunning. Judging from the way the women in the store are staring at her, she might as well be walking on water. She moves between the racks of clothes like a butterfly pollinating a flowering plant.

She talks, and her friends hang on every word. They giggle together and hold up dresses, twirl around with them, then hang them up and move on to something else. Two attendants follow them around like puppies. I wonder what it's like to have money and be successful.

Irina jets off to look at something that catches her eye, leaving Francesca and me alone.

"Oh, I love this for you," Francesca hums, holding up a dress.

"Did you notice the model?"

"They are a dime a dozen in Italy's hot spots. Sure, they look incredible, but I'll never give up my pasta to be that thin."

"You work out," I reply.

"Yes, and I do it for myself. Good for the young women who make it in the fashion industry. It's brutal." She puts a finger under my chin so I have to look her in the eyes. "Don't underestimate yourself. You can't compare yourself to someone who won the one-in-a-million lotto in looks and luck. You can become someone on your own. Besides, Roman notices you."

Irina rushes to rejoin us. "I found a dress, too." Then the two of them steer me into a fitting room.

"They are both lovely," I say as they place the dresses in my cubicle and close the door, leaving me alone with my thoughts of Nadia.

I have to dazzle Roman tomorrow night, and I wonder if Nadia and her entourage are here for the gala as well. I hate to ask. I don't want to come off as the jealous type.

"You have to model them both for us," Irina calls over the particle-board door.

"I'll be out in a minute." Quickly pushing my jeans down around my ankles, I step out of them and unbutton my top. The gown has a V in the front, so I take my bra off and pull the glamorous black dress off the hanger. It's silky and has silver sequins that catch the light as I step into it. I find the zipper on the side, and it glides up as if it's greased with butter.

I observe myself in the mirror. The gown is fitted, so fitted that I wonder if I should be seen in something this revealing. My boobs are barely contained, the fabric scarcely covering the nipples.

*Relax, Dasha. You're in Monaco, and sexy is the acquired taste for fashion here.*

I take a deep breath and exhale before I open the door.

I walk out, the long gown dragging on the floor.

"Oh, my." Irina's smile hits me like a car light on a dark road. She approves of the dress.

"Wow, well, Roman won't be able to keep his hands off you," Francesca says, her arms filled with more dresses. "It's amazing. Try on the other one and then decide."

I return to the fitting room, take a look at myself, and change. The dark green dress is a light fabric, airy, more like summertime. It does make my eyes sparkle.

I step out, gaining confidence, and walk a few steps, turning so the flowing dress twirls around me. It's long and reminds me of a similar one worn by an Aussie actress I saw on pirated intranet.

"Stunning," Francesca says, straightening the back of the dress so that it lies nicely on the floor.

"Can you walk in it?" Irina asks.

I take one step, then another. It's as if I'm pretending to be a princess. "Will I be able to dance in this?"

"Oh, my dear, dancing is slow, and fashion is not meant to be comfortable. It's meant to make a statement," Francesca says.

"What statement?" I ask.

"That you're untouchable, off-limits. You're a class above everyone else. It exudes power. That's the statement the woman with Roman needs to convey."

"I'm not powerful," I reply, confused.

"You're with powerful men. One is in your bed, and he doesn't do sleepovers." Irina winks at me, conveying a secret message.

"Roman loves me. But I can't believe it. It's so new. It hasn't sunk in yet."

"Duh." She chuckles. "Francesca is right. Wear green. It's a dress few women can pull off. Use it to your advantage."

"Fine. Have you found a dress?" I ask Irina.

"Yes, I'm going with plain black. I don't need to be pimped out for photographs. Tomorrow is about you and Roman."

"But his brothers will be there."

"I think Nikolay is missing his wife, and I doubt he'll go. Dmitry's wife is pregnant, and he'll probably hightail it out of here as soon as possible."

"Oh, I didn't realize. So, they love their wives?"

She laughs. "The men who appear to be above love fall the hardest, in my experience. For the right woman, a man can be conquered. I figure there is a message in this for me as well."

"I'm going with a dark blue," Francesca announces. "I love this designer It will fit me because Italian designers know a woman's curves. Let's get shoes."

An assistant gathers our gowns and disappears. I change into my clothes, and we pick heels to go with our dresses. At the register, there is a case with jewels.

"You have to wear something stunning with that dress," Francesca coos as her eyes rake over the gems and diamonds in the case.

"I'm sure it's all too expensive," I murmur. The fact that the items don't have price tags shouldn't surprise me, yet it does.

"Nonsense, you need to fit in." She looks at the sales associate and tells her we'll take the choker of diamonds.

"I don't know if I can wear that," I whisper.

"You can and you will. Trust me."

Oddly, I trust her with my life. I trust them both immeasurably.

I hand the woman the black card I've concealed in my tiny purse and try not to hyperventilate at the final number.

We're escorted to the vehicle. The attendant loads the car, and one guard holds my necklace for me. We arrive at a shop where three women are waiting for us to arrive and quickly take us to their station for assessment.

Francesca oversees me as if I'm a daughter. "She needs conditioners and a trim," she says briskly.

For over an hour, my hair is washed, infused with a moisturizer that smells good enough to eat, and placed under a hairdryer for it to activate. There are many stylists here, and everyone is chatting, so I tune it out so I can enjoy being pampered. Besides, I don't want to hear intimate details about the strangers around me.

I'm plucked out from under the hood of the dryer, my hair is rinsed, and I'm finally sitting in the chair to have a trim.

"You have beautiful hair, full, thick. You are very lucky," the French woman says in perfect English.

By the time we are done, my hair feels soft and silky. Francesca and Irina always look gorgeous to me, but they seem happy, and after we hand over our magical cards, we're out the door.

Irina instructs the driver to go to obscure, out-of-the-way stores. A guard goes with her as she darts into a store, returning five prominutes later carrying a bag. We repeat this a few times at different stores before driving back to the estate.

Staff take out packages and disappear.

I'm famished, and as luck would have it, the staff is prepared for our arrival. The terrace is set for lunch as a summer breeze blows in from the sea.

We drink iced teas with a slice of lemon and are served mixed green salads with salmon on top. A vinaigrette is drizzled over it. I'm too hungry to put my napkin in my lap before diving in. The salmon, greens, and pecans are sheer heaven to my taste buds.

"Okay, I'm going to need for you to wear a shirt that can get dirty and lie on the sofa in the study upstairs," Irina says. "I'm going to make a mask of your face."

"Will it hurt?"

"No, it's messy but perfectly safe."

"I call dibs on the pictures," Francesca teases.

"You wouldn't dare," I reply.

"It's all in fun. Besides, we didn't get many pictures on the yacht. When you get a phone, I'll text them to you."

"You took more pictures than of the three of us?"

"Oh, yes," she replies with a mischievous grin.

Mm. I have no idea what she found to be worthy of more pictures, and now I'm curious.

We retire briefly after our late lunch, and Irina comes to get me for the mask.

Just as she described, the goo on my face is unusual and takes time.

"This is a silicone mask. It will fit me perfectly. I have contact lenses and a wig the color of your hair. I'll be a double of you," she replies with satisfaction.

"You're enjoying this entirely too much, Irina," Francesca says from across the room, where she's sitting with a magazine in her lap.

"Well, I like being creative," Irina replies, carefully peeling the mask off my face.

"This is a bit freaky," I say when I see the final mask in her hands.

"It is a bit freaky. However, when one needs to look like someone else, it's highly effective."

There are voices in the house, and even though the brothers all sound very similar, I can tell Roman is laughing. Funny how I can distinguish his voice from others.

I scurry out of the room to clean my face before he sees me.

# CHAPTER 33

## ROMAN

My heart sinks when I enter the room, my smile and spirit fading because Dasha isn't there.

"Is everything okay?" Francesca asks. Damn her and her keen eye. It's not bad enough that Irina is telling me I love the Belarusian.

Fuck.

"Oh, yeah. Long day," I reply to hide my disappointment.

"Dasha will be down in a minute. I did a mask of her face." Irina reads me well, but it appears everyone knows my secret, as my brothers give me The Look.

I've done the same to them when I thought they were being sappy over the women in their lives. It appears it's my turn to fall for the young goddess who's transformed into an astute woman before my very eyes.

Dmitry can't hide a snicker.

A man on staff brings in a bottle of vodka I always have in the freezer. We love it cold, and a short drink is downed while it's still chilled. Alex opens the bottle, and the server returns with a tray of glasses, which he sets on the coffee table.

Dasha quietly enters the room.

The server collects drink orders from the women, and I hear Dasha politely ask for plain lemonade.

"Give me the details," Irina says abruptly.

"Well, we scoped out the area. We'll try to pin down where their guards are if we don't hear from Albert. Keep in mind that we don't know whether he's using Katsia and Dasha's goodwill or not." I have to be honest with my crew, even if it hurts Dasha's feelings.

She sits unmoved, but I know she's on edge, and I made it worse. We both have brothers who are putting their lives on the line tomorrow.

"I think Dasha should know how to fire a gun," Nikolay says.

"Oh, man, really?" I quip. After clinking my glass with the men, we all down the vodka.

"Great idea. We can show her tomorrow," Francesca says, solidifying the plan.

"Where? We have enemies in town. We can't run around like it's Bastille Day, for God's sake. Besides, I'm not sure I want her using a weapon."

"I'm right here, Roman." Dasha moves toward the center of the room. Good for her. She's moved out of the shadows. "I might be new to this, but everyone has a part to play but me. I can hold my own. Just show me what to do."

"Whoa, ho," Nikolay gasps. "Spoken like my wife. She has spunk, Roman."

Alex pours another round of vodka, and we all move out to the terrace.

"We walked the grounds at the warehouse. We can set off fireworks to get their men to shoot, find out where they are, and systematically take them out. Dmitry and Nikolay will work on that. Irina and I will be at the warehouse to make the exchange. We assume he'll have two guards. The building next to the warehouse is a perfect place for Alex to shoot the guards from the second floor. The warehouse doors will be left open once we go inside. We'll have our weapons. We'll go from there." I pause before I turn to Francesca, lounging on the patio fashioned with cream and terracotta-colored pavers. "You'll secure the house with my guards and keep Dasha safe."

"You've got it." She smiles and sips a limoncello, then turns her face toward the lowering sun. The terrace gains more shade as time ticks by. There are two clocks: one for the meeting tomorrow, and one to ensure everyone makes it home alive.

"I have the drugs in a van, and my buddies will plant them at the scene when we're done," Irina volunteers, taking a long swig of her gin and tonic.

Everyone is on edge. It's to be expected. I'd be more upset if they weren't concerned. We never take a mission lightly.

"Contingency plans?" Nikolay asks, adjusting his large frame in the wicker chair.

"Other than an all-out shoot-out?" My reply is half smartass and half truth.

"We don't have much room for error. I wish we had a man on the inside."

"Maybe Albert will come through," Dasha says.

"I don't know the number of men leaving Belarus, but we have to assume a minimum of twelve men will be there. There are only so many men Andrian can get into France illegally. We assume from Irina's intel that some might have visas, as he has moved drugs here before."

"Without a man on the inside, this is very risky," Dmitry reiterates.

"We live with risk. It has to be done," Irina says. She's committed to ending Andrian. She wants it as badly as my family does, and Francesca abhors human trafficking.

And Dasha will never have a life if we don't end this tomorrow.

"Suffice it to say everyone here is invested in the outcome," I tell them. It goes without saying, but I feel that if I'm to lead us into a war tomorrow, it's good to know we're all in this together.

My oldest brother stands and moves to the middle of the large terrace with his shot glass. Everyone conjugates around him, drinks in hand.

"To our health and our success tomorrow," he says.

The clink of our glasses rings out in the quiet afternoon.

My stomach knots, and not from lack of food. I will face the man who ordered my father's death and who will kill my lover if given the chance. He will certainly find Dasha as long as he's breathing. It was bad luck that Dasha crossed my path, or rather, a mixed blessing that neither of us knew the other's true identity.

Without me, she would be married to that insufferable prick. With me, she gained freedom from drudgery, but she has also has a price on her head. Andrian will know I've bedded his sweet virgin. He will not want to be reminded of it daily.

Dasha and I gaze at each other over our glasses, and she gives me a wry smile. I wish I could tell her I'll be home tomorrow night, but it's a crapshoot. This is why I use rifles. I'm good at it, and it keeps me at a safe distance. I'm not opposed to hand-to-hand if it comes down to it. But I'm usually taking out low-level thugs or men who left the military years ago and have gotten fat with their billions.

The group breaks into twos to chat after the toast.

Dasha walks to me, and my cock twitches. I can't forget how I buried myself in her on the yacht. The warmth of her surrounds me even now.

"Be safe tomorrow," she says. "I don't know what I'd do without you. Thank you for keeping me safe. Without you, I would have never lived outside the darkness."

"I'm a different type of darkness, mm?"

She chuckles. "I'll take your darkness over Andrian's. I know he'll kill me if he finds me."

"I'm to blame for that. I'm sorry." I put my arm around her shoulders and turn us to take in the view. I'd love to fuck right now, but it would be rude to my guests.

She shrugs. "There is always a price to be paid, no?"

"Sure. But you don't deserve what you've had to endure."

"Maybe not, but this week with you makes up for it."

I look down to read her face. "You had a good time?"

"The food was incredible."

"Fuck, and here I thought it was the fact that you love screaming my name when you come."

She pauses before she replies. "I'm not complaining."

"So, what's this with wanting to shoot a gun?"

"A woman needs to protect herself. I admire your friends."

"They have taken to you as well," I murmur.

I'm not sure I like sharing my little dove. What will happen when this is over? I can't keep her against her will. I want her to come to me because she loves me.

The sunlight fades, and brilliant colors grace the sea's surface. The air cools, and we gather for dinner.

The night before the event is heavy on our minds, and the conversation is sparse as wine is poured. At times, we carry on like it's a normal day, but the banter is followed by lulls where nothing but the sounds of our forks scraping our plates break the silence.

After dinner, I texted Andrian the location of the meeting. We retire to the living room as it begins to rain. I love the way the rain makes a rhythmic patter and find the raindrops relaxing.

Hours pass before my phone vibrates in my pocket. I look at the screen and see the coordinates where the guards will be.

I pull Alex and my brothers aside to inform them.

"We're setting off fireworks, and we're going to let them shoot first. That will give away their positions," I say. "I don't trust Albert."

"I agree," Dmitry replies. "We have to assume there will be twelve men."

"Let's try to keep the brothers alive if possible." I don't want to take out Dasha's siblings unless I have no other choice. I'm expecting flack over this, as they carried out the order to kill Dad, but as long as we get the man who wants us wiped off the planet, it's still a win. And the survivors will have a message to carry home. One that reminds them of what we're capable of.

"Sure, we might find out who has our weapons. We have to kill Andrian before he has a chance to transfer money," Nikolay says, thinking out loud.

"Agreed," Alex says.

"Great. I'll fill Irina in with the update," I reply as I head off to find our killer women, and I mean that both professionally and because they ooze sex appeal.

The night comes to a quiet end, and we all go to bed. I strip and crawl under the covers. Dasha has on a cute two-piece matching top and cheeky bottoms. She slips under the covers and lies next to me. I pull her into my arms.

"We're not trying to kill your brothers, but I can't promise that will be the outcome," I tell her.

"I know."

"It's going to be a long day tomorrow. Let's get some sleep."

"Sure."

I kiss her lips and roll over, lost in my thoughts. It's the first night we've not cuddled all night long, and as much as I want to hold her for what might be my last night alive, my mind is elsewhere.

* * *

"It's so early. Why are we getting up now?" Dasha asks.

"Because I have a farm where we can shoot, and no one will see us."

"Ugh," she groans.

I'm rethinking last night. Maybe if I had fucked her half the night and slapped her ass a few times, she'd be more appreciative that I'm taking the time to teach her about weapons.

"You asked, I'm delivering."

"Is Francesca coming?"

I go to my phone and look at the screen. "Yes, she's downstairs, so hurry the fuck up." I sit on the end of the bed, tug on my military-style boots, and tie them. Then I walk to the closet. Opening a gun safe, I pull out a bag and load three handguns in it and three boxes of bullets. The ear protection remains in the bag, but I count them and toss in a third set. I close the safe and set the heavy bag on the bench at the end of the bed.

Dasha is soon dressed in jeans and a dark blue T-shirt. She pulls her hair through the back of the ballcap. Smart, actually—it's a sunny day, and the cap will keep hot, ejected bullets from landing on her forehead.

"So, isn't it illegal to have firearms?" she asks.

"You wanted it, so here we are." I grab the bag as she slips into the sneakers sitting on the off-white carpet.

"Are you pissed at me?"

"No." I'm pissed that I haven't figured out a legitimate way to keep her bound to me after tonight. Without a price on her head, she's a free woman. And it pisses me off.

"Great, let's go." She scampers out of the room and down the steps. "Francesca," she says, beaming when she sees her friend.

It's only normal that the women have bonded. I shouldn't be surprised, and yet I am. Dasha was shy and timid over a week ago. She was thrown into my world, a world nothing like hers, and she's grown from it. She's no blushing virgin, and I have no clue what she'll want to learn next. A woman like her will keep me on my toes.

"Dasha." Francesca smiles and hands us both coffees to go.

"You're a lifesaver. I can't function without coffee," Dasha says.

"I figured. So, we'll go over the rules of the range on our way to the field."

It takes thirty minutes to reach the land I own. There's no one here to report unseasonal gunfire, another reason our meeting tonight has to be fast, and we need to be out of the warehouse. I chuckle because Monaco will spin this crime scene to serve their purposes. Not that I'm worried, but the crime scene will realistically pose a public relations nightmare.

Our driver pulls to a stop, and I get out. Dasha follows me, and Francesca gets out on the other side, a bag in her hand. The driver staples shoot-and-see targets on trees directly down range from us, approximately one hundred meters away.

"What's in there, Francesca?" I'm curious to know what she's brought to the party.

"I'm good with knives. And it's legal to have one on you almost anywhere, so you know, why not?"

Knowing her, she has one or more handguns in there as well.

"Interesting. I don't know if the thought of Dasha with a knife in her hands makes my cock hard or scares the shit out of me."

"It you're a smart man, it's a bit of both," she replies with a wink.

These women are out of control, for sure. I thought I'd had some wild nights. However, Francesca's demeanor makes me think I've only scratched the surface. "Point taken."

We move to the field, where my driver sets up a small table. I hand ear protection to Dasha and Francesca, then put plugs in my ears and slip on earmuffs as well.

"This is a Beretta, a 9mm," I explain to Dasha. "It's a good gun if you're carrying a concealed weapon. It doesn't have much kick, which means your hand won't jerk when you fire." I hold the weapon and show her how to use the sight, then fire a round while she watches. "Your turn."

"What are you aiming at?" she asks.

"The target the driver put up on that tree, the middle one. Range is hot," I yell.

Dasha takes the gun confidently. She holds it correctly. I make sure her stance is solid and tell her to fire at will.

She fires and hits the target.

"Damn, that's impressive."

"It is?"

"Hell, yeah."

"I'm going for the high one." Francesca fires and hits the bullseye on her target. I see the green splat.

"You're awesome," Dasha murmurs.

"Practice. Shoot more, so you're comfortable with it. Then I'll show you how to throw a knife."

# CHAPTER 34

## DASHA

Once we're home, I shower the gunshot residue off my body. The little flecks of black stick to my skin. I assume it's in my hair. Thankfully, my shirt protected my skin from the hot brass that went flying when I fired the gun.

Once shooting practice was over, Roman nailed a board to another tree, and Francesca showed me some moves with the knives. I had fun throwing them. I got lucky a few times and hit the board. I don't want to use these skills unless it's necessary. However, I'm relieved I learned how to shoot today. The fact that Roman had his chest pressed to my back while I practiced turned me on, the warm day turning into a cloud of steam when he had his arms around me and we held the gun together. He helped me aim, correcting me when I fired too far to the right. I'm sure he didn't need to get so physical. But I enjoyed it, and the practice session boosted my confidence. I don't want to be the only one who doesn't know how to fire a weapon.

I exit the shower as Roman enters the bathroom. He has the gun bag in his hand.

"How did you like it?" he asks.

"Great. I want to know how to defend myself." After years of mistreatment, I don't have to live to win the approval of others. If I have something to say, I'm going to speak my mind. I'm not going to be less of a person for anyone ever again.

"Good. I thought you'd say that. You did great out there. I'm impressed." He reaches into his bag and hands me the Beretta. "It's for you. I want you to have it. There are no serial numbers on it, so it won't be traced back to you. Not like it's legal to have guns for our purposes here, anyway." He gives me a knowing smirk. "Keep it close to you tonight, just in case. I'm sorry I can't be here."

"Thank you." I take the gun from him. "I love it." I look at it for a second, relishing my new ownership, before placing it on the bathroom counter. He lays a box of bullets next to it.

"I'm sure Francesca will keep me safe."

"Me, too. It makes sense with my brothers there, division of the manpower and all that…"

"Yeah." Is he trying to say something to me? If so, he's not being clear.

"Right, well. I'm going to shower." He dips into his closet; I hear the gun safe open and close. He returns as I finish braiding my hair so it will be wavy tonight. "I'll meet you downstairs for lunch."

I don't understand why he's being so cold. We were fine up until things changed last night. I'm sure he has larger problems to deal with, and worrying over me is the least of them. For all I know, he's sexting Nadia.

Nadia. I can't believe he never mentioned her. Irina knew they were an item. Sure, she and Roman are friends. Roman knows more about me than I know about him.

I have no way to look Nadia up on the internet. Not having a phone is a pain in my ass. I thought Roman would trust me by now. I console myself with the fact that this entire affair will all be over tonight.

I pull clothes from my drawers without even thinking about it. I've never had more than two pairs of jeans; now I have twenty. To hell with the posh lifestyle, I'm going barefoot today. I return to the bathroom and apply lotion to my skin. I can't resist the urge to look into the mirror to catch a peek at Roman in the shower, but the door is foggy. I doubt I'll ever forget the curves of his shoulders or his hips.

Or his dick, for that matter.

I groan quietly.

Fuck.

I'm addicted to him, the way he smells of the evening air mixed with musk. It's the scent I smell on his pillow after he's left the bed. His magnetic smile draws me in and turns my legs to gelatin. I love the incredible sex that has me moaning and ahhing for hours.

The fact that I scream his name when I come.

I beg him to fuck me.

I crave his touch. I want his fingernails dragging down my hips as he groans with pleasure.

I love him.

And I'll never see him after tonight if he doesn't make it home.

I shake my head to clear the turmoil in my head and my heart and go downstairs to join the others on the terrace. Staff members set the table and move about silently. Water pitchers clink with ice, and plates rattle in the background. I resist the urge to observe them as they work. That used to be me.

Roman joins us five minutes later. He slips his arm around my waist and hugs me close. He pulls my chair out for me at the table.

"I hope you ladies had fun shopping," he says.

"Great, thank you for the dresses, Roman. You didn't have to do that," Irina says, holding up a glass of water as if to toast him.

"Yes, thank you. You must come to visit Sal and me in Italy. I insist."

"It was my pleasure, and I'll take you up on the offer, Francesca." He nods to her, and she returns it. It's like a gentlemen's agreement. I bet there will be more than pasta cooking in that kitchen. Social gatherings are for work, and I assume private meetings are as well.

Does this mean he's getting in bed with the Italian mafia? I don't know anyone's last name but the Volkovs. Having lived with criminals, I've picked up on what's not being said, and the people at this table are very different. They are polished. They might have started as thugs in the streets, but it's clear they've removed themselves from it. Now, they are circulating among the elite and attending social events with affluent members of society. They have become legal criminals, and no one would suspect they have a shady empire under them.

"How are the hotels doing, Nikolay?" Francesca asks. "I must say, we stayed at one in the Alps, and it was amazing. I love your designer."

"Great," he quips. "It's my mother."

"Really? Well, she's amazing with colors."

"I'll pass it on," he replies as a server slides a plate of salad before him.

"Hotels?" I whisper to Roman. "You never mentioned hotels."

"You never asked," he retorts.

"How about Nadia?"

His body is so still that I wonder if he's breathing. Oh, boy. Did I piss him off?

"How did you hear of Nadia?" he asks.

"I ran into her at the shop today. Actually, I watched her and her entourage of young women waltzed through the store as if they owned it. Did you invite her here?"

"It's no concern of yours, is it?"

Wow. I didn't see that coming. It would hurt less if he hit me.

"You should tell me if you're involved with her."

"I'm not," he replies. "I was, but it was over around the time of our vacation. She would have loved the yacht but I wanted you with me."

"So, that's your type?"

"We met." He shrugs his shoulders and stabs the lettuce on his plate. "She's becoming famous. She travels for photoshoots. It's not as exciting as you would think."

"It sounds incredible to me."

"Believe what you will, but I don't cheat. She knows we're over. She's here for the gala, I'm sure. It's free publicity, and she'll get more offers for endorsements after the event. Just watch, you'll see."

I'm not sure what I'm supposed to see.

Hell, I don't even know where I'll be next week.

The next course arrives. Dmitry leaves the table to take his wife's phone call.

I turn to others at the table and join conversations that flow between us like we've known each other for years.

We finish the main course and have a light flourless chocolate cake Alex calls the Black Beast. It has a French name I can't pronounce, but the rich chocolate flavor is unforgettable.

It's been a long day for me, and it's not even four in the afternoon. I head to bed to rest. I drift off, and then I'm yelling.

Someone has their hands on me, and I try to shake them off.

"What is it?" Roman asks.

"I don't know. I wish I did."

"You had a nightmare."

I sit up, hoping it's not an omen. I'm not normally superstitious, but then again, my life isn't very normal at the moment. I've never felt further from Roman, and he's beside me.

Is he a different man now that he's working?

I get up and follow him downstairs. Irina joins the men as they have a cigar and sip brandy outside.

"What's on your mind?" Francesca asks.

"Roman is acting strange."

"Men fuck up good things all the time. Let's head to the library. I hear there's one on the second floor, and I'm curious to see what's in it."

"What are they doing out there?"

"Telling war stories and planning tonight is my guess. We'll have four guards outside, two on the roof and two on the ground. The camera feeds will be sent to my phone."

We walk up the staircase, and she leads me to a room with a toffee-colored leather sofa. Long windows overlook the sea, and bookcases are filled with leather-bound tomes.

"I love books. I never knew this was here," I say.

"Mm. Well, Europeans are avid readers." She walks along the shelving, her fingertips lightly tapping the spines of the books as she passes them.

A large skylight in the ceiling lights the room. I follow behind Francesca and fall in love with the navy-blue chaise longue sitting on a white shag rug. I sit on the chaise and lean back, and all my worries seem to melt away.

"This room suits you," she says.

"I love it."

She plops onto the couch. "There's nothing not to like, that's for sure."

"This is where the men must sit. Do they really read?"

"Who knows?" She shrugs.

"Are you worried about tonight?"

"I have an easier job than the others."

I think about it for a minute and see her point.

"How is your husband?" I ask. "I take it he's in the business as well."

"Yes. I have my own, and he has one with his family. It's made working together and living together better and worse."

"You *are* together, right?"

"Oh, yes. It doesn't mean there aren't arguments from time to time. You'll get used to it."

"What do you mean?"

She purses her lips and takes a beat before she replies. "You'll find out one day what marriage is like."

I roll my eyes. "I got out of one prison. I don't want to jump into another."

"Not even for the right man?"

"I don't know what right is. I've been with one man. I might not know much, but I know that. You and Irina are incredible. I never knew women could be involved in the men's world."

"It's not the norm, trust me." She puts a hand on the sofa and leans on it. "Well, I'm going to rest and call Sal. I'll see you later."

I read over the titles as I walk down the bookcase. I find *Made in New York* written on a spine and pull the book. I begin to read, and before I know it, it's late, and Roman is in the doorway. He's dressed in black and wearing his boots. A gun is clipped to his belt.

"Am I interrupting?" he asks.

I shake my head.

"We're getting ready to head out."

"Oh, my."

"Yeah, well." He nods in the direction of the hallway, and I follow him. Everyone is in black gear, but Irina looks exactly like me. She's my identical twin, from the light mole on my right cheek to the color of my hair and how it's curly with the humidity.

"You look incredible, Irina. I never doubted you, but holy shit."

"Great. I did a good job." She smiles. "It takes hours to do this."

She's wearing jeans and white sneakers.

"Change into workout wear. It's flexible," Irina suggests.

I nod. Then I swallow my saliva as if it's a pill and choke.

"We're heading out. Francesca has the house covered," Roman informs me.

I nod, and he gives me a hug and a short kiss. I hug Irina as she passes me on her way to the door. She returns my embrace and proceeds to the SUVs waiting in the driveway.

Roman pauses at the door. "Keep your gun by you, and if anyone comes through that door, shoot them."

That's it. Those are his final words to me?

Francesca locks the door and bolts it.

"Where is the staff?" I ask.

"All of them have the night off. It's just us now."

Francesca has knives, a handgun, and numerous magazines strapped to her legs.

Holy shit.

"Are you okay?" she asks.

"I think so. I'm going to change quickly and put on sneakers. Roman gave me the Beretta."

"Good man. I knew I liked him."

I'm nervous and try to get my foot in the leggings twice. I pull a long-sleeved dry-fit shirt over my sports bra. I need to be able to move. I tug my socks over my toes. My old sneakers worked for me once before. I walk to the close and pull them out of their hiding place. I slip them on, taking care to tie them perfectly. I grab the gun from the bathroom counter and the box of bullets. It's wise to be prepared.

When I return downstairs, Francesca has a pot of coffee going and is drinking hers in the kitchen.

"Coffee?" she offers.

"Sure. It's going to be a long night."

"You're right." I put the gun and box of bullets on the counter and helped myself to a cup, pouring the coffee slowly.

I pull up a chair, and we hang out at the kitchen counter. The pendant lights are hand-blown glass and remind me of the chandelier on the yacht. It was only a day ago, but it feels like a lifetime since we were on the water, enjoying the best life had to offer.

"It's too quiet," I say.

"It's the noise that will get to you. Let's hope it remains quiet, for your sake."

"Do you think my brother is helping us?"

"There are few you can depend on in life. When you find those few, treat them with respect and hold them tightly because those are the greatest treasures in your life."

"Like you and Irina and Sal?"

"Yes. I understand your concern for your brothers, but they made their decisions. We all make bad choices at times. The bloodshed tonight isn't on you. It would have happened in time. The fact that you and Roman found one another–you might have saved his family from being eliminated."

"It's weird. What are the odds we'd even meet?"

"Slim." She takes a sip of coffee and wraps her hands around the cup.

"What time is it?"

"Too early for any news."

"Are you connected to them with the coms in your ear?"

"Yes, but if they go out of range or there's interference, I won't hear them."

"That's amazing. Can you hear them now?"

She nods. "They are close to the warehouse."

"I wish it were on speaker."

"No, you don't." Her eyes stare ahead into the open space. I wonder if she has night terrors. I can't imagine what her life's been like, and then I realize bad things might happen tonight, and she'll be listening to it as she sits here, helpless to do anything about it.

# CHAPTER 35

## ROMAN

"Francesca, make sure she has her gun with her."

"She does." I can tell by the echoing sound that Francesca has gone into the bathroom to speak to me privately. "We're going in. Their vehicle is coming. Our scout saw them heading this way. Are you sure this is going to work?"

"It has to."

My phone pings. I copy the text and send it to my brothers. I'm sure I have the correct coordinates for Andrian's men. If I'm wrong, we're all screwed.

My guard drives me to the meet with Irina beside me. She's the spitting image of Dasha, but I notice subtle differences. Andrian won't know. By the time he suspects anything, it will be too late.

I speak in the coms and check on my brothers. We all rode in different cars for safety. I look behind my vehicle and see them getting out of their SUVs.

I check in with Francesca one last time before the meeting.

"All is quiet here so far," she replies.

"Just how I want it to stay."

Two of my four SUVS are here. I have guards in the other car. One will man the vehicles, and the other will escort us to the warehouse.

I get out, my boots making a crunching sound on the gravel as I walk around and pull Irina out. I pull her close to me, and she plays her part perfectly.

"Stop pulling me," she whines.

"Shut up, bitch," I growl.

We are at the warehouse entrance. The back doors are open, so Alex has his rifle set if anything happens.

Andrian stands beside his Hummer. What a showboat. Beside him are an unknown man and Vlad. Vlad is stiff but professional. He rubs a thumb over his nose before we turn to enter the building.

"You know, you should have delivered her to me." Andrian is dressed in an ill-fitting suit. He smells of cigars and whiskey. It makes my stomach sour to think of his hand being on Dasha for a second.

I hear shots ring in my coms.

"One down." Nikolay took out his target. I'm still on edge.

"Let's discuss this inside," I say. My guard opens the door for us and enters through a narrow doorway.

"Your guard needs to remain outside."

"Did you transfer the money?" I ask.

"In good time." His lecherous eyes are bloodshot. "I want to touch her first," he replies.

"Only after the money is transferred."

"You are so trusting, Roman. Right now, I have my men hunting for your brothers' wives."

"You'll never find them," I bluff.

"I found your warehouse, didn't I?" He rubs salt in the wound.

"You got lucky."

"Maybe I'll take a hotel next." He rubs his hands together with excitement at the game he's about to play.

"Come on, Dasha," I cajole.

"Stop, you're hurting me," Irina says as I pull on the back of her shirt and wrap my arm around her neck.

"Shut up." My voice is stern, and I flick my hand out, looking at my watch to divert attention and give Irina time to pull her gun.

I hear "Two down" in my ear. *Dmitry, you're a pro*, I think. Nikolay is great, but Dmitry used to do more of this shit.

My hearing is keen, and I detect a slight pump of air. I pull Irina along and hear Alex announce, "Three."

Good, now there is no one at the back door.

"Four," a random guard announces.

"Five," Nikolay is up again. *Good job, brother.*

She's wearing jeans, a thin Kevlar vest, and a shirt over a shirt. I have on a similar vest in case shit happens.

Andrian has a guard in front of him and Vlad at his back. We're all inside the warehouse.

"So, why all the fuss, Roman? You could have sent her back to me. I wanted to hunt you, not have you served on a platter." He runs his hand over his face. He hasn't shaved in several days, from the looks of it.

I want to strangle him with my bare hands.

Now I understand why Dasha feared him. She must have listened to her gut instinct. There is nothing redeemable in Andrian.

Another guard announces a kill, bringing the total to six.

There are four more. I need to buy time.

We're now standing on opposite sides of a long folding table.

"The Volkovs aren't easy, you know that," I say. "My father was better than you. Do you think he didn't teach his sons how to live in this world?"

"If your father knew so much, he would still be here." He beams at me, and I see his yellow teeth. He's like a rabid dog, a dog that needs to be taken down.

"We still haven't hit Albert," Dmitry says. "Did anyone kill him and not identify him?"

There are noes from my team.

At this point, I don't know if I'm being double-crossed. Where the hell is Albert?

"Vlad, who is your friend?" I ask so my team knows there are two men here.

"Oh, you like the fact I have two men with me, and you only have Dasha? I said come alone, and you listened." He laughs, and the guard to his left chuckles. By this time, Irina has the gun in her hand behind her because I feel it on my cock.

"You're an asshole, Andrian. You want a piece of this?" I hug Irina to me. "You need to transfer the million now."

"Settle down, let's negotiate. I need to know if she's still a virgin. I have to stick my dick in her and find out for myself. Then we'll talk."

"I don't think so," I reply in a make-my-day tone.

And with that, Vlad falls back, shooting Andrian's guard in the head.

The gunshot echoes off the metal walls, and Andrian's eyes grow wide as brain matter splatters his face. He stares into my eyes, realization dawning. The moment is brief but entirely too long in some ways.

Irina fires her gun, hitting Andrian in the chest. Pulling my 9mm Glock from the holster in the back of my jeans, I shoot Andrian in the head before he hits the ground.

He relied on his henchmen to do his dirty work. Now I understand why Dad hated him. He's a coward. Dad told us we had to know how to do everything in business, and to always stack the odds in our favor if possible. He also told us to take care of our men. We can't make them happy all the time, but they all have to be happy some of the time.

I hear gunshots outside and hope my brothers are alive.

Nikolay and Dmitry enter from the front, and I step to Vlad and shake his hand. "Thank you."

"My pleasure. I hated him. Has anyone found Albert? He was supposed to be at the entrance of the warehouse."

I turn to the back door and see Alex heading toward me. "How many men were out front?"

"Two, why?" Nikolay asks.

"We're missing two!" Chills run over my body as if I'm burning from a fever, and I start to sweat.

"Fuck!" Alex exclaims as we all run out of the building.

"Francesca, come in. Do you copy?" I yell into the coms, hoping we're not too late.

# CHAPTER 36

## ROMAN

*I*'m behind the wheel of the SUV, and my foot is heavy on the pedal. I press the accelerator to the floor.

"Jesus, Roman, we need to get there in one piece." Dmitry clutches the back of my seat as I zip into oncoming traffic, passing the geezer in front of me.

"We'll be just fine," I reply, but my heart is in my mouth.

Fuck. Anxiety wells in my chest. I can't focus on anything but the dark road in front of me.

I look in the rearview mirror.

"Good thing the coppers are all in Monte Carlo for the gala," Nikolay replies. Funny, he's practically a Brit now.

"There are four men at my house right now!" I shout.

"We'll get there in time." Nikolay tries to pacify me, but it's not possible. "Anya is fine. The house is fine. Everything has been checked."

"We're good, too," Dmitry says. He slides his phone back into his pocket and checks his gun.

# CHAPTER 37

## DASHA

Francesca narrates the meeting from her coms, informing me that Roman and Irina are in the warehouse. I ask her for more details, but her eyebrows furrow, and she breaks away from the security feed on her phone.

"Fuck." She stands and pulls her gun from her hip.

"What?" I keep my eyes focused on her like a laser.

"Someone's breached the gate. They went over it. Four men."

"Shit. Four? How are we to take on four?"

"Stay down. Remember, if anyone comes into the house, they are an enemy. Even if it's your brother," she warns, as if she knows who's coming.

"Right." I grab my gun off the counter, holding it like Roman taught me.

I move into the inner kitchen and sink to the floor, my finger on the trigger, wondering if I can shoot someone. Adrenaline flows like the Amazon River, and I know that given the circumstances, yes, I'll fucking kill anyone who touches me.

My heart is beating like a patient having a heart attack, the sound maddening in my ears. I hold my breath. I'm afraid I'll give away my location.

I hear grunting and groaning from the foyer. A gun clinks to the floor, scraping and sliding over the tile.

Glass shatters, and then more. It must be the huge mirror in the foyer. I tuck my head and hope Francesca is okay.

More glass breaks behind me. "Where are you, Dasha? A male's voice calls to me.

Someone is coming for me. His low voice is close, and it's like playing a game of hide and seek as a kid. I use this information to assess which direction he might be heading.

Fuck.

I move into a squat position, teetering on my toes. My heart races, as if horses are stomping over my chest.

More grunts and groans are coming from the living room now, and shit is hitting the tile.

A shot rings out, and a man yells, "Fuck you," in Russian.

I put my back against the cabinets. In the noise and commotion, it occurs to me that am a sitting duck.

I inch to the end of the kitchen and crouch closely to the ground, knowing it's only a matter of time before the man walks around to check for me before continuing his search elsewhere.

I take a shallow breath and peek my head out ever so slightly.

Feet. Boots like Roman's.

I have to shoot him, or he will find me at any second.

Holding the gun securely like I was taught, I lean out and pull the trigger. I'm not nervous anymore. It's similar to the fight or flight response I had at the church, only there is no second guessing.

He curses in Russian and drops, firing his weapon.

There are four of them and two of us.

Fuckity fuck.

I glance around to make sure I'm in the clear. I stand, firing at his chest before he can squeeze another round out of the chamber. He goes down and I walk past him, kicking his gun across the kitchen floor.

I cautiously creep toward the living room. I know the layout.

*Think, Dasha, think.*

The foyer is destroyed, and a man is bleeding out. Another man has his face badly smashed.

Francesca's work, I'm sure. Irina let it slip that she used to be a boxer. I'm in good hands.

I slip closer to the living room and remember there is a mirrored wall to the right of the refrigerated wine wall. I bend down and look in the mirror. Albert is fighting Francesca.

My brother, the one I thought was helping us, is here for me.

Did Katsia know he's on the wrong team? Did Francesca know? She made it clear that if anyone who showed up here tonight was an enemy. I have a feeling she's been in on more of Roman's planning of tonight than I thought.

How the fuck did this even happen? I thought Vlad hated me and

Albert loved me. How did I get this so wrong? And did I inadvertently set Roman up?

I'm in a state of denial. None of this is making sense.

Francesca throws a kick, and he attempts to catch her foot but only succeeds in knocking her off balance. She recovers and pulls the knife from the elastic holder attached to her leg. She lunges at Albert, who pulls back just in time. He has good reflexes.

Francesca drops to the floor, catching Albert off guard. She balances herself on her arm and swings her legs wide, knocking him to the floor.

She and Albert wrestle. I stare at them in shock, mesmerized by the fight. They hit each other, and Albert grabs her hair and neck. His face is heated.

Francesca flips to her back and puts her legs around his neck, then pulls him down to her. Keeping her head close to his, she rolls and pops out her leg so she's half standing. She moves quickly, pinning his arms behind his back.

She pushes his face to the tile. "Fuck you bitch," he yells in Russian. "You're going to die."

"Perhaps, but not today," she replies coolly.

I enter the room and point my gun at him. "It's me, Francesca."

"Great, find me some rope," she says, a bit breathless.

I run into the kitchen. Nothing, so I dash into the garage. There are three sports cars inside. I throw open cabinets until I find some thin rope. I rush back inside and give the rope to Francesca.

"Albert, why?" I ask as Francesca swiftly ties Albert's hands in a peculiar knot.

We're interrupted by the sound of skidding tires and numerous male voices, all jabbering simultaneously.

Roman rushes into the room and catches us standing there as if we have our hands in a cookie jar. He takes one look at my brother's bonds, and the tense atmosphere in the room breaks. "The twisted monk, seriously?" He smirks. "You are one twisted wench."

"Stick with what you know." She shrugs. "That's what they say."

She picks up her knife and puts it back in the holder on her leg.

Roman, Francesca, and Irina crack up. Dmitry, Nikolay, and Alex are laughing, too.

"What's so funny?" I ask.

Roman comes close to me and leans in close. "That knot is used for bondage," he whispers.

My eyes must have grown ten sizes larger. "Oh."

The house is in a shambles.

"Lucky for you, Roman, your wine collection is safe," Alex says, looking around.

"It can all be replaced," he replies. He turns to me. "Are you okay?"

"Yeah, yeah. I even shot a guy. He's in the kitchen. I made sure he wasn't getting up again."

"Good girl." He beams and pulls me into his arms.

The tension in my body evaporates. I'm safe.

"Andrian is dead, and your brother is being traded to your father for a million dollars," Roman informs me.

I'm blown away. Speechless.

Albert won't look at me as Roman's men escort him out of the house. Vlad enters, and I'm stunned.

"What's going on?" I'm confused.

"I helped Roman. I never wanted you to go to Andrian. I hated him."

I hug him. "I thought you hated me."

"It was a cover to eventually get us away from Andrian." My brother hugs me back.

I cling to him in shock.

"Hey, we have to get moving. The cleaners are coming to deal with all this. We need to get the fuck out of here," Alex informs us, ending a conversation with someone on his phone.

* * *

As we all shower and change to attend the gala, Roman fills me in on the back story. It appears that Vlad is the one who helped me escape the church.

Roman sent men to Belarus to find Vlad. He confessed that he had convinced Albert to chase me in the car but pretended the car didn't start because it was old. He also downloaded a virus on my father's computer so he wasn't able to get GPS tracking on the chip in my ring until long after it was off the grid.

"He never told you about the chip because he knew it would push you over the edge, and you'd never be allowed out of the house." Roman ends the story on this note.

"Jesus," I huff, gliding a blush stick over my cheeks. The shimmery formula catches the light in the room and makes my face shine.

I step into my gown and zip it. Roman is dressed in a tux and smells like summer with a hint of tobacco.

"You are so beautiful, Dasha," he says. "I'm really impressed with your shooting, too."

I roll my eyes. "Just what I wanted to hear."

He pulls me close. "It's a compliment. I've never had these feelings for anyone else. You know me. All of me, the billionaire and the criminal. What do you think of it?"

"Like it's a few bars above what I've ever known in all areas, and some of those areas are heavenly."

"Okay," he replies.

I slip out of his arms and step into my heels. Irina showed me how to walk in them on the yacht. She also helped me with my makeup. And with Francesca's fashionista's eye, I'm more than pleased with how I look tonight.

"What do you think about giving us a go?" Roman asks.

"A go at what, exactly?" I'm no longer afraid to ask for what I want.

"Us."

"Well, that would depend on a few things."

"Like what?" he asks cautiously.

"Do you think I'm beautiful?" I turn to face him.

"Of course, how could I not?" His eyes hold my gaze as I slip the diamond earrings onto my lobes.

"Do you like to travel?"

"It's the best. We've survived a road trip and being aboard a yacht for a week."

"Did you mean it when you said you love me?" I ask.

"Unequivocally, yes."

"Then I don't know why we're standing here discussing this. Let's go to Italy. I hear they have Fra Divola. I also hear that Positano is incredible. We can get there by sea, right?"

"Music to my ears." He beams, and his lips are so close to mine, I want to bite them. He slips his hand into his pocket and pulls out another box. "Then this is for you, Dasha."

He holds the box and lifts the lid. I try to peer inside, but he snaps it shut, making me squeal in surprise.

I squint at him. He's teasing me.

He grins and opens the box. A huge emerald ring is inside, surrounded by small diamonds set in gold.

"Will you marry me, Dasha? You'll make me the happiest man alive."

Considering how many we left dead in the living room, I want to enjoy life with the man I love.

"Oh, Roman," I exclaim. "Yes."

He slides the ring on my finger.

"I told you, I'm a man of my word." He waits for my eyes to meet his. "I will love you until the day I die."

"I love you, Roman Volkov." I smile, remembering his promise to replace the ring that contained a tracker with an emerald.

So far, he's kept all his promises.

# CHAPTER 38

## DASHA

The Casino in Monte Carlo is not just one casino but many. The enormous compound sits facing the sea, and the glitz and glamour make it worthy of the buzz it generates. Expensive sports cars and limos are seen for miles, Lamborghinis and McLarens waiting for staff to park them. Attendants dressed in the hotel colors of red and gold rush to and fro to service everyone as quickly as possible.

I fidget with my earring. My clutch purse rests in my lap.

"Stop, you're perfect." Roman gently takes my hand from the dangling jewels. "This should be fun."

I take a deep breath. "I think I'm still processing tonight's events."

"Fair enough," he replies, tracing the large emerald on my ring finger. "It's all new to you, and it is tragic to take a life, but the bastard had it coming to him. I only wish I could have been there to do it myself."

"I was so nervous. I'm surprised I hit him."

"You have a natural ability. You took to it immediately. I didn't have any doubt you'd hit your mark, though I might have underestimated your willingness to protect yourself."

"Oh, you did, did you? Well, if that man was going to take me to Andrian, then he was a dead man walking," I scoff.

"Spoken like a Volkov, and we're not married yet. I love it." He plants a kiss on my lips. I used a pencil to outline and accentuate them before I applied gloss to make them look plump.

"You are gorgeous. Please remind me to thank Francesca for helping with your dress. Green is your color."

"That's what she said." I rest my hand on my lap. The emerald is stunning, and the diamonds glimmer in the light of the art deco streetlamps, which give the night a 1920s vibe.

I look over the black and dark beige hood of the Bugatti Roman is driving. The car eases forward another meter. I can vaguely make out the shimmer of window glass in the distance and the lights glowing in the hotel rooms.

The hotel we're approaching is French in design. Shrubbery lights project a blue glow on the off-white building, giving our destination the allure of something decadent. The building represents the Belle Époque of architecture between 1871 and 1914. The copper dome in the middle is patina green.

"The opera house is over there." Roman points to another structure. "I'll take you there for a performance. I'm sure you will love it."

"I'm sure." I've never seen a live performance, musical or dance, only a few plays in school.

"We're next. Let them open your door for you."

"Okay," I reply nervously.

We roll to a stop, and Roman puts the car in park. My door is quickly opened. Gathering my clutch and dress, I allow the attendant to help me. I thank him and join my fiancé.

Roman slips my arm through his, and we stroll through a courtyard filled with exhibits, couches, and artwork on display. We walk down a red runner lined with photographers. The couple in front of us pauses to have their picture snapped.

Roman pulls me closer. "Ready?"

"I guess so."

"Smile."

I smile and place my ringed finger on his muscular forearm. Bright light bathes us, and then we're ushered along the procession to marble steps covered by a red carpet.

I take my time on the stairs. I don't want to trip and embarrass myself.

We enter a large receiving area with gleaming floors stretching endlessly. Every doorway is framed by columns. Grecian, I think, but my knowledge of art and history is limited.

Roman produces our tickets, and we are screened by security.

Once inside the massive building, we wait in line for an elevator to the second floor and step off with other elegantly dressed couples. We follow the crowd, and I smell the sweetness of magnolias.

There are strobe lights over a stage set up for a band. At one end of the large room, frozen sculptures of icebergs are on display. The walls of the room also have holographic images of icebergs, a fitting theme for a Gala for Global Change. Someone bumps into my arm, an actress from India. To the right are two large staircases with side steps that frame a podium.

The tables are as elegantly set as those on the yacht. Servers in crisp blue and white uniforms walk around with trays of appetizers. Roman and I walk to a bar hung with golden chandeliers where bartenders busily mix drinks.

"I wonder where the girls are," I muse.

"Rubbing elbows with the hottest singer performing tonight, no doubt."

"Really? That's going to happen?"

"Oh, yes. What do you want to drink?"

"I'd like a lemon drop martini," I reply, watching the women swirling around the room dripping with jewels. This is a thieves' paradise, and I wonder who's working the crowd to steal a few trinkets.

Roman hands me a lemon drop. His martini is garnished with a stick of olives. "Let's find everyone, shall we?"

I nod and scan the room. Alex is chatting with Nadia, and I give him a stern look for fraternizing with Roman's ex.

"Hello, Nadia," Roman says, his tone coolly polite.

"Roman, I see you've become engaged." Nadia gives me a cold look. She's stunning in an alluring dress and no bra. She's rail thin, almost hipless, and her jewelry looks heavy on her slender neck. I almost feel sorry for her. "The lack of replies to my texts suggested that you were otherwise engaged." She looks me up and down. "I didn't think you were the marrying type."

"I wasn't until now." He nods at her and walks away.

I hear Alex murmur an apology, and then he's on Roman's heels. "Everything at the house is being taken care of," he says, "and a tip will be dropped off to the police as soon as it's finished."

"Great, thank you, Alex."

Alex catches up to me with a grin. "I hear congratulations are in order."

"How did everyone know so quickly?"

"Oh, Roman did a press release, and it hit social media. Nadia couldn't miss your ring. No one can." He winks at Roman. "Impeccable taste, if I say so myself."

"Are you referring to the woman or the ring?" Roman asks.

"Both."

"Thank you." Roman sounds smug.

"I wish Katsia were here," I lament.

"She'll have to come to see us."

"Really?" I take a sip of my delicious drink. I hope we'll be eating soon. I'm starving. I snag a cracker with caviar topping and nibble on it.

"Anytime," Roman says. "She didn't know Albert was playing her. Vlad is a wealth of information."

"What's my brother going to do now?"

"Lie low, for the moment. We're getting him a new name. He can't be the only one who survived the events. It would look suspicious. We'll take him in and see where he fits."

"Really? He wants to work for you?"

"It's what he knows. Granted, he won't move up the ladder, but he can make a decent living. He saved our asses."

"That needs to be rewarded. How did you know Albert was bad?"

We pause beside a magnificent column. Alex is on his phone, texting.

"The information he gave us didn't match the number our man in Belarus gave us. When I said we had a source on the ground, we were already working on finding Vlad. We slipped a phone on him and a note for a meeting.

"How James Bond of you," I joke.

"Mm. Well, we aren't new to the game." He takes a long sip of his drink.

My eyes drift from Roman's handsome face to a pair of familiar faces.

"Aren't you a sight," Francesca says. She's covered the bruises she received earlier tonight in her battle with three men using artfully applied makeup.

"How are you feeling?" I inquire.

"A bit sore, but overall, pretty good." Her gown is dark blue, and she fills it perfectly. It clings to her in all the right places.

"Irina, you look fantastic." We give each other an air kiss on each cheek.

"Yes, you do, Irina." Alex drinks in the sight of her, his dark eyes intense. "You are a great shot, as always."

"Close range," she replies, lifting a champagne flute to her ruby lips.

Reading between the lines, I'm sure they are talking about how she and Roman ended Andrian.

"Well, look at that," Francesca murmurs, gazing at a man in the crowd. "The man himself."

"An American movie star?" I ask.

"Yes." She rattles off an A-list of celebrity names. "It's a who's who of Hollywood and Europe."

"There's the Princess of Monaco," Irina says, nodding toward a woman in a light blue dress with a flowing cape to match.

There is an announcement for us to take our seats, and soft classical music surrounds us. The evening's event is about to start.

I don't mind the long evening, as the food is exquisite. I converse with my new friends, laughing at Alex as he pops nicotine gum in his mouth. Irina teases him, but there's an approving smile on her face. Alex must be interested in her. He's trimmed his hair, and his tux and dress shoes are impeccable.

I gaze at Roman, who is focused on the famous musician on the stage. I don't hear a word. I'm lost in observing the man at my side.

He feels my eyes on him and turns to meet my gaze. "Everything all right, my love?"

"Perfect." I smile.

My hands are folded in my lap. He slides his large hand over mine, giving them a squeeze.

It's a new beginning, and I can't wait to see what the next chapter brings.

I HOPE you enjoyed Volkov Bratva's Promise Series as much as I enjoyed writing it. For more mafia, click here for my next mafia series, Borrelli Mafia, as it kicks off with MAFIA KING: MATTEO

The **bonus scene** for the Sinful Promise can be downloaded here **A Bratva Affiare or the link below**

https://dl.bookfunnel.com/y33l7umtvf

Antonio
&
Caitlin
Zoe Beth Geller

Nanny for the Bodyguard Antonio & Caitlin
the prequel to the Borrelli Mafia is free!

https://dl.bookfunnel.com/yyb5esazmh

356

The Player's Obsession

Scoring with the Coach's Daughter

**Maine Maulers Series (Pro Series)**

Maine Maulers Hockey Series

Rookie in Love (now in audio)

Jagged Ice

Hotter than Puck

Benched by the Nanny

Puck in the Oven

Pucking the Team Captain

Pucking with the Goalie

Pucked Over by Cupid

**Sin Bin Hockey Series (College Series)**

Tyler: Hooked (Free prequel to the series)

The Sin Bin Hockey Series

Jackson: Against the Boards

Alan: Between the Pipes

Erik: Fire and Ice

Blayze: Slap Shot

Paavo: The Defender

Spencer: Penalty Box

Isak: Coach

Kaden: Game Time

Liam: The Enforcer

Jake: Roughing

The Sin Bin Hockey Series Box Sets

The Sin Bin Hockey Series Box Set Books 1-4

The Sin Bin Hockey Series Box Set Books 5-7

The Sin Bin Hockey Series Box Set Books 8-10

Zoe Beth Geller's Hockey Pond Reader/Fan Group